A Deadly
Edition

Also available by Victoria Gilbert

A Deadly Edition

A BLUE RIDGE LIBRARY MYSTERY

Victoria Gilbert

CROOKED
LANE

NEW YORK

Published in the United States by Crooked Lane Books, an imprint of The Quick Brown Fox & Company LLC.

Crooked Lane Books and its logo are trademarks of The Quick Brown Fox & Company LLC.

Library of Congress Catalog-in-Publication data available upon request.

ISBN (hardcover): 978-1-64385-476-2
ISBN (ebook): 978-1-64385-477-9

Cover design by Griesbach/Martucci

Printed in the United States.

www.crookedlanebooks.com

Crooked Lane Books
34 West 27th St., 10th Floor
New York, NY 10001

First Edition: December 2020

10 9 8 7 6 5 4 3 2 1

For my brothers and sisters-in-law:
George and Jennifer
and
Joel and Soledad

"You don't choose your family. They are God's gift to you, as you are to them."
—Desmond Tutu

Chapter One

S ometimes chocolate is the only thing standing between me and murder.

I popped another delicious truffle into my mouth and peered out the half-closed door. From the intermittent bustle in the kitchen and the sound of music wafting throughout the house, I could tell the party Kurt Kendrick had thrown to celebrate my upcoming marriage to Richard Muir was still in full swing. I knew I should be mingling with the guests in the spacious living room of Kurt's historic home, Highview. Instead I was hiding in his pantry. All because my future father-in-law had decided to launch into a monologue about the decline of the arts in modern society.

Not that James "call me Jim" Muir knew anything about the arts. He simply "knew what he liked," or so he'd informed our host, who was, among other things, a respected art collector and gallery owner.

As I pressed my face to the crack in the door, a bright-blue eye peered back at me.

"Amy Webber," said my friend Sunshine "Sunny" Fields. "What in the world are you doing in there?"

"Hiding out long enough to conquer my urge to shout down my future father-in-law," I replied, opening the door.

Sunny's golden eyebrows shot up. "Do you think there's enough time in the world to accomplish that?"

"Probably not. But maybe at least I can now speak without sputtering out obscenities." I brushed a few traces of confectioners' sugar from the full skirt of my poppy-patterned sundress.

"Well, you'd better get back out here and calm down your fiancé before he resorts to swearing, or worse." Sunny flipped her long blonde braid behind one slender shoulder. "He's been furiously rubbing his jaw with the back of his hand, and you know what that means."

"Oh dear, I hadn't thought about that." I stepped out of the pantry, blinking in the light of the overhead fixtures. Unlike the rest of Kurt's elegantly restored eighteenth-century home, his kitchen was a paeon to modern functionality, designed for a chef rather than a family cook. Which made sense. Kurt was wealthy enough to hire chefs or caterers on a regular basis. He probably never lifted a finger in the kitchen himself.

"I can understand not wanting to curse out your future in-laws," Sunny said, as she turned to cross to the massive work island in the middle of the room. She cast a smile at me over her shoulder. "But maybe abandoning your fiancé wasn't really the best idea."

I sighed as I followed her. Somehow, Richard had grown up to be one of the kindest and most open-minded people I'd ever known, despite his difficult and judgmental parents. I wasn't sure how that had happened. It was, in my opinion, one of life's rare miracles.

"In my defense, Richard knows how to handle them better than I do."

"You'd better learn," Sunny said. "You're going to have to deal with them for the rest of your life. Or at least I hope so."

"I hope so too." I grabbed a napkin from the work island to wipe any traces of chocolate from my fingers. "I certainly don't plan on ever divorcing Richard, no matter how difficult his parents are."

"Good to hear," Sunny said with a grin. "Of course, you know I'll be waiting to scoop him up if you ever kick him to the curb."

I smiled in return, knowing my friend was just teasing. Not only was I certain that Sunny viewed Richard as simply a good friend, but I also knew she was not interested in marrying anyone. She was a free spirit who preferred to date men on her own terms, without any serious commitments. And that sort of relationship wouldn't suit Richard at all.

"Sorry, but I'm afraid you're never going to get that chance," I said.

"Figured as much. I mean, you two are so obviously in love, it's disgusting." Sunny's indulgent tone took any sting out of her words. She tugged up the drooping shoulder of her white peasant blouse. "But before you face the outlaw in-laws again, you might want to wash your hands. There are still a few smears of chocolate you missed with that napkin. As for me, I think I'll make a stop in the little girls' room. All that champagne." She grinned. "But I promise to wait for you in the hall. We can make a grand entrance into the living room."

"One for all and all for one," I said, giving her a mock salute before she exited the kitchen.

I crossed the room to reach the sink, tossing my napkin into one of several metal trash containers stationed along the way. A movement in an adjacent room—a narrow butler's pantry that housed a wine fridge and Kurt's eclectic collection of spirits— caught my eye.

An older woman with the slender but well-toned build of a dancer was pouring some type of amber liquor into a cut-crystal tumbler. She turned at the sound of my approach and set the bottle down with so much force I was afraid it might crack.

"Oh, hello, Amy," said Adele Tourneau, Richard's coach from his early days in the dance world. Although in her seventies, she was always stylish. Today she wore a short-sleeved eggplant-purple dress that featured tiny fabric-covered buttons running from its high neckline all the way across one shoulder.

"Sneaking a little something stronger than champagne?" I asked, with a smile. "Not that I blame you."

"Not really. I'm just . . . fixing a drink for someone else." Lines creased Adele's forehead, and she fiddled with one of the silver Art Nouveau–style combs that held her silky white hair away from her face.

My curiosity was piqued by this display of nerves. I wouldn't have expected fluttering hands and hesitant speech from the normally serene dance instructor. "Are you okay? You look a little flustered."

"I'm fine. Perfectly fine. Just getting too old for these types of events, I guess." Her laugh rang false to my ears.

I pointed at the glass. "Kurt's hired plenty of waiters who could take care of that. I know you've been acquainted for many years, but I'm sure he doesn't expect you to serve the guests."

"Oh, it isn't that." Adele stared down into the depths of the tumbler. "This was something I just wanted to do. Sort of a surprise, really." As she looked over at me, she kept her eyes shadowed by her pale lashes. "Something I wanted to take care of myself."

"Okay, sure," I said, certain my confusion was evident in my tone. "I'll leave you to it, then." I turned, but paused to add, "Maybe we can talk more later?"

"That would be lovely," Adele called out as I walked away.

When I left the sink area after washing and drying my hands, I noticed that Adele was still in the pantry, stirring the contents of the glass with a swizzle stick. I shrugged and walked out of the kitchen, convinced that she was fixing the concoction for herself. Why she felt the need for a strong drink was another question. But then again, I didn't know her that well. I was aware that some performers were shy offstage. It was possible that large social gatherings unnerved her.

Sunny was waiting for me in the wide main hall, which looked more like a museum than part of a private home. Paintings lined the walls, and antique tables held a variety of beautiful—and extremely valuable—artifacts.

"Ah, ladies, how lovely you look, standing side by side." A short, rotund man wearing an immaculately tailored gray suit blocked our entry to the living room. His silver-streaked dark hair was swept up and away from his face with copious amounts of gel, creating a pompadour that would've been the envy of any 1950s dandy. He pressed together his plump, beringed hands. "One so tall and fair, and the other petite and dark. It's like a portrait from Shakespeare's *Midsummer Night's Dream*. The beautiful Helena and exquisite Hermia in the flesh."

I narrowed my eyes, suspicious of the man's effusive praise. I was rather short but, with my curvaceous figure, not exactly petite. However, his voice held a trace of an Italian accent that leant grace to such flattery. I forced a smile, assuming it was his habit to speak admiringly of all women. "Thank you, but I'm afraid I don't know you. Should I?"

"Excuse me, I forgot that we had not yet been introduced." The man extended his hand. "Oscar Selvaggio. A friend of your host, Mr. Kendrick." The man's dark eyes sparkled almost as brightly as the gold cuff links studding his pale-blue shirt. "Or, perhaps not quite a friend, to be honest. We have been simpatico in the past but unfortunately are currently engaged in a bidding war over a rather delightful little artifact."

"You're an art dealer as well?" Sunny gripped Selvaggio's hand with a firmness that betrayed a lifetime spent milking the cows and goats on her grandparents' organic farm.

"Exactly." Selvaggio shook out his fingers before taking hold of mine. "You must be the bride. I just spied a picture of you and your fiancé in Kurt's living room."

"Yes, I'm Amy Webber. Nice to meet you."

Selvaggio released my hand. "Your photo doesn't do you justice, Miss Webber. You are much prettier in person." He tipped his head and studied me for a moment. "I think the picture doesn't quite capture the charming expression in those lively dark eyes, yes?"

I shrugged. "Perhaps. I don't photograph very well."

Sunny tugged on my arm. "It's lovely to meet you, Mr. Selvaggio, but we really must be getting back to the party." She flashed him a brilliant smile. "We don't want the groom thinking the bride has run off, now do we?"

"No, no, that would be terrible." The sardonic edge to Oscar Selvaggio's tone clued me in to his true personality. *His charm is all on the surface. I bet he's totally ruthless when he needs to be.* This didn't surprise me. It was in keeping with Kurt's business acquaintances, or at least the few I'd met.

Selvaggio stepped out of the way and motioned for us to move forward. "I was just heading into the dining room to grab another one of those exquisite canapés."

Walking past him, I couldn't help but notice Oscar Selvaggio's gaze darting from the back end of the long hall to the front door. *Like he's looking for something,* I thought. *Or someone.*

As Sunny and I stepped into Kurt's spacious living room, I once again noticed how it resembled a gallery rather than a room in a typical home. Although buttery leather sofas and upholstered chairs anchored by worn Oriental rugs offered comfortable seating and a stone fireplace provided a rustic touch, paintings and objets d'art dominated the spacious room.

Catching sight of the photo Oscar Selvaggio had mentioned, perched in a place of honor on the fireplace mantel, I pondered the odd feeling the art dealer had sparked in me. I whispered to Sunny, "I think Selvaggio had an assignation. But with who?"

Sunny cast me an amused glance. "Don't be silly. Not everything is a mystery. Even if you do tend to stumble over dead bodies far too often."

I groaned. "Don't remind me. Hopefully, I've left all that behind."

Sunny elbowed me. "Unless Richard decides to shut his dad up for good."

Jim Muir, abandoning what appeared to be a heated conversation with Kurt, stalked off to the other side of the room, where his wife Fiona was sipping a glass of champagne while staring darkly at one of Kurt's more explicit nudes.

"Fortunately, Richard isn't violent. Despite the provocation offered by his parents," I said, as Sunny and I joined a group that included my fiancé, Aunt Lydia, her boyfriend Hugh Chen, and Kurt.

"Where did you run off to?" My aunt, the picture of elegance in a lilac dress tailored to hug her slender figure, nudged my sandal-clad foot with one of her beige pumps.

"Just had to get some air," I said. It wasn't a good excuse, but it would have to do.

Richard wrapped his arm around my shoulders and drew me close to his side. "The air in here wasn't quite fresh enough?" As he gazed down at me, his dark lashes, far thicker than any man deserved, fluttered over his gray eyes in mock dismay.

I wrinkled my nose at him. "To be perfectly honest, I was afraid I might turn it blue."

"You shouldn't have worried. I've dealt with much more difficult people than Richard's father. One must simply smile and nod and not actually listen to anything they say." Kurt Kendrick, who at seventy-three looked every bit as fit as men half his age, offered me a smile as he swept his hand through his mane of white hair. In his youth, Kurt had been called "The Viking." It was still a fitting nickname for the tall, broad-shouldered man who'd made a fortune by mysterious, and undoubtedly dubious, means and now owned a few prestigious art galleries along with this gorgeous home and a townhouse in Georgetown.

"I wish I could learn to do that," Richard said. "I'm afraid I tend to lose my temper when Dad goes off on one of his tirades."

I slipped my arm around his waist. "Me too, which is why I disappeared. I was afraid I'd say something that would enrage both your parents. I'd hate to be the cause of their refusal to attend the wedding."

"Four weeks to go, so there's still time," Sunny said with a grin.

Hugh Chen, who was a match for my aunt in height and build but whose dark hair and eyes were in vivid contrast to her pale coloring, cleared his throat. "I doubt you have to concern yourself with that. I'm sure Richard's parents wouldn't think of missing their only child's wedding."

Hugh's earnest statement garnered a side-eyed glance from my aunt. "I'm afraid not everyone has your manners and good sense, dear." She patted his arm.

"Sad but true," Sunny added.

"As for Richard's parents refusing to show up for the wedding . . . If necessary, I will find a way to ensure that the Muirs attend the ceremony." Kurt's grin displayed large, white teeth.

I widened my eyes. "From William Morris's personal press? Wow, that must be worth a fortune."

Aunt Lydia stiffened, as if the mention of this particular book pained her. Before I could ask her what was wrong, she adjusted her expression to something more pleasant and fixed her gaze on Kurt. "I didn't know you collected and sold books. I thought you specialized in art and antiques."

Hugh took hold of Aunt Lydia's hand and slipped her arm through his. "It's an illustrated manuscript, dear. William Morris designed the title, borders, and initials, and it also includes eighty-some woodcut illustrations by Edward Burne-Jones. It was typeset by Morris himself, on handmade paper."

"And only four hundred and twenty-five copies were printed." The gleam in Kurt's eyes betrayed his desire for this particular object.

"So quite rare," Richard said.

"Exceedingly. Which is why Oscar is determined to buy it." Kurt shrugged. "As am I, but not with quite the same level of desperation."

I considered the dapper older man I'd run into earlier. He had seemed rather on edge, as if his effusive banter was masking anxiety. "He came here today to convince you to back off and allow him to purchase the book?"

"Something like that. I told him we'd talk later and suggested that he enjoy the party in the meantime."

Sunny shot Kurt a speculative glance. "It almost seemed like he was sneaking off to meet someone, didn't it, Amy?"

"Maybe he was just snooping around. Trying to scope out Kurt's property in case he needed to make a hasty exit later. After you two had your little talk, I mean." I gazed up into Kurt's impassive face. "I know how intimidating those talks can be."

"Nonsense. I am the gentlest of souls." Kurt bared his teeth in another grin.

Aunt Lydia audibly sniffed. "Right. Anyway, I wish you luck with your little competition over that book. I suppose I can say that?" she added, turning to Hugh.

Her companion inclined his head in acknowledgment. "I think this time I can approve Mr. Kendrick's efforts." He met Kurt's sardonic expression with a cool smile. "This appears to be a wholly legitimate enterprise."

I bit back a snarky comment. Hugh, an art expert who was often called on to establish the authenticity of acquisitions for the National Gallery of Art and other prestigious institutions, had long sought evidence to prove Kurt's guilt in various illegal art operations. But so far—and much to Kurt's amusement—Hugh had experienced no success in this endeavor.

"I'm sure that disappoints you," Kurt said, before his gaze swung up and over Hugh's head. "There's Oscar and his assistant now, making a beeline for us. No doubt to bend your ear about some piece of art he'd like you to authenticate, Dr. Chen. Be forewarned."

As Selvaggio joined our group, I noticed that his breath was labored, as if he'd just run in from somewhere. *Or away from someone?* I thought, as he clasped his hands in front of his chest. The young woman trailing him was dressed in a simple gray dress that hung loosely on her slight frame. She kept her head down and her gaze focused on her plain black loafers.

13

"But here's the happy couple, together at last. Congratulations upon your upcoming nuptials," Selvaggio said.

Richard shook the hand Selvaggio had thrust out like a rapier. "Thank you, Mr. . . . ?"

"Selvaggio. Oscar Selvaggio," the man replied with a quick glance at Kurt. "But surely Mr. Kendrick has told you all about me."

"Not so much," Aunt Lydia said. "Only that you also deal in art and antiques and that you are both vying to buy some rare book."

"Not just any book—a Kelmscott Chaucer." Selvaggio met Hugh's speculative gaze. "Dr. Chen, how delightful to see you again. We met at the opening of that Picasso exhibit in Madrid, if I recall correctly. But"—his eyes glittered like chips of onyx—"on that occasion you did not have this lovely lady on your arm. I would certainly have remembered her."

"We hadn't yet met at that time," Hugh said, pulling Aunt Lydia a little closer. "May I introduce Lydia Talbot? She lives in Taylorsford in a beautiful Queen Anne revival home that her family built around 1900."

"And she was my former neighbor." Kurt moved to stand beside the rival dealer. "When I was young, that is. As a child, she lived next door to my foster father, Paul Dassin. Actually, she still lives there, but now Richard is her neighbor. He inherited Paul's house."

"Ah, yes, I see." Selvaggio's bewildered expression belied this statement.

"Paul Dassin was my great-uncle," Richard said, offering Selvaggio a warm smile. "But don't worry about trying to figure all this out. It's pretty complicated. The short version is that Paul was a foster father to Kurt for several years, and my mother was Paul's niece. That's how we're connected."

"And Lydia is my aunt," I volunteered. "I live with her."

"For now," Aunt Lydia said.

"Of course, I'll be moving into Richard's house, that is, Paul Dassin's old house, after we're married."

"Of course," Oscar Selvaggio said, with a bright smile that didn't hide the confusion in his eyes.

"One big happy family," Kurt said dryly.

Sunny snorted in a decidedly unladylike fashion that raised Aunt Lydia's eyebrows. "Sorry," Sunny said. "I guess I just hadn't realized how convoluted all your relationships were until you attempted to explain it to poor Mr. Selvaggio." She flashed the plump art dealer a smile. "I'm Sunshine Fields, by the way. No relation to anyone here. Just a friend." She peered around him to stare at the woman standing a few paces behind. "But you haven't introduced your friend, Mr. Selvaggio."

The art dealer shot a quick glance at the quiet young woman. "Ah yes, I almost forgot. This is my assistant, Honor Bryant."

"Nice to meet you," Sunny said, before the rest of us offered our greetings.

"Can I get you a drink, Ms. Bryant?" Richard asked.

"Thank you, but I'm not a guest," said Honor Bryant. "I'm just here to help Mr. Selvaggio." Her tone was as subdued as her expression.

"Nonsense, I insist you enjoy yourself. Oscar shouldn't force you to work at a party," Kurt said, his gaze shifting to focus on something he'd apparently glimpsed over my shoulder. "Here come your parents, Amy. Accompanied by a young man I don't believe I've ever met."

Turning to face the archway that led into the hall, I noticed the immediate change in Oscar Selvaggio's expression. His mouth opened as if he'd just spied a monstrous spider as he stared directly at the man who stood in front of my parents—a young man with dark hair and deep-brown eyes, wearing khaki slacks, an ivory cotton sweater, and heavy tortoiseshell glasses.

My younger brother, Scott Webber.

Chapter Two

I quickly crossed to the archway, Richard following right behind me. "This is a surprise," I said to Scott, while Richard greeted my parents. I gave my brother a hug before stepping back to look him over.

It had been a while since we'd seen each other. With Scott's erratic schedule, frequent work-related trips, and almost pathological aversion to chatting by cell phone or text, we weren't in contact much. But he hadn't changed. He still presented the image of a stereotypical computer nerd, downplaying his good looks.

I'd always suspected that his understated appearance was calculated. He claimed to be a cybersecurity expert, but my parents and I had long suspected that his silence about what he really did on the job, his frequent mysterious trips, and his high level of government clearance meant he was actually working for one of the U.S. intelligence agencies. Perhaps not just behind a desk.

"I knew Mom and Dad were coming but didn't realize you could make it," I said.

Scott shrugged. "I was visiting, and when they told me about the party, I thought, why not? I did follow them out here in my own car, though, so don't be surprised if I leave a little early."

He turned to shake hands with Richard, whom he'd met a few times and seemed to like. Although with Scott, it was hard to tell. He was the type of person who kept his opinions to himself.

"You look happy," my mom said approvingly before giving me a quick hug.

My brother and I had both taken after our mother, whose short, compact build and cap of silver-winged brown hair was a vivid contrast to our dad's tall, gangly figure and shoulder-length dark locks, which he kept pulled into a tidy ponytail. After Mom stepped back, Dad swooped in to give me another, more exuberant hug.

"I hope she's happy. Or else I'm doing something wrong," Richard said.

"Your parents are here?" Mom asked, her tone as light as meringue.

Richard shot her a conspiratorial look. "They're around some-where. Nursing grudges." He grinned. "I mean, glasses of champagne."

Dad guffawed as Scott's eyebrows rose above the frames of his glasses. "Sounds like an interesting party," my brother said.

"Always is when the parental units are involved," Richard replied. "But let's not talk about that. You should check out the spread Kurt's provided. It's quite impressive."

"I wouldn't expect anything less," Mom said. "I still remember that dinner we had here. The meal was just superb."

"Hard to forget that dinner," my dad said with a chuckle.

Richard's grin broadened. "And not just because of the food."

"Welcome, Debbie and Nick. So glad you could make it." Kurt circled around Richard and me to shake hands with Dad and kiss my mom on the cheek. "And this must be the elusive Scott."

As my brother shook Kurt's hand, he gazed up into the older man's face. Although Kurt towered over him, Scott's expression betrayed no trace of intimidation. "Nice to meet you, Mr. Kendrick. I've heard a great deal about you too."

"Have you now?" Kurt's fingers tightened as he studied my brother. "Well, don't believe everything you hear. My reputation includes some rather egregious exaggerations."

"I know how to sift fact from fiction," Scott said, pulling his hand free of Kurt's tight grip.

"I'm not sure if anyone's told you, Kurt, but Scott works in computers like his dad," Mom said. "But he specializes in cybersecurity rather than programming."

"How interesting," Kurt said, in a tone that told me he already knew this and that he, like me, might suspect Scott of being involved in activities that went beyond a computer screen.

I frowned as I stared at the art dealer, wondering just how much he knew about all of us. I was aware that he ran a network of unofficial spies who kept him informed on matters related to his businesses.

Not all of which might be entirely legal, I thought, as my gaze slid from Kurt's rugged face to Scott's disinterested smile. I'd seen that look before. It usually meant my brother was processing vital information. I pondered this as Kurt welcomed Aunt Lydia and Hugh into our little group. Glancing around the room, I realized Sunny had wandered over to the room's large front windows to talk with some of our other friends, including Walt Adams and Zelda Shoemaker.

It's obvious Kurt has done a little digging into Scott's background. What isn't clear is exactly how much Scott knows about Kurt. I side-eyed my brother as he shook hands with Hugh before hugging our aunt. *But he knows something.*

I also noticed that Oscar Selvaggio and his assistant hadn't followed the others. In fact, Honor Bryant had disappeared, while Selvaggio was loitering by a door at the back of the room that led into the hall. I moved closer to Scott and tapped his arm. "Have you ever met that man before?" I asked, surreptitiously pointing toward Selvaggio. "He seemed shocked to see you here."

Scott shrugged. "People always think they've met me before, even when they're complete strangers. I just have one of those faces, I guess."

Which wasn't really an answer. I considered saying more but decided to drop my inquiry when I heard Aunt Lydia say something about Scott staying with her for a few weeks.

"Until the wedding, actually," she said, when Kurt murmured something about that being a pleasant surprise.

"I've neglected her for far too long, to be honest." Scott cast a bright smile at Aunt Lydia. "And since I had a little time off, I figured it would be nice to hang out in Taylorsford. Especially with the wedding coming up. Thought maybe I could help out with a few things."

"Sounds good," Richard said. "But be warned—since you're my only groomsman, I may need to lean on you quite a bit."

Scott threw his arm around my shoulder. "That's okay. It's not every day that my older sister gets married."

"And you won't actually be doing everything on your own," I said. "Richard's best friend, Karla, will be glad to help."

"That's right, she's going to be the 'best woman,' isn't she? Interesting choice," Hugh said, directing his comment to Richard.

"My parents would call it a misguided one, but everyone else seems cool with it." Richard shrugged. "Not that I really care what other people say."

"I think it's lovely," Mom said. "Especially since you two have been friends since, what? College?"

"High school," Richard replied. "Although we did have that span of years when we lost touch. But I'm working with some of Karla's dance students now, and the two of us are back collaborating on dance pieces. Oh"—Richard turned to Kurt—"I forgot to tell you that we've raised some additional money to fund the mountain folktale project."

"That's wonderful. Just remember—I hope I get invited to a rehearsal or two," Kurt said.

"Of course. Especially since your seed money helped get the ball rolling. Thanks again for that."

"Always happy to support the arts," Kurt said.

Glancing across the room, I noticed Oscar Selvaggio checking out a tall, statuesque woman who was striding toward the position he'd staked out at the door to the hall. He looked her up and down as she swept past him.

"Speaking of Karla, will you all excuse me for a moment? I have something I wanted to ask her." I held up my hand as Richard took a step forward as if to join me. "In private."

Richard's eyes brightened. "Is this in relation to some surprise for me?"

"Maybe. And no, I won't tell you what it is," I said, sliding my hand across my lips as if zipping them shut.

"I bet I can make you tell me, sooner or later," he said, leaning in to brush my lips with his.

I gave his chest a playful push with the palm of my hand and stepped back. "I bet you won't."

"What's the wager?" he asked, as my parents grinned and my aunt rolled her eyes.

"Enough, you two." Aunt Lydia shared a look of mock exasperation with my mom. "Sometimes I think they're in their teens instead of their thirties."

"It's love," my dad said. "Makes you act silly."

"On that note, I think I'll go ahead and talk to Karla. Before I receive any more compliments from my loving family." I patted Richard's arm. "If you're sure you'll feel safe left alone with this vicious crowd, that is."

Richard grinned. "I think I can manage."

"All right. See you all in a few minutes." I dashed off to follow Karla, who'd stepped into the hall.

"Hold up," I said when I reached her. "I wanted to ask you a favor. You can say no," I added as she paused midstride.

She widened her hazel eyes as she gazed down at me. "I was just headed to the dining room for a glass of water."

Karla Tansen was tall and big-boned for a woman, and especially for a female dancer. While I thought she resembled the stature of some ancient Greek goddess brought to life, her larger-than-average build had caused most dance companies to reject her back when she'd first left college. Since she was one of the most brilliant dancers I'd ever seen perform, this was a travesty. Fortunately, she'd made a name for herself as a dance instructor specializing in working with children with special needs.

And now she was also once again dancing with Richard, whose choreography was in demand by many of the very companies that had rejected his close friend and partner when they were young. *Poetic justice*, I thought, offering Karla a warm smile. "Sorry, didn't mean to ambush you. I just want to ask if you'll help me with a little surprise for Richard. For the wedding, I mean."

"Of course. Whatever you need," Karla said.

As we strolled into Kurt's elegant dining room, Honor Bryant swept past us, clutching a brown glass mug by its handle. She didn't make eye contact.

Focused on getting a drink for her boss, I thought. *He seems like the type who'd demand his subordinates to jump whenever he says so.*

Thanking my lucky stars that I was basically my own boss and only had to answer to the Taylorsford Town Council, I glanced at the long dining table that stretched beneath two sparkling crystal chandeliers. It was draped in white linen tablecloths and laden with a colorful array of hors d'oeuvres and desserts.

Karla crossed to a side table that held cut-glass pitchers of water, lemonade, and tea, as well as iridescent glass tumblers. "Only Mr. Kendrick would have amassed such a collection of carnival glass and actually use it," she said as she filled a tumbler with water.

"And the china is Limoges. No paper plates or plastic forks in this house, that's for sure."

Karla took a sip of water before replying. "I guess it's just how the other half—no wait, the other one percent—lives. But anyway, what is it you wanted to ask me?"

"Well"—I glanced around to make sure none of the other people in the dining room were close enough to hear—"I wondered if you would give me a few dance lessons. Before the wedding, I mean."

Karla arched her feathery eyebrows. "For the first dance or something?"

"Exactly. Richard's taught me to waltz, at least to a somewhat respectable level, so he thinks our first dance is going to be a waltz. At least, that's all we've ever discussed. But I thought it would be fun to surprise him with another style. A more difficult dance, like a tango or something." I drew imaginary circles on the hardwood floor with the toe of my sandal. "I mean, I don't expect to be brilliant at it in such a short time, but I'd like to be able to at least execute the basic steps."

Karla examined me for a moment. "Ballroom isn't my specialty, but I suppose I could teach you the basics." She smoothed her chin-length cap of sienna-brown hair with her free hand. "Good enough for social dancing, anyway. It's really all Richard knows in that style, to be honest, so it's not such a leap."

"Yeah, it's not like I'm going to compete with either of you in a contemporary routine. You'd wipe the floor with me. But I thought maybe a ballroom dance would work. Not competition level or anything. Just simple steps for me. Richard can add the flourish."

"It would be fun," Karla said, taking another sip of water as she studied me. "But I warn you—I can be a demanding teacher."

I grimaced. "And I can be a klutz. So we both have our work cut out for us."

"Rich *would* be pleased, though." Karla drummed her fingers against the tumbler. "I'd love to see his face when the band breaks into a tango or salsa or something for the first dance."

"I'd like to see that too. The thing is, he's always teasing me, and I thought maybe I could finally spring a surprise on him in return." I cast Karla a smile. "Anyway, I'd just like to try. Take a few classes with you—privately, of course—and see how it goes. If I turn out to be a hopeless case, you can always tell me to abandon the idea."

"No one is hopeless," Karla said firmly. She placed her tumbler on one of the small tables set up to collect used glasses and dinnerware. "You just have to concentrate and practice. I can't turn you into a ballroom champion in a few weeks, but I think I can teach you one dance."

"Thank you." I reached out and clasped one of Karla's hands. "I really am happy that you and Richard have grown close again, you know. It may seem weird to other people . . ."

Karla gently squeezed my fingers. "Have you heard any talk? From people at Clarion, I mean. I hope no one is implying that there is anything between us besides friendship, but I know how catty some of our colleagues can be."

"Campus gossip can be the worst," I said, releasing Karla's hand. "It was the same when I was working at Clarion, but no, I haven't heard anything. It's just something Richard said, about looks he's gotten when he's brought you in as a guest artist."

"From Meredith Fox and her crowd? You know that's just because Rich didn't run back to her after she left her husband. As if." Karla sniffed. "She's the one who dumped him when they were engaged and ran off to marry someone else. If that marriage didn't last, too bad for her. Of course," she added, "Meredith leaving was the best thing that ever happened to Richard. Because then he was single when he met you."

"And I can't hate Meredith for that reason alone. Her dumping Richard without a word killed any feelings he might've had for her. Too bad for her; good for me." I offered Karla another smile. "So, if you're really up to working with a very poor dancer, I'll be in touch. We can set up some sessions at your studio, maybe?"

"Sounds good," Karla said.

"Oh, and don't forget—you're supposed to accompany Sunny and Mom and me when we go for our final dress fittings. I'll let you know the time. Since you couldn't go with us when we chose my gown and Sunny's dress, I thought it'd be an opportunity for you to pick out something for yourself. Unless you've already found a gown?"

"I haven't. But are you sure this shop will have anything that will fit me?" Karla swept her hand in front of her body. "Without alterations, everything's usually too short or tight."

I nodded. "Which is why I made the owner promise to have their seamstress available to make any adjustments, or at least to mark your dress for any necessary tailoring. They also said they'd make sure it would be done in plenty of time for the wedding."

"Okay, I can work with that." Karla glanced at her watch. "Heavens, is it that late? I'm afraid I have to dash."

"I hope there's no emergency."

"No, it's just one of my dance students. He's playing in a piano recital, and I like to support all my students' creative efforts. The thing is, when I promised to attend, I didn't expect a conflict. Honestly, I didn't think I'd be here that long, but it seems time has slipped away from me." Karla cast me an apologetic smile. "Would you give Mr. Kendrick and everyone my thanks and good-byes? Tell Rich I'll call him soon. And you"—she pointed a finger at me—"text me about setting up those lessons."

"I will," I said, following her as she strode into the hall. I gave her a hug before she hurried out the front door.

Wandering back into the living room, I noticed that several other people were missing, including Kurt and my brother.

"Scott didn't leave yet, I hope," I said as I joined my parents.

"No, Lydia and Hugh just took him off to introduce him to some other people," Mom said. "Her friends Walt and Zelda. Then he headed outside, for a walk, he said."

"And I suppose Kurt's mingling with guests in another room?" I breathed a sigh of relief. Even though I wasn't sure why, I didn't like the idea that Kurt had somehow cornered my brother in a private conversation. There was a crackle of tension between those two that made me uncomfortable. *It might have something to do with Kurt's business interests*, I thought, remembering that the art dealer had some mysterious connections with government agencies like the FBI. *And then again, maybe it's what Kurt knows about Oscar Selvaggio, who seemed shocked to encounter Scott. If Selvaggio has been involved in any shady art transactions, it's possible both Kurt and Scott have access to that information.*

"I'm not sure where our host is right this minute," Mom replied. "I saw him chatting with that Selvaggio fellow right after you left the room, but both of them seem to have disappeared since."

"Chatting? Looked more like an argument to me." Dad tapped his chin with one finger. "Probably fighting over that book they both want to buy. Although Kurt did hand the other guy a snifter of what looked like brandy, so they can't be too much on the outs."

"Probably cognac. That is Kurt's favorite," I said, distracted by Richard's appearing at my elbow with a glass of champagne.

"Thought you might want another," he said, tapping the rim of his own full glass against mine. "I know I do."

28

"Must be nice to be rich enough to hand this stuff out like water." Dad lifted his own glass in a little salute. "Anyway, here's to you, daughter and future son-in-law."

"Thanks," I said, before taking a sip. Over the rim of my glass, I noticed Aunt Lydia and Hugh approaching, with Fiona and Jim Muir in tow. "Listen," I said to Richard in a low voice. "Do you want to slip away for a minute? Take a stroll outside or something? Not sure I'm up to chatting with your parents at the moment."

"Good plan." Richard winked at me. "Let's deposit these glasses and take a walk around the grounds," he said in a louder voice, taking my arm and sweeping me away from his approaching parents. We dropped our half-empty champagne glasses on one of the small tables set up in the hall before heading outside.

"Dodged that bullet," he said, as we followed the path that led around to the back of the house.

"Leaving my parents, aunt, and poor Hugh as targets." I shook my head. "I suppose that was wrong of us, but . . ."

"You really don't care?" Richard's lips twitched.

"I wouldn't say that. But I think they have the fortitude to handle such situations."

Richard's grip on my arm tightened. "Unlike us, cowards that we are."

"Smart cowards," I said with a smile.

Richard paused on the path that led into the trees surrounding Kurt's manicured backyard. "To be honest, I really just wanted a moment alone with you."

"To do what, exactly?"

"Kiss you properly, for one thing," he said, pulling me behind the screen formed by a tall lilac bush before proceeding to do so.

Some time passed before I was aware of anything besides the two of us, but at one point, as Richard lifted his lips from mine, I caught a glimpse of something moving through the trees to my right. There was a flash of purple amid the green undergrowth. I stepped back, pulling free of Richard's arms. "Someone's out there, walking through the woods."

"Probably a guest getting some air." Richard turned to follow my gaze. "Wait, that's Adele. What the heck is she doing, tramping through the woods?" He frowned. "She's had some balance problems lately, and when I talked to her earlier, I noticed she was wearing pretty flimsy heels. She has no business hiking across uneven ground."

"That is odd. Kurt doesn't clear his woods either. He says he likes to allow them to remain natural for the benefit of the wildlife. So trying to navigate that area in heels has to be rough."

"Good way to break a leg." Richard rubbed his jaw with his clenched fist.

"Speaking of Kurt, there he is, popping out of the woods on the other side of the yard." I glanced up at Richard. "What's going on here? Some strange game?"

"A secret assignation?" Richard widened his gray eyes. "Kurt and Adele have known each other for a long time . . ."

"True, but they're old enough not to have to sneak into the woods for a rendezvous. Anyway, I've never gotten the impression that they were that close, and Adele could just as easily stay after the party if they wanted private time alone. Who would know, or care?"

"No one, I suppose." Richard's gaze followed Adele as she crossed the yard and entered the house through the back door.

Kurt, who'd paused at the edge of the yard until Adele went inside, waited a few additional minutes before following her. As he opened the back door, I was surprised to see my brother stroll around from the other side of the house. *That's right, he went out for a walk for some reason*, I thought, reaching for Richard's hand.

"This is starting to remind me of one of those French farces— people coming and going from all directions." Richard's fingers curled around mine.

Looking over the area as if to make sure no one was watching, Scott also used the back door to enter the house.

"It is peculiar," I said, "but I'm sure there's some reasonable explanation."

A loud crash silenced Richard's response.

"Sounds like it came from that direction," he said, dropping my hand to sprint down the path.

I followed, running to match his longer strides. The path curved off to the right, ending at a wooden garden shed.

Richard paused, grabbing the edge of the half-open door. "Hold on," he said as I reached him. "We should be careful. It could be some sort of wild animal, and if we back it into a corner, it could turn violent."

"But it also could be hurt," I said, pulling the door wider to peer inside the shed. "Can't see much."

"There's something on the floor." Richard pointed toward a large, shadowy object sprawled across the center of the small room.

I backed away. "Not a bear, I hope."

"It's not moving. Maybe just some tarps that tipped off that top shelf." Richard grabbed a rake that was propped next to the door.

As he crept closer to the shadowy object, holding the rake like a weapon, I stepped in behind him and moved to the side to allow light to spill in through the door.

It was a tarp—a cracked blue tarp dusted with mold. But it was draped over something else.

Richard tentatively reached out and flipped up an edge of the thick plastic covering.

I gasped as an expensive leather shoe was revealed.

We both rushed forward to fling back the rest of the tarp. Then stood in silence, holding hands, as we stared down at the body of Oscar Selvaggio.

Chapter Three

Chief Deputy Brad Tucker offered a thin, gray wool blanket as Richard and I huddled on one of the wooden benches in Kurt's back yard.

"So we meet again, under way-too-deadly circumstances." Brad, a tall, broad-shouldered man in his early forties, loomed over us, his sheriff's department hat dangling from his right hand. "I'm beginning to think you two attract dead bodies like sugar draws ants."

"Not our intention," I said, after stilling my chattering teeth. It was still pleasant outside, but the shock of stumbling over yet another lifeless body had given me the shakes.

Richard draped the blanket over my shoulders. "Not the way we wanted to end this event, believe me."

I glanced over at the perimeter the sheriff's department had established around the shed before looking up into Brad's blue eyes. "Any idea what killed Mr. Selvaggio? We were thinking maybe a heart attack or a stroke, since there was no sign of blood."

"Too soon to tell. The coroner will have to do a more thorough examination before I can say anything conclusive." Brad covered his short blond hair with his hat before pulling a small notebook and pen from the pocket of his uniform jacket. "Just to be clear, you really didn't see anyone in the direct vicinity of the garden shed?"

"As we told the other deputy, Selvaggio was alone," Richard said. "We did see some people outside right before the time he must've collapsed, but they were either in the woods or the yard."

Brad peered at the notebook. "Right. That was Adele Tourneau, Kurt Kendrick, and"—he glanced down at me—"Scott Webber."

"But Scott entered the backyard from the other side of the house," I said. "He was nowhere near the shed."

"Still outside, like the others." Brad tapped the notebook with a ballpoint pen. "We are interviewing all three of them, along with others at the party."

"Of course." I drew the edges of the blanket together, creating a cocoon-like wrap around my body. "It was probably natural causes, though. Don't you think?"

The lines bracketing Brad's lips deepened. "I'm not going to speculate on that," he said, pocketing the notebook and pen.

"Are we done here?" Richard stood to face the chief deputy. He was a few inches shorter than Brad, but his perfect posture always leant him the air of a taller man. "Sorry, but I'd like to get Amy home as soon as possible. She's pretty shaken."

"We're finished, although we may need to call you into the station to clarify your statements." Brad tugged his hat lower on his forehead. "You'd just met the victim, from what I understand?"

"Barely spoke two words to him," Richard said.

I rose to my feet, still wearing the blanket like a cape. "Neither of us ever saw him before today. As I told the other deputy, it's my understanding that Mr. Selvaggio showed up to talk with Mr. Kendrick about some rare book they both want to buy, and Kurt asked him to stay. I mean, it's not like he was actually invited as a guest." I lowered my lashes to shade my eyes. Although both Brad and his significant other, Alison Frye, were our friends, they hadn't been invited either. Which probably said more about Kurt's relationship with law enforcement than anything else.

Brad cleared his throat. "And of course we'll follow up on that. I am sorry this happened during your party," he added in a gentler tone. "You do seem to have the worst luck with these sorts of things."

"Tell me about it." Richard managed a wan smile. "But at least this time it doesn't appear to be a murder."

"Not at first glance. But the investigation isn't over yet. Now, if you've told us everything you can remember, I suppose you might as well head home. Just remember that you will be on call for any further questions."

"Naturally," I said, leaning into Richard.

He threw his arm around my shoulders and drew me closer. "Always happy to help. But I doubt there's anything more we can add to our original statements. It's all pretty cut-and-dried."

Brad's expression hardened again. "I hope so. Taylorsford doesn't need another murder on the books."

I shivered under the blanket. "That's for sure."

After Brad wished us a "better rest of the day" and strode off, Richard turned to me. "Let's get out of here."

"Should we try to find Kurt and thank him?"

"I think he's probably too involved with the authorities to talk to us." Richard gave me a quick hug. "We'll call him later. For now, let's go home, or rather, to Lydia's house. I'm sure your family will be anxiously waiting for you there."

"Yes, I saw them leave earlier, after briefly talking to one of the deputies. I think they were told they had to go, just to clear the scene." I shrugged off the blanket and tossed it onto the bench, hoping Brad or one of his team would pick it up later.

"Except for Scott," Richard said, his gaze fixed on something over my shoulder. "I see Brad's talking to him now."

"Poor thing. He comes for a visit and this happens." I tapped Richard on the shoulder, drawing his eyes back to me. "Are we really bad luck or something? I'm beginning to wonder."

"Don't be silly. We just have an unfortunate habit of being in the wrong place at the wrong time." Richard's eyes narrowed. "You aren't really worried about Scott being mixed up in a suspicious death, are you?"

"Of course not," I said, tossing my head as if such an idea were completely out of the question.

But although I knew very little about my brother's career, I was aware that he'd been engaged in top-secret work for the government, among other things. There were many previous missions he wouldn't discuss. Which made his involvement in something like a suspicious death all too possible.

*   *   *

My parents, huddled together on the sofa in Aunt Lydia's comfortable sitting room, looked up as Richard and I entered.

"Glad you could finally get away from that awful scene. You didn't happen to see Scott outside, did you?" Mom asked.

I shook my head. "I didn't realize he'd beaten us back here."

"We just heard his car pull up a few minutes ago, but he hasn't come into the house yet," Dad said, his expression troubled.

"Maybe he decided to walk off some stress." I turned to Richard. "Sit down and chat with the folks. I'm going to pop into the kitchen and see if Aunt Lydia needs help with anything."

"All right," he said, after giving me a raised eyebrow look.

I left him making small talk with my parents and headed down the main hall of Aunt Lydia's turn-of-the-century home. Stepping just inside the kitchen archway, I asked my aunt if I could offer any assistance.

"No, I'm fine. Just brewing some coffee." She held up a bottle of brandy. "I thought perhaps a little shot of courage wouldn't go amiss either."

I leaned against the wall. "Good idea. Mom and Dad look pretty shaken. I think they're more upset about Scott being questioned so intently than the death of the unfortunate Mr. Selvaggio."

Aunt Lydia set down the bottle and grabbed a small tumbler, which I noticed already held some brandy. "Surely they aren't worried that Scott would be considered a suspect? He only attended the party at the last minute, you know."

"That may be true. And Selvaggio may have simply shown up today on a whim as well, but . . ."

Aunt Lydia swirled the liquor in the glass as she intently studied me. "You're afraid it might not be quite that random?"

I shrugged. "I don't know. It's just that Scott has done some work in the past, helping the authorities track down evidence on fraudulent businesses and embezzlers and things like that. Who's to say he hasn't run up against Selvaggio in the past? I mean, if the guy is one of Kurt's colleagues, he might have a shady past."

"Or present." Aunt Lydia took a swig of her brandy. "I have to admit I've been wondering the same thing. Especially since Hugh told me that Oscar Selvaggio had been implicated in some dubious art sales. Although, like Kurt, he's never been charged with any wrongdoing."

"If he's moving stolen goods or laundering money or something, Scott might be on his trail. Which could explain why Selvaggio blanched at the sight of him."

"But how would he have known someone like Scott? I'm guessing your brother conducts most of his work from behind a computer screen."

"I wouldn't necessarily assume that," I said. "It's what he leads us to believe, but he's never actually claimed that explicitly."

My aunt polished off the small amount of brandy left in her glass before speaking again. "He probably can't, if what Hugh thinks is true." She set the glass on the counter. "Hugh says Scott has the air of a government man. The type who works in the field, not just in an office."

"You mean, an agent of some kind?" I rubbed the back of my neck with one hand, trying to loosen my stiff muscles. Although

I'd already suspected this, it was interesting to get confirmation from someone like Hugh. "Like FBI or CIA, that sort of thing?"

"Yes, although there are many other agencies engaged in similar activities." Aunt Lydia pulled a white cotton handkerchief from her pocket and dabbed at her lips. "Hugh's worked with several of those, tracking down art forgers and exposing illegal sales of antiquities."

"I suppose it's possible." I tucked a lock of my dark hair behind my ear. "Anyway, if you need help serving the coffee, let me know. Otherwise, I think I'll head out back and see if I can track down Scott. Dad said he heard his car but hadn't seen him come into the house. I thought he might be in the garden."

Aunt Lydia waved me off. "I can handle this. You go and see if your brother is outside, and if so, if he'll talk to you."

"Neither of which is guaranteed," I agreed. "Okay. Just save me one shot of that brandy, would you?"

"I'll put a glass aside for you," Aunt Lydia said with a smile.

I left the kitchen and crossed through the enclosed sun porch to reach the back door. Pausing on the outside stoop, I caught a glimpse of dark hair through the fluttering leaves of a tall rosebush.

"Hey you," I said when I reached Scott. He turned away from his contemplation of the concrete birdbath set in the junction of crisscrossing pea gravel–covered paths. "What's with the disappearing act?"

Scott used one thumb to shove his drooping glasses up the bridge of his nose. "I just needed some fresh air."

"Like earlier?" I tipped my head and surveyed him, noting his calm, unreadable expression. "When you were at the party, I mean. Richard and I saw you walking into the backyard from around the far side of the house. Right before we stumbled over Oscar Selvaggio's body." I twisted a strand of my hair around one of my fingers. "We had to tell the sheriff's department, I'm afraid."

"It's all right. No big secret." Scott brushed a rose petal from the shoulder of his sweater. "I told the deputies I'd been taking a stroll outside around that time."

"You weren't the only one, though."

"No?" Scott's dark eyebrows rose above the top rim of his glasses. "I didn't see anyone else, except for some young woman in a baggy gray dress."

"That would've been Honor Bryant, Oscar Selvaggio's assistant," I said with a frown. "Kurt was taking a walk as well, but he'd headed inside by the time you reached the house, I guess," I said, not sure that was entirely accurate. Kurt had entered the house by the back door prior to Scott crossing the yard, but not so long before that Scott should've missed seeing him.

"Must have." Scott turned back to the birdbath. "Anyone else?"

"There was someone hiking through the woods," I said, debating whether to mention Adele's name. "An older woman in a purple dress. You didn't see her either?"

Scott flicked his fingers across the surface of the water. "No, but I wasn't in that area. I didn't think the woods would be kind to my good shoes, so I just walked down the paved driveway to the main road and back."

"Someone probably saw you, then."

"Not sure. As I said, I didn't encounter anyone else, except that assistant. She kept her head down and was intently focused on her cell phone, though, so it's questionable whether she even noticed me."

"That's unfortunate."

Scott turned around to face me. "Why? Because it leaves me as a possible suspect in Selvaggio's death?"

"I didn't mean . . ." I took a few steps back before stiffening my spine and looking Scott in the eye. "Actually, I did mean that. Brad Tucker, the chief deputy, singled you out for special interest, along with Kurt and that woman in the woods. So it would've been better if Honor Bryant or someone else had seen you when you were out taking your stroll down the lane."

Scott shrugged. "Not that it matters. Selvaggio's death isn't necessarily due to foul play. Could have been natural causes."

I exhaled a gusty breath. "That's true. I guess I've just had so many bad experiences over the last few years. I tend to jump to conclusions."

"You have run into more than your share of murders." Scott's lips twitched into a smile. "Mom and Dad have despaired over your unfortunate habit of encountering killers."

I shook my head. "It has happened far too often recently. But I swear, I don't seek them out. It's just that when there's a mystery to be solved . . ."

Scott laid his hand on my arm. "You can't help but investigate? I know. In that regard, I think we may be more alike than anyone suspects."

"Could be." I covered his hand with mine and looked him up and down. "Now tell me—why are you staying with Aunt Lydia until the wedding? That's a full four weeks. You've never taken that much time off work before, at least not to my knowledge. And don't tell me it's to help out with the wedding preparations. I know better than that."

"You're right, it's not, although I am happy to help. No"—the brightness fled Scott's eyes—"I do have another reason for staying here for a while."

I lifted my hand and stepped away. "You're either working a case or hiding out. Or both. But of course, you can't say."

"That's right." Scott rubbed the side of his nose with one finger. "But don't feel left out. I can't tell Aunt Lydia or Mom and Dad either." He shrugged. "I don't know if they, like you, suspect anything, but can we continue to pretend they don't?"

"In other words, you don't want me discussing it with them."

"In those very words, no, I don't." Scott flashed me a smile. "I won't tell you not to talk with Richard, as I would hate to create secrets between you. It's too rare to see people who really seem to trust one another for me to mess that up. But I hope you'll keep your suspicions to yourself otherwise."

"I promise," I said, before tapping my lips with two fingers. "Speaking of relationships, are you still in one? Last time I saw you, you mentioned some guy named Sean."

"Alas, Sean is long gone. Like all the rest. Unfortunately, I don't seem to have your ability to find the right person."

"Don't give up hope. It took me a while," I said dryly. "Besides, I have a feeling that your job isn't very kind to long-term relationships. All that jetting off here and there."

"It's true. And despite your clumsy attempt to catch me off guard, I'm not going to tell you anything more." Scott offered another smile before strolling past me to reach the main path. "You coming, or do I have to make excuses for you as well to Aunt Lydia and the parents?"

"I'm coming," I said, following him. "And as for excuses, who was the one who always came up with the best ones? The ones that saved us from being sent to our rooms?'

"That was me," Scott called back over his shoulder.

Since he was right, I didn't bother to reply.

Chapter Four

The next morning we accompanied Aunt Lydia to church, which resulted in too many questions from curious parishioners, not just about my family, who rarely visited Taylorsford, but also about the tragic outcome of Kurt's party. After fielding the fifteenth inquiry into Oscar Selvaggio's sudden death, I was happy to spend the afternoon concentrating on an entirely unrelated activity.

Right after we returned home, Richard had left for Clarion University, where he planned to coach a few of his choreography students on their graduation projects. "He's a dedicated teacher," I'd told my family, who, being equally committed to their jobs, understood. Hugh had also headed out, claiming he had to meet up with a friend.

When Dad, who always grew restless if unoccupied for too long, suggested a hike, I'd asked my mom to stay behind with me. It was clear that Scott and Dad were eager to spend the rest of the day outside. Which meant I had to recruit my mother as a cake taster.

"They're off being healthy, and here I am, stuffing my face," Mom said, in an indulgent tone that told me she wasn't actually upset over this turn of events.

I cut a thin slice of caramel-frosted spice cake and slid it onto a paper plate. "One more piece to try."

My mom groaned. "Really? I think I've reached my limit."

Aunt Lydia pointed a silver-plated cake server at Mom. "Now, Debbie, when you agreed to help test options for the wedding reception, I warned you I was making several varieties."

"I know, and they're all delicious. It's just a lot more cake than I'm used to." Mom tapped her temple with two fingers. "My head is spinning from the sugar rush."

"This really is the last one." I carried two slices over to the table. "We do need to narrow it down to three or four options. I think anything more would feel overwhelming."

"Agreed," Mom said, as I sat down across from her.

The center of the table was filled with other plates holding cake slices—some half-eaten and some untouched. Mom had already dug into the various selections, as had I, but Aunt Lydia, who'd been occupied with cutting the samples, had yet to taste anything.

I grabbed a piece of red velvet cake with cream cheese frosting. "Like I mentioned earlier, Mom, we're going to have a local bakery make a small decorated cake that we'll cut for the photos and so on, but we didn't want one of those giant, inedible concoctions that would only please a few guests." I paused to take a bite of my cake. "This way," I said, after licking the frosting from my fork, "people will have several flavor combinations to choose from."

"And Lydia's cakes are amazing, so there's that," Mom said, casting her sister a smile.

"Thanks." Aunt Lydia sat down beside me. "I just thought it was something I could do that would save Richard and Amy some money, as well as offer the guests a choice."

I pushed the red velvet slice aside and reached for a rich chocolate with mocha icing. "We're going to use one of Aunt Lydia's special serving trays. It has several tiers, which will allow us to arrange the slices decoratively. I thought it could be used to create a centerpiece in place of the traditional multitiered wedding cake."

"You know your dad and I would help out with the wedding expenses if you asked," Mom said.

I waved my fork through the air. "I know you would, and I also understand it's tradition for the bride's parents to foot the bill, but it isn't necessary. I mean, I'm thirty-five and Richard is thirty-seven. I think we're old enough to pay our own way."

"I'm going to pay for your dress, though," Mom said firmly.

I smiled. "That I will accept. Fortunately, the one I've chosen isn't going to break the bank."

"Can't wait to see it," Mom said. "When's that fitting again?"

"This coming Saturday. Oh, by the way, Karla will be joining us. She needs to pick out something for herself."

Mom grinned. "Fiona won't be tagging along, I hope."

"I'm not a masochist," I said. "Besides, she's still bent out of shape over the fact that Richard is having a best woman rather than a best man."

"Don't I know it. When she cornered me at yesterday's party, she was quite eloquent in expressing her dissatisfaction with that plan." Mom laid down her fork and pushed her chair back from the table. "I simply told her I thought it was a charming idea, which sent her off, grumbling."

"Fiona does have very strong opinions about any number of subjects," Aunt Lydia said, her expression thoughtful. "But I suspect she's less hard-nosed than she appears."

I side-eyed my aunt. "What makes you say that?"

"Her face when she caught sight of you and Richard standing together. Her expression softened, and she made some offhand remark about being pleased that her son seemed so happy." Aunt Lydia tapped my thigh with her finger. "I think she really wants a closer relationship with Richard. It's just that dreadful husband of hers, with all his bluster and biases, standing in the way."

"You think he runs her life?" my mom asked, with a lift of her dark eyebrows.

"It appears so. To me, anyway." Aunt Lydia shrugged. "I admit she comes off as very opinionated, but I wonder if all those opinions are her own."

I considered this nugget of information as I sampled the chocolate cake. My future mother-in-law, who always seemed so formal and detached in her relationship with her only child, had taken to Aunt Lydia in a surprisingly friendly fashion. Perhaps she'd actually let her guard down around my aunt. It was something worth considering, anyway. Although I doubted I could ever win over Richard's dad, I still hoped to eventually establish a rapport with his mother. Or at least, something more than the polite frostiness that constituted our current relationship.

"Jim Muir does come across as a bully," Mom said. "It amazes me that Richard emerged from that situation as kind and affectionate as he is."

"That constantly astounds me too." I laid my fork across the edge of the plate. "Okay, ready to vote?"

"I don't know how to choose. They're all so delicious," Mom said.

Aunt Lydia toyed with her fork, stirring a few crumbs on her plate. "What would offer the best variety?"

"I think you need the chocolate, because there are always chocolate lovers," Mom said.

"And the vanilla cake with the icing that has that touch of almond flavor." I looked over the selections. "The red velvet for a different color and texture."

"How about one more?" Aunt Lydia tapped the side of her plate with her fork. "The spice cake, perhaps?"

"I think that would round out the flavor options," Mom said as the front door opened.

All three of us turned toward the thump of hard-soled shoes resounding against the wood plank hall floor.

It couldn't be Dad and Scott, I thought, remembering that they'd been wearing sneakers. *But it has to be someone with a key . . .*

"What's this?" Hugh strolled into the kitchen, followed by a younger man I'd never seen before. "Serving up cake without me?"

"You said you'd be out all day, dear." Aunt Lydia rose to her feet to greet Hugh with a peck on the cheek. "Anyway, you aren't that fond of sweets."

"That's true, although you should know I might make an exception for anything you bake." Hugh leaned in and kissed my aunt on the lips before turning to his companion. "Sorry, Fred, I don't mean to leave you just standing there."

The stranger's chestnut-brown eyes swept over Aunt Lydia. "I can see why you'd get distracted," he said, before offering her his hand. "Frederick Nash, but you can call me Fred."

"Lydia Talbot," she replied, grasping his fingers with a firmness that seemed to surprise him. "I suppose you're the friend that Hugh was meeting with today?"

"Yes, ma'am."

Fred Nash's polite but clipped tones, along with his ramrod posture and air of quiet confidence, betrayed a background in either the military or law enforcement. I studied him with interest, puzzling over his connection to Hugh. He looked more like a body builder than anyone involved in the arts.

But that's a stereotype, I chided myself. With a voluptuous figure and a face that resembled a 1920s film vamp more than a nun, I didn't present the image most people expected of a librarian either. Which could be frustrating. All the more reason for me *not* to stereotype others.

Aunt Lydia waved her hand toward the table. "This is my sister, Deborah Webber, who goes by Debbie."

"Hello," my mom said. "And this is my daughter, Amy."

"The bride-to-be?" Fred Nash turned to face Mom and me. "Hugh said there was a wedding on the horizon."

"That's me," I said, meeting his smile with a questioning gaze. "He's never mentioned you, I'm afraid."

"Oh, sorry." Hugh swept back a lock of silky dark hair that had fallen over his forehead. "I've been remiss." He shot Aunt Lydia an apologetic glance. "Fred's actually a colleague as well as a friend. He's assisted me with some investigations into art thefts and other criminal matters."

So he does have a law enforcement background, I thought, as I observed the slight sheen of perspiration beading Fred Nash's upper lip. "You're working a case, Hugh?"

The art expert looked down and shuffled his feet before meeting my gaze. "Yes. An inquiry involving . . . someone you know."

Aunt Lydia stepped back to look Hugh up and down. "Not Kurt Kendrick?"

"I'm afraid so," Hugh said, after sharing a swift glance with Fred Nash.

My aunt wrinkled her brow. "I thought you'd given up digging into his past."

Hugh frowned. "I never said that."

Mom sat up straighter in her chair. "What's Kurt got to do with anything?" She shifted her gaze from her sister's concerned face to Hugh. "I didn't know you were investigating Mr. Kendrick."

"I've actually been doing so for a long time," Hugh said. "There are questions about the legality of some of his art deals, among other things."

Aunt Lydia crossed to one of the butcher-block kitchen counters. "Can I get anyone some coffee, or tea, or anything?" she asked, keeping her back to us.

"You've never found any definitive evidence to indict Kurt, though." I shared a look with Mom. "At least, that's what I've always understood."

Fred Nash leaned against the doorjamb and surveyed me with interest. "That's true; Mr. Kendrick is very good at covering his tracks. But this latest feud with Oscar Selvaggio appeared to offer a way to dig a little deeper. Until Selvaggio was found dead, of course."

"But surely Kurt had nothing to do with that." Mom's brow wrinkled. "I mean, we don't even know that Mr. Selvaggio was murdered, and even if he was, I find it hard to believe that Kurt would be involved. Don't you agree, Amy?"

I stared down at the table, brushing a few cake crumbs into my palm before dumping them back onto one of the plates. "I can't imagine him murdering a visitor to his home. Even if he does tend to avoid talking about his past," I said, remembering a few times when Kurt had refused to answer my questions about whether he'd ever killed anyone.

"Anyway," Mom continued, "enough shop talk. You should both pull up a chair and taste some of this amazing cake. Lydia's testing out some recipes for the wedding reception."

"It does look good." Fred Nash strolled over to the table and sat down next to my mom.

"We'll need extra forks," Aunt Lydia said, with a glance toward Hugh. "Could you bring over a couple, dear?"

"Of course, although maybe just one for Fred." Hugh headed straight for the cutlery drawer and grabbed a fork before returning to the table. "No offense to Lydia," he said, handing the implement to Fred. "She's an excellent baker. It's just that, like she said, I'm not much for sweets."

"It's okay; we know you love her cooking otherwise," I said.

Hugh patted his flat stomach. "A little too much, I'm afraid."

I shot him a sarcastic smile. "Oh right, like you have to worry. You and Richard can both eat like there's no tomorrow and never gain weight. Unlike me, who only has to look at food to add a few pounds."

"And me," my mom said, although her trim figure belied this remark.

I decided to switch the subject back to what really interested me, which was Hugh's investigation into Kurt's business dealings. "So you work with Hugh?" I asked Fred.

"Sometimes," he replied, after swallowing a bit of cake. "It's all delicious, Ms. Talbot. I wouldn't know how to choose between them."

She brushed off this compliment with a wave of one fine-boned hand. "It's fine. We'd pretty much decided anyway. And please, call me Lydia."

Hugh, sitting at the head of the table, surveyed the array of cake slices. "What are you going to do with this? I don't think we can finish them off, even with Nick and Scott's help."

"I've already decided to take most of the leftovers to the church," Aunt Lydia said. "They have a preteen hangout event every Sunday night. I can't imagine those young people refusing free cake."

"I'm sure they won't," I said, before turning my attention to Fred. "What is it exactly that you do, Mr. Nash?"

"It's Fred, and as far as Hugh's investigations are concerned, I just help with some of the legwork. Tracking down forgers and art thieves and that sort of thing."

"You're a police detective?" Mom swiveled in her chair to study Fred more closely.

"Not officially. I do work with the police and other authorities, but I'm not on the force." Fred lowered his gaze and toyed with his fork. "Not anymore."

Hugh crossed his slender arms over his chest. "I call in Fred when I need to track the movements of certain individuals. He has the experience with fieldwork that I lack."

"So you're a PI," I said.

Fred looked up and met my inquisitive gaze. "Basically. I hunt down information. And people, if need be."

I narrowed my eyes. "And you're looking into Kurt Kendrick?"

"And Oscar Selvaggio. Among . . . others."

"Is this connected to something called the Kelmscott Chaucer?" Aunt Lydia asked. "Kurt mentioned that both he and Oscar Selvaggio were interested in that book. They seemed to be rivals for its acquisition. Of course, that was before Mr. Selvaggio died so unexpectedly."

"Which is unfortunate," Fred said, after sharing a swift glance with Hugh. "I'd hoped to question him about a few matters, but that's obviously off the table now."

"Do you think the book is stolen property or something?" Mom asked.

"Let's just say we aren't certain of its provenance," Hugh replied.

"But that wouldn't have anything to do with Kurt, or Mr. Selvaggio, would it?" Aunt Lydia fixed Hugh with her brilliant blue gaze. "As I understand it, they were only seeking to buy the thing, not sell it. Wouldn't the crime, if any, be connected to the seller? Even if it was stolen property, how could Kurt have known that?"

Hugh's thin lips twitched. "Trust me, if this Kelmscott Chaucer was illegally acquired, even years ago, Kendrick and Selvaggio would've known. They both have—or had, in the unfortunate Mr. Selvaggio's case—enough contacts in the art world to at least suspect an item of having a questionable past."

I stared at Hugh. "I know you've been looking for some hard evidence to pin on Kurt for many years. Without success. Did you think this particular investigation might lead to something more damning?"

"Possibly. It's hard to say." Hugh's gaze swept around the table before landing on Aunt Lydia's face. "There were rumors of Kendrick's involvement with this particular item in the past. Which made me question whether he was buying it to display or sell, or whether he just wanted to cover up one of his earlier indiscretions."

Aunt Lydia shoved back her chair and stood up. "Really, Hugh, you need to get over this obsession with Kurt. You've been at it for years, trying to find the evidence to put him away, and haven't been able to make a case stick yet. So why bother? Just let it go."

Mom's brown eyes widened. "I didn't know you were that fond of Mr. Kendrick, Lydia."

"I'm not," my aunt said, her tone tinged with exasperation. "I just don't like to see Hugh wasting his time on something that will give him ulcers."

Hugh rose to his feet to face off with Aunt Lydia. "I think I'm the best judge as to what information I should or shouldn't pursue."

"Fine. If you think it's worth sacrificing your health to chase after nebulous rumors . . ."

"Come now, Lydia, it's a little more than that." Hugh extended his hand. "If this is really about what we might dig up on Andrew, you know I won't share such information with anyone."

My aunt's sharp intake of breath hung in the air as my mom turned to me, holding up her hands as if to ask, *What gives?*

I shook my head. My uncle, Andrew Talbot, who'd died in a tragic accident before I was born, had been an artist. He'd also been Kurt's closest friend, staying in contact with him even after marrying my aunt. Although she'd learned that fact only recently.

Among other things, I thought grimly. Kurt had tried to help my uncle when he'd gotten mixed up with some less-than-honest individuals. Something I suspected my aunt appreciated and resented in equal measure.

Aunt Lydia lifted her hand, palm out, in a *stop* gesture. "No more," she said, after a swift glance at Fred Nash.

"I will protect your late husband's good name any way I can," Hugh said, his expression hardening into an implacable mask. "But I must reveal the truth, when I find it. If that implicates Andrew . . ."

"You don't care?" My aunt's fine features appeared chiseled from ice. "Well then, I suppose it's just as well I learned this now. Before our lives became more entangled." She lifted her chin and stared at Hugh for a moment before turning on her heel and marching out of the kitchen.

"Lydia, please wait a minute." Hugh cast the rest of us an apologetic look before following her.

Fred absently tapped the table with his blunt fingernails. "That took a turn."

"There's some history behind it," I said. "But it's a little personal. If Hugh hasn't told you anything about my late uncle . . ."

"He hasn't," Fred said.

"That's good. Maybe that will be enough to mollify Aunt Lydia."

"I wouldn't bet on it," Mom said, her expression darkening. "What's all this talk about Andrew, anyway? I thought you were helping Hugh investigate Kurt and that Selvaggio fellow."

"That's what I thought too." Fred's thoughtful tone warned me that he might be putting two and two together.

I decided I'd better try to refocus his attention. "Do you really believe you can catch Kurt Kendrick involved in something illegal? I'm not saying he isn't, or at least, hasn't been in the past, but it seems he always expertly covers his tracks."

"Perhaps, but in this case, with someone dying on his doorstep . . ."

My mom made a derisive noise. "No offense, Fred, but I think you are jumping to some very strange conclusions. I admit Kurt can come off as mysterious, but I can't imagine him harming anyone." She ran her fingers through her feathery cap of dark hair. "I may not be a trained investigator, but I think I'd know if I was in the presence of a murderer."

I opened my mouth and then snapped it shut before speaking the words that had popped into my mind. *No, you wouldn't. I didn't. I haven't. More than once.*

Chapter Five

Since Mom and Dad weren't scheduled to leave until Tuesday morning, I'd arranged to take Monday off. Sunny was happy to work some extra hours to fill in, claiming that her duties as mayor could wait one day. "The former mayor didn't do anything for years," she told me with a smile. "What's a missed day or two on my watch?"

Although I'd planned to spend the day with Scott and my parents, touring a few of the wineries in the surrounding area, my nagging curiosity got the better of me and I begged off the excursion. I was anxious to do some research on the Kelmscott Chaucer and knew that online searching would yield only so much.

"There's something I'm researching that requires a little extra digging," I said at breakfast. "For work, you know. Anyway, I think I'll check out the resources at the Clarion library." I met Scott's inquisitive gaze and gave a little shake of my head. He'd obviously guessed my true intention, but as always, he kept his opinions to himself.

Aunt Lydia set another plate of her famous pancakes on the dining room table. "Please, eat up, everyone. These aren't as good reheated."

I eyed her with concern, noting the shadows under her eyes. Hugh had left after dinner the evening before. That was significant, as he always stayed over until Monday morning during his weekend visits. I knew this signaled some rift between him and my aunt and suspected it had to do with his bringing in a PI to investigate Kurt—a choice he'd staunchly defended throughout the previous day.

My dad waved his fork at me. "Work? Admit it—you just want an excuse to have lunch with Richard. I remember you telling us that he has another rehearsal tonight and you probably wouldn't get to see him today."

"Guilty," I said, although this wasn't quite true. Of course, I'd be happy to see Richard, but what I really wanted was to find more information on the rare Kelmscott edition that both Kurt and Oscar Selvaggio had hoped to buy. I didn't clarify that point, as I wasn't sure my parents would approve of my obsession with such research, especially since it was connected with yet another suspicious death. They would, on the other hand, understand me ditching them to spend time with my fiancé.

I sent all of them off after extracting a promise that they'd bring back a few bottles of wine that we could taste test for possible use at the wedding reception. Dad drove, leaving me the car I shared with my aunt.

Fortunately, Clarion University was only a thirty-minute drive, a fact that made Richard's daily commute bearable. I parked in one of the visitor lots and hiked across campus to the library, where I'd worked before taking the director position in Taylorsford.

I stopped by a few offices to say hello to some of the librarians I'd known during my tenure at Clarion. They all seemed happy to see me and to hear updates about my new job and the wedding.

Not even one disapproving look, I thought as I took the elevator to the reference department. Ironically, I'd fled my job at Clarion because I'd thought I'd made a fool of myself over my cheating former boyfriend. But it appeared that no one had actually cared about my childish actions. Honestly, it seemed I could've stayed at Clarion and everything would've simply blown over.

But if I'd stayed, perhaps my life wouldn't have turned out so well, I thought. *I might not have met Richard in a setting where we could really get to know each other. I wouldn't have been able to spend as much time with Sunny, or become so deeply involved in the life of my new hometown either.* I smiled as I walked off the elevator. *I'm glad I'm a stronger, more confident person now, but leaving Clarion was a hidden blessing. My past behavior might've been foolish, but in the end, its result was the best thing that ever happened to me.*

I chose a seat at one of the wooden carrels that lined one wall of the reference department, draping my jacket over the chair to reserve it while I perused the stacks. After a short search, I tottered back to my carrel, my arms laden with books, including a facsimile copy of the original Kelmscott Chaucer. Settling into the armless task chair, I opened my laptop to take notes.

The story of the Kelmscott Press, founded in 1891 by William Morris, was a fascinating one, and I was soon lost in my research, oblivious to the passing of time and anything happening around me. So oblivious, in fact, that I didn't hear my name being spoken until someone tapped my shoulder and repeated it.

"Amy, so nice to see you again," said Emily Moore, a celebrated poet I'd met when she'd moved to Taylorsford the previous autumn.

I spun around in the chair and looked up into her square-jawed face. Her dark eyes blinked owlishly behind the round frames of her glasses.

"Emily, hello." I motioned toward the chair at the next carrel. "Please, have a seat. If you have a minute, I mean."

"I have all the time in the world." Emily's smile illuminated her strong-featured face. "I just finished teaching a class and that was it for the day, so I thought I'd do a little digging for a new project." She pointed at my pile of books. "I see you're also engaged in research. I hope I'm not bothering you."

"Not at all." I brushed a lock of dark hair away from my face. "I just had a free day, and thought I'd look into something for work."

Scooting closer, Emily peered at the spines of my books. "The Kelmscott Press?" She sat back in her chair and looked me over. "That's not something I'd expect one of your patrons to be asking about."

"You'd be surprised," I said lightly. I didn't want to go into my reasons for this research. Particularly not with Emily Moore, who was savvy enough to make connections, given any hints.

"It's a fascinating period. I studied some of the Pre-Raphaelite poets once upon a time." She smiled. "Many of them led such tumultuous lives—even put some of the antics of my hippie generation to shame."

"It is interesting. I have an undergrad degree in art history, so I knew about William Morris's design influence. Father of the Arts and Crafts movement and all that. But I didn't know much about his work as a publisher."

Emily shrugged. "That was just an extension of his design work, though, wasn't it?"

"I suppose so. Definitely the Chaucer, with the Burne-Jones woodcuts and Morris's elegant designs for the borders and initial words, is as much a work of art as it is a printed book." I pulled the facsimile copy from the stack of books and passed it over to Emily. "Only four hundred and twenty-five copies were printed. On handmade paper, no less."

"And typeset by Morris, I believe." Emily flipped through the facsimile. "The originals would be stunning, wouldn't they?"

"I'm sure. I haven't seen a real one, although my research turned up a copy at the University of Maryland, so maybe"—I met Emily's interested gaze with a smile—"a road trip is in order."

"You probably need an appointment," Emily said absently, her eyes fixed on one of the illustrated pages of the facsimile. "You know, this reminds me of something. Some conversation I was involved in once. What was that?" She tapped her chin with one finger. "Oh yes, I remember now. It's a funny coincidence, really, because it involved someone whose name I heard again recently."

"Who might that be?" I asked, leaning forward to take the book from her hands.

"That poor man who died out at that art dealer's house. You know, he collapsed and died at some party . . ." Emily covered her mouth with one hand for a moment before speaking again. "Oh dear, you were there, weren't you? I remember hearing your name mentioned in the news."

"Actually, my fiancé Richard and I discovered Selvaggio's body," I said grimly. "The party was in honor of our upcoming wedding. Kurt Kendrick hosted it for us."

"That's right, Kendrick. The art dealer. Which was what Selvaggio was too, you know."

"I'm aware." I twisted the hem of my cotton tunic between my fingers. I wasn't sure if Emily had actually forgotten Kurt's name or was just trying to pretend she'd never met him when they were both much younger. In any case, that wasn't the mystery I wanted to pursue. "What did you hear about Selvaggio in the past? I'm just curious, having been thoroughly interrogated by the sheriff's department about the man."

Emily rolled her shoulders in a mock shiver, reminding me that she was almost as well-known for her dramatic readings as for her poetry. "Oh dear, I know how dreadful that can be. To be honest, it was so long ago. I was still in New York at the time, so it must be more than forty-five years." Emily lowered her lashes to veil her eyes. "But I remembered the name, because I thought it had a poetic ring to it. Sel-vag-gio," she said, drawing out each syllable.

"He was already an art dealer at the time?"

"Oh yes. He apparently dropped by the Factory to speak with Warhol once or twice, although Andy never sold him anything.

Didn't like the look of him, or so I heard." Emily shrugged. "I'd left the Factory by then, so this is all hearsay."

"Why did his name come up in a conversation then?"

"Because there was a scandal, and if there was anything my artsy New York pals liked better than shocking the public, it was a scandal involving someone else in the arts scene." Emily adjusted her tortoiseshell glasses and fixed me with her slightly myopic stare. "Oscar Selvaggio apparently sold someone a stolen Kelmscott Chaucer, and when the poor fellow tried to subsequently insure it, the truth came out. He was investigated, and even though it was eventually proven that he had nothing to do with the theft and no knowledge of receiving stolen goods, it affected him so adversely that he died from a heart attack. Or so his children claimed."

"Really? Was Selvaggio ever arrested?"

"No. Strangely, he was cleared, or at least never prosecuted. No one knew why at the time, and one of the dead man's children— his daughter, I believe—was absolutely furious over the whole affair. Made a big noise in art circles, but her accusations never seemed to affect Selvaggio, at least from what I know." Emily shrugged. "At any rate, the last thing I heard was that he continued to buy and sell art without any interference from the authorities."

"That is interesting," I said, filing away this information to consider later. "It sounds like Mr. Selvaggio wasn't exactly the most honest of individuals."

"Apparently not. Just like . . ." Emily closed her lips over whatever words she'd meant to say next and simply lifted her hands. "But that's not such an unusual thing in the art world, I'm afraid."

"No, it isn't, as I sadly found out not too long ago," I said, thinking about my own run-in with forgers and thieves.

"Well, now that I've bent your ear about some ancient history, I should go and let you get on with your research." Emily rose to her feet. "We should get together sometime. I've discovered a few nice little restaurants not too far from Taylorsford. Maybe we can meet up when you can get away from the library for a longer lunch?"

"That would be nice," I said, adding with a smile, "But not at the Heapin' Plate, I take it?"

"Heavens no." Emily flung one dangling end of her paisley scarf over her shoulder. "The diner's good for a quick bite, but hardly haute cuisine."

"True, although I don't think Bethany is aiming for that." I held out my hand. "Good to see you again, Emily."

"You too." Clasping my fingers tightly for a moment, she stared directly into my eyes. "I didn't realize you were such close friends with that Kendrick fellow. I'd be careful there. I mean, I don't really know the man, but I've . . . heard things. Just a word to the wise." Dropping my hand, Emily scurried off before I could reply.

I stared after her for a moment before turning back to my pile of books. *Everyone's heard things*, I thought with a sardonic smile. *But I can do better than that, Ms. Moore. I actually know a few things.*

Enough to always be careful in my dealings with Kurt Kendrick, no matter how much he seemed to care about me, Richard, or the rest of my family. Enough to believe he could've had a hand in Oscar Selvaggio's death, if anyone had.

I checked my watch and realized I needed to leave soon if I hoped to make it across campus to meet Richard at his studio by noon. But before I deposited the books I'd pulled on a reshelving cart, I opened the Kelmscott Chaucer facsimile one more time. Staring at the beautifully decorated title page reminded me of something I'd just typed into my notes—a quote from a letter Edward Burne-Jones had sent to Charles Eliot Norton in 1894:

> *Indeed when the book is done, if we live to finish it, it will be like a pocket cathedral . . .*

And it had been exactly that—a magnificent edifice captured on paper, a work that captured the soul of two great artists. Something rare and wonderful.

And sadly, I thought, as I closed down my laptop, *perhaps something worth killing for.*

Chapter Six

After our parents departed on Tuesday morning, Scott and I shared a second cup of coffee while Aunt Lydia headed outside to work in the garden.

"I'll join you in a minute," Scott said before she left the kitchen.

Aunt Lydia just raised her eyebrows and mentioned something about an extra pair of garden gloves in the hall closet.

"I can tell she doubts me," Scott said.

I sipped my coffee and studied his unreadable expression. "You have to admit that garden work has never been your thing."

"True." Scott waved his mug at me, sloshing a little coffee over the rim. "But I do want to help out while I'm here. I know you're busy, with the wedding planning as well as your job, and I don't think Aunt Lydia should be doing all the heavy lifting."

"Besides, you're looking for something to do." I cast him a smile. "I know how restless you get when you aren't occupied with work."

"I am used to being busy," he admitted with an answering smile.

"I'm sure she'll appreciate the help. Just be willing to take direction." I absently swirled the remaining coffee in my cup. "She has her way of doing things."

"I don't doubt it." Scott pushed his chair back and stretched his arms over his head. "What are your hours today?"

"Eight to five," I said. "The library is actually open until eight, but Sunny will be coming in around noon and staying on to cover the later hours. Along with a volunteer or two, of course."

"That's right, you told me Sunny's only working part-time now because she has her mayoral duties too. How's that going?"

"Fine. I was able to hire someone who lives in town to fill in the other hours. One of our regular patrons, Samantha Green. She's actually quite good."

"You mean Sunny had better watch out?" Scott shot me a grin, but his expression grew immediately thoughtful. He took a long swallow of his coffee before speaking again. "On another subject, and just between you and me, I was a little surprised Hugh left right after dinner Sunday night. When I met him the other day, he said he'd be staying until Monday morning."

I shrugged. "To be honest, I suspect he and Aunt Lydia are on the outs."

"There was definitely some tension crackling over the dinner table Sunday night." Scott set down his mug. "You think it's because he's asked that Nash guy to dig into Kurt Kendrick's business interests?"

I finished off my own coffee before replying. "I believe she's more concerned with what they might unearth from Kurt's past."

"I see. Something to do with Uncle Andrew, then."

"Exactly. Remember that whole mess about a year and a half ago? All that stuff about forgeries?"

"You told me a little about it." Scott slid one finger around the rim of his empty mug. "Although I think you were deliberately vague about some of the details."

I wrinkled my nose at him. "There are some things that Aunt Lydia prefers to keep quiet."

"Especially from me?" Scott adjusted his glasses. "I know you all suspect that I'm too closely tied to a few government agencies."

"Aren't you?" I asked as I rose to my feet, my empty mug dangling from my fingers.

"I think I'll leave that alone." Scott stood up as I reached over and grabbed his cup with my other hand.

"Which answers my question." I carried both mugs to the dishwasher.

"I'm not trying to be evasive," my brother said.

"I know." I turned around. "You can't say. Just like you can't tell me why you're staying here for several weeks." I looked him over as he stood to face me. "It does seem like an odd choice, though. Wouldn't anyone tracking you discover such a close family connection?"

"Are you worried?" Scott's expression darkened. "Don't be. You should know better. I'd never draw danger anywhere near my family."

"But if you have to lay low, doesn't that mean you're in hiding?"

Scott shook his head. "It isn't that people are looking for me. It's that they need to think I've been put on indefinite leave."

"That you've been suspended, you mean." I tapped my temple with my forefinger. "I get it. Whoever it is needs to think you've been removed from whatever mission you were on."

"Something like that." Scott shoved his hands into the pockets of his jeans and rocked back on his heels. "Still determined to sleuth out all the answers, aren't you? You just can't let things go until you solve the mystery."

"Seems like that runs in the family." I grabbed my purse from the table and strolled out into the hall.

*   *   *

As I did on most fine-weather days, I walked to work. It was a pleasant way to incorporate more exercise into my schedule and also allowed Aunt Lydia and me to share one car. Besides, I enjoyed the ever-changing landscape. Every season had its own charm, but I especially loved the late spring, when the gardens that filled the fenced front yards of many of the houses overflowed with color and fragrance.

Taylorsford dated back to the eighteenth century, so historic properties lined the main street. Toward the center of town were a few businesses housed in brick buildings erected in the late 1930s or '40s, but most of the private homes were older. They came in a variety of styles: simple, two-story wood structures with plain black shutters and stoop porches rubbed elbows with elegant Victorians sporting gingerbread trim. The oldest and rarest were built in the style of English cottages from the fieldstone once prevalent in the area. It was the same mottled gray stone that had been used to build Kurt Kendrick's home, as well as the low walls dividing farm fields outside of town.

Strolling beneath the arched canopy formed by the trees that lined the sidewalk gave me the feeling of walking under the intricately beamed vault of a cathedral. As I gazed up into the interlaced branches to watch bright-red male cardinals and their dull-brown mates flit through the crisp green leaves, the toe of my leather loafer caught on a loose piece of cement, sending me staggering forward.

"Oh dear, do be careful," said the person who grabbed my shoulder and righted me before I tumbled to the ground.

"Thank you." I turned to face this savior of my dignity. "Hello. I don't believe we've met."

"Probably not. I'm a visitor to Taylorsford."

"Welcome, then. I'm Amy Webber, director of the public library."

"Very nice to meet you. Cynthia Rogers," the stranger said, offering me her hand.

I looked her over as she gave my hand a firm shake. She was my height, but certainly older—in her early seventies, or at least her late sixties. Her pale-pink cotton tunic-and-slacks set was complemented by magenta sneakers, a choice that made me suspect she was one of those feisty older ladies who enjoyed being fashionable as well as comfortable when they traveled.

"Is this your first visit to Taylorsford?" I asked.

"Not at all." The older woman patted her short gunmetal-gray hair. "I've been here before, on day trips. Always loved it, so I swore I'd come back to spend a little more time exploring the town and surrounding areas."

As Cynthia Rogers widened her eyes behind the round lenses of her pewter-framed glasses, I noticed their unusual shade. *Gray, but they can probably look green, or even a dusky blue, depending on the light or the color she's wearing.* "Are you staying at the inn?"

"No, the Hill House bed-and-breakfast."

"I've heard that's very nice. I'm sure you'll enjoy it." I brushed a crab apple petal from my amber silk blouse. "And thanks again for preventing my tumble, but I'm afraid I must get going. I have to open the library"—I glanced at my watch—"very soon."

"Perhaps I could accompany you? I've been wanting to stop by. I understand it's a Carnegie building?"

I set off at a brisk walk. "Yes. There's an addition that was added later, but it's at the back, so the facade still looks like it did when it was built in 1919."

"Lovely." Cynthia Rogers easily kept pace with me. "I can take pictures, I assume?"

I shot her a sidelong look. "Of course. Inside as well. We just ask that you don't take any photos of our patrons without their permission."

"For privacy reasons, I assume?"

I paused on the sidewalk in front of the stone library building. "Exactly. We're careful about that, especially when it comes to children and young people. I mean, anyone can walk into a public library, and that's fine, but . . ."

"You don't want to encourage any exploitation? Very sensible." She slid a cell phone from her pants pocket.

I looked at my watch again. "I must leave you now. I need to get everything set up before we open. It'll be about fifteen minutes, so feel free to take some outdoor shots. You might want to get a few of the Lutheran church across the street too." I offered her a smile before striding toward the staff door located on the side of the building.

Inside, I crossed through the workroom to reach the main part of the library, then turned on lights and brought up the circulation system computer before making a sweep of the building.

The high-ceilinged main room, with its dark wood trim and tall, deep-set windows, housed the main desk, public computers, current periodicals and general book stacks. It was separated from a small reading area by an arched opening decorated with carved-wood trim. After scanning the main space, I headed to the back of the library. The 1960s addition lacked the charm of the original structure but did provide space for a children's room and staff break room.

At exactly nine AM, I opened the front doors, where I was greeted by Bill Clayton, one of our most reliable library volunteers, and Cynthia Rogers.

"Got some good shots of the outside," she said, waving her cell phone as she strode past me. "By the way, where are the public restrooms? All that coffee I sucked down at the B and B is running right through me."

Bill pointed down the short hall that led off the flagstone-floored foyer. "That way, ma'am."

Cynthia thanked him before disappearing into the ladies' room.

"Nice woman, but nosy," Bill said, as we passed through the open inner doors and circled around behind the circulation desk. "While we were waiting, she bombarded me with questions about how long I'd lived here, who my family was, and stuff like that. Like I was supposed to know her or something."

I straightened some local-attraction flyers in a display rack on the desk. "I think she's just a curious traveler. You know, one of those people who likes to learn everything about every place they visit."

Bill shook his head of shaggy gray hair. "I don't know. She seemed familiar somehow. Maybe it's just that she has an extremely average appearance. Like she could be anyone."

"That's probably it. She does look like a lot of the other tourists who visit Taylorsford. Especially the older ladies," I said. "Now—I need to pull some materials for our homework crowd later today. There's a big English project they all seem to be frantically trying to finish at the last minute." I grinned. "You know how students are."

"Don't I ever. Don't miss that," said Bill, who'd taught algebra and other math classes at the local high school for over twenty-five years. "Well, to be honest," he added, "I really mean the bureaucracy. I do miss the students."

I patted his arm. "You get to see them here. And I'm thankful to have you to assist with any math questions. Not my forte."

"Happy to help," Bill said.

I flashed him a smile before heading out into the stacks. Pushing a metal rolling cart, I perused the list of books I'd printed at home after searching the online catalog over the weekend. I normally encouraged the students to find their own research materials, but occasionally, when they were all looking for the same items, I pulled a few ahead of time. It eased the panic over projects that were almost always due the next day.

As I knelt down to search one of the lower shelves, something blocked the light falling in from the windows. Looking up, I spied Cynthia Rogers standing over me.

I used the metal support post on the range of shelves to pull myself to a standing position. "Hello again, Ms. Rogers. Something I can do for you?"

She offered me an apologetic smile. "Please, call me Cynthia. And sorry to bother you while you're obviously busy, but I did have a question. It's a local-history thing, really. I thought perhaps you'd know the answer, since I've heard you manage the town archives as well as the library."

I brushed some dust off my black slacks. "Maybe. If I don't know off the top of my head, I can certainly do a little research and find out."

"It's about a novelist. Someone local, so I figured you'd know of him, even though he passed away many years ago." Cynthia fiddled with her glasses, adjusting the earpieces over her exposed ears. "Paul Dassin— ever heard of him?"

"Why yes, I know quite a bit about him." I rolled the cart back against the shelves to clear a path in the aisle. "As a matter of fact, he's my fiancé's great-uncle."

"Really?" Cynthia widened her eyes. "What a coincidence!"

I smiled. The woman did give off a nosy vibe, but that didn't bother me. I exhibited that trait myself when something interested me. "What do you want to know?"

"I read a couple of his books, and I'm just fascinated by the details he includes about the area. Was it based on fact?"

"Some of it. Look, why don't we sit in the reading room, where we can talk more comfortably." I motioned toward the tables and chairs in the open area beyond the archway.

"I don't want to pull you away from your work."

"No problem. I can finish this later." I walked into the reading room and pulled out a heavy wooden chair at one of the round tables.

Cynthia followed and sat down across from me. "It's very kind of you."

"Really, it's okay. Answering questions is a big part of my job." I leaned forward, resting my arms on the table. "You said you'd read some of Dassin's books. Was one of them *A Fatal Falsehood*?"

"Absolutely. That was actually my favorite."

"It's one of his best. And that one is definitely based on a true event, a local murder trial from 1925. Although he did change names and several other details when he wrote the novel. To protect the privacy of the real people involved," I added, recalling Paul Dassin's love for the woman who'd inspired his main character.

"I'd heard that." Cynthia balanced her elbows on the table. "Paul Dassin's home is still standing, isn't it? I'd love to see it. From the outside, of course. I hear it's a private home."

I sat back in my chair. "It is. It was originally owned by Daniel and Eleanora Cooper, the couple Paul Dassin based his victim and accused murderer on in *Falsehood*. Paul Dassin lived there later on."

"After Eleanora Cooper, who was Lily in the book, disappeared?"

I tapped my foot against the carpet. It was obvious that Cynthia Rogers had done her homework, which made me wonder why she needed answers from me. But I figured there was no harm in indulging her desire to chat. Perhaps she was just one of those people who enjoyed talking about things they'd learned, which was, I had to admit, another trait we shared. "Right, although the book's ending is quite different than reality. Happier than what actually happened to Eleanora. And Paul too, I suppose." I examined Ms. Rogers's face, which was alight with curiosity. "Ironically, it's the same house where my fiancé lives now, next door to where I currently share a house with my aunt. Lydia Talbot," I added, when my companion quirked her eyebrows. "She's the granddaughter of Rose Baker Litton, who was also represented by a character in *Fatal Falsehood*."

Cynthia rested her sharp chin on her interlaced fingers. "Let me guess—the next-door neighbor to the poor accused woman? But her name wasn't Rose in the book. Something else—I forget exactly what."

"Correct." I shifted in my chair, not sure I wanted to follow this train of questioning. References to my great-grandmother Rose, whom I apparently resembled, always made me a little uneasy. "Anyway, the old Cooper place, where the events related to the murder trial took place, was later purchased by Paul Dassin. He lived there the rest of his life, and then bequeathed it to his niece. Who happens to be the mother of the man I'm going to marry. I'll actually be living there soon." I lifted my hands. "Which does make it quite a coincidence that you should ask me these questions."

"Really? Who would've thought?" Cynthia sat back, dropping her own hands into her lap. "Perhaps I could visit sometime? After your marriage, of course. I'd love to see the interior and relate it to the book."

I shook my head. "It doesn't look the same. Paul Dassin made changes, and then Richard had it completely renovated. He mostly kept the 1920s style of the house, but I'm afraid it wouldn't match what you read in the book."

"Too bad." Cynthia traced an old set of initials carved into the tabletop with one finger. "So Paul Dassin didn't have any children?"

"He never married." I opened my mouth to add that he'd taken in a foster child named Karl Klass for several years, but thought better of it. Although Karl, who'd later changed his name to Kurt Kendrick, made no secret of his former association with Paul Dassin, it wasn't something recorded in any information about the novelist. At least nothing I'd ever seen. Which meant it wasn't necessarily something I felt I should share with a stranger, no matter how pleasant she was.

"That doesn't always mean he didn't have a child." The other woman's gaze swept over me. "But apparently there were no known heirs. Other than his niece, I mean."

"That's right," I said, pushing back my chair and standing up.

"So you'll be living in the old Cooper place. How romantic." Cynthia rose to her feet with a bright smile. "Anyway, I've taken enough of your time. Thanks so much for allowing me to ambush you with my questions."

"You did save me from a tumble," I said. "I think we're even."

"Not so sure about that." Cynthia extended her hand again, but this time she firmly clasped my fingers without shaking them. "I hope we'll meet again soon, Ms. Webber. Although I probably won't return until the summer, and I suppose you'll be Mrs. Muir by then." She flashed another smile and released my hand. "I guess I should offer my congratulations now."

I pulled my hand free and stepped back as Cynthia turned and strolled away.

Staring after her, I puzzled over the fact that she was familiar with Richard's last name. I hadn't mentioned it, which meant either that the owners of Hill House had been gossiping too freely about matters that didn't concern them or that Cynthia Rogers was definitely one of the most inquisitive people I'd ever met. *Which isn't*, I reminded myself, *such a terrible character flaw.*

Or at least I hoped not, considering it was one we shared.

Chapter Seven

Sunny arrived around noon and immediately demanded an update on the Oscar Selvaggio case. I had to tell her I didn't know any more than she did.

"It's not like Brad is keeping me posted, and since you guys broke up, we don't have that direct line of communication anymore," I said as I waved good-bye to Bill, who had completed his volunteer hours.

"Sometimes he still tells me a few things." Sunny swept her long blonde hair away from her face and tied it into a ponytail with a scrunchie. "We're still friends, you know."

"I think we're friends as well, but I doubt I could get him to tell me more than what he's willing to share with the public." I studied my friend's classic profile. "But then again, I don't possess your charms."

"I don't think Richard would agree with that assessment," Sunny said. "Oh, by the way, how's that good-looking brother of yours? I heard he was hanging out in town for a few weeks."

"My brother is gay, as you well know."

Sunny cast me an amused glance. "Of course I know that. I wasn't thinking of dating him myself. But there might be someone else who'd be interested." She elbowed me and surreptitiously pointed toward the *New Books* rack, where firefighter Ethan Payne was perusing the latest additions to the collection.

A handsome, well-built man in his late twenties, Ethan had been one of my rescuers a couple of years earlier, when I'd suffered a traumatic tumble into an abandoned well. I'd gotten to know him a little better when our paths crossed again about a year ago. But that brought up another point. "He has a boyfriend, remember? He and Chris Garver are a couple."

"Not anymore." Sunny held one finger to her lips as Ethan approached the desk.

"Hi, Ethan, how are you today?" I asked, shooting Sunny a warning glance.

"Doing great," he said, as he laid a new James Patterson novel on the circulation desk. "Just grabbing this before a hundred other people find it." He offered us a lopsided grin. "There's a lot of waiting around at the station. Which isn't a bad thing. When all's quiet, that means no emergencies. But I like to keep occupied, and I'm not much for playing video games or cards."

"Books are better anyway," Sunny said. "A truth you seem to have discovered fairly recently. I don't remember you using the library much before this year. Now you're here all the time."

Ethan rubbed one temple, mussing his well-groomed short hair. "Never did much reading before last year. Didn't like it in school. But then someone introduced me to some more entertaining stuff and changed my mind."

I suspected that this someone had been Chris Garver but decided not to mention that name. "You're still living out on Logging Road?"

"Yeah. But"—Ethan met my inquisitive gaze squarely—"by myself now."

"Oh? Sorry to hear that." Noticing the delight brightening Sunny's face, I nudged her sandaled foot with my loafer. "Things didn't work out between you and Chris?"

Ethan shrugged. "We parted on friendly terms, but yeah." He pulled his wallet out of his pocket and extracted his library card. "Here you go," he said, handing the card to Sunny.

"It happens, doesn't it?" Sunny scanned the card under the bar code reader and handed it back to him. "I'm between significant others myself. Not that I mind. I've got so much to juggle these days, between this job and my duties as mayor, I don't have time for dating."

"That was part of my problem. My hours are so weird, it's hard to make plans." Ethan refiled the card and pocketed the wallet. "At least, it's difficult if the other person really craves routine. Not something I can offer, I'm afraid."

"You need someone who's willing to be more flexible," Sunny said. "Maybe even someone with a job that isn't so nine-to-five."

I side-eyed her. "Not that you need anyone to set you up, I'm sure."

"Oh, I don't know." Ethan flashed a grin. "If you know any guys who are as nice as they are nice looking and who aren't ready to settle into a routine, I'm all ears."

This time I pressed my foot over Sunny's before she could offer up my brother's name. This earned me a dirty look, which I ignored. "Sorry, can't think of anyone right now. But if I do, I'll be glad to point you in the right direction."

"Thanks." Ethan stepped through the security gates as Sunny slid the checked-out book to the end of the desk. "I'll probably be back in a couple of days, so if any names do come to mind . . ." He winked at Sunny as he picked up the book.

She opened her mouth and snapped it shut again when she caught a glimpse of my face. "Enjoy your book," she told Ethan as he headed for the exit.

Sunny rapped the pitted surface of the desk with her knuckles. "I don't see the harm in introducing him to Scott."

"I think we'd better ask first," I said. "Given the nature of his job, Scott has to be careful about his associates, romantic or otherwise."

"I doubt Ethan presents a national security risk."

I straightened a pile of bookmarks. "You never know. Maybe being a firefighter is just a cover for clandestine activities."

"Oh sure." Sunny cast me an exasperated look. "Because Taylorsford is such a hotbed of espionage."

I looked up and noticed the man who'd just walked in from the foyer. "Speaking of secret investigations, there's the guy I told you about."

Sunny pressed her palms against the desktop so she could lean forward. This action caused her low-cut peasant blouse to gape, exposing a little more of her cleavage than might be considered appropriate in a library setting. "That's Fred Nash?"

"Yes." I wrinkled my nose as I observed the sparkle in my friend's blue eyes. I knew what that meant. "He's just here to help Hugh for a week or two. I doubt he'll be hanging around for long."

"Maybe so, but then again"—Sunny's ponytail bounced as she tossed her head—"I'm not really looking for a long-term commitment."

"Just be careful. We don't really know anything about him," I murmured. Raising my voice, I addressed the private investigator. "Hello, Mr. Nash. How can we help you?"

"By calling me Fred, for one thing." As soon as he reached the desk, he thrust out a hand to Sunny. "Fred Nash, and you are?"

"Sunshine Fields," she replied, dropping back down on her heels. She shook Fred's hand firmly. "But I go by Sunny."

Fred held on to her hand a little longer than I thought necessary. "That name sounds familiar. Wait, aren't you the mayor?"

"I am, but I also work here. Part-time for now. Until someone replaces me as mayor, which will probably happen in the next couple of years."

"That's not what I hear." Fred looked her up and down with a gaze that was as appreciative as it was appraising. "I'm doing a little investigating to aid an art expert who has some business in Taylorsford . . ."

"I know Hugh." Sunny cut him off with a flick of her hand. "I'm good friends with Lydia Talbot as well as Amy, so I've had the opportunity to spend time around Mr. Chen." Her bright-eyed gaze swept over Fred's muscular body before focusing on his handsome face. "But I bet you knew that already."

He shrugged. "As I said, I've heard several people talk about the new mayor. All good things," he added. "Although they didn't tell me that she was quite so young and beautiful."

I cleared my throat. "Now that we've all been introduced, was there something that you needed, Fred? Related to the library, I mean."

"Probably more so the archives," Fred said, tearing his gaze away from Sunny long enough to look me in the eye. "Hugh told me the library manages the town history and records. Is that right?"

"They're housed in a separate building out back." I glanced around the main room of the library. It was a fairly quiet day. I could probably spare the time to escort Fred Nash to the archives and perhaps even pull him a box or two of material.

"I'll go," Sunny said, before I could voice this thought. "I mean, if it's all right with you, Amy. And if Mr. Nash—sorry, Fred—has the time to look at anything now."

"I can make the time," Fred said, his gaze resting on Sunny. "This is as good a time as any," he added, shooting me a quick glance.

"That's fine, we aren't really busy . . ."

Sunny turned on her heel and headed for the staff workroom, which was located right off the desk. "I'll get the key," she called over her shoulder.

"What exactly you are looking for in the town records?" I asked.

Fred shifted his weight from one foot to the other. "Just corroboration for some info I've already gathered."

"Nothing to do with my uncle Andrew, I hope. I know you may feel it's ancient history, but my aunt's very protective of his legacy. She doesn't want anyone tarnishing his reputation." I met

Fred's laser-sharp stare with a lift of my chin. "You might want to remind Hugh of that. If he wants to continue to date her, I mean."

"Here it is!" Sunny bounced back behind the desk, the archives key dangling from her fingers. "Ready, Fred?"

"Lead the way," he said, with a sweeping gesture worthy of an eighteenth-century courtier.

Sunny immediately headed for the back door of the library, with Fred right at her side.

"You know that fellow?" asked a familiar voice.

I turned to face Brad Tucker.

"Not really. I only met him yesterday." I noticed that Brad was staring down the hallway that led to the back door. The door that had just closed behind Sunny and Fred Nash. "He wanted to search the archives, and Sunny offered to help."

"Department gossip says he's a private investigator now, working with Dr. Chen." Brad twisted the brim of his hat between his fingers. "But he was a cop once. Worked his way up to become part of some high-level task force in DC."

"Really? I figured he'd been with the police, but . . . high up, you said.? I wonder why he left."

"Had to, from what I hear." Brad's eyes narrowed. "Some sort of scandal. I guess it didn't involve anything criminal, or if it did, there must not have been enough evidence to charge him. Anyway, he has a clean record."

I raised my eyebrows. "You checked?"

"Felt I had to. Some guy shows up in my jurisdiction, running his own private investigation . . ." Brad shrugged. "I thought it wise to check him out."

"That makes sense." I took a deep breath. "By the way, I wanted to apologize to you and Alison. I didn't realize Kurt hadn't invited you to the party, or I would've insisted he include you."

Brad shook his head. "Don't worry about that. We understood. Between you and me, I think Kendrick is a little leery of inviting the authorities to his home, even as guests."

"But you've been there before," I said, and then cursed my stupidity. Yes, Brad had once attended a holiday party at Kurt's home. But only because he'd been Sunny's date.

Fortunately, Brad didn't appear disconcerted by this remark. *I guess he's really, truly over Sunny.* It was a thought that made me happy, for Alison Frye's sake as well as Brad's.

"You could be right," I said, keeping my tone light. "By the way, is there any news on Mr. Selvaggio's death? Any that you can share, I mean."

Brad's pleasant expression turned stony. "Unfortunately, yes. And I can tell you one thing, because it will be all over the evening news anyway—it wasn't a natural death."

"What?" The pitch of my voice made Mrs. Dinterman, one of our regular patrons, turn from the cookbook section to stare at me.

"Yes," Brad said grimly. "He was killed."

"But there wasn't any blood . . ." I pressed my palms against my temples. Despite our vow to avoid such things, it looked like Richard and I *had* stumbled onto another murder.

"Because Mr. Selvaggio died from ingesting a poison." Brad straightened the brim of his hat before placing it back on his head. "The coroner confirmed that easily enough. Aconitum. Even though it does occur naturally, it's not something Selvaggio could've accidentally ingested, especially not in that concentration."

"That's from a plant, right?" I leaned into the desk to brace my wobbly legs.

"Yeah, aconite. Commonly called monkshood or wolfsbane or blue rocket." Brad shrugged. "I'm no gardener, but I was told that it's common enough and can be found in flower beds all over this region."

"But how would Mr. Selvaggio have ingested it?"

"Someone obviously made a tincture out of the roots, which are the most poisonous part, according to our expert. It could've then been slipped into a drink, something with a strong enough taste to mask the poison, and Selvaggio wouldn't have necessarily noticed."

An image of Adele stirring a dark liquid in a glass flashed through my mind. And then there was my dad's remark about Kurt handing his rival a snifter of cognac . . . I cut Brad off with a wave of my hand. "But regardless, why did Mr. Selvaggio end up out in that shed? You think he was lured there by his murderer?"

Brad's frown deepened. "We aren't sure, although Mr. Selvaggio's assistant, a young woman called Honor Bryant, claims that he rushed outside after receiving a text. Unfortunately, Selvaggio's phone is missing, so we have no way to verify that yet."

"You think someone drew Oscar Selvaggio out to that shed and then gave him a drink laced with poison?"

"Not necessarily. He could've been poisoned a little earlier. Not long before, as aconite in that dosage tends to kill pretty quickly, but there could've been a short gap between him drinking the poison and collapsing in the shed. Long enough for him to stumble out there and die, anyway." Brad pulled at his tight collar. "Our expert says the symptoms can be mistaken for a stomachache, or just a racing heart and difficulty breathing. Which wouldn't have been that unusual in a man of his age and physical condition."

"So, deliberately poisoned." I traced a question mark across the surface of the desk with my finger. "But why?"

"Over a valuable artifact, maybe? Sorry, Amy, but from everything I've learned, Oscar Selvaggio appeared at that party uninvited and unannounced. In fact, at this point it seems unlikely that any of the guests would've known he had any plans to visit Highview, that day or any other." Brad's steely expression softened. "Which points to the one person who might've expected his arrival. Someone battling him for possession of what I understand is an extremely valuable book. A man who had a reason to want Selvaggio out of the way. Your host, and sadly, now our primary suspect."

"Kurt Kendrick," I said, my fingers clenching as Brad nodded.

Chapter Eight

I was doubly glad for my date at Richard's house after work. It was one of the rare days in April when he didn't have to stay late at Clarion University for an end-of-semester dance rehearsal, which meant I'd actually get to see him before ten or eleven in the evening. It allowed me to share Brad's information with him face-to-face.

"The authorities really think Kurt is the most likely suspect?" Richard leaned back against the sofa cushions and stared up at the high ceiling of his living room. "It just doesn't compute with me. Kurt's too clever to murder someone on his own property. And he certainly wouldn't do so at a party where any number of people could have seen something."

I shot him a sidelong glance. "I notice you aren't claiming he wouldn't ever kill anyone."

Richard met my raised-eyebrow expression with a wry smile. "Should I?"

"Probably not." I stroked the sleek fur of the tortoiseshell cat curled up on my lap. "But I agree it seems out of character. Not the murder, perhaps, but the sloppy way it was handled."

"What's your opinion, Loie?" Richard asked, leaning in to pet the cat. She rolled over and stared up at him with her bright-green eyes. "No comment? A lot of good you are."

Loie yawned, displaying her sharp white teeth.

"She finds our human concerns beneath her," I said. "By the way, where's Fosse? He's usually looking for a lap the minute Loie finds one."

"Basking in the sunshine on the porch, last time I looked." Richard draped his arm around my shoulders. "They were both out there before you arrived, so I'm sure he'll bound into the room as soon as he wakes up and realizes Loie has disappeared."

"No doubt. By the way, there's another thing I wanted to mention related to the party." I tightened my lips as I considered my next words. I had to tread carefully. Adele Tourneau was someone Richard cared about deeply.

"What's that?" Richard's fingers caressed my shoulder. "Not something about my parents, I hope. I know they were being . . . well, I guess *less than congenial* is the nicest way to phrase it."

"Nothing like that. It was something else that gave me pause." I took a deep breath. "When I was in the kitchen, I saw Adele in the butler's pantry, pouring a very stiff drink."

Richard's dark eyebrows arched. "You're afraid she's turned into a secret alcoholic? I wouldn't worry too much about that. I know she likes a shot now and then, but she's never been one to overdo it."

"It wasn't that. As far as I'm concerned, she can grab a drink whenever she wants. It's just the way she was acting, like I had caught her doing something she didn't want anyone to see." I leaned closer to Richard and looked up at him from under my lowered eyelashes. "Like spiking a drink, maybe?"

Richard sat back and pulled his arm away. "With what? I hope you aren't suggesting she poisoned Selvaggio."

"Of course not," I said, straightening until my back didn't touch the cushions. Loie glared at me before making a disgruntled noise and leaping onto the coffee table. "But if someone else saw her, they might've wondered."

"Did you mention this encounter to the authorities?"

"No, because frankly, I forgot all about it until Brad mentioned that Selvaggio had been poisoned."

Richard's gaze slid to the wall behind my shoulder. "I imagine they can figure out whether he had a particular liquor in his system. That will clarify things."

"Which is why I still see no point in mentioning the incident. If I hear that it was whiskey or brandy or anything that color"—I crossed my arms over my chest—"I may have to say something. I couldn't see any label on the decanter, but the color was distinctive enough to know it wasn't a clear liquid like gin or vodka."

When Richard lowered his gaze, I could read the distress in his gray eyes. "I've never seen Adele drink whisky or brandy or any dark liquor."

I reached out to clasp his hands. "Maybe she was making it for someone else. I mean, I got that impression, and it's actually what she told me. Perhaps for Kurt. She could've just been looking out for him. You know how it is when you're the host—sometimes you don't have time to snag any food or drink for yourself."

Richard tightened his grip. "Maybe. That would be something Adele would do. She's always looked after others."

"Right." I gave his fingers a gentle squeeze before releasing his hands. "Anyway, my dad mentioned something about Kurt handing Selvaggio a cognac too, which I guess keeps him at the top of the suspect list."

"Better him than Adele," Richard said, meeting my inquiring gaze with a tight smile. "Let's face it—if anyone could outwit a murder charge, it would be Kurt."

"True, but let's not worry about all that right now. Especially where Adele is concerned. I mean, what possible reason could she have to harm anyone?"

"None I can think of." Richard exhaled a gusty breath that made Loie jump off the coffee table. "I just don't like the thought of either Kurt or Adele being under suspicion."

"I'm not too fond of that idea myself. But seriously, I'm sure neither one of them are involved." I leaned in and gave Richard a swift kiss. "No reason to worry."

"Are you trying to distract me?" he asked, taking hold of my shoulders.

"Is it working?"

"Always does," he replied, before pulling me in for a more serious kiss.

After several minutes, a paw batting my bare foot made me pull away. "What do you want now?" I asked Loie, who stared up at me innocently before casually nipping my big toe.

I yanked my foot away, sharing a few choice words about Loie's parentage.

Richard laughed. "That's one way to get your attention."

I made a face at him. "Oh yeah, very nice. Let her bite you and see how funny it is."

"She's done it plenty of times. Often while I'm dancing, which is even worse," Richard said, his expression sobering. "Look, she has something wrapped around her tail. What is that?"

I leaned down and pulled a fragment of fabric from Loie's fur. "Bit of ribbon," I said, before a crash resounded from the back of the house. I jerked up my head to meet Richard's horrified gaze.

"The gifts!" we shouted in unison as we both leapt to our feet.

Richard, with his longer stride, beat me to the small room located directly across the hall from the kitchen. Normally used as an office, it had been commandeered as storage space for the wedding gifts we'd already received. The gaily wrapped packages were piled on an old wooden desk that filled the center of the room.

Or they had been stacked on the desk. Now half of them lay in a jumble on the floor.

"Thank goodness there's a thick rug," I said, hoping none of the tumbled gifts held breakable items.

"Another reason I'm glad we didn't request any formal china or crystal," Richard said, scooping up one of the packages. He shook it near his ear. "Nothing rattling."

"Except my nerves." I grabbed a couple of smaller boxes. "How did the cats get in here? I thought you were keeping the door closed."

"I was, but I swear that one"—Richard pointed toward an orange tabby crouched inside one bookcase shelf—"has opposable thumbs."

The cat turned his golden-eyed gaze on me. "Fosse, did you really open the door?" I asked as I placed the gifts I held on the desk.

"It's possible, especially if the door wasn't tightly latched, which would've been my fault." Richard sighed. "I've caught him before, sticking a paw under and wiggling it back and forth until the door popped open."

"Naughty cat." I picked up a small blue box with a tightly fitted lid. "Hold on, I don't remember seeing this one before. Did someone just recently drop it off, or was it mailed?"

Richard deposited the last of the tumbled boxes on the desk before turning to look at the gift I held. "Who's it from?"

"I don't know. There isn't a tag." I turned the box over, but found nothing to indicate the sender.

"Maybe it's inside." Richard frowned as he moved closer. "That's odd. I don't remember receiving that box, and it isn't even wrapped . . ."

"I know. Just a box without wrapping paper. And the box looks old too, doesn't it?" I held the gift up to the light spilling in from the back window. "Like the color has faded over time."

"Could've been stored for a while before it was used. But yeah, it's a little unusual." Richard tapped the box lid with his forefinger. "This doesn't feel like the typical cardboard used in boxes today. It's a much heavier material."

"Should we open it? I think we should," I said.

"I thought we were waiting a few weeks to unwrap everything. Hasn't Lydia planned some sort of family dinner around that?"

"Yes, but"—I touched the lid with my fingertip—"for some reason, I feel we should open this one now. I mean, it's one mystery we can easily solve, and I could use one of those."

"Okay, why not." Richard offered me a warm smile. "You do the honors."

I smiled in return before popping off the lid to reveal a smaller hinged box covered in white velvet flocking. "Looks like a jeweler's box."

"Also looks old."

"It does, doesn't it? Well, here goes." I lifted the lid. Nestled in a bed of sapphire blue silk lay an antique-looking pendant on a gold chain.

Richard leaned in to peer at the contents. "That's different. Is there a card?"

I gently peeked under the lining, then glanced at the underside of the hinged lid, thinking it might be taped there. "No, I don't see anything."

"Strange," Richard said. "Who'd send jewelry without a note? Especially since it looks like an antique."

I lifted the pendant from the box. At first glance, I'd assumed that the decoration had been painted on a convex oval of ceramic or metal enclosed in a gold frame, but then I realized it was actually real flowers under glass. Dainty sky-blue petals and fragile gray-green stems and leaves were pressed against a feathery background of white milkweed floss.

"This must be old. It's something they did in the late nineteenth or early twentieth century," I said, setting the box on the desk as I handed the pendant to Richard. "Although I suppose it could be a modern reproduction."

Richard held up the pendant by its chain. "From the look of the goldwork, I'd say it's probably original. Mom has a lot of antique jewelry, and this chain and bezel are similar to her pieces." He dropped the pendant into his palm and looked at it more closely. "What are the flowers?"

"I think they're forget-me-nots."

Looking up, Richard gave me a knowing look. "It's something old and something blue."

"What?" I crossed over to the bookshelf and pulled a protesting Fosse into my arms.

"You know, the old rhyme—something borrowed, something blue, something old, something new?"

"Oh, right." As soon as I set the wriggling cat down on the floor, he dashed out the door and into the hall. "Someone obviously sent this for me to wear on our wedding day." I took the necklace from Richard and held it up to my neck. "But who?"

"A mysterious benefactor, apparently." Richard looked me over. "It does look good on you. But I don't know how well it will go with your dress."

"Quite well, I'd say. I might need to adjust the chain, but otherwise it will probably work." I balanced the pendant in one palm, allowing the chain to drape over my hand. "Anyway, I think I'll take this back to Aunt Lydia's and keep it with my other jewelry."

"Are you going to show it to her? She might have some idea where it came from. Maybe one of her friends?"

"I'll ask, for sure." I grabbed the white box from the edge of the desk and carefully placed the necklace back inside before slipping it into the deep pocket of my cotton dress. "But what do you say we head into the kitchen? I don't know what you've planned for dinner tonight, but whatever it is, I'm happy to help put it together."

"No need," Richard said, as he followed me out of the office. "I confess to cheating and buying premade dishes at a gourmet shop near Clarion. All that's required is removing some packaging and microwaving."

"Good, 'cause I'm suddenly starving." I watched as Richard closed the office door and then double-checked that it was secure. "Cat-proofed now?"

"If anything can be," he said with a grin.

We were greeted by both Loie and Fosse, who were sitting smack-dab in the middle of the archway that led into the kitchen. I slipped past them while Richard headed for the cabinet where he stored the dry cat food. "I know, I know," he said. "I have to feed you two first. Or I'll never hear the end of it."

"They have their priorities," I said.

"Yeah, themselves," Richard replied, in an indulgent tone that told me he didn't really mind. He filled their bowls before turning back to me. "Sometimes I think we're their pets, to be honest."

I slipped my arms around him and looked up into his amused face. "You ever doubted that?"

"Not really," Richard said, before kissing me.

Chapter Nine

My new library assistant, Samantha Green, had quickly learned that spotting the "The Nightingale" meant a dash into the stacks. This particular patron had earned her nickname by her habit of trying to "help" by shelving any books left out on tables or elsewhere. The only problem was that the Nightingale, who'd never learned the Dewey decimal system, tended to shove books anywhere. Adult fiction ended up in the auto repair section, while children's picture books were interspersed among the cook-books. Knowing this, the library staff and volunteers had learned to shadow the Nightingale as she made her rounds.

"Back in a minute," Samantha said, as soon as we both noticed the tall, bony figure appear Wednesday morning and immediately disappear into one of the far rows.

I gave her a mock salute. "Your sacrifice is appreciated."

Samantha grinned before heading into the stacks.

Left alone, I checked the integrated library system, or ILS, on the desk computer, searching for any new interlibrary loan requests. As I compiled a file of titles to search later, my aunt's best friend, Zelda Shoemaker, appeared at my elbow.

"Oh, hi," I said, saving my file before turning to face her. "I didn't realize you were volunteering today."

"I switched with Denise. She had a doctor's appointment." Zelda patted her expertly dyed curls. Unlike my aunt, she eschewed her natural color, claiming that her hair had turned an unattractive yellowish gray rather than Aunt Lydia's pure white. While that might've been true, there was also the fact that with Zelda's relatively unlined face and rosy cheeks, the blonde tint of her permed curls made her appear ten years younger than her sixty-seven years.

I frowned. Denise, who typically volunteered more hours than Zelda, had originally signed up to work into the evening. Since Samantha was working the late shift, she'd be alone after I left around five. "Are you planning to stay later? Denise had signed up for that."

Zelda rolled her eyes. "Don't worry, we worked it out. Bill's coming in at five. He'll stay with Samantha until closing."

"That's great. I just wish you'd told me ahead of time," I said, fighting a twinge of irritation. I appreciated the library volunteers, but sometimes they forgot to include me in their schedule changes. I was concerned that this might cause a major problem one day. "You know I like to be informed when you guys switch things around. Just in case I need to cover in an emergency."

Zelda tapped my arm with her pale-pink polished nails. "You worry too much, Amy. It's going to age you before your time."

"That's not the only thing that will do it," I said, thinking of my unfortunate habit of stumbling over dead bodies. "I guess you heard that the sheriff's department is focusing their investigation into Oscar Selvaggio's death on Kurt Kendrick?"

Zelda pursed her lips. "There were a lot of other people there. Maybe more than one with a reason to want to kill that rather obnoxious man."

"What do you mean? Did you see something?"

Zelda's light-brown eyes sparkled. I loved her dearly, but I had to admit that she liked nothing better than sharing juicy gossip. Something I always had to remember when I spoke with her. "Just one of the guests being manhandled by that Selvaggio fellow, that's all."

"Are you serious? I hope you informed the authorities," I said, my mood brightening as I realized that this might take some of the focus off Kurt. *Or Adele, or my brother*, I thought.

"Of course I did." Zelda stroked her plump jawline with one finger. "I don't know who it was, as we weren't introduced, but I definitely caught Selvaggio grabbing the woman's arm and giving it a pretty rough shake. They were alone in the kitchen at the time. When I walked in, Selvaggio dropped the woman's arm and strode past me without meeting my eyes."

"Really?" The kitchen . . . I realized she could be talking about Adele, and if so, I'd better tread carefully. "Did the woman say anything?"

"Not really. She thanked me for walking in when I did and made some small talk about the party, but that was all." Zelda's expression turned thoughtful. "Now that I think about it, it seems even stranger that she didn't introduce herself. But maybe you know her—a slender older woman in a purple dress?"

I coughed to cover the swear word that almost escaped my lips. It looked like I would be forced to lie, or at least skirt the truth, to prevent my aunt's inquisitive friend from jumping to any unwanted conclusions. Gripping the edge of the circulation desk with both hands, I forced a smile before speaking again. "That would be Adele Tourneau, a former dancer who was once Richard's coach. She's known Richard and his friend Karla for a long time, and Kurt Kendrick has been a patron of some of her dance charities for many years, so it's not surprising she was invited."

"Seems like she also knew Oscar Selvaggio before the party."

I shook my head. "I'm not sure about that. Maybe Selvaggio grabbed her because he was trying some sort of clumsy advance. He came off as overly flirtatious to me, and Adele is a very attractive lady."

"I don't think it was that." Zelda narrowed her eyes. "Because the guy said something like 'Don't forget I know what you tried to do,' which made me think they were already pretty well acquainted."

I swept up a scattering of loose bookmarks from the desktop and shoved them back into their plastic display holder. "But even so, he might have had a thing for her for years and finally took the opportunity to make a move."

"That doesn't quite fit what I observed." Zelda's expression brightened as her gaze flitted toward the entry doors. "But look— it's your brother. I didn't realize he was still in town."

"He's staying with us for a few weeks. A little break from work." I caught Scott's eye and waved him over.

"Brought you some lunch, courtesy of Aunt Lydia," he said, holding up a brown paper bag. "She said you'd left without packing anything and was worried you wouldn't have time to run out to the diner."

"Thanks," I said, taking the bag. "Let me just set this in the back."

As I turned away to head into the workroom, I heard Zelda bombarding Scott with questions about his visit. I smiled grimly. I was grateful he'd shown up to distract Zelda before she could pry any further into Adele's connection to Selvaggio but sorry he'd also be obliged to lie to her if she asked too many personal questions.

Returning to the desk, I was greeted by another familiar face. "Hi, Ethan," I said, as the firefighter slipped a book into the return slot in the desk. "Finished with the new Patterson already?"

"Yeah, it's been slow at the firehouse—which is good, of course." Ethan nodded at Zelda and Scott. "Hello, Ms. Shoe-maker, how are you?"

"Very well, thank you," Zelda replied, motioning toward Scott. "This is Amy's brother, by the way. I doubt you've met. He doesn't visit us rustic folks in Taylorsford much."

Ethan extended his hand. "Ethan Payne," he said.

As the two men shook hands, I noticed them checking each other out. Something Zelda also seemed to observe, if the sudden spark of glee in her eyes was any indication.

"Scott's another brilliant member of the Webber family, or so I'm told," she said. "One of those computer experts, doing stuff I can't for the life of me understand."

"Cybersecurity, for the most part," Scott said, his gaze fixed on Ethan. "You're a firefighter?"

"Yeah." Ethan rubbed his short hair with one hand. "I some-times help out the EMTs too. I work for the county."

"I thought the local firefighters and EMTs were mostly volunteers."

"They are. But the county hires a few professionals to supervise the volunteers and do training and that sort of thing." Ethan shifted his weight from one foot to the other. "Anyway, we're happy to have Amy here, running the library. She's done a great job."

"I'm sure," Scott said, with a swift glance at me.

"Ethan's the one who helped rescue me that time I was trapped in the well," I said.

Scott raised his eyebrows at me before focusing on Ethan. "So you're the guy? Thanks for that. It could've been a tragedy, if what I heard later was true."

Color rose in Ethan's cheeks. "I was just doing my job."

"We still appreciate it." Scott pushed his glasses up to the bridge of his nose as he continued to examine Ethan intently.

I had talked to Scott about my rescue, but I knew that wasn't what had captured his attention. Recently I'd also mentioned Ethan's involvement in a later investigation. One that had included his then boyfriend, Chris. "I'd hate to have lost my big sister, especially that way," Scott said.

Zelda shuddered. "Oh, don't remind me. That would've been horrible." She tossed her head, bouncing her crisp curls. "But thankfully that's all in the past. Now we can happily look forward to celebrating her wedding."

"Right, that's coming up soon, isn't it?" Ethan asked.

"Less than four weeks now. That's one reason Scott's here," I said, thinking it wouldn't hurt to add verisimilitude to my brother's cover story. "He had a break from work and wanted to visit Aunt Lydia, then just decided to stay for the wedding."

"You'll be around for a few weeks?" There was no mistaking the interest brightening Ethan's expression.

Zelda gave me a knowing look. "That's right. Come to think of it, Ethan, maybe you could show him around town. Amy and Richard are so busy with work and wedding preparations, and while Lydia would probably be happy to play tour guide, Scott might prefer the company of someone closer to his own age."

I groaned inwardly. Zelda was an inveterate matchmaker. Not that I minded the thought of Scott dating Ethan, but I also knew my brother. He resisted outside involvement in his personal life like a cat fighting a leash.

To my surprise, Scott simply tipped his head and studied Zelda for a second before turning his gaze back on Ethan. "That would be nice, although I don't want to insert myself into your undoubtedly busy schedule."

"It really wouldn't be a problem. I have two days off a week. It's just that I don't always know when they'll be. But if you're flexible about the timing, I'd be happy to show you some of the sights. Although"—Ethan fiddled with his collar for a moment—"haven't you seen everything already? I mean, you have family living here and all."

Scott's smile broadened. "I do, but I don't get to visit much. In fact, it's been quite some time since I was here. I'm sure many things have changed."

"Well, it was nice to see both you boys, but I suppose I should get back to work," Zelda said, circling around to stand next to me behind the desk. "If I don't do my fair share, Amy might not allow me to volunteer anymore."

I snorted. "As if I'm going to turn away free help."

Scott and Ethan, discussing some of the recent changes in and around Taylorsford, didn't appear to hear me.

Zelda nudged my foot with her shoe. "I'll watch the desk if you want to eat lunch," she said in a quieter voice. "I know Samantha has to lead story hour in the children's room as soon as she's done correcting the Nightingale's shelving."

"If you're sure that's okay, it would be a help." I cast one final glance at Scott and Ethan, who'd moved away from the desk but were still chatting. "I'll just take a half hour today, though. Eating alone in the break room isn't really something that makes me want to linger."

"No problem, dear. Take as much or as little time as you want. I'll be here." She winked. "And maybe they will be too," she added, bobbing her head in the direction of Ethan and Scott.

"Hmmmm . . ." I shook a finger at her. "Now, promise you'll behave. You're looking far too much like a cat among the canaries. No more blatant matchmaking, okay?"

Zelda grinned. "Don't worry. I think my job is done."

After I grabbed my lunch from the workroom, I cast one last glance at my brother and Ethan before I crossed to the children's room. They certainly seemed to be enjoying their conversation, which was fine, although . . . I chased this thought away for a moment to let Samantha know she was free to set up for story hour, since Zelda was covering the desk.

But as I slumped into one of the break room's hard plastic chairs, I analyzed the bubble of concern that had risen in my chest when I'd observed Ethan and Scott.

I loved my brother, but his track record in the romance department was not the best. Mainly due to his work, of course. Ethan might think his career, with its erratic schedule, was a detriment to establishing a long-term relationship, but Scott's globe-trotting, secretive job was even worse. *Honestly*, I thought as I gnawed on a piece of celery, *I'm worried about Ethan, not Scott. My brother won't mind if a new relationship turns out to be just a fling. I'm not so sure Ethan will feel the same.*

These thoughts were interrupted by a knock on the break room door.

"Come in," I said, after swallowing a bit of celery.

Samantha poked her head around the door. "Sorry to bother you, but there's a lady here who said she knows you. Adele Tourneau?" There was a wariness in Samantha's dark eyes. Aware of my history of helping the authorities with murder investigations, she knew that not everyone who wanted to talk to me was a friend.

"It's okay. She can come in," I said. "Thanks."

As Samantha ushered Adele into the break room, she said, "If there's anything you need, just shout."

I cast her a warm smile. "Don't worry. You have enough to do, dealing with the little monsters."

Samantha returned my smile before gently closing the door.

I wiped my mouth with a napkin as I motioned toward a chair. "This is a pleasant surprise. I thought you would've left town by now."

Adele sat down, facing me across the table. "I decided to spend a few extra days." She shrugged her slender shoulders. "I have so little to do these days outside of my charity work. So whenever I travel, I like to take my time."

"Are you staying at Highview?"

"Oh no, Kurt and I are friendly, but we aren't that close. I have a room at one of the local B and Bs." Adele fanned her face with both hands. "It's rather stuffy in here, isn't it? And a trifle drab and closed in, especially in comparison to the main part of the library."

"Welcome to the 1960s. Unfortunately, this space was an add-on, like the children's room just outside." I looked around, taking in the plain painted drywall and acoustic-tile drop ceiling. "It doesn't have the charm of the original, that's for sure. Or the high ceilings and natural ventilation."

"No, I'm afraid it is lacking in all those aspects." Adele looked drained. Deep lines grooved her forehead, and her elegant features appeared pinched.

I pushed my lunch to one side and leaned forward, resting my forearms on the table. "What can I help you with, Adele? It seems like you want to ask me something."

"Not so much help as . . ." Adele tucked an errant strand of silver hair behind one ear. "To be honest, dear, I'm afraid you might've gotten the wrong impression of me at the party." She twitched her thin lips into a smile. "I'm really not a lush, you know, despite you catching me depleting Kurt's liquor stores."

"I never thought you were."

Adele fluttered one of her slender hands. "I got the feeling you were taken aback when you found me in the butler's pantry, and then we didn't really have time to talk later, so I just wanted to be sure."

"I wasn't concerned about the drink; I was worried because you seemed agitated. Not that there was anything wrong, but I felt you just weren't your usual calm and graceful self, that's all." I studied the older woman's lovely face for a moment as my mind calculated the timing of our encounter. If it had been *after* Oscar Selvaggio accosted her, perhaps that explained everything. "Someone told me that you had an unpleasant encounter during the party. Was that before I saw you?"

"What?" Like a deer sensing danger, Adele stiffened. "I don't know what they could possibly be referring to. I had no such issue at the party."

"You didn't have a run-in with Oscar Selvaggio?" I narrowed my eyes as I kept my gaze fixed on Adele's wan face. "Someone said you did."

Adele stared down at her hands, which she had clasped together on the table in front of her. "Heavens no. I never even spoke to him."

"But you've met before?"

"Not really," Adele said, without looking up. "I've seen him at some events, that's all. He and Kurt run in the same circles, and you know Kurt has supported many of my charity efforts." She lifted one hand and examined her unpolished fingernails. "But I've only seen him in passing, and I certainly didn't know he was invited to Kurt's party."

"He wasn't." I sat back, dropping my hands into my lap. "He just stopped by to talk to Kurt about some item they both wanted to buy. A Kelmscott Chaucer, from what I understand."

At the mention of the book, Adele's fingers clenched into her palms. "Really? Well, I wouldn't know anything about that."

I was sure she was lying but decided not to call her on it. "Anyway, that's one reason why the authorities are focusing on Kurt as a suspect. I guess they think he has a motive, although I can't imagine Kurt killing someone over a deal. Other things, maybe," I added, with a little laugh.

When Adele raised her head to meet my gaze, her eyes were wary. "Be careful, Amy. I am fond of Kurt, but he does associate with people I find . . . distasteful."

"Like Oscar Selvaggio?"

Adele sniffed. "I'd say Selvaggio would've been one of the least dangerous of Kurt's associates. There are far worse."

"I don't doubt that, but I also don't think Kurt would allow them to get close to anyone he cared about."

"One can't always control such things. Not even someone like Kurt Kendrick." Adele shoved back her chair and rose to her feet. "I don't want to see you or Richard or Karla or anyone, really, harmed due to the actions of people who are willing to take risks for gain. Or even," she added, her voice dropping to a lower register, "someone who made a mistake, once upon a time."

"What are you saying, Adele? That I should stop asking questions? Or answering them?"

"I'm just suggesting that you concentrate on your upcoming wedding and leave investigating to the authorities." Adele crossed to the door but paused with her hand on the knob and turned back to look me in the eye. "Whatever you think you saw, whatever you hear, and no matter what gossip falls into your lap, please leave this alone, Amy. For Richard's sake as well as yours."

She opened the door and fled before I could ask additional questions, like why she'd been wandering in the woods around the time of Oscar Selvaggio's death. Rising to my feet, I repacked my half-eaten lunch and walked out into the children's room, where Samantha was reading from Henry Cole's picture book *A Nest for Celeste*. I tiptoed through the room, earning a few glances from parents, although the children were too interested in the book to pay me any attention.

As I crossed into the main room of the library, a tall, raw-boned woman stepped in front of me.

"I need to tell you something," said the Nightingale.

"Can it wait?" I asked, maneuvering my way around her.

Undaunted, the Nightingale followed at my heels. "It's about that woman. The one who just talked to you."

I stopped in my tracks and turned to face her. "What about her?"

The Nightingale tugged down the hem of her rumpled blouse. "I saw her fighting with that man that got himself killed at that party."

I stared into her angular face, worried by her triumphant expression. "What do you mean, fighting? And how did you see any such thing?"

"I was walking by that B and B in town. Hill House, they call it. Crossed around back to take a shortcut and there they were— your friend and that foreign man I saw on the news. The murder victim," the Nightingale added with relish.

"When was this?"

"Day before that party where he got himself poisoned, as best I recall."

I took a deep breath to calm my racing heart. "But surely they weren't actually fighting?"

"Maybe not hitting or anything, but there was yelling and threats and stuff like that." A cunning look crossed the Nightingale's face. "Suppose I should tell the sheriff that, shouldn't I?"

"Have you?" I asked, furiously considering whether I should tell Brad about this information before the Nightingale provided her undoubtedly embellished version.

"Not yet. But I think I will. Duty as a citizen, don't you think? Yes," she added, as she moved away from me, "I think I will."

As soon as she disappeared out the front doors of the library, I sprinted over to the circulation desk. "Don't ask," I told Zelda as I slipped around behind her and dashed into the workroom.

Before I called the sheriff's office, I made sure to close the workroom door. Given the Nightingale's sudden realization of the importance of what she'd seen, she was bound to spread the story of an argument between Adele and the murder victim far and wide. I didn't need anyone else, especially Zelda, involved before I had a chance to talk to Brad.

I sighed as I waited to be connected to Brad's office. I knew I'd have to tell him everything I'd seen and heard involving Adele, even the scene in the butler's pantry. It wasn't what I wanted, but there was nothing else I could do. The truth had to come out before lies and fabrications spun by town gossip made everything that much worse.

Chapter Ten

I didn't hear more news from Brad after I shared my information on Adele, which I hoped was a good sign. In the meantime, I had to focus on a few other things, like dress fittings for the wedding. With only three weeks until the ceremony, I was getting anxious to have this task completed.

"Sorry, too frilly," Karla said as Sunny pulled another dress from the rack. "Besides, since you're wearing blue, I should have something that will blend well with that." Karla cast me a glance. "There's another bridesmaid too, isn't there? What color is her gown?"

"Jessica's wearing a shade of blue as well," I said. "She sent me a photo, and it looks like it will work well, color and style-wise. It's a darker shade but in the same hue, so it should complement Sunny's gown just fine."

Aunt Lydia, who was seated in one of the velvet upholstered chairs provided for guests, pursed her lips. "A pity that she can't come until a few days before the wedding. I hoped she'd be able to offer more help with the preparations."

"She wanted to. But then her university insisted on scheduling a mandatory training session that ruined her original plans." I turned to Karla. "Jessica and I were in library school together and have remained friends. But she took a job at a music library out in California right after graduation, so we rarely see each other these days. We stay in touch through social media and phone calls, though."

"Which means I definitely need something that will work alongside various shades of blue, I guess," Karla said as she looked over the rack of gowns.

Sunny popped on the glasses she wore only when she needed to closely examine things. "I was thinking something in the purple family. The kind with underlying bluish tones, not red."

"That would work." Karla flipped through the selections available in her size. "A bit limited, I'm afraid."

"We can order items in any size," said the store clerk, who'd introduced herself as Deanna.

Karla frowned. "Can you get it in time? The wedding is only three weeks away."

"That won't be a problem. Our suppliers will expediate shipping if we ask," Deanna said.

"But I wouldn't know how it would fit."

Deanna looked Karla over. "Well, you have a great figure. I think almost anything would work, as long as it's long enough in the torso and arms and so on."

"Okay, I guess I could deal with that." Karla's expression was decidedly dubious.

"Let me get our catalog. That might help," Deanna said, before scurrying off into a back workroom.

A jangle of bells made Aunt Lydia glance over at the main door of the shop. "Hold on, here comes Debbie. Maybe she'll have some ideas."

"Hello everyone. Sorry I'm late. Traffic was awful," said my mom, hurrying over to join us. "I hope I haven't missed Amy's fitting."

"You're fine," I said, giving her a hug. "They're still setting up things in the fitting room for me and Sunny. In the meantime, we're searching for something that might work for Karla."

"Oh right, the best-woman dress." Mom dropped her purse into the chair next to Aunt Lydia before turning to the rack that held a selection of bridesmaid dresses. "Well, I'm no fashion maven, but maybe we should look in the mother-of-the-bride section as well. When I was looking for my outfit, I noticed that many of those gowns were more sophisticated than the bridesmaid choices." She smiled. "I guess everyone assumes that bridesmaids will all be in their twenties or something."

"That's a good point," Karla said. "All of us are a little older than the typical bridal party."

"Way to rub it in." I shot her a grin to let her know I wasn't offended. I didn't really mind being a thirtysomething bride. Whatever my age, I was marrying the man I loved, and the person I knew I wanted to live with the rest of my life.

"But you didn't get your dress here," Aunt Lydia said. "We went shopping together for that, remember."

Mom nodded. "And got cocktail-length dresses instead of long gowns. Just made more sense, particularly for an afternoon wedding. But I do think Karla needs something more formal."

"What color did you end up buying?" Sunny asked, shifting her attention from the rack of gowns to address my mom.

"Indigo for me. Lydia went with a pale, almost icy, blue." Mom smiled. "Looks great with her eyes."

"Really?" My aunt arched her feathery brows. "Are you saying my eyes are cold?"

"No, just a gorgeous pale blue, as you well know," Mom replied, wrinkling her nose at her older sister.

"I definitely want something in blue or purple hues, then," Karla said. "Especially since a little bird told me that Amy is including purple wisteria in her bouquet."

"Had to," I said with a smile. "And I expect that little bird also told you that we're using those colors in all the flower arrangements."

"He did." Karla turned away from the dresses to give me a wink. "I have to say that he's gotten more involved in the wedding planning than most guys I know."

"Come on, Karla, you know Richard. He's a choreographer. He's all about the visuals."

"True." Karla's light-brown eyes sparkled with amusement. "He showed me his outfit, by the way. A lovely morning suit. I think you'll approve."

"Hey, no fair," I said, without rancor. "But of course, I'd approve of anything as long as it's Richard wearing it."

Sunny made a show of elaborately fanning herself. "Richard in tails. Lord help me."

Mom laughed as Aunt Lydia once again raised her eyebrows. "Sunshine Fields, sometimes you are too much," my aunt said.

I slipped my arm around Sunny's slender waist. "No, she's perfect, and you know it."

"Thanks, bestie," Sunny said, leaning her head against mine.

"Now there's a picture," Mom said. "Especially with Karla in the frame too. Three beautiful women."

"I think you're a little biased," I said as Deanna reappeared, clutching something that looked like an oversized magazine.

"Here you go," she said, handing the item to Karla. "Take a look through this and see if something strikes your fancy. We can order anything and get it here within a week, so there'll still be plenty of time for a fitting." She turned to me and Sunny. "We're ready for you now, if you want to follow me."

Mom circled behind Aunt Lydia's chair, snatching up her purse. "Here, Karla, sit down and let's look through the catalog while Amy and Sunny are getting dressed."

"No, no. You should sit beside your sister, Ms. Webber," Karla said. "I'll stand behind you. Trust me"— she grinned—"I'm tall enough to look over your shoulders."

Sunny and I left them to peruse the catalog and followed Deanna into a large fitting room with a gold-and-silver-patterned carpet and mirrors lining three walls.

The attendants helped Sunny into her gown first. A simple sleeveless column of peacock-blue silk with a draped scoop neckline in front and low-cut back, it didn't possess much pizzazz when dangling from a hanger. But draped over Sunny's slender but well-proportioned figure, it looked sensational.

"Wow, we'd better hire some bodyguards to keep the men at bay," I said with a smile.

Sunny spun this way and that to admire the gown from all angles. "Oh, don't go to that trouble," she said, flashing me a grin. "I'll manage."

I was next. My white silk gown was also sleeveless but featured a full skirt and fitted bodice. The front neckline was cut in a modest, draped vee, but the back spilled from my shoulders in a deep cowl. It fell in folds so low that I'd had to buy a special, almost backless corset to wear under the gown.

Sunny whistled. "Gorgeous! I mean, it looked lovely when you picked it out, but now that it's been fitted, it's simply perfect."

I turned slowly, examining my reflection from all sides. It was the most flattering dress I'd ever worn, highlighting my curves with elegance and style.

"Now the veil," said Deanna, holding out the flowing expanse of airy white lace with reverence. She fitted the halo of silk, which would be decorated with real flowers for the ceremony, over my hair, adjusting the lace so it fell in a sheer panel from the back of my head to the floor.

"With the flowers and your hair pulled back, it will be stunning," she said as she stepped back to allow me to study the finished ensemble.

Sunny clapped her hands. "Even more perfect. We'd better warn Karla and Scott to be ready to catch Richard, because he'll probably fall over when he sees you."

I laughed. "I doubt his reaction will be quite that dramatic."

"Let me go and bring the others in," Deanna said.

As she hurried out into the shop, I tipped my head to one side and marveled at the woman staring back at me. I'd never considered myself beautiful, even though Richard insisted it was true. But now, in this dress, with the happiness I couldn't hide shining from my eyes, even I could believe it.

Mom, Aunt Lydia, and Karla appeared behind me, their reflected faces expressing joy, delight, and admiration.

"You look truly splendid," Aunt Lydia said. "Just like Debbie did on her own wedding day," she added with a swift glance at my mom.

My typically pragmatic mother was too busy wiping away tears with a tissue to respond.

"Rich will lose his mind," Karla said, casting me a warm smile. "I mean, he thinks you're gorgeous anyway, but wow."

"I need to do something different with my hair," I said, tucking a lock behind my ear. "It's not long enough to put up into a twist or anything, but maybe just the sides . . ." I held back the front sections of my hair with both hands. "What do you think?"

"I think we'll make an appointment for hair and makeup so you don't have to worry about it," Aunt Lydia said. "I'm sure Zelda knows someone who could come to the house right before the wedding."

Sunny nodded. "If anyone does, she would."

As if drawn out of a reverie by Sunny's words, my mom glanced over at her. "You look pretty spectacular yourself, Sunny."

"Thank you," Sunny said, making a little curtsy.

"I really do have to find a dress that complements you two," Karla said.

I pulled the veil forward so that it draped over my shoulders and admired the delicate lace. "Did you see anything in the catalog that you liked?"

"One. It's silk like your dresses and equally elegant, but it has one shoulder bare, and I don't know if that will work with your design aesthetic."

"I don't see why not," I said, turning to look her over. "Is it a Grecian sort of style?"

"Exactly," my mom said. "It drapes from one shoulder, then falls fairly straight, but with enough shape to show off Karla's lovely figure. But it has that soft, flowy effect, like you see in ancient statures. It comes in a wonderful shade of deep violet too."

I gave a thumbs-up. "I think that would be perfect. I've always pictured Karla as a Greek goddess anyway."

Color flushed Karla's cheeks. "I don't know about that, but I think it's a style that would work for me. So if it's okay with you, that's what I'll go with."

"As long as you can dance in it," I said. "Because you know you'll have to dance with Richard. He'll insist."

"Pretty sure it will work just fine." Karla looked me over. "As will your dress. Minus the veil, perhaps."

"This lace part detaches," I said, touching the back of the silk-covered frame. "And I plan to wear flat slippers. I know heels are more fashionable, but . . ."

"Not for dancing. I mean, if you aren't used to them, that would be dangerous." Karla shot me a conspiratorial look. We'd already met once to begin my training for the first dance, and it had gone about as well as expected. Which is to say, not exceptionally well. But I was determined to conquer my doubts as well as my limitations.

Deanna tapped Karla's arm. "If you're set on that dress, why don't we go ahead and order it?" She glanced at her watch. "If we put in the request soon, it will get here a day earlier."

"Sure thing," Karla said, before following Deanna out of the room.

Sunny, who'd been staring into one of the mirrors, experimenting with pulling her long hair into different versions of buns and twists, cast me a side-eyed glance. "Well, dancing or no dancing, you'll be more comfortable in flats. Especially since you don't often wear heels. And we'll all be on our feet a lot, I'm afraid."

"Not this old lady," Aunt Lydia said. "I plan to spend a good bit of time sitting on one of my garden benches."

I rolled my eyes. "As if that will happen. You'll be rushing around, instructing the musicians, directing the caterers, greeting guests, making sure everything is perfect, and so on. I know you."

"Honestly, Amy, I don't know where you get these ideas," my aunt said. But she smiled.

"And you need to squeeze in a few dances with Hugh as well." Mom's expression was perfectly innocent, but I knew what she was up to.

So did her sister. "If Hugh is even at the wedding," Aunt Lydia said, her tone suddenly as icy as her eyes.

Sunny smoothed her dress over her hips. "Oh now, you can't break up with him right before the wedding. I mean, it's bad enough I don't have a date."

Unmoved by this playful comment, my aunt lifted her chin and stared my mom in the eye. "It's not me who's causing the problem."

"Come now, Lydia, he's just doing his job," Mom said firmly.

Aunt Lydia sniffed. "Hugh hasn't been assigned to look into Kurt's past. That's something he's chosen to do. I suppose now, with this murder at Highview, it fits in with the official investigations, but that's not how it started."

"Hugh has had suspicions about Kurt's business practices for some time," I said, keeping my tone mild. "You can't really blame him for digging a little deeper when someone dies on Kurt's property. Someone who was vying with Kurt over an acquisition, too."

"Perhaps not, but when I've asked him not to look into certain things . . ." Aunt Lydia tightened her lips.

"I don't think you need to worry," Mom said. "Hugh loves you. He isn't going to deliberately do anything to hurt you."

My aunt swept one hand through the air. "Enough. I don't care to discuss the matter any further." She turned on her heel and marched out of the dressing room, but not before calling out, "You do look beautiful, Amy."

My mom shared a concerned look with me before following her.

I sighed. "I guess I should get out of this now. Although it is hard to go back to wearing my street clothes." I poked my foot out from under the gown's full skirt. "But I have no glass slippers and it's past midnight."

"I'll help you, since Deanna is apparently still busy with Karla," Sunny said. "Just unzip me first, please."

I obliged, allowing her to change back into her sage-green cotton tunic and denim shorts before she assisted me. We carefully draped our gowns over two upholstered chairs, assuming that the store would prefer to handle hanging them.

"I just hope Hugh and Aunt Lydia make up before the wedding," I said as I gently laid the veil on a padded bench. "I hate to see them on the outs."

"It is sad. But I think it will blow over." Sunny slipped her bare feet into a pair of open-backed sandals. "I mean, they're both adults. And once Kurt is cleared from having anything to do with Oscar Selvaggio's death . . ." She grimaced, obviously catching my expression reflected in the mirror. "You do think he'll be cleared, right? I know he has kind of a secretive past, but I can't imagine him doing something as foolish as killing a rival."

"At least not in a way that might guarantee him getting caught," I said as I tugged on my jeans. Looking up, I met Sunny's concerned expression with a grim smile. "He's a charming devil, and I know he's been a wonderful friend to Richard and me, but honestly, I wouldn't put anything past him."

Sunny ran her fingers through her hair. "You really think he could murder someone? I mean, selling some art pieces with dubious backgrounds is one thing. Killing is another."

"I'm not sure." I brushed my own mussed hair behind my ears. "But either way, that isn't what's worrying Aunt Lydia. She's concerned that Hugh and his PI friend might dig up something unsavory connected to my uncle Andrew."

"Oh right. He and Kurt were good friends, and Kurt helped Andrew out when he got in trouble back in the day, didn't he?"

"Yeah. I thought we'd learned all there was to know about that unfortunate period in my uncle's life, but it's possible there's more to uncover."

"And Lydia is determined to prevent that, I suppose." Sunny's expression grew thoughtful. "Maybe I can help. It's possible I could find out what's going on with Hugh's investigation."

I turned to look at her. "How exactly?"

Her golden lashes fluttered over her bright-blue eyes. "Let's just say I might be able to ask someone about some details. Discreetly, of course."

"What makes me think you're talking about pumping Mr. Fred Nash for information?" I tipped my head and studied her deceptively innocent face. "Don't tell me you're already dating him."

"I do have plans to go out with him tonight." Sunny beamed. "So I can see what I can find out. In a roundabout fashion, of course."

I shook my head. "Don't jeopardize a possible relationship just to get info for me."

Sunny threw her arm around me and turned us so we were reflected side by side in the mirror. "Who's more important? Some guy I've only known for a hot second, or my best friend and her family?" She pointed at me with her other hand. "You know the answer to that."

I leaned into her and studied our reflections. "Selvaggio was right, you know. We could pose for Hermia and Helena."

"Maybe. But we've never fought over a man like they did." Sunny tossed her head. "And if it means helping Lydia, and by extension you, there's only one choice I'm ever going to make."

"I know," I said. "But I'm always going to push you toward your own happiness. Which might mean another choice."

Sunny's smile illuminated her lovely face. "If it's real happiness, it can't be destroyed by me being true to my family and friends."

Which was, all in all, probably the wisest thing I'd ever heard my very intelligent friend say.

Chapter Eleven

On Sunday afternoon, I was left alone. Richard had dashed off to another rehearsal, Scott was touring the area with Ethan, and Aunt Lydia was having lunch with Zelda and Walt. Determined to keep the weeds at bay, I decided to do a little work in the garden.

It was in good shape, due to my diligence as well as the recent efforts of Aunt Lydia and Scott. But I knew we had to stay on top of it if we hoped to keep it tidy for the wedding. The spring rains caused new weeds to sprout every day, and the early roses needed to be regularly deadheaded so they'd continue blooming into late May.

As I wielded my clippers, cursing the thorns that somehow managed to pierce my suede garden gloves, my cell phone buzzed in the pocket of my worn cotton slacks. Yanking off my gloves, I fumbled the phone from my pocket and glanced at the number displayed on the screen.

It was Sunny. "Hi there," I said, crumpling my gloves in my other hand. "What are you up to today?"

"Not much. Had a late night, so I'm basically in recovery mode," Sunny replied.

"Oh, that's right. You went on a date with Fred Nash. How did that go?" I strolled over to one of the white benches at the edge of the garden path. I sat down, dropping the gloves onto the wooden plank seat.

"Fine, but that isn't why I called." Sunny cleared her throat. "Along with the normal getting-to-know-you questions, I did manage to slip in a few inquiries about the investigation into Mr. Kendrick. I thought you might like to know what I found out."

I stretched out my legs and leaned against the back of the bench. "Of course I do. Spill."

"Well, here's the thing. Fred isn't just digging into Mr. Kendrick's business. He's also involved with something connected to your brother."

I sat bolt upright. "What? Why would he be doing that?"

"I don't know. He didn't go into any details. Just mentioned it in an offhand way. Actually"—concern tinged Sunny's tone—"I think it was a slip. Because as soon as he mentioned something about Scott, he changed the subject. I couldn't get anything else out of him after that."

"I guess he realized that you're my friend and might share info."

"That's what I figured. Anyway, as far as Mr. Kendrick is concerned, Fred and Hugh are looking into his past involvement with the Kelmscott Chaucer. Apparently, he might have been secretly involved in a deal over a copy of that book many years ago."

I stared blankly out over the garden as I recalled what Emily Moore had told me about a scandal surrounding the Chaucer. I frowned. "A stolen copy sold to someone unaware of its questionable provenance?"

"Exactly. Fred told me there has always been a shadow hanging over that situation, even though no one was ever charged with wrongdoing. But when the buyer died, his kids sued or something. Anyway, it was a big scandal in the art world."

"Emily Moore told me something about that. She said the buyer died unexpectedly and the accusations of buying stolen property created so much stress that it contributed to his death. At least according to his children."

"Really? I guess that might be the reason why Hugh is still digging into that old scandal. He must be trying to close a cold case."

"And he wants to lay the blame on Kurt, I bet," I said. "Although, according to Emily, it was Oscar Selvaggio who was directly involved in the sale."

"Maybe Mr. Kendrick was a silent partner or something?"

"It's possible." I focused on a butterfly perched on one azure blossom in a bed of decorative thistles. "What did you think of Fred Nash? I mean, I know he's handsome, but is there more to him than that?"

"He's also smart and easy to talk to." Sunny sounded guarded, which told me she was far more interested than she wanted to admit. "He used to be a cop, you know."

"I'd heard that." I didn't mention that Brad had been the first person to share that information with me. Although I believed Sunny was totally over any romantic feelings for Brad, I still sometimes hesitated to bring him up in conversation.

"Anyway, I liked him well enough to see him again. After that, who knows?" Sunny tossed off this information with a nonchalance I suspected she didn't feel. I'd never seen her react to any man as strongly as she had to Fred Nash upon meeting him. There'd been a sense of electricity sparking between them that made me question whether this might not be the start of a more serious relationship. But I wasn't about to say anything about that. I knew such words would drive my free-spirited friend into denial.

"Okay, I'll let you go. I just wanted to share that bit of info, but I'm sure you have things to do, and honestly, I just want a nap," Sunny said, before telling me good-bye.

After we hung up, I continued to watch the butterfly dance over the spiky purple thistle flowers for a few minutes, then decided the rest of the garden work could wait. Sunny's mention of my brother had unnerved me. The fact that he was on the radar of a PI as well as the sheriff's department was something that required action. I needed to find a way to untangle the sticky threads of coincidence that seemed to be entrapping the truth.

I wanted to question Kurt Kendrick, who appeared, as always, to be at the center of the web.

*   *   *

Fortunately, Walt and Zelda had picked up Aunt Lydia after church, so I had access to the car. Driving out to Highview, I reminded myself that this might be a fool's errand. Even though Kurt often spent weekends at his country house, he also traveled a great deal and sometimes stayed in Georgetown at the townhouse next door to his gallery. There was no guarantee that he'd even be home today.

Turning off the gravel mountain road onto Highview's paved driveway, I was surprised to see the gates standing open. Typically the gates were left unlocked only during parties or other events. At any other time I had to use the intercom attached to a pole near the gates to introduce myself before Kurt or one of his staff would buzz me through.

I hope I'm not crashing a party, I thought as I drove down the gently winding driveway. Lined with trees and shrubs, the drive masked the view of the house. There would be no way to know if Kurt had guests until I pulled into the circular parking area at the end of the drive. *But there's really no harm. If I spy vehicles, I'll just turn around and leave.*

When I reached the house, I realized I'd been mistaken. Only one vehicle sat in front of the picket fence—enclosed cottage garden that separated the driveway from the house, and that was Kurt's glamorous black Jaguar.

I parked, sitting in my car for a moment to consider my next move. Something was off—I'd never seen the Jag parked in front of the house. A smaller driveway led to a garage behind the house, where the expensive sports car was normally kept under lock and key. Added to the oddity of the gates being open, this was a definite red flag.

Don't be silly, I chided myself. *Kurt might have simply forgotten to close the gates after returning from some errand. Maybe he was in a hurry and just parked out front for convenience. Perhaps he plans to drive out again soon.*

That would explain everything. I shook off my sense of unease and climbed out of my car. Smoothing my loose T-shirt over my worn slacks, I reached the gate that led into the cottage garden.

As I strolled the flagstone-paved path to the small covered porch, I admired the myriad colors of the blooming garden. Kurt's landscaper had planted old-fashioned flowers and shrubs, most of them native to the area, and so the air was filled with fragrance—seductive scents that modern, genetically modified flowers just couldn't match.

Remembering Brad's words about aconite being a common garden plant in this area, I surveyed the kaleidoscope of brightly colored flowers for any traces of blue. And there it was, in the far corner—a tall plant with feathery silver-green leaves. The spiky stems were covered in purple-blue blossoms shaped like a cap, or like the monk's hood that had given the plant one of its common names.

Another of which is wolfsbane. I considered the irony of this as I climbed the steps to Kurt's front porch.

As I reached out a finger to press the doorbell, I noticed that the forest-green front door stood slightly ajar. Like the open gates, this gave me pause. Kurt wasn't fanatical about security, but he kept his doors locked unless he was throwing a party. And then, as I'd discovered, he always hired private security to blend in with the guests. Which made sense, given the value of the art and antiques that filled his home.

I considered returning to my car to immediately call the sheriff's department but decided that Kurt would probably not appreciate such an action, no matter the circumstances. I was concerned, though. Not so much about thieves, since I'd seen no other vehicles, but rather that Kurt could've suffered some sort of medical emergency. Despite his air of strength and vitality, he was in his seventies. He could easily have experienced a spell of light-headedness, if not something worse.

Since Kurt didn't keep a full-time staff, preferring to hire in a chef, cleaners, or other workers only when they were needed, I knew that he might be alone in the house. If he was incapacitated, no one would know . . . I pulled out my phone and held it in one hand, prepared to punch in 911.

Before I could even lower my fingers to tap the phone, the door was yanked open and I found myself face-to-face with a strange man.

He was almost as tall as Kurt but much thinner. *Almost skeletal*, I thought. There was nothing weak in his appearance, however; lean muscle sheathed his bare lower arms, and the hollows of his bony face were sharpened by genetics rather than illness. His dark hair, worn longer than most, flopped over his wide forehead, shadowing his deep-set, pale eyes.

Eyes that blazed as he stared at me for a second before shoving me aside and barreling down the porch steps. I grabbed one of the railings to steady myself as he disappeared around the side of the house. Clinging to the balustrade, I puzzled over his lack of transportation. How had this strange man traveled to Highview without a car?

My question was answered by the roar of an engine. The stranger, his face now covered by a black helmet, spun his oversized motorcycle out from the side of the house and raced off down the driveway.

Recovering my balance, I dashed into the hall, allowing the door to slam behind me. I knew from other visits that a hard close would engage the automatic lock mechanism, which would hopefully keep any other strange visitors at bay.

"Hello," I called out. "Kurt, are you here?"

A groan, followed by a swear word, answered me from the living room.

I ran into the room, stopping short at the edge of one of the Oriental rugs that covered the weathered wood floor. Kurt was sprawled across the rug, his white hair stained red at one temple.

Blood, I thought, and again raised my phone, prepared to call for help.

"Don't." Kurt lifted his head and fixed me with a piercing glare.

"You need medical attention," I said, my fingers hovering over my phone screen.

"Do. Not. Call." Kurt spat out the words like bullets.

I grimaced but pocketed my phone. "All right, but let me help you." I crossed to him and knelt down. "I can try to lift . . ."

Kurt's laugh was raspy as a saw cutting through cement. "You can't possibly do that, little girl. Just help me sit up. I can do the rest."

I didn't even try to mask my displeasure at being called a child. "All right, old man," I said, emphasizing the last two words.

Kurt's laugh roared out again, but with a more cheerful ring this time. "Touché, my dear. Now, if you don't mind—sit down with your back to me and allow me to use your shoulder to hoist myself into a less embarrassing position."

I did as he requested, wincing as he reached out and pressed his heavy palm into my shoulder. He pushed off, almost shoving me over.

I spun around to face him, eyeing the blood staining the linen handkerchief he'd pressed to his temple. "That might need stitches."

Kurt adjusted his legs, crossing them one over the other in a yoga pose. "I have some butterfly bandages and antiseptic upstairs. I can take care of it."

"Don't you want my help?"

"No." Kurt looked me over. "I may be old, but I'm not feeble."

"I wasn't suggesting that you were. Just that it might be easier for someone else to place the bandage properly. And"—I met his sardonic gaze with a lift of my chin—"a blow to the head can be dangerous. You should have someone stay with you for a while, in case you develop symptoms of a concussion."

"Please don't fret. I've had concussions before. I know what they feel like. This is just a minor wound."

I scrambled to my feet, glad I was wearing long pants and a baggy shirt. I might look awkward, but at least I wasn't showing any skin. "A minor wound that knocked you to the floor."

"That wasn't the blow. That was someone kicking my legs out from under me." Kurt motioned toward a heavy wooden chair. "Can you push that over here? I think I can stand if I have something to pull up on."

"Okay, but if you get dizzy and fall over again, I'm calling 911, no matter what you say."

"Fair enough." Kurt waited for me to scoot the chair over, then pulled himself up to a point where he could slump into the seat. "Thank you. Now, if you could just grab me a glass of water from the kitchen, you will have fulfilled your mission of mercy and can go."

I crossed my arms over my chest. "I'll get the water, but I'm not leaving. Not until I see you stand and walk around without assistance."

Kurt quirked his lips. "Making sure the old man doesn't keel over?" His expression sobered as his gaze raked over me. "I don't mind being old, you know. Not most of the time. Although, occasionally, I admit to wishing I was young enough to . . ." He laughed and dabbed the handkerchief at his temple, where the blood had dried to a dark blotch. "Never mind, my dear. Just make that drink Scotch instead of water. I think you know where to find the booze."

"In the butler's pantry," I said, cursing the heat that had flushed the back of my neck. "Oh, by the way, I caught Adele in there during the party, pouring herself a stiff drink."

Kurt's blue eyes went cold. "Did you?" he asked lightly. "Not that I mind. She's welcome to whatever she wants."

"I figured. It was just odd . . . But never mind. Let me get you that drink." I turned on my heel and headed out of the room, considering Kurt's reaction to my mention of Adele. He had seemed perturbed by my words, which was curious. Very little rattled Kurt Kendrick.

Certainly not a blow to the head. It's almost as if he's survived plenty of those in the past, I thought with a wry smile, as I returned to the living room carrying a glass of water in one hand and a tumbler of Scotch in the other. I set them down long enough to slide a side table close to Kurt's chair. "Here you go—water and liquor," I said, placing the drinks on the table. "Pick your poison."

"Hmmm, perhaps that isn't the best choice of words, all things considered." Kurt grabbed the tumbler.

I pulled another chair around so I could sit facing him. "Yeah, speaking of that . . ."

"I prefer not to." Kurt eyed me over the rim of his glass.

"I'm sure you don't. But I have to tell you that I heard the sheriff's department has placed you at the top of their suspect list."

"Not surprising, considering that the murder happened at my house, during a party I was hosting, and the victim was a business rival." Kurt took a slug of the Scotch.

"You don't seem particularly concerned."

"I'm not. I didn't kill Oscar. Where would be the fun in that? Yes, I wanted to beat him out to acquire the Kelmscott Chaucer, but only if I could do it fair and square." Kurt leaned back in his chair, stretching out his long legs. "Despite the suspicion in your eyes, I promise I don't murder people over such things."

I almost asked if he'd killed anyone over other things, but decided against it. He would undoubtedly find a way to prevaricate without telling an outright lie, as he had many times before. "Speaking of criminal actions, who was that guy who knocked you down? A thief?"

Kurt took another swallow before replying. "I have a better question—why are you here today, Amy?"

"You aren't going to tell me why someone attacked you and fled?"

"Not unless you tell me what you want. You obviously drove all the way out here to satisfy that insatiable curiosity of yours." Kurt tipped his head to one side. "What are you trying to find out?"

"If you are somehow involved in Oscar Selvaggio's death, of course. You've already told me no, so I guess that's that."

"It should be, but I'm sensing that you don't necessarily believe me."

"You do have a motive, and you had the opportunity." I fixed him with an unwavering gaze. "My dad saw you hand Selvaggio a snifter of cognac, which is apparently what he drank right before he died. And Richard and I caught a glimpse of you outside the house that day, you know. You walked out of the woods and into the backyard right before we found Selvaggio's body."

"Did you? And I suppose you've already informed the authorities about that, since they questioned my whereabouts at the time rather intensely. I told them the truth, of course."

"Which was?"

"That I was out looking for Oscar, but not to harm him. Actually, I saw him right before he rushed outside—due to some text message, according to his assistant—and he looked ill to me. He was breathing irregularly. I was afraid he was having a heart attack. So I went outside to see if I could find him." Kurt lifted his glass. "I didn't think to check that shed, because why would he have gone there?"

"Why indeed? Unless someone asked him to meet them there."

"Not me, I assure you. Anyway, as for me being outside, I wasn't the only one. There was Adele, for one. Oscar's mousy little assistant for another. And"—Kurt's eyes narrowed—"your brother."

I stiffened my spine, pulling my back away from the chair. "True. But they don't have a motive to murder Selvaggio. You do."

"Are you so sure they don't?" Kurt swirled the remaining Scotch in the tumbler. "People can keep secrets, even from friends and family. Sometimes quite deadly ones."

"I know that all too well." I rose to my feet. "Are you going to report what happened today to the authorities?"

"I wasn't planning on it. Are you?"

I looked him over. Despite the dried blood darkening the white hair over his temple, he appeared totally at ease and, as always, in control. "Not immediately. I'll give you time to reconsider and report it yourself. That could be beneficial, in terms of helping to clear your name, I mean."

Kurt bared his teeth in his typical wolfish grin. "Why, Amy, I didn't know you cared so much."

I bit my lower lip to stifle a rather unsavory comment before replying. "I'm thinking of Richard. He considers you family. And honestly, I'd hate to see you incarcerated right before the wedding. That kind of scandal is the last thing we need."

Kurt set down his glass and stood to face me. "More importantly, the last thing you need is to get tangled up in another murder investigation. Leave it alone, Amy."

"You always tell me that."

"And you never listen." Kurt held up his hands. "But this time, you must. That man today is not working alone. And, as you can see"—he touched a fingertip to his temple—"he and his cohorts are playing hardball."

"Is this all connected to the Kelmscott Chaucer?"

"Perhaps. And perhaps not. But that is irrelevant. What's crucial for you to understand is that the people involved in this situation are not amateurs." Kurt's rugged face could've been sculpted from stone. "This is not something you can fumble your way through. Walk away. Leave it alone."

He took a step toward me, his blue eyes cold as a glacier. I backed away but met his imperious gaze without flinching. "Are you really all right?"

"Fine, as you can see." Kurt moved closer.

"Then I'll leave. But I hope you'll call someone to come and sit with you tonight, just in case."

"My chef is coming over shortly. I'm sure she'll be happy to keep an eye on me." Kurt reached out and took hold of my shoulder, giving me a little shake. "You haven't promised to stay out of this investigation yet."

I pulled free of his grip. "I never make promises I'm likely to break," I said as I strode off into the hall.

A string of colorful swear words followed me out the front door.

Chapter Twelve

Since we were closed on Sundays, the library was always busy on Mondays. Which meant my research on the earlier scandal surrounding Oscar Selvaggio and the Kelmscott Chaucer had to wait until the next day.

Sunny, who was working all day on Tuesday, was stationed at the circulation desk while Bill shelved books. She was equally anxious to dig into some of our research databases. "Why don't you use the workroom computer while I do a little poking around here at the desk." She swept her hand through the air. "It doesn't look like we're going to have much business today, at least not until the after-school crowd drops in."

"All right, but let's divide and conquer," I said. "I'll check the papers that might've covered the incident while you look into Selvaggio's past. I'm not sure there'll be anything on him in the digital sphere, especially from the past, but you never know."

"Okay, boss." Sunny gave me a mock salute. "By the way, where did you run off to Sunday afternoon? I stopped by the house when I was out, checking on some town properties, but no one was home."

"Oh, you know, just went for a walk," I said, keeping my head down so Sunny couldn't read the lie in my eyes. "Everyone had abandoned me, and I just didn't feel like rattling around the house on my own."

"Okay, but I thought you must've driven somewhere because your car was gone." Sunny shrugged. "I guess Lydia took it?"

"Hmmmm . . ." I fiddled with the pamphlets in our desk display rack. "She had lunch with Walt and Zelda." I looked up at that point. That statement, at least, was true.

"But not with Hugh? I guess they're still not talking?" Sunny shook her head. "Sad."

"It's not quite that bad. They have talked on the phone. It's just that"—I pushed the rack up against the side of the desk computer—"Aunt Lydia doesn't feel like she can trust him as much as she used to. Or so she tells me."

"That rack's going to be in the way there," Sunny said, moving the display back to its former position. "And as for Lydia, I think she's blowing the whole thing out of proportion. Fred says that Hugh has no intention of revealing any information he might turn up on Andrew Talbot. He doesn't want to make Lydia's dead husband look bad; he just wants to prove Mr. Kendrick's ties to questionable art deals."

"Well, Hugh should know how sensitive my aunt is to anything that might tarnish Andrew's name." I shot Sunny a sidelong glance. "Although maybe she has no reason to worry. It seems to me that Hugh's bloodhound is hot on another trail at the moment."

Sunny whipped off the scarf tying back her locks, allowing her golden hair to spill over her shoulders. "It isn't like that. We're just friends."

"Uh-huh. Friends don't get that dreamy look in their eyes when they talk about their pals."

"Behave. I do like Fred. I just don't want to talk about him."

I raised my eyebrows. "Which tells me that you have fallen for him, fast and hard."

Sunny snapped the scarf at me. "No such thing. Now, are we going to research or what? If you want to gossip, I suggest you wait until Zelda gets here this afternoon. I'm not interested."

"Okay, okay." I lifted my hands in a mea culpa gesture. "Let's do some research."

I left her working at the desk and slipped into the workroom, where we had another computer set up on a desk in the corner. It was where I usually conducted my behind-the-scenes work, like handling interlibrary loan requests, paying invoices, and ordering new materials.

Settling into the task chair, I considered my search strategy. We fortunately had online subscriptions to a few major newspapers, like the *New York Times*, that included digitized back files. Surely, if there'd been a major scandal in the art world, the *Times* would've provided some coverage.

But first . . . I glanced over my shoulder at the workroom door, which was slightly cracked open. Not enough for Sunny to peek in and see anything on my screen, though. I absently picked up a pencil and twirled it between my fingers. I was happy that Sunny had apparently embarked on a new relationship, but also a little leery. She'd had some bad luck before, and I didn't want her embroiled in another situation that might end badly.

Switching to the *Washington Post*'s digital archives, I searched on the name *Frederick Nash*. There were immediate hits—a full-page list, in fact. Leaning forward, I squinted at the small print on the screen.

The most prominent headlines all referenced a major drug bust. I clicked on the most recent post, which was still six years old, and pulled up the article.

A quick read-through confirmed my suspicions. Fred Nash had been part of a task force charged with bringing down a multistate drug ring. Unfortunately, the task force was infiltrated by a couple of corrupt officers who were in cahoots with the criminals running the drug operation. During a sting that was intended to catch the leaders of the cartel, the task force was betrayed, resulting in an ambush that killed several officers and severely injured others.

Fred Nash was one of those seriously injured. His longtime partner, Trudy Klein, had died.

I sat back. No wonder Fred had left the force. That sort of loss, especially brought on by betrayal, would've traumatized anyone. As I considered the impact this might have had on Fred's behavior, something else I'd glimpsed in the article swam to the surface and grabbed my attention.

Esmerelda. That was the street name of the leader of the drug ring that Fred's team had been attempting to bring to justice. It was a nickname I'd heard before, in connection with another crime—the name of a female dealer who'd supplied drugs to people in the Taylorsford area during the 1960s.

I gnawed on the pencil. It seemed a strange coincidence. Fred might be investigating Kurt, but it was possible he was also digging into the past of another dealer from that time. Back in the 1960s, Kurt Kendrick, whose nickname had been "The Viking," had moved in the same circles as the dealer known as Esmerelda. Which made me wonder exactly what Fred Nash was investigating, and why.

He might be working for Hugh, but I had a suspicion there was more to his sleuthing than that. Which didn't make him a bad romantic partner for my best friend, but it certainly made him someone to watch.

I sighed and switched back to the *New York Times* database, refocusing my thoughts on the questions surrounding the stolen Kelmscott Chaucer that Oscar Selvaggio had supposedly sold to an unsuspecting buyer.

This was a more complicated search. I found a few references to the sale, but it wasn't until I included the term *lawsuit* that more useful information surfaced. I found what appeared to be the most comprehensive article covering the matter and printed it out.

Reading the first few paragraphs only confirmed what I already knew—Selvaggio had brokered the sale of one copy of the Kelmscott Chaucer to a collector, who later learned that the book's provenance was suspect. An art expert who'd been called in to offer a second opinion on the book's value for insurance purposes discovered that the chain of ownership behind the Chaucer was incomplete. The person who'd supposedly owned the book before teaming up with Selvaggio to sell it did not exist. This had raised serious questions about the legality of the sale.

Hearing a bell, I rose to my feet. Still clutching the printed article, I hurried out to check on the circulation desk.

As I suspected, Sunny had been called away by someone needing help in the stacks at the same time another patron approached the desk, arms laden with books. "I can get this," I told Sunny, who'd poked her head around the end of a range of shelves.

As I waited for Sunny's return to the desk, I checked our integrated library system, or ILS, for any messages or email reference queries. With my gaze focused on the computer screen, I didn't notice that another patron had approached the desk until they loudly cleared their throat.

When I saw who it was, I took a step back. "What are you doing here?" I asked, not bothering to temper the sharpness in my tone.

The tall, dark-haired man standing in front of the desk offered me a thin-lipped smile. "So sorry to startle you, Ms. Webber. I know we met under strained circumstances the other day, and I just wanted to stop by and offer my apologies."

I looked him over, noticing that he was dressed more professionally today. Although his navy suit hung loosely over his skeletal frame, it was perfectly tailored to fit his broad shoulders, and both the collar and cuffs of his white dress shirt were crisp as autumn leaves. "We weren't really introduced Sunday, unless you call shoving me aside an introduction."

The man swept the fall of dark hair away from his forehead. "Again, I apologize. That was incredibly rude of me. But, you see, I was in a rather distracted state."

I crossed my arms over my chest. "After knocking down Mr. Kendrick, you mean."

"An unfortunate accident." The man thrust out one bony hand. "Lance Dalbec. I'm another art dealer, or perhaps I should say broker. I tend to work as a middleman or finder rather than directly buying or selling pieces myself."

"So, one of Mr. Kendrick's business acquaintances," I said, without taking his hand. "Or rivals, perhaps?"

"You could say that." Dalbec flashed me a humorless smile. "We are both vying for the right to buy a particular object at the moment."

I shifted my weight from foot to foot. "A Kelmscott Press edition of the complete works of Chaucer? It seems everyone has an interest in that book. I heard the unfortunate Mr. Selvaggio was also looking to purchase it."

"That's correct. But as you say, he is now out of the picture." Lance Dalbec stared down at his hands, which he'd pressed against the counter top. "At any rate, I just stopped by to assure you that I mean no harm Sunday. I hope I didn't injure you in any way."

"No, I'm perfectly fine. I wish I could say the same for Mr. Kendrick."

Dalbec looked back up at me, his pale eyes clear and cool as water in a mountain stream. "I suspect you won't believe me, but I intended my visit with Mr. Kendrick to be a friendly discussion. I thought perhaps we could work together to acquire the Chaucer. But he became enraged at the very suggestion and lunged at me. I was merely defending myself. Unfortunately, as I was pushing back against his attack, he had the misfortune to fall. I suppose I should've stayed with him, but he ordered me to leave in no uncertain terms."

"He was quite angry," I said, examining Lance Dalbec with a critical eye. I wasn't convinced that he was telling the truth, but it was entirely possible that Kurt had lost his temper with this man. Especially since Dalbec projected an oily insincerity that would've undoubtedly gotten on Kurt's nerves.

As it does mine, I thought, before forcing a smile. "Anyway, thank you for your apology, although it really wasn't necessary for you to track me down to offer it. How exactly did you do that, by the way?"

Lance Dalbec lifted his hands. "It wasn't difficult to connect a rather unlikely visitor to Kendrick's home with one of his local acquaintances. It's not like he has that many friends, you know."

"Actually, I don't, but then, I try not to dig too deeply into Kurt's personal life. Which is, frankly, none of my business." I tipped my head and looked Dalbec up and down. "Or yours either, I imagine."

"No, of course not." Dalbec stepped back from the desk. "The truth is, I'm going to be staying in the Taylorsford area for a bit and might want to use your lovely library from time to time. I didn't want you to feel the need to call the authorities on me if you spied me in the stacks, so I felt it prudent to offer my apologies for shoving you. Which was entirely unacceptable, of course. And quite out of character for me, I assure you."

"That's good to know," I said, eyeing him with distrust. Nothing he'd said had alleviated my initial negative reaction to him. But I had to admit that it wasn't surprising that he knew Kurt, since, as Adele had said many times, Kurt had many questionable business associates. Dalbec was probably one of them, which meant that his claim to be involved in the art world might be entirely legitimate. "Anyway, I promise not to call the sheriff's department on you simply for using the library."

Although I will inform Brad of this encounter, I thought as I mirrored his insincere smile and wished him a good day.

He exited the library before Sunny returned to the desk. She apologized for leaving so long.

"It's not a problem," I said absently, still processing my encounter with Lance Dalbec. "I assume you were helping someone in the stacks."

"Mr. George," she said, as she circled around to join me behind the desk. "He's giving a talk to the historical society and needs information on the lumber mills that used to operate around here."

"Like the one owned by the Baker family?" I made a face. My great-great-grandfather, William Baker Senior, had established a successful lumber business back in the late nineteenth century. It had created great wealth that had unfortunately dwindled away by the time the inheritance was passed down to my aunt and mother. "You should tell him to talk to Aunt Lydia. She may be able to offer some useful family anecdotes."

"I'll do that," Sunny said. "Now—what did you find out?"

I wasn't about to share my research into Fred's past, so I waved the piece of paper in my hand instead. "More details on that old scandal concerning a copy of the Kelmscott Chaucer."

"Do you think it could be the same copy? I mean, the one that Mr. Kendrick and Mr. Selvaggio were fighting over?" Sunny twirled a strand of her long hair around one finger. "I thought maybe it was back on the market and that was one reason Selvaggio was so determined to buy it."

I opened my mouth and shut it again without saying anything. Although Kurt had mentioned something about Oscar Selvaggio being desperate to purchase the book, I hadn't thought of that possibility. I gave Sunny an appraising look. Sometimes I forgot that behind her beautiful, flower-child exterior lay a woman with a shrewd and brilliant mind. "I suppose it's possible," I said at last. "If it came on the market again, he might have thought it was his chance to put those rumors to rest, once and for all."

Sunny flicked the coil of hair off her finger. "That was my first thought when I heard about him being involved in some old scandal involving that particular book."

I laid the printed page on the desk. "I'd just started reading this article. Maybe we can look through it together."

"Sure, but wait a minute." Sunny pulled her aqua blue–framed glasses from the pocket of her sundress and popped them on her head. "Now, let's see what this furor was all about."

The article named the collector who'd been sold the questionable book as Jasper Brentwood, a wealthy philanthropist. He'd apparently inherited his fortune and had chosen to become a clergyman rather than pursue a business career. That made the charge that he'd participated in a fraudulent sale particularly damaging, as his reputation had been built on a life of honesty and moral rectitude.

"Sounds like someone had it in for that buyer," Sunny said. "Like they were just waiting for him to slip up and used this incident as a way to tear him down."

"Possibly. Or maybe it was engineered by someone who was angry because they wanted to buy the Chaucer and he beat them to it." I frowned. That sounded more like something Kurt would do. He certainly wouldn't have cared about anyone else's morals, or lack thereof.

"Well, whatever the reason, they sure did a good smear job on the guy. It seems it contributed to him having a heart attack too."

"Or so his children claimed." I leaned in closer to read the final paragraphs of the article. "They brought a lawsuit against Oscar Selvaggio after the authorities refused to charge him with anything due to lack of evidence. Or at least one of them did."

"The daughter, Maria." Sunny looked off into the distance, as if contemplating the effect such a scandal would've had on a young woman whose father had just died. "I wonder what happened to her."

"Something else to research," I noticed that a couple of young women with small children clinging to their hands had cornered Bill at the edge of the stacks. They appeared to be peppering him with questions, which wasn't really his responsibility. "But perhaps not now. It looks like Bill might need some help."

"I'll go," Sunny said. "You can stay here and dig a little deeper into the unfortunate Brentwood family."

I waited to dive back into my online research until I'd reviewed the status of a few books that had been dumped onto a table near the circulation desk. None were checked out, so I simply placed them in call number order on a book cart, hoping Bill would have time to return them to the shelves before his volunteer shift ended. After that, I turned to the desk computer to see if I could find anything more on Mr. Brentwood or his family.

It wasn't difficult, especially after I pulled up the digital archives for a few papers that had been active in his home city during the sixties and seventies. I found a few mentions of Jasper Brentwood Junior, who'd continued his father's charity work but also embarked on a successful legal career. Maria was a little harder to track down. There didn't seem to be any mentions of her after her failed attempt to sue Oscar Selvaggio.

I widened my search to include any Brentwoods in the area. After several false hits, I spotted the name *Maria* in a heading and homed in on the attached article.

It was a wedding announcement, one of those extensive puff pieces detailing the nuptials of people who were part of high society. I peered at the grainy photograph for a moment, which showed a lovely blonde woman in a gorgeous pearl-encrusted lace gown, before reading the article.

All it took was a couple of sentences to make me step back from the computer, holding my hand over my mouth.

The bride, only twenty, already had an impressive résumé as a dancer, having studied at Jacob's Pillow and performed for Agnes de Mille as well as the Martha Graham Dance Company. Although her first name was Maria, she always performed under another name.

She used her middle name, which was Adele, and she'd married a businessman by the name of Nathan Tourneau.

Chapter Thirteen

As soon as I collected my thoughts, I printed out the newspaper article and shoved it into my pocket. When Sunny returned to the desk, I pulled her into the workroom and explained what I'd found out about Adele's connection to Oscar Selvaggio, but asked her not to share that information with anyone until after I'd had a chance to talk to Brad.

"I also want to give Richard a heads-up about the situation," I said. "He's known Adele a long time and respects her as a person as well as a dance coach. I don't want him blindsided if the investigation's focus suddenly shifts to her."

"Understood. I will keep it to myself until you let me know otherwise," Sunny said, making a zipper motion across her lips.

"Thanks. I guess I should inform Brad right away. Can you keep an eye on the desk while I make that call?"

Sunny gave me a mock salute. "Sure thing, boss. And . . . tell him hello from me," she added, in a softer tone.

"I will." I examined her face for any signs of sorrow but found none. "You really are over him, aren't you?"

"Absolutely. Anyway, he's involved with Alison Frye now, and it seems to be serious. Which is great, as far as I'm concerned. I still like him as a friend and wish him all the best."

I patted her hand. "Someday, some other guy is going to luck out. Or maybe"—I winked —"that day is already here?"

An uncharacteristic blush colored Sunny's cheeks. "Don't go all matchmaker on me. You always complained about your aunt and Zelda doing that to you."

"Sorry," I said, turning to head into the workroom. But I really wasn't. Even though Sunny always swore she would never get married, I still hoped she'd find a more serious, long-term relationship one day.

Calling Brad Tucker's office, I shared the information I'd uncovered about Adele Tourneau's past.

"Combined with her wandering through the woods, you spying her filling a glass with a dark liquor in that pantry, and the info about Mr. Selvaggio having cognac in his system, this is pretty vital information. Too bad we didn't know all the details earlier." Brad's stern tone betrayed how displeased he was with me. "You should've disclosed everything you knew about Ms. Tourneau's actions at the party right away, Amy."

"Sorry, but I didn't immediately think her behavior had any possible connection to Selvaggio's death. I mean, I didn't know it wasn't a heart attack or something natural until just the other day, and I did share the information about Adele fixing a drink then. Anyway, I just discovered her connection to Selvaggio, which I admit does put another spin on things," I said, before promising to email him a copy of the wedding announcement as well as the information concerning Adele's father.

"Good work." Brad's voice betrayed the fact that he was mollified by this offering. "We really should put you on the payroll."

"I wouldn't object, especially since I seem to be your go-to person for research," I replied. "But honestly, I enjoy being able to help. Although I don't like the fact that this might implicate Ms. Tourneau in any way."

"We won't take any direct action until we check all this out," Brad said. "And of course, there are others we're looking into as well."

"I know." I grimaced as I thought about my recent visit to Kurt's home. Respecting his wishes, or perhaps I should say *demands*, I didn't want to share all the details of that encounter with Brad, but I thought I should at least mention the presence of a suspicious stranger in town. "By the way, I saw something curious the other day. There was a man on a motorcycle who almost"— I fumbled for words that covered the incident without giving too much away—"knocked me over."

"You didn't recognize him?"

"No, and he has a very distinctive appearance. If I'd ever seen him before, I'm sure I would've remembered him. Then to further complicate things, the same man showed up at the library, after apparently tracking me down, in order to apologize to me. Which struck me as very suspicious. He told me his name is Lance Dalbec."

Brad asked for a description of both the man and his motorcycle, which I provided. "Thanks, Amy. We'll keep a lookout for the guy, as we do for any strangers. Especially ones that show up around the time of a crime."

"That's good," I said, glad that I could at least put Kurt's attacker on the sheriff's department's radar. "And I'll keep digging into the past. Maybe there's more information connected to copies of the Kelmscott Chaucer that can help your investigation. It's worth a try, anyway."

"Definitely, and thanks again, Amy," Brad said, before telling me good-bye.

Glancing at my watch, I realized that it was about time for me to head home. Or rather, to Richard's house, as we planned to have dinner together. But instead of immediately grabbing my purse, I stood in the middle of the workroom for several minutes, tapping my cell phone against my palm while I pondered the best way to tell my fiancé that one of his favorite mentors might be a murderer.

*　　*　　*

"Lydia had no idea who might've sent that necklace?" Richard asked as we cleaned up after dinner.

I slapped my forehead, forgetting that I'd just stuck my hand into a pot of soapy water. Bubbles burst and ran down my cheeks, prompting me to grab a kitchen towel to blot my face while I let loose a few choice phrases.

"Nice language," Richard said, amusement rippling through his words.

I turned to face him, waving the towel. "You'd swear too. Admit it."

"I would, and worse than that. Did you get any soap in your eyes?" He placed one hand on my cheek, his gaze searching my face.

"No, thank goodness." I leaned my face into his hand. "It's still embarrassing, though. I'm such a klutz sometimes."

"An adorable one," he said, before kissing me.

After a few minutes of this delightful distraction, I pulled away and looked up into his face. "And no, to finally answer your question, I completely forgot to ask Aunt Lydia about the necklace. I carried it up to my room with the intention of questioning her later, but then other things came up and I never did." I ran my fingers through his dark hair. "I promise I'll mention it to her tomorrow."

"It's no real crisis. I'm just curious, that's all."

"Me too, but then there's all this other stuff . . ." I dropped my hand and stepped back. "Could we go sit in the living room? There's something I need to share with you."

"Sure." Confusion flitted across Richard's face. "Nothing bad, I hope."

"Not really. Maybe a little worrying, but I'm sure it will turn out to be nothing."

"Now you have me intrigued." Richard motioned toward the sink. "You go ahead and grab a seat on the sofa. I'll put these pots in the drying rack and join you in a minute."

"Okay." I flashed him a smile. "Maybe bring along some wine?"

"Sounds like a plan," he replied with an answering smile.

When I reached the living room, I noticed a slight problem with our plan. Two cats had already staked a claim to the sofa. "Hey, guys," I said as I stood over them. "You're going to have to move."

Loie opened one emerald eye and twitched her tail, while Fosse just rolled over, all four paws waving in the air.

"Yes, you're cute, but you still have to move." I scooped up Fosse and sat down still holding him. "You can sit in my lap if you want."

Fosse sprang out of my arms and stalked off, his yellow-and-orange-striped tail switching like a windshield wiper set on high. "Or not," I said.

Richard appeared, holding a full wineglass in each hand. "I'm going to need that seat," he said, directing his words at Loie.

"You'll have to remove her. I've already ticked off Fosse. I don't need two cats angry with me at the same time."

"Take this." He handed me a wineglass before setting the other down on the coffee table. "Now, Loie, are you going to get down on your own, or must I move you?"

The tortoiseshell cat simply yawned, displaying her needle-sharp white teeth.

"Forcible removal it is, then." Richard lifted Loie, ignoring her yowl of protest. He sat down, placing her on his lap.

"Watch your glass," I said, as the cat leapt onto the coffee table.

Fortunately, Richard grabbed his wine just as Loie's tail sliced the air beside it like a rapier.

"That was close," I said as he settled back against the sofa cushions.

"Catlike reflexes." Richard opened and closed his free hand. "Beats cats behaving badly."

I took a sip of my wine before shooting him an amused glance over the rim of my glass. "This time."

He grinned as Loie dashed up the stairs, followed by Fosse. "Look at them. They're probably on a search-and-destroy mission."

"Did you close the bathroom door? Because you know how Fosse likes to unroll the toilet paper and drag it all over the house."

Richard narrowed his eyes as he gazed at the now-empty steps. "Hmm, good point. I think I did, but if not, I'll sort it out later. For now"—he turned to me—"I need to know what you're so eager to discuss."

"I'm not really that eager; I just feel it's necessary." I set my glass on the coffee table before pulling my legs up onto the sofa and stretching them across Richard's knees. "It concerns a friend of yours."

"Oh?" Richard rested a hand on one of my upper thighs. "Who might that be? Not Adele, I hope."

"I'm afraid so."

"You really think she might be involved somehow? I know she was acting a bit suspicious at the party, but surely she has no reason to murder anyone." Richard's fingers nervously tapped my leg.

I took a deep breath before launching into what I'd discovered about his former coach. "Maybe it's all coincidental," I said as I finished my spiel, "but I did find her messing around with a drink in the privacy of the butler's pantry, and from what I've read about aconite, when dissolved in a tincture, its presence can easily be masked by something with a strong taste."

"Like cognac, you mean." Richard's expression shifted from thoughtful to concerned. "I suppose you told Brad Tucker this already?"

"I felt I had to. Not that I wanted to get Adele in trouble, but facts are facts, and where murder is concerned . . ."

"No one is above suspicion?" Richard leaned back, staring up at his high ceiling. "You did the right thing. I just hate that you had to."

I swung my legs off his lap and scooted close enough to lay a hand on his shoulder. "I know. It's terrible to think that Adele could've taken such a drastic step. But if she believes Selvaggio's behavior was a factor in her dad's untimely death, it's almost understandable."

"I suppose." Richard covered my hand with his. "I do remember her once alluding to some tragedy in her past. It was when she coached me on *Fall River Legend*. I was having trouble getting in touch with the proper emotion for a dramatic scene, and she talked about using a memory to access the anguish I needed for that moment."

"That's the Agnes de Mille contemporary ballet?"

"Yes, the one based on the Lizzie Borden case." Richard lowered his head and met my questioning gaze. "Not a cheerful story."

"I guess not. So Adele said something about a tragedy in her own life?"

"I thought it was a reference to the death of her husband." Richard released my hand, adjusting his position to allow him to slip his arm around my shoulders. "He died young. Some sort of boating accident. She never really talked about it, so I figured when she mentioned a tragedy, that had to be what she meant."

I leaned into him, resting my head on his chest. "But now you wonder if it was her father's death instead?"

"It would make more sense, actually. Because I always thought what she said was odd in terms of her husband's death. That was obviously an accident, but when she talked about a tragedy in her past, she used the word *betrayal*."

"Which would tie in with Selvaggio duping her father, and then allowing him to be accused of buying stolen property."

"Exactly." Richard kissed the top of my head. "Maybe she carried that resentment for years and finally decided to do something about it when she saw Selvaggio again at Kurt's party."

"But wait a minute." I sat up, dislodging Richard's arm. "Kurt said Selvaggio just showed up at Highview that day with his assistant. He wasn't an invited guest. So even if Adele somehow knew everyone Kurt had invited to the party, which I doubt, she couldn't have known that Selvaggio would be there . . ." I sucked in a sharp breath. "Except Adele *did* see Selvaggio before the party, I'm afraid." I clasped one of Richard's hands before divulging the information the Nightingale had shared with me about Adele and Selvaggio's altercation at the bed-and-breakfast. "Maybe he mentioned planning to visit Kurt at Highview the next day?"

"Possible, but I sure hope not. That wouldn't look good for Adele," Richard said, frowning.

I squeezed his fingers, forcing him to look at me. "I know, but consider this—whoever murdered him had to already possess the poison used to kill him, wouldn't they? I mean, they'd need to have brought it with them. If Adele simply ran into Selvaggio the day before, how could she have come up with something like a poison solution so fast?"

"Unless it was something Kurt kept hidden at his house."

"He does grow aconite in his garden, so he had access to the original plant material needed to make the poison," I said. "But how would Adele know that? They've been acquainted for many years, but she wasn't staying at Highview. They're not that close, according to Adele, so I doubt she knows all his secrets."

"Hard to say." Richard's gray eyes searched my face. "And, don't forget—we only have Kurt's word that Selvaggio showed up uninvited. It's possible Adele could've known he'd be there, from Kurt if not from Selvaggio himself." He grimaced. "I hate to admit that option, but we can't discount it."

"Is it possible that they were in on it together? Kurt because he wanted to eliminate a rival and Adele for revenge?"

"Possible, but . . ." Richard slid his hands from my grasp and rubbed at his jaw. "I have a hard time believing Kurt would be so sloppy. I think if he planned to murder someone, he'd carry out the deed somewhere other than his own property."

"I've puzzled over that too. But he's the only one who could've had the poison stashed away ahead of time. The only other option is that Adele, or someone else, knew Selvaggio would be at High-view that day and came prepared."

"As for someone else . . ." Richard's expression brightened. "That isn't impossible, if you consider the fact that Hugh and Fred Nash were looking into Selvaggio's business practices as well as Kurt's."

I frowned. "I doubt either of them would kill the man. What would that get them? They wanted to bring him, and maybe Kurt, to justice. Not kill anyone."

"But what if they weren't the only ones keeping tabs on Selvaggio?" Richard jumped to his feet and began to pace. "I mean, he was accused of selling stolen goods in the past. Maybe he was still mixed up with some criminals. They may have been tracking his movements too."

"That's true. He did have a dubious reputation. He could easily have gotten on the bad side of thieves or forgers or other dangerous individuals. Maybe they decided to take him out at the party precisely because there would be so many possible suspects." I stood up and crossed to Richard, who'd paused beside one of the bookcases that lined the side wall. "As a matter of fact, I ran into a rather suspicious-looking stranger out at Highview on Sunday. A guy who also showed up at the library today."

Richard's brows drew together. "Why were you at Kurt's house on Sunday?"

I met his intense stare squarely. "I wanted to ask him a few questions. You were busy with a rehearsal and everyone else was out, so I just thought, why not take the opportunity to track down some more info?"

"Okay, fine, but why didn't you tell me anything about this?" Richard took hold of my hands. "I don't like you keeping secrets from me. Especially when they involve risky situations."

"I didn't think visiting Kurt would be dangerous," I said, lowering my lashes to veil my eyes.

"But it sounds like you weren't right about that. Listen, Amy"—Richard squeezed my fingers, forcing me to look back up at him—"it's fine that you want to help the authorities with these investigations, but I worry about you getting hurt. It's happened before, you know, so I hope you understand why I'm concerned. If you'd just waited, you could've asked me to go out to Highview with you later that day."

I opened my mouth to tell him that if I had waited, Kurt might've been left lying on the floor for far too long, but thought better of it. "Nothing really drastic happened. There was just a strange man who dashed out of the house right when I arrived, that's all. He jumped on a motorcycle and drove off without a word to me. Then I simply headed inside and talked briefly with Kurt."

"Who wouldn't tell you who the guy was, I bet." Richard sighed and dropped my hands. "Okay, I admit this particular incident doesn't sound too extreme. And I can easily imagine Kurt having visitors who lack manners and are the type of acquaintances he may prefer not to disclose. I know parts of his life are mysterious, if not downright morally questionable." He tipped up my chin with one finger. "But we've talked several times since Sunday. Why didn't you tell me about this before today?"

Because Kurt asked me to stay silent, I thought, and then realized how strange that sounded. I didn't owe Kurt Kendrick more loyalty than Richard. No matter how forcefully he'd demanded it. "I'm sorry. I wasn't thinking clearly, I guess. Anyway, after the guy showed up today and gave me his name, I called Brad. So at least the department will be keeping an eye out for him."

"Good. Now, how about we drop the discussion of this latest murder?" Richard quirked his eyebrows. "You know I have to leave tomorrow morning for that choreography gig, and I'll be gone for the rest of the week. I'd rather enjoy the rest of the evening, if you don't mind."

"I think that sounds like a splendid idea," I said, rising up on my tiptoes to brush his lips with mine.

As I dropped back down on my heels, Richard swept me up in his arms and kissed me, as he put it, "thoroughly enough to drive all thoughts of murder" from my mind.

Chapter Fourteen

I didn't get a chance to talk to Aunt Lydia until the following afternoon, a Wednesday. Arriving home after work, I ran upstairs and changed my clothes before grabbing the box containing the mysterious necklace.

Aunt Lydia was in the sitting room, comfortably ensconced in her favorite armchair with a book open in her lap. She looked up at me over the rims of her reading glasses. "What do you have there, Amy? Looks like a jewelry box. Did Richard give you a gift?"

"No. Well, it is a gift, just not from Richard. It was stuck in the pile of wedding presents, and we don't know where it came from. There wasn't any tag outside or card inside. I thought maybe you'd have some idea." I crossed over to her chair and popped open the hinged lid of the jewelry box. "See—it looks like an antique."

My aunt laid aside her book and lifted the necklace from its silken nest. "It does look old. But I'm afraid I can't help you. I have no idea where it came from."

"Really?" I stared at the gold-framed pendant dangling from the golden chain. "I hoped maybe one of your friends had mentioned sending it. Or maybe gave it to you to hand over to us? It was inside a blue box that looked rather old, if that rings any bells."

Aunt Lydia coiled the chain and laid the necklace back against the silk. "It doesn't. Sorry."

"Richard thinks someone sent it for me to wear at the wedding. Something old and something blue."

"That makes sense, but I must confess my ignorance as to its origins." Aunt Lydia held out the jewelry box. "Maybe ask Fiona? You know how she loves antiques. It could've come from her, or even one of her friends."

I took the box from her hand. "I suppose that's possible. We were just baffled by the fact that it wasn't wrapped as well as the absence of any sort of card. We don't even know who to thank."

"It probably had a tag that fell off. That's why I always slip them inside the package," my aunt said.

Setting the box on an end table, I flopped down on the suede sofa that faced her chair. "I guess I'll check with Fiona next time we see her. I can't think of anyone else to ask. None of my friends are likely to send a gift like that."

"That sounds like a good idea." Aunt Lydia slipped off her reading glasses and set them on the side table next to her chair. "I suppose I should expect you to join Scott and me for dinner for the rest of the week, since Richard's out of town?"

"Until Sunday. He's supposed to get back late that afternoon."

"Which means we won't see you Sunday evening." Aunt Lydia stretched out one leg, wiggling her foot in her satin slipper. "Maybe I'll plan the main meal for after church, then."

"I thought you were heading into the city this weekend," I said, widening my eyes in feigned innocence.

Aunt Lydia tapped her foot against the multicolored rag rug that covered the hardwood floor. "My plans have changed."

"I'm sorry to hear that." I scooted to the edge of the sofa. "You and Hugh seem to be going through a rough patch. Want to talk about it?"

Aunt Lydia's eyes narrowed. "No."

I clasped my knees as I leaned forward. "He really doesn't plan to reveal any information concerning Uncle Andrew, you know."

"What makes you so certain about that?"

"Because Fred assured Sunny that he, well actually that *they*, wouldn't."

Aunt Lydia sniffed. "From what you've told me about his immediate attraction to her, Fred Nash would tell Sunny anything if he thought it would garner him another date."

"Come on, you can't believe that Hugh would do anything that might hurt you. That's just not who he is. And there's no doubt that he loves you."

"I'm not sure I know who he is. Not entirely." Aunt Lydia waved her hand as if tossing something aside. "Embarking on an investigation of Kurt without telling me, for example. Does that sound like love to you?"

I tightened my lips, remembering my conversation with Richard the evening before and how I'd withheld information from him about my visit to Kurt's house. "I'm not sure love comes into it in a case like this. It's part of Hugh's job to track down illegal art sales and expose the people behind them. He probably just thought of it in terms of his work rather than his relationship to you."

"Oh, I don't know." Aunt Lydia sighed deeply. "I suppose I may be overreacting . . ."

I slumped back against the sofa cushions. "You think?"

"But I've been kept in the dark by someone I loved before." Aunt Lydia cast a swift glance at her side table, which held family photographs. Including, I knew, one of my late uncle Andrew. "I didn't press the issue then, even when I had my suspicions that vital information was being kept from me. I swore I wouldn't ever be so naïve again."

"I don't think this is the same thing."

"Maybe not, but I would've felt better if Hugh had just told me what he was doing up front. Yes, I might've still been upset"—she shrugged her slender shoulders—"but at least I wouldn't have felt quite so betrayed."

I stared at the picture that hung on the opposite wall. A landscape painted by Andrew, it captured the beauty of Aunt Lydia's garden in a realistic style that still somehow evoked mystery and magic. "The stuff that Uncle Andrew hid from you wasn't just about his work, though. I mean, he never told you he'd stayed in touch with Kurt, his best friend from his teenage years, either. Hugh hasn't kept secrets about personal things from you, has he?"

"Not to my knowledge." Aunt Lydia's strained expression relaxed. "Maybe you're right. Perhaps I'm dragging issues from the past into the present. Mixing up my feelings about some of Andrew's behavior with Hugh's. That probably isn't fair." She absently drummed her fingers against the padded arm of her chair. "You know, I heard Andrew speak about the Kelmscott Chaucer once. He just mentioned it in passing, so I never thought about it again until Kurt brought it up at the party."

I straightened and sat forward. "Why would Uncle Andrew mention that particular book?"

Aunt Lydia blinked and raised a hand to wipe one finger under her eye. "Oh, it was really nothing. Andrew just mentioned some legal hassle over one copy of the book. It was a scandal in the art world at the time."

"A pretty big one, from what I discovered when doing some research on that edition of the Chaucer. A man named Jasper Brentwood, who purchased the book, was hounded by the press and others after it was suspected that the item had been stolen. His children thought it contributed to his death."

"You always need to know more, don't you?" my aunt said, pulling a tissue from her pocket. "Drat this eye. Got a lash in it or something. Anyway," she added, dabbing at her eye with the tissue. "The truth is, Andrew didn't go into any details about the matter. He basically just asked me if I'd heard anything about a lawsuit involving a copy of that book, and when I said I hadn't, he dropped the whole discussion." Aunt Lydia finally looked up at me, her expression as calm and collected as ever. "Although he did throw in some remark about the whole thing being blown out of proportion and that if I did hear anything to just ignore it."

"Do you think he could've been trying to protect Kurt?"

Crossing her legs at the ankles, Aunt Lydia placed her hands, one over the over, in her lap. *Like a prim schoolmarm*, I thought.

"Why would he have needed to do that? I know they stayed friends, and even saw each other from time to time without my knowledge. But I don't think Andrew would've gone out on a limb for Kurt. They weren't that close."

I wasn't about to contradict her. The truth was, I didn't really know anything about the relationship my uncle had had with Kurt Kendrick. I knew Kurt had loved Andrew, but that was all. I had no knowledge of how my uncle had truly felt about his childhood friend.

"I just wondered if Kurt was somehow involved in the sale of the Chaucer to Mr. Brentwood. Sort of a silent partner, with Oscar Selvaggio being the public face of the arrangement."

Aunt Lydia straightened in her chair. "You think Kurt killed Selvaggio to keep something like that quiet? But why, after all this time? It doesn't make sense."

There was an eagerness in her tone that made me purse my lips. My aunt was acting a little odd about this Kelmscott Chaucer business. Perhaps it was because it touched too closely on Kurt's relationship with her late husband? "No, it doesn't, and I can't imagine Kurt being that concerned about an old scandal that never really went anywhere. Selvaggio wasn't even charged with anything, and the lawsuit was thrown out. I mean, even if Oscar Selvaggio was trying to blackmail Kurt . . ." I shook my head. "It just doesn't track with Kurt's character for him to murder someone so publicly, especially over something that happened years ago."

"No, it doesn't." Aunt Lydia's expression turned thoughtful. "And if Oscar Selvaggio engaged in such questionable business practices over the years, there could've been any number of people who wanted him dead. "

"They'd have to have attended the party, though. That narrows the field," I said, thinking about Adele. I didn't want to mention her connection to Selvaggio to my aunt. Time enough for that if Brad found any solid evidence to link the former dance coach to the crime.

"True, but not everyone there was a guest," Aunt Lydia said, her eyes narrowing. "Selvaggio's assistant, for one. Maybe she had a reason to kill him? I mean, it isn't unknown for employees to want to murder their bosses, and while she didn't seem like the vindictive type, you never know." Aunt Lydia again drummed her fingers against the arm of her chair. "And there were also the people Kurt hired in for security, and waiters, and so on. It's possible one of them could've slipped under his radar."

"But again, no one knew Oscar Selvaggio would be there," I said.

Aunt Lydia tipped her head and studied me for a moment. "Good point, but there's another possibility. If someone had him under surveillance for some reason, they could've easily figured it out. Perhaps he wasn't that careful about keeping his plans a secret."

This meshed with the thoughts I'd had while talking with Richard. I leapt to my feet. "I have to admit that's the most reasonable explanation. Someone tracking Selvaggio for other crimes could've known about his plan to visit Kurt and followed him. Maybe they arranged to get a job working the party." I used both hands to shove my hair behind my ears. "They could've even simply blended in with the guests. There were a lot of people there, and some brought companions I'd never seen before. It could've been one of them."

"Definitely a possibility," my aunt said. "Now, I really must get supper together. I know you don't mind foraging for yourself, but with Scott here . . ."

"You mean, he's a guest and I'm not," I said, without rancor. "By the way, where is Scott? His car's parked outside, but I haven't seen or heard anything from him all this time."

"He took a walk. At least, that's what he told me he planned to do. I suggested the trails through the new park next door to Richard's house, so I imagine that's where he went."

I crossed over to the doorway of the sitting room. "Maybe I'll go and see if I can catch up with him. I can let him know that dinner will be ready soon, if you want."

"Thanks, that would be helpful." Aunt Lydia followed me out into the hall. "I tried to call him to let him know what time we'd be eating right before you came in, but his phone was busy." She turned and headed toward the kitchen as I grabbed my keys from the ceramic bowl set on the hall side table.

"Oh, sorry. I should have asked if you needed help with dinner," I called after her.

She waved her hand over her head in a dismissive gesture. "No need. I actually made a casserole earlier. It just needs to be reheated."

Outside I took a right, following the sidewalk to its end, past Richard's front yard. The land beyond that point had recently been converted to a town park. It was still a work in progress, so there was a stretch of open field before the small parking area that served the park. A trail led into the woods that bordered the field. That was the most likely place for Scott to have chosen to take a walk, if he'd followed our aunt's suggestion.

The path had been cleared of any undergrowth or large stones, but it was still littered with fallen twigs and smaller rocks. Not wanting to trip, I kept my eyes focused on the ground, but the beauty of the branches arching over my head soon drew my gaze upward. Since it was early May, the trees had already leafed out, but the foliage retained a translucent green newness that spoke of fresh beginnings. Tucked in among the taller deciduous and pine trees, dogwoods bloomed, their white and pink blossoms shining like stars amid the dark green needles of the spruces.

As I breathed in the scent of pine mingled with the earthy perfume of the woodland's leaf-carpeted floor, a sound broke through my reverie. I immediately recognized Scott's voice and realized he must be just around a bend in the trail. Although I couldn't initially make out what he was saying, from the lack of response to what sounded like a question, I assumed he was on his phone. I paused, not wanting to intrude. If my brother had sought out such an isolated spot to make a call, perhaps it was something personal. *Maybe he's talking to Ethan*, I thought, hoping this was true. Despite my earlier misgiving, given his romantic record, I'd decided my brother deserved a chance to prove me wrong. Everyone could grow and change. *I certainly did,* I thought, smiling as I recognized my newly awoken tendency to encourage relationships—first with Sunny and now with Scott. My matchmaking tendencies had blossomed since I'd gotten involved with Richard. It made sense. I was happy, and I wanted my brother and best friend to find happiness as well.

But Scott's next words, spoken in a louder voice, shattered this daydream.

"As I told you, things did not go as planned. Tracking Selvaggio wasn't difficult, but then everything fell apart."

I swallowed an exclamation. So Scott wasn't just here to visit Aunt Lydia while pretending to be on a "suspension" from work. He had come to pursue one of his mysterious missions. It all smacked of 007-type shenanigans.

"Well, obviously, him dying was not part of the plan." Scott's tone was ragged as a hangnail.

Part of me wanted to hear more, but a sensible voice in my brain warned that it was probably better if I stopped this right now. I didn't want to get my brother in more trouble than he might already be in. I coughed and shuffled my shoes through the desiccated leaves at my feet before moving forward on the trail.

As I rounded the bend, I spied Scott pocketing his phone. "Hey there," I said, lacing as much cheerfulness into my voice as possible. "Aunt Lydia sent me out to find you. She wanted to let you know that dinner would be ready soon. She said she tried to call but your cell was busy." I forced a bright smile. "Romantic complications or something, I bet."

"Um, yeah." Scott brushed a lock of his dark hair away from his glasses. "You know how it is."

"Don't I ever. Well, not now, fortunately."

A wave of relief washed over Scott's face. He seemed to have bought my story.

Which is a little odd, given that he's trained to read people, I thought. But I knew all too well how personal feelings could color perception. I'd made plenty of mistakes in reading people's true intentions in the past. Obviously, Scott didn't want to believe I'd heard anything, because that would involve his family in his work, something he always strove to avoid. So he'd accepted my false words without questioning them as much as he should have.

He isn't infallible, I thought, fighting the urge to clench my fingers. I didn't particularly like this idea. While it might give me more clues as to what happened to Oscar Selvaggio, it also meant my brother could be more likely to make a mistake that might land him in danger.

"Let's head on back, then," Scott said. "I don't like to keep Aunt Lydia waiting."

"Wise choice." I kept pace with him as he strode back toward the trailhead, sneaking covert glances at his stoic profile.

He wasn't giving anything else away, and I didn't dare ask him what plan had involved him tracking the whereabouts of a somewhat disreputable art dealer. All I knew was that someone *had* been keeping tabs on Oscar Selvaggio, just like the scenarios put forth by Richard and Aunt Lydia.

Of course, my aunt had also suggested that the person tracking Selvaggio could be the one who murdered him. I side-eyed Scott as we approached our aunt's house, trying to decide whether he could kill anyone. It seemed ridiculous, and yet . . .

Just like Kurt, my brother was enough of a mystery to make the idea a possibility.

Chapter Fifteen

I didn't mention my suspicions about Scott to anyone, not even Richard. I considered telling him when we talked over the phone on Wednesday night but decided I would prefer to have that discussion face-to-face. Even though I was desperate to share my concerns, I felt it would be better to wait to broach this particular subject when he returned home from his choreography gig.

Despite my determination to keep silent on this matter, I was so distracted the next day at work that I kept making stupid mistakes. After discovering that one book was still checked out, Samantha had to redo an entire cart of returns just to make sure I'd cleared them.

"I'm so sorry," I told her. "My mind is scattered today, it seems."

"Don't worry about it," Samantha said. "It's wedding jitters, I bet. I was completely useless a couple of weeks before my own ceremony."

I didn't correct her. The truth was, the mystery surrounding Oscar Selvaggio's death had driven concerns about the wedding completely from my mind. Anyway, everything seemed to be on track—we'd already arranged everything with the caterer, florist, and musicians and had met with the pastor of the Episcopal church, who'd agreed to conduct the ceremony. I was scheduled to pick up my dress and veil over the weekend and already had my shoes, undergarments, and other necessities. All I really needed to do now was keep practicing my dance steps with Karla. Something I planned to do later. With Richard out of town, we'd agreed to meet at his home studio.

When I arrived at Richard's house after work, Karla was relaxing on one of the Adirondack chairs on the covered front porch. "You have keys, I assume?" she asked, jumping to her feet.

"Of course," I said, opening the door. "Just like Richard has one to Aunt Lydia's house, in case of emergencies. Anyway, I take care of the cats and collect the mail and that sort of thing when he's out of town. Speaking of cats," I added, as Loie and Fosse dashed up the stairs, something they did when anyone but Richard or me entered the house, "they've headed upstairs for now, but we'll have to keep an eye out for them. I don't want them running around underfoot, causing a dangerous situation for them as well as us."

Karla hoisted the strap of her dance bag up over her shoulder as she crossed into the dance studio that occupied half of the front room. "I'll warn you if I see them sneak back down." She glanced around the room, which ran the entire width of the house. "It's kind of funny, you just moving next door when you get married. I moved halfway across the country."

"It's true, it won't be that big of a transition for me. I'm here a lot anyway, and I plan to continue to help my aunt with the upkeep on her home and garden after the wedding."

"I wondered about that," Karla said, dropping her dance bag near the wall of floor-to-ceiling mirrors. "Your aunt's house is so big. I hope she won't feel too lonely when you move out."

"We kind of hoped that someone else might move in with her, but now"—I paused with my hand on the dead bolt as I heard a nearby car rev its engines—"it doesn't look like that's likely to happen." Peering out the window near the door, I noticed Scott's car backing out of the adjacent driveway.

"You mean because she and Mr. Chen aren't on great terms right now?" Karla stripped off her loose T-shirt, exposing her sleeveless black leotard. "Rich told me they were having some problems."

"Which is really too bad. They've always gotten along so well before." I watched Scott drive away toward the main part of town. *Perhaps he's meeting Ethan*, I thought, hoping it wasn't a more dangerous assignation.

"You'd better switch into some decent shoes," Karla said, eyeing my leather loafers. "Did you bring the slippers you plan to wear for the wedding, like I asked?"

I fished them out of my soft-sided briefcase and held them up for inspection.

"Very good. Now, enough procrastination. March over here and let's get to work."

"Yes, ma'am," I said, giving her a mock salute.

Karla ignored this attempt at humor, instead tossing me a bundle of white material she'd pulled from her dance bag. "Here, put this on over your slacks. Now that you have the basics down, you need to get used to dancing in a long skirt."

"Yikes, more complications," I said as I tied the strings of the practice petticoat at my waist. "I don't know. Maybe this wasn't such a good idea. I can just see me doing a face-plant in my wedding gown."

"Nonsense," Karly said firmly. "Besides, you'll be dancing with Richard, and I guarantee he won't let you fall."

"There is that." I kicked off my loafers and slid my stockinged feet into the hard-soled white ballerina flats I'd bought to wear with my gown. "At least I'm not trying to attempt this in heels. I don't know how those professional ballroom dancers do it."

"Neither do I, honestly. They have my true admiration. As do ballerinas, with their toe shoes." Karla pointed the toes of one of her feet, which were clad in black jazz flats. "I'm more used to wearing something like this, or even dancing barefoot. Now," she added, after adjusting the ties of her flowing cotton dance pants so that they hugged her sculpted waist, "let's get to work."

We had settled on the American rumba, which was more of a partner dance than some while still being, as Karla had told me with a wink, "sexy as all get-out." With Karla playing the male role, I had finally mastered the basic steps, but the addition of the petticoat did present new challenges.

"Quick, quick, slow," Karla chanted, as we moved around the wooden dance floor Richard had installed in half of his front room.

I stumbled a few times, catching my foot in the petticoat, but after a while, with Karla's help, I began to find my way. We practiced to a mix of songs, all with a rumba beat.

"Better to learn to various songs rather than just one," Karla had said when I'd questioned this approach. "Unless you've definitely settled on one yet."

"No. Richard hired a student group from Clarion that plays big band and jazz and so on. They're really good, but I haven't found the prefect song for this dance yet," I took a deep breath. I still got winded during rehearsals, unlike Karla, who seemed unaffected by any exertion. "I have their lead player's number, though, so I can give them a heads-up when I finally settle on something."

"Good idea. Unless it's already in their set list, they'll need to practice it before the wedding." Karla looked down at me, widening her hazel eyes. "In other words, you'd better decide soon."

"I know," I said, as the music ended and we took a break. "I just want it to be the perfect choice."

"After all this work, I agree with you," Karla said, rolling her head in a stretch that swung her chin-length cap of brown hair.

I stepped back to lean against the wooden barre that ran the length of the mirrors. "I want you and Richard to dance together too."

Karla raised her eyebrows. "When have you ever known us not to, given a dance floor and music?"

"Right. What was I thinking?" I pressed my lower back into the barre. "I think I need some water. Can I get you some?"

"Sure, that would be great," Karla said.

I headed into the kitchen to grab two bottles of water, but as I returned to the front room, the doorbell chimed. "Wonder who that could be?" I handed Karla one of the bottles and crossed to the front door. Peering out through the peephole in the door, I saw Brad Tucker.

"Hello," I said, opening the door. "What's up? Richard's out of town if you were looking for him."

"I wasn't." Brad removed his hat and nodded an acknowledgment to Karla, who'd hung back near the studio's wall of mirrors. "Sorry to bother you, but Ms. Talbot told me you might have a better idea about your brother's whereabouts."

"Scott? Why are you looking for him?"

Brad twisted the brim of his hat. "We need him to come into the station. There's some questions we'd like to ask him."

"In relation to the Oscar Selvaggio case?" I asked, fighting to keep my tone light.

"I'm not at liberty to confirm or deny that," Brad said.

I stared into his steely blue eyes. They gave nothing away, which frustrated but didn't surprise me. "The thing is, I'm not going to be able to provide any more help than Aunt Lydia could. I really don't know where Scott is. I saw him drive off about forty-five minutes ago, but I have no idea where he was going." I wiped a trace of sweat from my upper lip with the back of one finger. "Sorry, we were rehearsing something, as you might've guessed," I added, holding out a section of my practice petticoat. "Anyway, you could check with Ethan Payne. He and Scott have been spending time together. Maybe Scott went to visit him."

"No, we checked that already. Mr. Payne is on duty at the fire station today."

I shrugged. "Then I have no idea."

"All right. It was worth a shot." As Brad put his hat back on, amusement softened his stern expression. "Rehearsing, huh? This wouldn't be for a first dance or something, now, would it?"

"Maybe, but please don't mention anything to Richard."

"A surprise? Sounds like fun. By the way"—Brad tugged his hat down a little lower on his forehead—"you might as well know, since I'm sure it will get around soon enough. Alison and I got engaged over the weekend."

I clapped my hands. "That's wonderful!"

"Yeah, so maybe I should start taking notes on all your preparations." Brad's smile turned boyish and shy. "Never done this before, you know."

"The most important thing is to do what you and Alison want, not what anyone else tells you to do." I stepped forward and impulsively gave Brad a quick hug. "I'm very happy for you. And Alison, of course."

As I stepped back, I noted Brad's flushed cheeks, which I knew indicated embarrassment rather than disapproval. "Thanks. Well," he said, glancing into the studio, where Karla was stretching at the barre, "I'll let you get back to it. And I promise to keep my mouth shut about this." His lips quirked into a smile. "To tell you the truth, I'm looking forward to seeing Richard's face when you spring this surprise on him."

"Me too," I said with a wink. "And as for Scott—he can be something of a loner. He may have just decided to take a drive to collect his thoughts. He does that sort of thing quite often."

"That may be, but when you do see him, tell him he needs to contact the department right away. It's important." Brad gave a tip of his hat. "Have a good day, Amy."

"You too," I said as he turned away.

I waited until he was back in his cruiser before closing and locking the door. Wandering back into the studio portion of the front room, I met Karla's inquiring gaze with a little shake of my head. "He just wanted to talk to my brother."

"So I heard." Karla crossed to the sound equipment set up on the far wall. "From what Richard's told me, Scott's a bit of a mystery." She flipped through a stack of CDs piled on top of the shelves.

"He has a classified job, so yeah, he tends to keep things pretty close to the vest," I said.

Karla held up a CD. "Here's an option. Part of a mix that Rich apparently recorded for his studio. 'Sway,' sung by Michael Bublé. That has a rumba beat, and it would be wedding appropriate."

I burst out laughing. "Sorry, sorry," I said, as I collected myself. "I should've thought of that right away. It would be perfect. It's actually something Richard played for me on one of our first dates."

Karla grinned. "Seducing you with dance, was he? The naughty boy." She looked me up and down. "Did it work?"

"Absolutely," I said.

"Then it *is* perfect. Your chance to seduce him back. Although you don't really need to. He's already mad about you. But still—it will be fun to see you match his moves with finesse." Karla popped the CD into the player and turned to face me. "That being said, maybe we should rehearse a little more."

"Must we?" I flexed my right foot, which was sore.

"If you want to keep up with your husband during your first dance, yes, we must. Besides"—Karla tossed her hair as she strode toward me—"my reputation as a teacher is at stake."

"Well, in that case," I said, stepping forward to meet her, "we'd better practice the rest of the evening."

Chapter Sixteen

Scott never returned Thursday evening, which left Aunt Lydia and me stirring food around our dinner plates, pretending not to worry.

"He's a grown man," my aunt said. "If he wants to go off somewhere without telling us, I suppose that's his prerogative."

"But it isn't like him not to call. I mean, I'm not around him much these days, but I never remember him being impolite. Especially not to someone who's housing and feeding him, free of charge." I recognized the sharp tone that had crept into my voice and cleared my throat. "Anyway, I'm done eating. If you are as well, let me help you clean up, and then maybe we can watch that music program you recorded from PBS. We shouldn't let this ruin our evening."

Of course, it did anyway. To the point where we both went to bed early. Not that I slept much—I sat up in bed every time I heard anything that sounded like a car.

Friday morning, with Scott still absent and no messages on either of our phones, my concern turned to anger. Observing the strain on Aunt Lydia's face, I decided to give my brother a good talking to the next time I saw him.

"The least he could do would be to leave a message, just saying he's okay," I told Sunny as we stood behind the library circulation desk later that morning.

"I agree, but what can you do?" Sunny flicked her long golden braid behind her shoulder. "Young men tend to be thoughtless when it comes to stuff like that."

"Scott isn't that young. He's thirty-three, for heaven's sake."

"For a guy, that's still early on the 'how to be a decent human' learning curve," Sunny said, her smile fading as she added, "And some apparently never learn. Take Fred, for example. Or rather, don't."

"What do you mean?" I asked, turning to examine her face. "Did you guys have a fight?"

"No. Not yet, anyway," Sunny said grimly. "But we probably will next time I run into him." She inhaled an audible breath. "I found out he's the one who put the sheriff's department on Scott's trail. I mean, he actually told me that he'd uncovered some information that linked Scott to Oscar Selvaggio. Can you imagine?"

"When was this?"

"Just last night. I guess he'd already shared the discovery with the authorities, and that's why Brad showed up yesterday evening asking you and Lydia for information on Scott's whereabouts."

"Well, to play devil's advocate, it is Fred's job."

Sunny's blue eyes flashed. "But it's *your* brother. Fred knows you're my best friend, so he should've waited before spilling that info to Brad and his team. At least, that's my humble opinion."

I laid my hand on her bare forearm. "And I love you for that. But if Scott has hidden secrets tying him to Selvaggio, it was bound to come out sooner or later. He probably should've told Brad everything up front." I pulled my hand back and looked her over. "My point is that you shouldn't throw Fred under the bus for doing what he was hired to do."

Sunny sighed. "If it doesn't bother you, I guess I can get past it. But I'm not sure I like the work that Fred does. All this snooping into other people's lives . . . You know what my grandparents would say—better to focus on your own affairs than meddle in other people's business."

"That's because they were part of the counterculture," I said mildly. "They've always lived outside society's rules and still don't trust authority."

"True." Sunny grabbed her braid and fiddled with the elastic band tying it off. "Maybe I'll return Fred's calls. If you aren't really angry about him sharing that info on Scott."

"Has he called often, then?" I asked, with a lift of my eyebrows.

"Oh, a few times." Sunny grinned. "Like every hour. Not to mention the texts."

"Seems he's a tiny bit invested," I said. Looking up as the front doors opened, I nudged her. "Speak of the devil."

Fred Nash strode over to the desk. "Listen, Sunny, I want to clear this up right now."

"Not here," I said, pointing over Sunny's head. "Workroom. That is, if Sunny agrees to talk with you."

Sunny rolled her eyes. "Yeah, sure, why not," she said, before flouncing off into the back room.

Fred held up his hands. "I do want to apologize; I guess I got your brother in trouble. But facts are facts. There was nothing I could do, not if I wanted to retain my integrity as well as my job."

"I know." I motioned for him to step around behind the desk. "Go talk to her. I think she may be more receptive now that she knows I'm not terribly upset."

As Fred slipped past me, I stopped him with one hand on his wrist. "Can you tell me what you discovered that connected Scott with Oscar Selvaggio, or is that privileged information?"

He paused, his brown eyes narrowing as he met my inquisitive gaze. "It's no secret. Not anymore. I found out that your brother was assigned to shadow Selvaggio. Something to do with the art dealer's connection to organized crime. From what I can tell, Scott was trying to catch Selvaggio in a secret convo with some mysterious leader of a criminal organization. A big fish. Someone who's evaded capture for years."

"Oh, really?" I tossed this off with a little smile, although inside I was fuming. "Does that mean you no longer think Kurt Kendrick has any connection to Selvaggio's death?"

"Honestly, we aren't really sure one way or the other. We haven't cleared Kendrick of that or . . . a few other things." Fred massaged the back of his neck with one hand. "It simply means that there could be someone else with just as much of a motive. In a nutshell, it doesn't appear that his bid to acquire the Kelmscott Chaucer was the only thing that would've put a target on Selvaggio's back."

"Right. It could've been his connection to illegal activities," I said. *Or perhaps a vendetta from the past,* I thought, remembering Adele's connection to the art dealer. But I wasn't about to share that with a private investigator. Let the sheriff's department follow that lead first. I shifted my weight from foot to foot. "So you're saying that Scott was sent here to track Selvaggio to help apprehend someone? That's odd. He's always told us that he was a security expert. I assumed he had a desk job. Maybe classified, but not anything out in the field."

Fred's gaze flitted to the half-open door to the workroom. "I'm afraid you've been misinformed. My investigation turned up something quite different. Yes, Scott Webber is a computer expert. But he also does a few other things."

"Apparently," I said, my smile tightening into a grimace. So my brother had not come to Taylorsford for a long delayed visit as he'd told Aunt Lydia. Or even because his superiors had asked him to pretend he'd been put on suspension. No, he'd come to town tracking a man who was likely to be connected to a criminal network.

He's brought that danger into my aunt's house, I thought, clenching my fingernails into my palm. I was so angry with my brother that if he'd walked into the library at that moment, I would probably have thrown him out. But I simply forced another smile and urged Fred to head into the workroom and talk to Sunny.

As I stared blankly out over the quiet library, I considered Fred's description of my brother's work. *He's a field agent*, I thought. *Something he's never admitted to. Not to me or, to my knowledge, to our parents. A field agent who's now gone missing. Why? If it's connected to his mission to track down a dangerous criminal, it's possible he's in serious trouble. Fred actually did us a favor, telling the authorities what he knew. At least now they know that my brother could be in danger.* I glanced at the closed door of the workroom. I'd have to share this revelation with Sunny. It might change how she looked at Fred if his words didn't do the trick.

For now, I decided to call someone who might have additional information, or at least a few contacts, and could be of assistance. Because if anyone outside law enforcement knew who my brother might be tracking now, it would be Kurt.

I pulled out my cell phone and texted the art dealer. I knew he often left Georgetown early on Friday to spend the weekend at Highview, so there was a chance he was already in town.

After asking Kurt to meet me later, I laid my phone facedown on the counter and knocked on the workroom door. "If you guys are done talking, could you please come out? I need Sunny to watch the desk while I do some shelving," I said.

Sunny strolled out of the workroom looking like a cat who'd finished off a bowl of cream. Fred, following her, appeared rather pleased too.

"Seems like you sorted things out," I said, reaching over to tug Sunny's sleeve back over her shoulder.

"We did." Sunny made a shooing motion. "Now go and get back to work, Fred, so I can do my own job."

He gave her a mock salute. "At your command," he said, walking around the desk. As he turned to face Sunny and me, his merry expression melted into something more serious. "But as I said, Sunny, be careful. And warn your friend here to stay safe as well."

"I will do my best." Sunny blew him a kiss. "See you later."

After Fred left, I picked up my cell phone and took a quick glance, but there was no answering text from Kurt yet. Curling my fingers around the phone, I turned to my friend. "It looks like all is well again."

"Except he thinks I'm going to prevent you from doing any more amateur sleuthing." Sunny rolled her eyes. "As if I have that power."

I tapped my phone against my other palm. "Not even Richard can do that,"

"Oh, I know." Sunny pointed at my phone. "In fact, I bet you're calling someone right now to try to track down more information."

"Texting, but yeah." I lifted my shoulders. "My brother could be in trouble. I have to do something,"

Sunny tipped her head and surveyed me with a critical eye. "Brad and his team can take that on. It's what they're trained to do."

"Says the woman who's helped me investigate several other cases Without keeping the sheriff's department entirely in the loop." I grabbed the smooth metal handle of the book cart we kept behind the desk. "I would like to shelve these items, if you don't mind watching the desk."

Sunny *hmph*ed and placed her hands on her hips. "So that's the end of the conversation? Okay, sure. I'll stay here while you shelve and plot your next bit of sleuthing."

I cast her a smile as I pushed the cart around the desk. "Research," I called over my shoulder, heading into the stacks. "Just research."

In the general fiction section I ran into Zelda, who was doing some shelf-reading as part of her volunteer duties.

"This area is such a mess." Zelda's blonde curls bounced as she shook her head. "And we can't blame all of that on the Nightingale."

"Unfortunately, many people pull books to look at the jacket info and then just shove them back any which way," I said.

Zelda pointed at an empty cart sitting at the end of an adjacent range of shelves. "I know. Even though you put up prominent signs asking that books be returned to the carts rather than reshelved."

"You should know by now that people don't read signs. I mean, we still need to have them, just so we can point to them when patrons question the rules, but that's about all they're good for."

"Sad but true." Zelda paused midmotion and pressed the book she held to her chest. "By the way, there's something I've been meaning to mention to you. Ever since I heard all the talk about that rare book that might've gotten poor Mr. Selvaggio killed."

I leaned into the metal frame of my book cart. I knew I shouldn't encourage Zelda's tendency to gossip, but sometimes she provided useful information. *All's fair*, I thought, before asking, "What's that?"

Zelda's light-brown eyes sparkled like water in a fast-moving stream. "Well, dear, I don't want to talk out of school, and you know Lydia is my dearest friend, but this whole mess about that Chaucer book . . ." She laid the book she was holding on a shelf and glanced around, as if making sure no one else was listening. "That Kelmscott thing, I mean. I've heard that edition mentioned before, a long time ago. By your aunt, of all people. Now she's acting like she's never heard tell of it."

My fingers tightened on the cart handle. "What do you mean? Aunt Lydia talked to you in the past about the Kelmscott Chaucer?"

"She did. I remembered it because I thought the phrase was so interesting. Kelmscott Chaucer," she said, widening her eyes. "Sounds like some name for a wealthy aristocrat, don't you think? Some fellow wearing a velvet dressing gown and smoking a pipe while his valet serves him a brandy on a silver tray. Anyway"—Zelda's hands fluttered like butterfly wings—"years ago, Lydia shared her concern that Andrew was getting in over his head, trying to break into selling art objects as well as his own paintings. They were always a little short of money. If Lydia hadn't had the inheritance from the family . . ."

"I know," I said, cutting her off. "What was Uncle Andrew trying to do? I mean, I wouldn't have thought he'd have had the funds to invest in purchasing items for resale."

Zelda arched her golden brows. "He didn't, poor lamb. This was something that someone had given him in exchange for a painting. Or so he told Lydia. Apparently, the person who did the trade didn't know the value of the item, which was an old illustrated book."

"A copy of the Kelmscott Chaucer? But that sounds impossible," I said.

"Well, I guess Lydia didn't realize what it was worth. Anyway, she didn't seem to think much of it. She was just concerned about Andrew getting into art sales in general. She didn't think he had the head for that sort of business."

"I can understand her concern," I said. "I never met my uncle, but from what I've heard, he was more a creative dreamer sort. Definitely not a businessman."

"That was Andrew, all right. Darling man, but a bit . . . scattered. Head always in the clouds. Anyway, Lydia didn't like him trying to sell any artworks other than his own. She felt he might get mixed up with the wrong sort."

Sadly, he did anyway. I didn't voice this thought, instead focusing on Zelda's comments about Andrew acquiring a valuable book from some unknown art lover. "So he decided to sell it? Did Aunt Lydia say to whom?"

"No. She didn't know anything except that he was working with an art dealer to broker the sale. When he collected a tidy sum, Andrew warned her not to say anything about the matter.

Which she said she never did, other than mentioning it to me in a moment of weakness." Zelda sniffed. "I know this is hard to believe, but Lydia was so besotted with that man, he could do anything and she'd just go along with it."

I thought about my very independent, self-contained aunt. "It's almost impossible to imagine, but she was rather young at the time. We all act a little foolish when we're that age."

Zelda patted her curly bob and smiled. "Don't I know it. Anyway, I'm not sure if Lydia's said anything to you about any connection with one of those Chaucer books, but I thought maybe it was something you should know. Just so you could ask her about it—in a roundabout way, of course. And without mentioning my name, if you don't mind."

"Thanks, that is interesting. I will see what I can find out," I said absently, my thoughts on what my aunt had already told me in relation to the Kelmscott Chaucer, or at least the scandal surrounding its sale.

She said Andrew told her there was nothing to it. That she shouldn't believe the rumors. Which now makes more sense. What if he was somehow connected to the sale of the copy that went to Adele's father? Aunt Lydia didn't mention anything about that, but maybe she didn't want to discuss anything else that might tarnish Andrew's name.

"Well, I just wanted to share, in case it sheds light on poor Mr. Selvaggio's death. Not that Andrew or Lydia would be connected to that recent event, of course." Zelda wrinkled her brow as if just realizing that none of this made much sense. "It probably means nothing, actually. Forget I ever said anything."

"Don't worry, I'll keep you out of it. And I'm not sure it matters either, so I may not even bring it up with Aunt Lydia. For now, I'd better see to this," I added, motioning toward the full book cart. "Books don't shelve themselves, you know."

"Sometimes I wonder," Zelda said, her face brightening again. "The way they end up in such strange locations." Her eyes twinkled. "Or maybe it's ghosts?"

I threw up my hands. "Oh heavens, don't say that. I have enough people trying to convince me such things are real as it is. Anyway, thanks for the info. It does give me a little more insight into the past, and that's always interesting, even if that doesn't have anything to do with the current murder investigation."

"Just thought I'd share. Have fun shelving," Zelda said as she went back to her shelf-reading.

"Sure, 'cause that's a thing," I said, flashing her a bright smile before I rolled the cart into another aisle.

Pausing for a moment, I allowed my mind to process the information that Zelda had just provided. She was right—it was unlikely that Uncle Andrew's participation in the sale of a copy of the Kelmscott Chaucer had anything to do with Selvaggio's murder.

But it could easily have had something to do with the dealer he'd used to broker the sale. I couldn't help but suspect that that had been his longtime friend Kurt Kendrick.

All these copies of a valuable book, and one man in the middle of every sale? I shoved a book into its rightful place on the shelf. That was a little too coincidental. I pulled my cell phone from my pocket and checked my messages.

Kurt had sent a text. *Will meet you in the garden at Lydia's around six*, it said.

I shelved the remaining books with renewed vigor, using the time to mentally compose the questions I wanted to ask Kurt.

There was quite a list. I wasn't afraid to ask, but whether I would get the answers I sought was another matter.

Chapter Seventeen

When I arrived home Friday evening, Aunt Lydia was sitting in the kitchen, staring at a plastic-wrapped platter of sandwiches on the kitchen table.

"Do you want to leave the lights off?" I asked as I leaned against the doorjamb.

"What?" Aunt Lydia looked up, her eyes wide as those of a startled deer. "Oh, sorry. I guess I was lost in my thoughts."

"Apparently." I pointed toward the sandwiches. "Are those for an event?"

"Actually, I made them for supper. I wasn't sure when your brother would return, but I thought he might be hungry, so . . ." Aunt Lydia rubbed her eyes with her fists as if awakening from a stupor.

"Still no word?" I asked as I strolled into the kitchen.

"No. Have you heard anything?"

I shook my head as I sat down, facing her across the table.

Aunt Lydia toyed with a loose edge of the plastic wrap. "I should put these in the fridge, then. Who knows when he'll show up."

"No one, apparently." I frowned. "I checked in with Mom and Dad, and they've had no messages from Scott either. He's gone dark."

"It might be something required by his line of work, but it is worrisome." Aunt Lydia stood and picked up the platter. "I guess I should ask if you want a sandwich before I carry these off."

"Don't worry. I'll grab one later." I glanced at my watch. Fifteen minutes until I was supposed to meet with Kurt in the garden. "While it's still light out, I'd like to get in a little weeding. Maybe I can also work off some of my nervous energy."

"Sounds like a good plan, but be sure to wear your gloves. The wedding is two weeks from tomorrow, and you certainly don't want chipped and broken fingernails for the photos."

I rolled my eyes, even though I knew she had a point. "I promise to protect my hands."

"You'd better. Anyway, it will be a help to me if you weed, especially since I need to do some laundry. Well"—my aunt said as she slid the platter into the refrigerator—"I don't absolutely need to. But it will keep me occupied."

I rose to my feet and patted my pocket. "I'll leave my cell phone on, just in case Scott does message me."

"Let me know immediately if he does," Aunt Lydia said, leaning back against the closed door of the fridge.

I assured her I would before dashing upstairs to change into proper gardening attire. Which, in my case, was a pair of cotton shorts and a well-worn T-shirt, along with a pair of battered sneakers.

Before I headed into the garden, I grabbed a pair of suede gloves and a trowel from the storage bin beside the back-porch steps. If Kurt kept his appointment, I probably wouldn't actually do any weeding, but I knew it was possible that he would bail on me.

But he was already waiting when I reached the middle of the garden, which was screened from view of the house by the lilacs and verbena that filled the beds surrounding a whimsical metal sundial.

"Fairies?" Kurt touched the delicately wrought wing of one of the two entwined figures that served as a base. They appeared to be dancing together as they balanced the face of the sundial on their uplifted hands. "That's a bit risky. Considering some of the local legends, I wouldn't think that Lydia would want to encourage a visit from the Fair Folk."

"Aunt Lydia—like me and, I suspect, you as well—respects the folklore as story but doesn't believe the fae are still roaming the Blue Ridge," I said, repressing the memory of orbs of light dancing above a mountain forest.

"'There are more things in heaven and earth,'" Kurt said, with a sardonic smile. "But never mind that. I don't want to waste your time with a lot of chitchat."

"That suits me. I have a list of questions for you. Most importantly, what you might know about my brother's business. Do you have any idea why he was sent here or who he might be tracking?"

Kurt held up one hand, palm out. "I have some suspicions, but I really don't think I should share them. Not even with you."

I placed my balled fists on my hips. "Why not?"

"For one thing, it's probably classified information." Kurt met my frown with a sardonic smile. "Yes, I often know things I shouldn't. That doesn't mean I share that information with others. I've helped out a few federal agencies over the years, you know. If I ever wish to work with them again or, more importantly, count on their assistance in certain matters, I must show the proper discretion."

"I should've known this would be all about what you want or need," I said. "So why exactly did you agree to meet with me?"

"That I can explain. I might have a story to tell you that will clarify a few things concerning this Oscar Selvaggio business." He motioned to one of the garden benches that faced the sundial. "Shall we sit?"

"If you wish," I said, following him to the bench. As I sat down, I noticed slight discoloration at his temple surrounding a gash almost hidden by his thick hair. "By the way, how's your head?"

"As good as ever," he replied. "And yes, I did see someone about it. They gave me a clean bill of health. Well"—he shot me a grin—"as clean as I can get at this point in my life, I suppose."

My lips twitched into a smile in spite of me. "I won't ask for any details."

"Probably wise." Kurt's expression sobered. "Getting back to the business at hand—I must delve into a little personal history to explain my connection to Selvaggio and the Kelmscott Chaucer."

I leaned against the back of the bench, stretching out my legs. "I thought the connection was that you both wanted to buy a copy."

"That's the most recent one." Kurt cleared his throat. "You already know your late uncle was involved with some rather dubious people in the art world."

"Wait, this has something to do with Uncle Andrew?" *Just like Zelda said . . .* Even though I knew Aunt Lydia couldn't see us from the house, I cast a quick glance toward the back porch.

"Unfortunately, yes. Which is one reason I've been trying to keep my history with Selvaggio under wraps." Kurt tapped my arm, forcing me to look at him. "Andrew got mixed up in a sale of a Kelmscott Chaucer, one that also involved Oscar Selvaggio."

My jaw dropped. "Not the one Selvaggio sold to Adele Tourneau's father?"

"I'm afraid so." Kurt ran his hand through his thick hair, wincing slightly as his fingers brushed over the injury at his temple. "I suppose he needed the money. If only he'd told me . . ." Kurt shook his head. "But I imagine he was too embarrassed. I'd given him the Chaucer as a gift, you see."

"And then he sold it?" I straightened, pulling my back away from the bench. "You gave him a Kelmscott Chaucer? That was quite a present."

Kurt shrugged. "I was assigned to read Chaucer in my junior year in high school and was at something of a loss, as my background hadn't included much exposure to classic literature. Andrew tutored me and helped me to understand it well enough to make a decent grade in that class. So years later, when a copy of the Kelmscott Press edition of Chaucer's works came on the market, I acquired it."

"Legally?" I asked, tapping the trowel against my bare knee.

"I think I'll take the fifth on that." The lines bracketing Kurt's mouth deepened. "I should've known better, but I thought it was just going to sit in the library at Andrew and Lydia's house, where few people would see it."

"But Andrew decided to sell it instead." I lifted the trowel and stared at my reflection, warped by the concave metal surface. "He was often short of funds, as we know from his unfortunate dabbling in forgery."

"And I suppose he didn't feel he could go to Lydia for the money. Or me." Kurt exhaled a deep sigh. "He suffered from a drug problem from time to time, you know."

"I'm aware." I laid the trowel next to me on the bench and swiveled to face Kurt directly. "You think he needed money to buy drugs?"

"No, he was clean at that point. But he still had debts. Not the kind anyone can avoid paying if they want to keep all their fingers." Kurt smiled grimly. "And being a painter, that was rather important to Andrew."

"Are you saying he sold the Chaucer because he owed money to dealers?"

"I assume that was the reason. He wouldn't have confessed that to Lydia, of course, and even though I knew about his on-again, off-again problems with drugs, he wouldn't have come to me either."

"Why not? Weren't you the one who introduced him to drugs when you were younger?"

"To my eternal regret." Kurt leaned back and gazed up into the sky, which was tinted violet as twilight approached. "I did help him out, quite a few times, including paying off some of his debts. I felt I owed him that much. But the last time I did so, Andrew told me he would never ask again. And he never did."

"He sold the Kelmscott Chaucer instead."

"Apparently." Kurt lowered his head and met my stern gaze. "I didn't know anything about it. Not until the scandal erupted and Adele's father was caught in the middle of it."

"But I researched that story, and no one ever mentioned Andrew Talbot. They all reported Oscar Selvaggio as the seller."

"Oscar was just a broker. He always claimed he had no knowledge about the Chaucer's provenance, which was actually true. Since Andrew didn't know that the book had a questionable background, Oscar wouldn't have known that either."

"So his innocence on that point was real. It must've convinced the authorities, anyway, since no formal charges were ever brought against him." I frowned. "But why didn't he name Uncle Andrew as the actual seller, then? There's no mention of that in any of the reports I read."

"Because I warned Oscar not to, of course."

I studied Kurt's face. It was shadowed by a weariness that betrayed, for once, his true age. "You threatened him?"

"Not exactly. Technically, I bribed him. But it had the same effect. He told the authorities he had bought the Chaucer in a bundled deal; that it was just one piece in a collection he'd purchased from someone overseas." Kurt bared his teeth in the semblance of a smile. "Someone who couldn't be located later, I'm afraid."

"One of your aliases?"

"Perhaps."

I leaned back, stretching one arm across the top rail of the bench. "I see. Employing the old quid pro quo. You helped Selvaggio by providing a cover for his supposed purchase of the Chaucer, while he kept quiet about Uncle Andrew's involvement in the matter."

"Exactly. And it would've ended there, but . . ."

"But Jasper Brentwood died, and his daughter, Adele, decided to sue Selvaggio when the authorities failed to charge him with a crime."

"They really didn't have a strong case," Kurt said. "But I was afraid the investigation launched by the private detectives Adele and her siblings hired would reveal Andrew's involvement. So I stepped in again to make the matter go away."

"Did you know Adele at that point?"

Kurt shook his head. "We were not yet acquainted. I knew who she was, but only because I had an interest in the arts and followed some dance companies."

"So what did you do?"

Kurt stretched his arm over mine. "I bought off Adele's lawyer. Which doomed her case to failure, of course. I wasn't proud of that," he added, laying his hand on my shoulder. "But I had to protect Andrew."

I wriggled my shoulder to try to loosen his grip, to no avail. "Is that why you were so generous about supporting Adele's dance charities later on?"

"Partially. But I also believed in what she was doing. And, of course, I wanted to help Richard. My belated way to repay the generosity of his great-uncle Paul."

I met Kurt's calm gaze with a glare. "You never told Adele any of this?"

"Of course not. And I would appreciate it if you didn't enlighten her. Or Richard, if you can see your way to keeping anything from him."

I finally yanked my shoulder free and dropped my arm into my lap. "I may keep quiet about it, if only so he's not completely disillusioned by you."

"As you are?"

"I never had any illusions to start with. Anyway, your story clarifies your connection to Oscar Selvaggio and Adele, but it doesn't exactly exonerate you. In fact"—I tipped my head to study his implacable face—"it gives you all the more reason to murder Selvaggio. I mean, you may have killed him to keep everything quiet about your involvement with another Kelmscott Chaucer in the past."

"That is a logical assumption, although I must correct one thing—it isn't *another* copy of the Chaucer."

I leapt to my feet. "You and Selvaggio were trying to buy the exact same copy that you originally gave Uncle Andrew?"

"We were." Kurt flashed me a humorless smile. "To be perfectly honest, I still am."

"Surely not from Adele," I said, crossing my arms over my chest.

"No, the family sold it to another collector soon after Jasper Brentwood's death." Kurt stood to face me.

Or rather, I thought, *to loom over me*. "And you want it back because it is another connection to my uncle?"

"Partially, but also because it will put a final nail in the coffin of one of my more foolish youthful indiscretions." Kurt shoved the sleeves of his ivory cotton sweater above his elbows, exposing his muscular forearms. "I preferred to bury the book in one of my storage vaults rather than have Oscar attempt to sell it again."

"Which might raise some ugly skeletons?"

"Indeed. Especially since there are a few people digging a little too deeply into some of my past actions."

I thought of Hugh and Fred Nash. They were trying to track down just this type of evidence of Kurt's questionable former art deals. "Why are you telling me this?" I asked, dropping my arms to my sides. "You know I could go to Brad Tucker and relay what you've just confessed. Not to mention I could tell Hugh Chen everything."

Kurt lifted his bushy eyebrows. "I am aware you can do so. But will you?"

Taking a few steps back, I dug my heels into the loose gravel of the path. "I should."

"Of course you should. That would be the sensible thing to do. After all, as you noted, I do have a reason to have desired Oscar Selvaggio's death."

"So why risk everything by talking to me?"

"Because I want you to know that I am doing whatever I can to protect you and those you care about." Kurt spread out his hands. "How do you think Lydia would feel if all this information about Andrew came to light?"

I narrowed my eyes. "That's not the only reason. You also don't want Richard or Adele to know the truth about your initial involvement in her affairs."

"True enough. But I'm more concerned about the safety of you, or anyone else, who digs too deeply into this matter. There are other factors that might have led to Oscar's death, things I can't discuss at this point. I just wanted to share what I could, so you would know that I am not trying to deceive you when I say that you, and Hugh, and anyone else, need to tread very carefully." Kurt's blue eyes grew icy. "There are more layers to this than you can possibly imagine. My involvement with the Kelmscott Chaucer in the past is only the tip of the iceberg. And trust me, my dear, this danger is just as unexpected and deadly as the one that sunk the *Titanic*."

A puff of wind ruffled my hair, carrying with it the scent of lilacs. "That man at your house, the one who struck you," I said, speaking slowly as the thought formed in my mind. "Is he connected to all of this?"

Kurt's sardonic expression shifted to stony stillness. "That's another thing altogether."

I looked him over, noticing that while his arms hung loosely at his sides, his hands were clenched into fists. "It occurred to me," I said, although the thought had just popped into my head, "that he might be the killer. He looked like hired muscle to me. I can't help but wonder if he was working for someone else who wanted the Chaucer. Maybe he was told to get you out of the way as well as Selvaggio."

Kurt's glower told me I might be on the right track. "He's nothing. Just one of those people I sometimes have to deal with in the course of doing business. Don't concern yourself with him."

"And then there's the fact that Oscar Selvaggio appeared to recognize my brother. Who works in some top-secret capacity for the government and just happened to show up here about the time Selvaggio did. It's all a little puzzling, to tell you the truth." I lifted my chin defiantly. "Perhaps I should at least mention that much to Brad Tucker."

"I wouldn't. Not before talking to Scott first," Kurt said, his tone razor-sharp.

Emboldened, I took a step forward. "Do you know why Scott was tracking Selvaggio? Because I now believe that's what he was really doing here."

"As I said before, I have my opinion, but it's not something I'm going to discuss." Kurt reached out and grabbed my hand. "Listen, Amy, you need to be careful. The Kelmscott Chaucer is one thing . . ."

I met his intense gaze and held it without wavering. "There's something else?"

"Isn't there always?" he said, his tone suddenly light. He squeezed my fingers before he released my hand. "You can tell the authorities whatever you want, as long as you allow them to do their job without your help. I'm sure they'll uncover Oscar's murderer soon enough."

"Even if it's you?"

Kurt grinned. "If it's me, they will find that out, but they may not find me." Sweeping one hand through his thick white hair, he added, "I do own a passport and a few properties overseas."

"So you'd run?"

"If necessary. But it won't come to that." Kurt gave a little nod. "Good evening, Amy," he said, before turning away and striding off.

I watched until he left the garden before I sat back down on the bench and considered the information he'd just shared, and why.

The *why* still puzzled me. Sure, he might be explaining his behavior and guaranteeing my silence by claiming that he was trying to protect the reputation of someone he'd loved. And by extension, protect that man's widow, who was someone I loved. It wasn't out of the realm of possibility. I knew how deeply Kurt had cared for my Uncle Andrew.

Unless, of course, everything he'd told me had been a lie. *Which also isn't*, I thought, *an impossibility.*

Chapter Eighteen

By Monday, Aunt Lydia was ready to report Scott as a missing person, but when she called my parents, they advised her against this action.

"They said it's happened before," she told me as I prepared my lunch before walking to work. "Debbie says Scott has always cautioned them not to get the authorities involved, as it might jeopardize a covert mission. So I suppose we should just sit tight."

"Sounds reasonable," I said, although I was also concerned. But knowing it was possible that our interference might actually place my brother in more danger, I agreed to wait before taking any action. "Besides," I said, dropping my plastic lunch bag into my briefcase and slinging the satchel's strap over my shoulder, "Brad and his team are already looking for Scott, although that's because they want to question him. But still—if he's in any real danger, the authorities are more likely to find him than not. They're already on his trail."

"True." Aunt Lydia drew in a deep breath before following me into the hall. "By the way, the caterers called. They need a final decision on the hors d'oeuvres options. Do you think you could stop by today? Hani said she'd hang out at the shop until six if you thought you could pop in after work."

"Sure, I can do that."

"You can take the car today, if that makes things easier."

I slipped out the front door, pausing on the porch to look back at her. "No, I can walk to Hani's place from the library easily enough. And the weather looks like it will cooperate." I flashed my aunt a smile. "I need the exercise anyway. I want to look good in that gown."

"You'll look lovely regardless," Aunt Lydia said, holding the door ajar. "But maybe that will work better. You can call Richard and ask him to meet you there. That way he can give you a ride home."

I made a face. "Richard won't be able to join me. He probably won't get home until ten or later. Another rehearsal."

Aunt Lydia frowned. "I thought the semester was winding down."

"This is for his studio's final production. And since he was gone for several days on that choreography gig, he feels compelled to work with them every night this week. So once again, I won't see much of him." I shrugged. "But the last performance is this Friday, and graduation is Saturday. After that, he'll be free."

"Good," Aunt Lydia said. "Because we're going to need his help with all the last-minute wedding preparations."

"Yeah. Especially since Scott bailed on us." I waved good-bye, waiting until Aunt Lydia closed the door before dashing down the porch steps and talking off at a brisk walk.

But despite my efforts, I was still running late. When I reached the library, I had little time to get everything set up for opening.

Fortunately, Samantha had arrived a few minutes ahead of me and had already done a sweep of the public spaces.

"No visible problems," she told me as we met up behind the circulation desk.

"Good. I could do with a quiet day," I said, knowing that this was not likely to be the case. It was a Monday, after all.

Fortunately, things ran smoothly until after lunch, when the Nightingale arrived. After informing me that she'd seen a UFO hovering over the mountains the night before, she disappeared into the stacks.

"My turn to follow," I told Samantha, who offered me a sympathetic smile before turning away to help a patron check out some books.

I trailed the Nightingale for half an hour, marking the locations of the items she shoved into various sections with sticky notes tacked to the shelves. When she completed her rounds and exited the library, I returned to the marked sections and pulled the books, placing them on a rolling book cart. We'd need to double-check their status at the desk before they were returned to their proper locations.

As I pushed the cart toward the circulation desk, a voice halted my progress.

"Hello, Ms. Webber. So nice to see you again." Cynthia Rogers stepped in front of my cart, waving a rectangular piece of paper. "I stopped by today, hoping to speak with you. Your assistant said you were in the stacks, so I thought I'd track you down. Hope you don't mind."

I surveyed the short figure in front of me, noticing that she was wearing more formal clothes today—a navy blazer over a white blouse and a pearl-gray pencil skirt.

"Hello, Ms. Rogers—sorry, Cynthia. I'm surprised to see you're still in Taylorsford."

"Oh, I've quite fallen in love with the place." Cynthia Rogers tapped the piece of paper, which I realized was a legal-sized white envelope, against her chin. "I've decided to spend the entire month here, to be honest. One of the benefits of being older," she added with a bright smile.

"I guess it is." I wheeled the book cart closer. "Was there something you wanted? More information on the history of the town, or . . . ?" I allowed my question to hang in the air.

"Not this time. Actually, I'm here to give you something." Cynthia slid past the book cart to stand in front of me. "A little gift for the library," she said, holding out the envelope.

I took it from her with a puzzled expression, which changed to astonishment when I opened the envelope and pulled out the check that had been placed inside. "My goodness, is this a donation? It's quite"—several words tumbled through my mind before I landed on the right one—"generous."

Cynthia Rogers waved her hands as if shooing away a cloud of gnats. "It's really not that much. I have been blessed in my life, and I like to share my good fortune with others. I thought your lovely library would be just the place to support, especially since you're also preserving the history of the town. I believe that's always an extremely important thing to protect, don't you?"

"Of course," I said, my gaze still fastened on the check. It had more zeroes than I'd ever seen since we'd received the money from selling Delbert Frye's donation of gold coins the previous spring. I glanced up to offer Cynthia a grateful smile. "Thank you so much.

I just never expected such generosity, especially from a visitor to Taylorsford."

"Well, to be entirely honest"—Cynthia tugged on one of the pearl earrings dangling from her ears—"I wasn't quite forthcoming with you the last time we spoke. I admit I have a few ties to the area. From many years ago."

"Did you live here?" I asked, sliding the check back into the envelope and laying it on the book cart.

"Not exactly. In the area, but not in Taylorsford proper. I never really spent much time in this town. But I do remember meeting some interesting people in those days. One in particular—an artist who was showing his work at the local fair. I really wanted to buy one of his paintings, but unfortunately I didn't. Not sure why." Cynthia smiled. "Just couldn't make up my mind which canvas I wanted and then I ended up with none."

"Not Andrew Talbot?"

Cynthia Rogers pointed a finger at me. "That's the one. He was forgotten for many years, by everyone it seems, as well as me, but about a year ago I heard about an event that revived his reputation."

"That's right." I eyed her intently, wondering just how well she'd known my uncle. "The art dealer, Kurt Kendrick, hosted a showing at his house. A lot of the paintings subsequently sold to galleries and collectors."

"Doesn't Kendrick live at a historic estate outside of Taylorsford? I read about that house in some literature on the area."

"It's called Highview." I studied Cynthia's eager face for a moment, debating whether to share any more information with her. "As a matter of fact, Andrew Talbot was my uncle," I said, after deciding that this was not a detail I needed to suppress.

"Was he? What a coincidence. I don't suppose you have access to any more of his paintings, do you? I really would like to buy one."

This put a different spin on Cynthia Roger's curiosity about my family. I looked her over, realizing that she was probably the right age to have been a contemporary of my late uncle. What if they'd been involved in the past and all this questioning was a roundabout way to acquire a memento from a lost love?

"That's not my call," I said, keeping my tone light. "My aunt Lydia manages my late uncle's estate. You'd have to speak to her about buying anything. Although I must warn you, she isn't keen on selling too many of Uncle Andrew's paintings. She did allow Mr. Kendrick to sell some, but she hasn't parted with any more after that showing."

"I'd be willing to pay a very respectable price." Cynthia Rogers beamed at me. "I do have the resources to meet any reasonable offer."

"That's nice, but again, my aunt is the one who would have to decide on selling anything."

"In that case, do you think you could introduce us? I hate to impose, but I have regretted not picking up an Andrew Talbot painting when I had the chance. I'd like to remedy that, if there's any way I can."

"Let me check with my aunt before I promise anything," I said, my smile tightening. I didn't like the thought that Cynthia Rogers had donated to the archives just to acquire an introduction to my aunt, and perhaps influence me to encourage Aunt Lydia to sell her a painting. "If you can give me your phone number, I can call or text you once I've had a chance to talk to Aunt Lydia."

"Of course, of course." Ms. Rogers rummaged through her purse and pulled out a scrap of paper and a pen. After jotting something down, she handed me the paper. "Here's my number. I'll be in town for a few more weeks, so just let me know."

I stared at the paper, noting that the phone number had a Washington, DC, area code. "All right," I said, as I pocketed the number. "I'll mention your request to Aunt Lydia and see what she says. It will probably be a no," I cautioned as I looked up to meet Cynthia's bright gaze, "but I promise to let you know, one way or the other."

"Thanks so much. Well, I don't want to take up any more of your time. Hope to hear from you soon." Cynthia turned away and strolled out of the aisle.

I picked up the check and absently studied the blank surface of the envelope for a moment. It was odd for someone who didn't live in Taylorsford to offer a donation to the library, but I suspected that Cynthia Rogers had betrayed her ulterior motive. For some reason, perhaps something linked to a romance in her past, she was intent on purchasing one of my late uncle's paintings. I stared after her retreating figure as she turned toward the front doors. It wasn't impossible that they'd been acquainted in the past, if she'd lived in the area. Uncle Andrew had actually grown up in a neighboring town, only getting to know Kurt and, by extension, Paul Dassin and Aunt Lydia and her family, through some countywide programs that he and Kurt had attended. So it was quite possible that Cynthia Rogers had known Andrew as a young man, even if she'd visited Taylorsford only once or twice before.

That might also explain her curiosity and questions about Richard's great-uncle Paul. Maybe she'd actually met him as well, if she knew Andrew. As my mind spun theories about Cynthia Rogers and her connection to my late uncle, I pushed the cart forward, finally parking it behind the circulation desk. "These will need to be statused," I told Samantha. "One of the volunteers can shelve them later. But right now"—I glanced at my watch—"I need to head over to Hani Abdi's to confirm a few things concerning the catering for the wedding. She said I could come after work, but I hate to make her wait around that long. She doesn't usually keep the shop open past two, so I thought I'd run over there during my lunch break. But don't worry, I'll be back in plenty of time for you to take yours."

"No problem," Samantha said. "I brought my lunch today, so I'll only need a half hour. Take as long as you need."

"Thanks," I said as I headed into the workroom to grab my purse.

Leaving by the staff door in the workroom, I was surprised to see Cynthia Rogers sitting on one of the benches outside the library. She was on her cell phone, so I didn't bother to speak to her as I hurried past.

Hani Abdi ran her catering company out of her home, which was located only a few blocks from the library. One of the few remaining fieldstone buildings in town, her house was a simple four-square structure with a stoop instead of a porch. Its beauty derived from the simplicity of its design as well as the stones themselves, which were mottled and streaked in tones of white and gray. Attached to the main structure, a smaller wood-frame addition clad in white siding housed Hani's catering business.

A bell attached to the heavy wooden door jangled as I entered the shop, drawing Hani from the workroom located behind the plain wooden counter.

"Oh, Amy, hello," she said, wiping her hands on her apron to remove a dusting of flour. "I thought you were coming by later."

"I decided to pop in during my lunch break instead so you wouldn't have to wait around for me."

Hani's black hair was cut short to hug her scalp, a look that not many people could pull off. *But she has the bone structure for it*, I thought as she headed back into her workroom and kitchen to grab some samples for me to taste. *Like that model Iman. Which isn't surprising, as both women were born in Somalia.* But since Hani's family had moved to the U.S. when she barely two, she had no accent other than the one most people raised in Taylorsford had.

"I just wanted to make sure we were on the same page with the vegetarian options." Hani placed a small pewter platter of hors d'oeuvres on the white quartz countertop. "I know that's important to you."

"Yes, as I mentioned, several of my guests are vegetarians, including my maid of honor and her family."

"The Fieldses, right? I know them pretty well. I buy organic vegetables and fruit from their farm."

"Which is exactly why Sunny suggested you to handle the reception," I said with a smile. "She told me you were more sympathetic to the needs of vegetarians and vegans than most other catering businesses in the area."

"I just think the client should get what they want. Speaking of which," Hani said, pointing to the samples, "try out these options and see what you think. I can spice them up or down, according to your taste."

I picked up a small cheese puff. It looked deceptively plain, but when I bit into it, an intriguing spectrum of flavors flooded my mouth. The puff was infused with a subtle blend of spices that made me immediately want to grab another piece. "Well, that's definitely a yes," I said as I wiped my hands on a napkin.

Hani beamed. "One of my favorites as well. But also try that one." She pointed at a date stuffed with what looked like cream cheese. "It's not quite what you might expect."

I tasted the sample and enthusiastically agreed with Hani's assessment. What I'd taken for cream cheese was a blend of whipped cheeses that had a goat-milk base. Along with the sweetness of the date and richness of the cheese, there was a faint trace of cinnamon and some other spice I couldn't determine.

"It's mace, which actually comes from nutmeg seeds," Hani said when I questioned her. "So that one's a yes too?"

"Absolutely." I reached for the third and final sample, which looked like a small rice ball. "Oh, by the way, I also wanted to pay you something on the total bill. I know you said we could pay the balance after the reception, but I'd like to stay ahead of that. Easier on my budget," I added, before biting into the sticky rice ball.

"Your bill?" Hani's black eyebrows arched over her dark eyes.

I finished off the rice ball, which tasted of coconut milk and raisins with a hint of cardamom. Giving that sample a thumbs-up, I wiped my hands again before replying. "Not the whole amount, of course. Just another third." Richard and I had paid Hani a third of the original quote as a down payment, but I wanted to pay a little more now so our final invoice wouldn't be quite so devastating.

"But the rest of your bill has been paid," Hani said. "I assumed you knew that."

"I had no idea. Who in the world paid it? Not my aunt, I hope."

"No, not Lydia. I know her. This was another lady. Actually, I wasn't here when she came in. My mother was working in the shop that day. But I can find out. Hold on." Hani bustled into the back. After a few minutes she reappeared holding a printed invoice. "Here it is. Mom said the woman was older, like your aunt, and just as elegant." She peered down at the invoice. "Okay, that makes sense. It was Fiona Muir. I assume she's related to your fiancé?"

I swallowed a shocked exclamation before answering. "She's my future mother-in-law."

"That's so sweet. I guess she meant it as a surprise." Hani offered me a warm smile.

It's certainly that, I thought as I smiled in return. "Let's just say it's the last thing I ever expected."

Chapter Nineteen

After agreeing to include all three hors d'oeuvres on the reception menu, I wished Hani a good day and headed outside.

As I walked back to the library, I mulled over Fiona's surprising gesture. Maybe I had misjudged her. I'd never been certain that she approved of me, but it seemed she'd finally accepted my relationship with her son. At least enough to support our celebration in a meaningful way.

Approaching the library, I was surprised again—this time by the sight of a young woman half-hidden by the forsythia bushes that formed a natural fence between the library and a neighboring house. It was Honor Bryant, and she was so absorbed in a cell phone conversation that she didn't notice me stopping to stare at her.

I paused, waiting for her to complete her call before I said anything. *It's odd that she's still in town, but perhaps the sheriff's department asked her to remain. Or return*, I thought, as I observed her strained expression and wildly gesticulating hands. Although I couldn't hear any distinct words, she was obviously embroiled in an argument with whoever was on the other end of the call.

When she pocketed the phone, I loudly cleared my throat. She jumped and turned to face me, meeting my gaze with concern clouding her wide hazel eyes. "Ms. Webber, you startled me."

"Sorry, I just saw you there and wanted to ask if you were doing okay. I know the investigation must be very stressful."

"It has been, yes." Honor rubbed her hands together as if she had a chill.

I looked her up and down. It was a warm spring day, but she was wearing a brown cardigan sweater over her plain ivory blouse and plaid skirt, along with short brown boots. Strangely, the boots were caked with dried mud, which spoke of either her distraction over her boss's death or a recent foray into a garden or field. "Have you been forced to stay here since the party?"

"Forced to?" Honor fiddled with one of the earpieces of her glasses. "No, not really. I just thought it was more convenient, what with the authorities pulling me in for questioning several times. And Oscar—Mr. Selvaggio, that is—had given me some money in an expense account for this trip, so I've been able to stay at the local inn."

"That's good."

Honor's gaze darted from left to right and back again, as if she expected to see someone else appear. "It's been useful. I'm trying to put Mr. Selvaggio's affairs in order. I didn't really have any other place to go, so I thought staying at the inn was as good a home base as anywhere else."

"Didn't he have an office somewhere?"

Honor's laughter stung, sharp as needles. "Oh no, he was always traveling. Never stayed in one place too long. We did business out of hotel rooms all the time."

"I see," I said, and honestly, the fuzzy picture I had of her boss's business practices became clear. Oscar Selvaggio had probably chosen to move around because it would make it harder for anyone to track him down. Sure, he was well-known in artistic circles, but if he was always here today, gone tomorrow, it would've made it more difficult for any disgruntled buyers to locate him. Especially if many of his sales were transacted overseas.

"I hadn't worked for him that long, you know. Only six months or so." Honor twisted one of the buttons on her cardigan so hard that it popped off in her hand. "We were in San Francisco and then Chicago before we came out here," she added, shoving the button into the pocket of her skirt.

"I hate to pry, and I'm sure you've already explained all this to the sheriff's department, but did you notice anything suspicious before Mr. Selvaggio was poisoned?" I held up my hands. "It's just that my brother mentioned seeing you when he was walking outside not long before my fiancé and I discovered the body. The authorities seem to be looking at him as a suspect, and I thought if you'd seen someone else, like maybe a bony, dark-haired man . . ."

Honor cut me off with a sharp swipe of her hand through the air. "I saw no one. Not even your brother." Her fierce expression melted to sadness as she gripped the edge of her cardigan. "I was only outside so I could make some private calls. It was time-sensitive stuff related to Oscar's business interests. I wasn't paying attention to anything else."

"I see. Well, like I said, I don't want to pry," I said, although of course I would've loved to do so, especially if it would help Scott.

"I bet you were trying to lock down the purchase of the Kelmscott Chaucer. That would've been a coup."

"Um, sure. That was part of it." Honor squared her hunched shoulders. "It was something Oscar wanted, of course. To be able to announce that he'd bought the Chaucer out from under Kurt Kendrick."

"A perfect way to trump him," I said, noting Honor's eyelashes fluttering behind the lenses of her glasses. I'd always heard that rapid blinking meant someone might be lying. Which wouldn't surprise me in this case. Honor Bryant was as edgy as a cat facing a vacuum cleaner. "But sadly, someone had other plans."

"I think it was Mr. Kendrick," Honor said, refusing to meet my inquisitive gaze. "Oscar rushed off after getting a text, you know. That's how he must've ended up in that shed—someone demanded he meet them there. And who else would know of the existence of that outbuilding along with wanting to confront my boss? Anyway, Oscar warned me to be on my guard around Mr. Kendrick. He said he was a dangerous adversary."

"Maybe in terms of business transactions, but I honestly can't imagine him poisoning a guest at his house," I said, examining the young assistant's face for any sign that she might've seen more than she was letting on.

"I don't know about that." Honor's expression hardened into a stony mask. "People saw Mr. Kendrick give Oscar a drink, you know. Maybe that was how he was poisoned."

I saw you carrying a glass too, I thought, but the remembrance of Adele Tourneau in the butler's pantry forced me to keep silent. No use pointing out everyone who might've had the opportunity to slip poison into Selvaggio's beverage. "Did you see Mr. Selvaggio after that?"

"Not after he got that text." Honor shoved her unruly bangs away from her forehead. "I headed outside right after that, but in the opposite direction. Oscar said he didn't need me right then, and I had those calls to make . . ." She squared her shoulders and lifted her chin as she looked straight into my eyes. "Anyway, since Oscar was poisoned, and I understand there was cognac in his system . . . Well, I expect the sheriff's department has marked Mr. Kendrick as the primary suspect."

"He's on the list, from what I hear," I said dryly. "But you know, any number of people could've slipped that poison into a drink and handed it to your boss." *Even you*, I thought, but I didn't think it wise to voice this idea aloud.

Honor crossed her arms over her chest. "I still believe Mr. Kendrick is the killer, and sooner or later the authorities will prove it."

I looked her up and down, noting how tightly she'd hugged her arms to her body. "If he was responsible, I'm sure they will. But fortunately, Brad Tucker and the rest of his team are not inclined to jump to conclusions. They'll conduct a meticulous investigation before they arrest anyone. Which should be what you want. I mean, you do want the right person punished for Mr. Selvaggio's death, I assume?"

"Of course." Honor's gaze flitted to something she'd glimpsed over my shoulder. "Doesn't everyone?"

"Not the actual murderer, I suppose, but yeah, everyone else." I glanced at my watch. "I'd better get a move on. My lunch hour is just about over." I considered the fact that I hadn't eaten anything but the sample hors d'oeuvres but shrugged this off. I could sneak a snack in the workroom if I got hungry later in the day. "Anyway, Ms. Bryant, I hope for your sake that this is all cleared up soon. I imagine you'll be happy to leave Taylorsford."

Honor grimaced. "Yes, although I'll have to start looking for another job. But I'd like to be able to do so sooner rather than later."

"I'm sure. Good-bye, and good luck with your job search," I told her before I strode away.

When I reached the library, I noticed that Cynthia Rogers had not moved from her spot on one of the concrete benches under the maple trees that shaded the front yard of the building.

"Still here?" I asked as I approached her.

"It's a pleasant place to sit and catch up with some old friends," Cynthia replied, holding up her cell phone. "I've neglected a few people for far too long, and when you get older, they have the unfortunate habit of disappearing on you if you don't keep in touch."

I studied her calm face. It sounded like she was on some mission to reconnect to her past, as I'd guessed. "I imagine you're right. Anyway, it is a nice day to be outside."

"Absolutely," she said, taking in a deep breath. "Such lovely weather calls for it, don't you think?"

"If you can, for sure. But for now I must get back inside. Talk to you soon, but please"—I held up one hand—"don't get your hopes up about that painting."

"All I request is that you ask," Cynthia said.

As I turned to head into the library, I noticed a car parked across the street, a few buildings up from the library. A glossy black sports car.

What is Kurt doing here on a Monday? I thought, shading my eyes with my hand to try to determine if anyone was sitting in the car.

Cynthia Rogers stood and crossed to stand beside me. "Someone you know, or just admiring the beautiful vehicle?"

"It's certainly not something I see in Taylorsford every day," I said, keeping my tone light. Cynthia might just be a nosy visitor, and maybe she had even met him in the past, but I knew how Kurt valued his privacy. His connection to the pricey car wasn't something I felt I should share with a relative stranger.

"Well"—Cynthia laid her fingers on my bare forearm—"I think I'll head over to the diner and grab something for lunch." Her fingers tapped against my skin, drawing my gaze to her pleasant face. "Even if your aunt doesn't want to talk to me, which I sincerely hope she does, we still need to arrange that luncheon date sometime before I leave town."

"What? Oh, right," I said, distracted by my realization that someone was sitting in Kurt's Jag. "Maybe we can talk about that when I call with any information on my aunt's response to your request."

"I look forward to it," Cynthia said, lifting her hand and giving me a cheery wave before she strolled off.

I glanced at my watch again. I was going to be late, but I had to do one more thing before I headed inside. Striding across the quiet street, I reached Kurt's car and rapped my knuckles against the driver's side window.

The glass slid down. "Spying on me now?" I asked, refusing to be intimidated by his stern expression.

"One of my many hobbies," he replied, before adding in a lighter tone, "Who was that woman?"

"Just some visitor," I said. "Cynthia Rogers. Ever heard of her?"

Kurt looked down at his fingers, which were clutching the steering wheel tight enough to blanch his knuckles. "I'm not familiar with that name."

"Honestly, she's a bit nosy, but she did give me a rather sizable donation for the archives, so I decided to overlook her tendency to ask a lot of personal questions. It seems that she's one of those people who likes to learn all they can about every place they visit."

"A donation?" Kurt looked up at me, his blue eyes glittering like sapphires. "That's rather unusual, don't you think? Some unaffiliated person just deciding to give you money."

I almost mentioned my suspicion of her connection to Uncle Andrew but thought better of it. I had no proof, after all, and I hated mentioning anything concerning my uncle's romantic past to a man who'd loved him as much as, if not more than, my aunt had.

"Not me, exactly. The library." I shrugged. "I got the idea that she has plenty of money and doesn't mind spending it."

"In other words, she likes to buy things."

I frowned. Kurt's typical sardonic smile appeared particularly fierce in the filtered light of the car interior. "You should understand that compulsion."

"I do. In fact, I understand it all too well." Kurt's hand shot out, and his fingers encircled my wrist. "As I've told you on many other occasions, you need to be careful who you trust, Amy."

"Most people would say that includes you," I said, shaking off his fingers and taking a step back.

"And they wouldn't be wrong." Kurt looked away to stare out his windshield, his gaze focused on something up the street. "Speaking of visitors, there's someone I really am keeping an eye on—Selvaggio's little assistant. Quite the church mouse, isn't she? Oscar did like to hire quiet types for his assistants, but she takes that to a whole new level."

I followed the trajectory of his gaze, observing Honor Bryant walking away from her hiding place in the forsythia bushes. "I just spoke with her. She seems to think you should be considered the primary suspect in Mr. Selvaggio's death."

"I'm sure she does," Kurt said, his voice so low I thought he might be talking to himself. He turned his head to look at me again. "I was Oscar's main rival, of course."

I twisted my hands together at my waist. "She told me that she's aware you gave him a drink. Something that could've held the poison that killed him."

"Ah, I see. Well, she isn't wrong, at least about me handing Oscar a drink. Despite being rivals, we were united in our love of a good cognac." Kurt placed his hands back on the steering wheel. "But I assure you there was no poison in that snifter."

"I suppose that's something the sheriff's department will have to validate," I said.

Kurt's bushy white eyebrows disappeared under the thick hair falling over his forehead. "It's my understanding that a few other people supplied Oscar with drinks, including little miss mousy over there. Anyway, the glass in question has not yet been located, and I suspect it may never be found." His bright-blue eyes narrowed. "Glass shatters, and the woods are dark and deep," he added, in a tone that reminded me of someone quoting poetry.

I took another step back, my heels falling off the sidewalk and onto a patch of grass. "That sounds like you know what actually happened."

Kurt flashed me a wolfish smile. "I may have an inkling. But never fear," he added, "justice will be served, one way or the other."

I eyed him dubiously. "I need to get back to work, so I'll overlook the implications of that remark. For now." As I turned and headed back to the library, I heard him call out. Pausing on the sidewalk on the other side of the street, I watched the passenger's side window roll down.

Kurt, leaning across the front seats, pointed his forefinger at me. "Watch your step, my dear. Don't jump into water that might close over your head."

I waved him off and headed into the library, realizing he was right on at least one point—when it came to Kurt Kendrick, I could never be sure what I was dealing with.

Chapter Twenty

On Tuesday, facing a slow afternoon at the library, I decided to do some additional internet sleuthing. I was curious to see what I could find out about the two women I'd spoken with the day before, Honor Bryant and Cynthia Rogers.

Also, since my aunt had informed me that she absolutely refused to consider selling any more of Andrew's paintings, to Cynthia Rogers or anyone else, I knew I had to deliver that bad news sooner rather than later. But before I did so, I wanted a little more information on a woman who, I suspected, had thought her generous donation would ensure my cooperation in her quest to acquire at least one of Andrew's paintings.

I expected to find information on Honor, since she was younger and likely to have an expansive digital footprint. But the hits, once filtered to remove other people with the same name, were actually rather sparse. She had no website or blog, and there were just a few mentions of her in posts from her university's art history department, along with a handful of appearances in group photos with friends. She didn't seem to have accounts on the main social media sites either. *A private person*, I thought as I scrolled through the group pictures that had tagged her. Surprisingly, she looked very different in these photos—much more vibrant and stylish. It seemed that she had adopted her rather dowdy appearance after college.

Or perhaps, I thought, chewing on the end of one of the golf pencils we provided for our patrons, *she chose to dress differently when she went to work for Oscar Selvaggio. Which is odd, since Selvaggio moved in trendy circles. But then again, as Kurt mentioned, he apparently preferred assistants who didn't draw attention to themselves.* I smiled as another thought occurred to me, based on my brief acquaintance with the art dealer. *He undoubtedly didn't want anyone to pull the spotlight off himself.*

Tossing the gnawed pencil in the trash, I turned my attention to Cynthia Rogers. Despite using varied search strategies, in this case I found nothing. Oh, there were plenty of mentions of people with that name, but none matched the woman who had introduced herself as a visitor to Taylorsford. It was like she didn't actually exist.

Of course, I told myself, *not everyone uses computers, much less has social media accounts.*

I drummed my fingers against the pitted wood surface of the circulation desk. Cynthia Rogers obviously had some deeper connection to the Taylorsford area that she hadn't as yet divulged. There was nothing wrong with that, of course, unless . . .

Unless she'd had a relationship with Andrew Talbot that was more than a friendship, which wasn't impossible. Andrew had been five years older than my aunt. He could've easily dated

Cynthia at some point before Aunt Lydia was even old enough to catch his interest. There would've been nothing wrong with that, but I knew how fiercely protective my aunt was over her memories of her late husband. The last thing she'd welcome was some old girlfriend turning up to reminisce about my uncle.

I gnawed on the inside of my cheek. I knew my aunt could take care of herself, but I still wanted to spare her more anxiety, especially now, when she was concerned about Scott's disappearance and conflicted over her relationship with Hugh. To shield Aunt Lydia, I'd have to be blunt with Cynthia Rogers, despite her generous donation. I'd just have to tell her that there was no chance of her buying one of Andrew's paintings, so there was no point in me connecting her with Aunt Lydia. It did feel a bit rude and wasn't a conversation I looked forward to, but I'd do it for my aunt's sake.

Samantha came in to relieve Sunny around five, but since she and I were the only staff, paid or otherwise, working until eight, I didn't get a chance to head out to the archives to look for any mentions of a Rogers family living anywhere near Taylorsford. I decided it could wait for another day. *Or maybe never*, I thought, my enthusiasm for this research waning as I realized that Rogers could easily be Cynthia's married name. Which meant I didn't have enough information to conduct a successful search anyway.

Besides, Cynthia Rogers's association with Taylorsford was the least of my concerns. While it might be interesting to ferret out her connection to my Uncle Andrew or even Paul Dassin, such research wouldn't be likely to help the authorities in the Oscar Selvaggio case. Not to mention that although I hadn't come into work until noon, I was exhausted and anxious to drive straight home once we closed down the building.

When I reached my car, which was parked in the library's back lot, I was surprised to see Ethan Payne standing in front of the driver's side door.

"Amy, hello. I hope I didn't startle you."

"A little," I said, lifting my chin to look him in the eye. "We just closed. What are you doing here at this time of night?"

Ethan ran his fingers through his short hair. "I was actually waiting for you. I need you to drive me home."

"Excuse me?" I pulled my keys from my purse. "Drive you home? Why, and how did you get here?"

"I had to drop my car by the shop after my shift. It needs a new battery. They promised they'd get to it early in the morning." Ethan's abashed expression was almost comical. "The friend that drove me here from the shop promised she'd pick me up tomorrow."

I raised my eyebrows. "Why didn't your friend just drive you home?"

"Because I had to see you. Well," Ethan held up his hands, palms out—"actually someone else wants to see you. I was going to stop by after work and talk to you, give you directions and all that, but then my car died and I was afraid the jump would only get me as far as the shop . . ."

I waved my hands at him, jangling my keys. "Whoa, what the heck are you talking about? Who needs to see me?"

"Your brother."

Staring into Ethan's wide eyes, I exhaled loudly before speaking. "Scott is at your house? Why? No, don't answer that. Just tell me why he suddenly needs to see me at eight o'clock at night, when he's been perfectly willing to remain incommunicado for days."

"I don't know." Ethan looked down and shuffled his feet. "He just asked me to bring you. Didn't really tell me why."

"Has he been staying with you this whole time? I saw him drive off Thursday evening, but no one in my family has heard from him since." I closed my fingers over my keys.

"Yeah, he's been at my place. I honestly don't know why he didn't call or text anyone, but I think maybe he was hiding out for some reason." Ethan squared his muscular shoulders. "He begged me not to mention where he was to anyone but didn't say why."

I pursed my lips and considered Scott's request to see me. I wasn't worried about driving Ethan home. I knew I could trust him. Scott, though, was another story.

What game is he playing? I thought as I motioned toward the car. "Get in, then. You'll have to play navigator, since I don't exactly know where you live."

"No problem." Ethan jogged around to the passenger's side, sliding in after I unlocked the doors and climbed into the driver's seat.

We drove outside of town, where, following Ethan's instructions, I turned onto a paved road, and then onto Logging Road, one of the many gravel-covered roads that led up into the mountains.

"You're out in the country, for sure," I said, as my car lurched over the washboard surface of the road.

"I like the solitude." As Ethan stared out into the dark expanse of pines that lined the road, a ghostly image of his face was reflected back by the glass of the side window. "Slow down; my driveway is just ahead."

I turned onto the dirt road Ethan indicated. As I rounded the corner in the drive, his house, screened from the road by tall, spindly pines, came into view. It wasn't the log cabin I'd expected but rather a simple brick ranch with a wooden deck that ran from the front door around the side of the house.

"Let me go in first," Ethan said, bounding out of the car as soon as I parked.

I glanced up at the picture window that looked out over the front yard, noticing the flick of a curtain. *Scott's checking to make sure who it is*, I thought, pondering the need for this type of caution as I made my way up the steps to reach the deck and front door.

Ethan waited for me, holding the door so I could enter in front of him.

The front entrance opened onto a long, narrow living room, with a brick fireplace filling one side wall. Seated in a worn but comfortable-looking leather recliner, Scott met my gaze with a wan smile.

"You don't need to pretend you were lounging there this whole time," I said. "I saw you peering out the window when we arrived."

Scott's smile faded. "I've been trained to take precautions," he said, as a silky-coated collie leapt up from a dog bed near the hearth and padded over to greet Ethan and me.

"This is Cassie." Ethan patted the dog. "She's a little wary of strangers, but well trained."

"You mean she won't bite, I hope," I said, holding out my fingers for the dog to sniff before I stroked her head.

"She never does that. Not when I'm giving off vibes that someone is a friend. Now, if someone tried to harm me . . ." Ethan allowed this thought to hang in the air.

I stared into the dog's liquid brown eyes. "All bets are off? But she seems like a good girl," I added, giving Cassie another pat before crossing the room to stand in front of Scott. "Unlike you, who's been a very bad brother."

Scott's expression grew somber as he met my gaze. "I didn't mean to be. Circumstances dictated that I disappear for a while."

I placed my balled fists on my hips. "One little text letting me and the rest of the family know that you were okay would've been enough. Aunt Lydia and our parents have been worried sick."

"Sorry," Scott said, although I noticed that there wasn't an ounce of contrition tingeing his tone.

"So why the sudden need to talk to me?"

Scott gestured toward a rocking chair close to the recliner. "Sit down and I'll explain. As much as I can, anyway."

I shot him a suspicious look before settling into the rocker.

"I'll just go and rustle up some food," Ethan said as he strode through the archway that led into the kitchen, Cassie trotting at his heels.

I leaned back, allowing my chair to rock a few times. *A comforting motion*, I thought, before I turned my head to look at Scott. "Spill. What sent you into hiding without a word to your family?"

"Work, of course." Scott took off his glasses and cleaned the lenses with the tail of his charcoal-gray shirt. "It was actually an order from above. Not something I could ignore."

"You were told to disappear?"

"For a few days." Slipping his glasses back on, Scott finally turned his head to meet my intent gaze. "I was doing surveillance on someone and the powers that be were afraid my target had gotten wind of me. They wanted me to vanish so our suspect wouldn't do the same. Others are tracking them now."

"You mean you messed up?" I asked, not bothering to temper the incredulity in my tone. I'd never known Scott to undertake a task without completing it to perfection.

"Not exactly. Someone I didn't expect to recognize me did."

"Wait." The memory of Oscar Selvaggio's reaction to seeing my brother at the party resurfaced. "It was the art dealer, right? The one who was murdered."

"Yes, Selvaggio. I knew as soon as I saw his face that he'd remembered me from a brief encounter a few years ago." Scott shrugged. "I didn't think he would make the connection. I looked different when he met me before."

I pushed off with my foot, allowing my chair to rock slowly. "When did you run into Selvaggio in the past?"

"It was a few years back, when I was working with a task force tracking some art thieves who also dabbled in financial fraud. Selvaggio had done some business with them, and while we didn't really have any reason to suspect him of being involved in cybercrimes or money laundering, we did question him for leads on the real criminals." Scott shifted in his chair, causing the worn leather to squeak. "But I didn't interview him directly. I'd just tagged along because I was working the cyber side of things. The other agents thought they might need me to access his computer. I was in the background the entire time, not to mention wearing contacts and dressed much differently." Scott's lips quirked into a sardonic smile. "They had me outfitted like the typical hacker-turned-consultant— spiked hair, black leather jacket, and ripped jeans."

"Really?" I couldn't help but smile in return. "Selvaggio must've taken notice, though, to recognize you when you appeared at the party."

"I suppose his work in buying and selling art made him more visually observant than most," Scott said, his smile fading.

"So you were sent here to keep tabs on him for some reason." I held up my hand, palm out. "You don't have to tell me what that is. I know you probably can't divulge too much."

"It's true, I can't say much. But I can tell you that Oscar Selvaggio was not my real target."

I slammed my heel into the floor, halting the movement of my rocker. "You were investigating Kurt?"

Scott shook his head. "I don't know about anyone else, but no, I wasn't."

"Really?" I slumped against the wooden back of the chair. "I can't think who else . . ." The image of skeletal, dark-haired man flashed through my mind. "There was a man I ran into, quite literally, when I visited Kurt not long ago." I cast Scott a glance. "I guess you could say he ran into me, since he shoved me aside when I was at the front door. A few days later he stopped by the library to apologize, which was also a little weird, since it meant he had to track me down. Told me his name was Lance Dalbec. Tall guy but not heavily built, although he looked like he was all lean muscle. He has dark hair and an angular face."

A shadow flitted across Scott's face. "Not my specific target, but he's definitely on my radar. He's a career criminal who always seems to slip through our nets. And yeah, he sometimes goes by the name of Lance Dalbec, although he uses other aliases as well."

"He and Kurt had an altercation. I didn't see it, just the result, after Dalbec knocked Kurt to the floor. I wanted to call the authorities, but Kurt ordered me not to."

"That doesn't surprise me," Scott said dryly. "Kurt Kendrick has a history of helping various federal agencies, but only when it suits him. And while that buys him some goodwill and several instances of the authorities looking the other way, his business practices are a little . . . murky, to say the least."

"I'm aware of that," I said. "But obviously he isn't one of this Dalbec guy's pals."

"Definitely not." Scott held up a finger as Ethan reentered the room.

"I'll disappear again if that's best," Ethan said. "But I thought maybe you'd like some water or coffee or something. I'd offer wine or beer, but I know Amy has to drive home."

I slid forward on the wooden rocker seat. "Thanks, but I don't need anything right now."

"I'm not driving, but I'll wait until Amy leaves to grab a beer." Scott offered Ethan a warm smile. "I don't want to taunt my big sis, at least not right now."

"So nice of you," I said, fighting the urge to stick my tongue out at him as I had when we were kids.

Ethan touched his forehead in a little salute. "I'll leave you alone again, then."

"So you and Ethan . . ." I said, as the other man headed back into the kitchen.

"Are friends," Scott said firmly. "And he very kindly offered me a place to hide out when I explained my dilemma to him. Not that I told him all the details, of course."

"Why doesn't that surprise me?"

Scott's lips twitched. "However, I think I may ask him to be my date at the wedding, if you don't mind."

"Of course I don't mind." I studied Scott's calm face. "But I thought you were going to escort Karla. She doesn't have a date, you know."

"Ethan and I can do that together, don't you think? Besides, from what I hear, he's a much better dancer than I am, if she's mainly needing a partner."

"That's part of it, although she'll probably dance with Richard quite a bit. Not that I mind," I added when Scott shot me a questioning look.

"No jealousy there, I take it?"

"There's nothing to be jealous about. She and Richard are just friends, like you and Ethan."

"Maybe that isn't the most accurate comparison." Scott flashed me a smile. "I hope we can be more, eventually. I wouldn't want to think that Karla felt that way about Richard."

"She doesn't," I said firmly. "And he doesn't. I mean, they had plenty of time to explore those feelings in the past, and nothing ever came of it. I honestly think they relate more like brother and sister, especially because they're both only children."

"That makes sense." Scott leaned forward, gripping his knees. "Getting back to the issue of my work, I can at least tell you that I should be free to return to Aunt Lydia's soon. I shouldn't have to hide out much longer, as my colleagues are closing in on our target as we speak. In fact, Fred Nash . . ."

I leapt to my feet. "What? You're working with Nash? I thought he was working for Hugh Chen."

"He is, as a cover. But his real mission is aligned with my agency's goals." Scott looked up at me, his eyes very bright behind the lenses of his glasses. "I thought you might have figured that out. Nash signed on to help us, while also working on Hugh's cases, because he has a connection to the individual we're ultimately attempting to bring in."

I stared down at him, my arms crossed over my chest. "A connection? Are you talking about his former work on a high-level task force? But that was intended to bring in some drug kingpin, or rather queenpin, I suppose. Someone called Esmerelda." I frowned. "I have to tell you that I've heard that name before, but it was someone in the past. I don't know what they'd possibly have to do with current events."

Scott shrugged. "My suspicion is that it's a code name that's been used by more than one person. So it might not be the same woman who was active back in the sixties and seventies. But it's definitely the same gang."

"That's what you're trying to track?"

"And shut down," Scott said. "We've set up a joint task force that includes federal agency reps as well as some local law enforcement and a few contract players, like Nash. This Esmerelda criminal network has been on our radar for some time, but their leader, whoever it is, has always escaped capture and even exposure. It was something law enforcement had been working on for years, but it's taken on new urgency now, because Esmerelda's organization has started dealing in fentanyl as well as other drugs."

"That's a lot more dangerous, isn't it?"

"Definitely. The truth is, there've been far too many deaths associated with the Esmerelda gang's drug sales recently. It sent our efforts to capture the head honcho into high gear."

"You really think this bunch of criminals will just disappear if you jail their leader?"

Scott stood up to face me. "No, but if we can get the leader to talk, maybe we can round up the rest."

"You mean you'll cut a deal with her."

"Hard to say." Scott laid a hand on my arm. "I'm not involved with that side of things."

"You're just the tracker, not the one who decides what happens after you catch someone?"

"Exactly." Scott lifted his hand to sweep the fall of dark hair away from the top rim of his glasses. "I help locate people and collect the digital evidence to cement a case against them. What happens after that is out of my hands."

"Were you or Fred Nash ever looking into Kurt? Or was that just a smoke screen?"

"I wasn't. I don't know about Nash. He may have been doing so as part of his contract with Hugh."

I looked my brother up and down, taking in his unprepossessing appearance and the wan smile that curved his lips. "I thought you were just a cybersecurity expert, working behind a computer screen."

"I am, but also"—Scott's smile broadened—"a little more. I don't mind you knowing that much. But I hope you won't feel the urge to confess everything to Mom and Dad, or Aunt Lydia. You know they'd just worry."

"I'll keep it to myself. But only because I think you should tell them. They might worry less if they knew the truth. Especially if you plan to disappear from time to time."

"I'll think about it." Scott tipped his head and examined me with a critical eye. "And you should tell me when you stumble onto dangerous information. I'm not sure how you even knew that Esmerelda existed, but as you've said, this wasn't news to you."

I thought back to the last murder investigation I'd been involved in. "The problem is, I don't always know the information is dangerous when I uncover it. But I take your point."

"Good. Now head on home and tell Aunt Lydia that everything is fine. Call Mom and Dad and tell them the same. Let them know I'll be back at Aunt Lydia's soon. Definitely before the wedding."

"Very well." I took hold of one of his hands. "But you'd better promise to never disappear like this again."

Scott shook his head. "Sorry, I can't promise that. All I can say is that I will try to let you know it's a work thing. Somehow." He squeezed my fingers before releasing my hand. "Maybe we need a code word?"

"How about what we used to say when one of us overheard that the other was just about to catch it from Mom or Dad?"

Scott grinned. "Okay. *Take a chill pill* it is."

"Not that we ever got in trouble," I said, arching my eyebrows.

"Of course not. We were perfect angels at all times." Scott raised his hand. "As God is my witness."

I pointed upward. "Don't call down lightning on poor Ethan's house."

"At least he knows how to extinguish a fire," Scott said, giving me a hug. "Go on, tell the fam I'm fine and that I'll talk to them soon."

I hugged him back, a little longer than usual. "Stay safe," I said, before calling out a good-bye to Ethan and leaving the house.

I wouldn't share my brother's mission with anyone yet, except Richard. But I would talk to someone who might have more information.

Fred Nash, I thought, *you'd better be ready to tell me the truth. Especially if you want me to support your romantic pursuit of my best friend.*

Chapter
Twenty-One

I didn't know where Fred was staying but managed to get his phone number from Sunny by claiming that I wanted to talk to him about alleviating the problems between Hugh and my aunt.

That was only a partial lie—I did want to mention something to him about encouraging Hugh to confess the entire truth to Aunt Lydia, but of course I also wanted to quiz him about his cooperation with Scott and other members of the task force.

Fred agreed to meet with me after work a few days later, on Friday. I suggested that he come into the library right before we closed at five. That way we could talk in private after I cleared and locked up the building. Fortunately, Sunny wasn't working at the library that day, and Samantha had also asked for the afternoon off. I told Fred to slip into the staff lounge and lock the door behind him right before we closed so he wouldn't be ushered out of the building with the rest of the patrons.

After encouraging Denise, the only volunteer working on Friday afternoon, to leave immediately after closing time, I knocked on the door of the staff lounge.

"All clear?" Fred asked, as he cracked open the door.

"Everyone's out." I led the way back to the main part of the building. "We can use the reading area to talk, if that's okay with you."

"Whatever you think best." Fred followed me to one of the round tables. As he sat down, he looked me over, his dark eyes filled with curiosity. "I had no idea you were so into spy-versus-spy techniques. Are you sure you're really a librarian?"

"Are you sure you're really just helping Hugh Chen investigate art crimes?" I replied, as I plopped down in a chair across the table from him.

Fred's dark skin didn't betray a blush, but he shifted on his wooden chair, signaling that my barb had hit home. "I'm not sure what you mean."

"Oh, come on. I know you're just using Hugh's investigation as a cover."

Leaning back in his chair, Fred studied me for a moment before answering. "Someone told you this? Let me guess—your brother? He really should know better."

"He knew I wouldn't say anything to anyone, and I won't." I leaned forward, crossing my arms on the table. "You're the exception, because I know you're actually working with Scott. Or with people on the same task force, anyway."

"It's true, I'm collaborating with his team. But I'm also helping Hugh. The two things aren't mutually exclusive. They're just two different jobs that happen to overlap." Fred's brown eyes narrowed. "I'm still an independent investigator, and I need the work."

"I'm sure that's true." I sat back and fixed my gaze on Fred's face. I found it curious that he was willing to talk to me so frankly but suspected that he was hoping to obtain some reciprocal information from me, given my connection to both Scott and Kurt. "Honestly, I thought you might have a personal interest. Tracking down someone called Esmerelda, perhaps?"

The change in Fred's expression was swift and devasting. "How did you hear about that? If Scott's sharing that much, I need to have a long talk with him." The fury in Fred's voice told me that talking was not all he had in mind.

I swept my hand through the air. "No need to go after Scott. I'd already heard that name last fall, during another murder investigation that I was unfortunately embroiled in."

"Then you know this involves a drug operation."

"I do. I also know that Esmerelda may or may not be the same person who was the leader of the drug cartel that infiltrated your previous task force and set up an ambush." I cleared my throat "Causing you serious injury and killing your partner."

"It's the same person, all right." Fred rubbed his forehead with one hand. "That much I know."

"Really? Scott wasn't sure if it was the same woman who'd run the gang back in the sixties and seventies or just a code name used by all their leaders over the years."

Fred's lips twitched into a grim smile. "Why? Because she'd be too old now? Trust me, that never stopped any of these criminals. They just hire muscle to do their dirty work and stay safe in their mansions, counting their money. Besides, Esmerelda was young in the early to mid-sixties. Barely twenty, from what I've learned. So she'd only be in her seventies now. Not too old to run a drug crew that has plenty of younger lieutenants to do the heavy lifting."

"How has she evaded capture all this time?"

"No one knows. She's clever, and not one to live a flashy life-style. Stays incognito, actually." Fred studied me for a moment. "You do know that your friend Kurt Kendrick was also active in the drug scene back in the day?"

"I believe he left that behind when he moved into dealing art instead."

"He did, as far as I can tell. Not to say all his art dealings are on the level, but that's another matter." Fred relaxed his tensed shoulders. "I'm also helping Hugh look into Kendrick's business dealings, you know."

"And have you found anything you can use against him?"

"No." Fred offered me a rueful smile. "He's even cleverer than Esmerelda, if that's possible. But Hugh is convinced that we'll uncover something sooner or later."

"Hugh's obsessed, and that isn't good. At least not as far as his relationship with my aunt is concerned."

Fred's expression softened. "I've told him as much. Especially after meeting Lydia and realizing how much he cares for her, and she him. As a sadly single guy myself, I believe that kind of relationship isn't something Hugh should throw away on a wild-goose chase."

But maybe not so very single for long, I thought as I examined Fred's handsome face and considered his obvious interest in Sunny. "Do you think you'll ever be able to indict Kurt?"

"Probably not. The Kelmscott Chaucer was a good lead, but even with that, we haven't found any definitive proof of wrongdoing. Although"—Fred pressed his hands against the tabletop—"I did uncover an interesting connection between Kendrick and another sale of one of those Chaucer books."

I decided I might as well share what I knew. Perhaps Fred would be willing to offer me more information in exchange for my honesty. "Something to do with Adele Tourneau?"

Fred's eyebrows drew together. "You are well informed."

I shrugged. "I'm a pretty good researcher, among other things."

"I see Scott isn't the only one in the family with skills." Fred slid his chair to the side so he could stretch out his legs. "Anyway, since you've already made the connection—Hugh and I believe Kendrick was involved in the sale of a copy of a Kelmscott Press edition of Chaucer's works to Adele Tourneau's father, using Oscar Selvaggio as a middleman. But we can't find the evidence to prove it."

And you won't, I thought, arranging my expression into a mask of surprise. "Really? I knew she was devastated when her father died and blamed Selvaggio, saying that he'd knowingly sold her dad a stolen copy of the book. She and her siblings believed the subsequent scandal brought on his heart attack. That much was in the news reports I researched."

"Right, but what wasn't in those reports was any mention of Kendrick, or the other thing that's added fuel to Hugh's fire."

"Which was?"

"The fact that Adele Tourneau, or Maria Brentwood, as she was known then, made an attempt to kill Oscar Selvaggio not long after the courts dismissed her lawsuit against him."

I shoved my chair back and jumped to my feet. "What? I can't believe that."

"Sadly, it's true. She accosted him at his hotel room, threatening to exact revenge. The authorities found a small but loaded pistol in her purse. It was hushed up at the time, of course. Ms. Tourneau, or at least her family, had friends in high places, and enough money to pay for lawyers who kept her from being charged. She had some psychiatric counseling instead, or so I heard." Fred shrugged. "You know how it is—the rich rarely pay the price for their actions, while the poor are incarcerated for minor crimes."

I paced the reading room, my mind spinning with this new information. "But how is this related to Kurt Kendrick? You said this information gave Hugh hope he could catch Kurt in some wrongdoing."

"Apparently, Kendrick helped to pay for some of the legal expenses in Ms. Tourneau's case. Anonymously at the time, but Hugh found someone who was able to provide enough info for me to track the source of a particular check back to one of Kendrick's business interests."

I stared out the library's tall front windows, keeping my back to Fred. I didn't want him to see my face and read the truth in my expression. I knew why Kurt had aided Adele—to protect Andrew as well as himself.

But Oscar Selvaggio probably knew that too. He protected Andrew because Kurt bribed him to do so. Perhaps, with the Kelmscott Chaucer back on the market, he thought he could use this old information as a weapon. He may have been trying to force Kurt to pass on buying the book so he could acquire it himself.

Blackmail. Which was a pretty good motive for murder. I turned around to meet Fred's inquisitive stare. "I'm not sure how that would connect Mr. Kendrick to any wrongdoing. Anonymously helping someone is not a crime."

Fred's gaze raked over my face. "No, but it might be a thread that links him to the original sale of stolen goods. But"—he lifted his hands in a dismissive gesture—"that's Hugh's theory, not mine. Honestly, I don't think there's anything to it. Kendrick was known to be an aficionado of the arts and had been seen attending dance performances that featured Ms. Tourneau. I think he may have had a little crush on her or something. He could've hoped to gain her affections by helping her financially."

"Not if it was anonymous." I tipped my head as I surveyed Fred, wondering if his own burgeoning interest in my best friend was coloring his thoughts. "Although I suppose Kurt could've secretly informed Adele about his financial assistance in her legal troubles."

I knew this was untrue but didn't want to share my belief about what had actually motivated Kurt. No use dragging my uncle, and by extension my aunt, into this story.

"Possibly." Fred stood up to face me. "I guess you've realized that I have more than a little interest in your best friend."

I widened my eyes. "Really? I couldn't tell. I mean, I'm sure no one's noticed that."

Fred's serious expression morphed into a grin. "Okay, okay, I guess I deserve the sarcasm. The thing is, I do really like Sunny. I know we've only just met, but there's this spark between us I haven't felt in a long time. The thing is . . ."

I thought of my brother's problems related to the unpredictability of his job. "You can't promise anything because you never know where your career will take you?"

"Something like that." Fred ran his fingers through his short black hair. "I'm not really looking to getting married or anything. Not anytime soon, anyway."

My lips curved into a smile. "Which is actually a factor in your favor. I don't know if Sunny's mentioned it yet or not, but she isn't eager to get married either."

"No, she hasn't said anything about that. Of course, come to think of it, she doesn't talk about long-term relationship stuff at all." Fred's expression brightened. "That's a refreshing change, you know. Being in my late thirties, the topic usually crops up pretty quick. With the other women I've dated, I mean."

"Well, you're in luck. Sunny's likely to bolt if she thinks a guy is determined to tie her down. She's a free spirit. Loyal to a fault, but not really interested in a typical romantic relationship. One leading to marriage, I mean." I pointed my forefinger at him. "In fact, it will probably end up that you'll be the one who wants a more serious relationship. So be prepared."

Fred grinned. "I'm willing to take that chance."

"Okay, but don't say you weren't warned. Now, since we've covered the important stuff, including Sunny, I think it's time for me to head home. I don't want my aunt to think I've gone missing along with Scott."

"You can at least reassure her that he's okay. I suspect from what you said earlier that you've seen him?" Fred turned and strolled toward the stacks.

"Yes, and he told me I could let Aunt Lydia and my parents know that he's safe and sound. Which I already did, of course. Wait"—I crossed my arms over my chest—"there is one more thing. Scott wouldn't tell me, but maybe you aren't under the same restrictions."

"What's that?" Fred paused and glanced back at me over his shoulder.

"Scott's real target. He told me he had to go into hiding because his superiors were afraid his cover might've been blown. But even though he was keeping tabs on Selvaggio, apparently the art dealer wasn't actually his focus. Neither was Kurt Kendrick. Which makes me wonder who it was."

Fred turned around and fixed me with a puzzled expression. "I thought it was Selvaggio. Something to do with his connection to Esmerelda."

"Oscar Selvaggio had dealings with a notorious criminal?"

"Not to buy or sell drugs." Fred frowned. "But he wasn't above acquiring and selling art to someone who had plenty of cash, no matter where their money came from."

I dropped my arms to my sides. "I'm surprised a drug dealer would be such an avid art collector."

"Well, I don't know if Esmerelda really cares about art. I think it's probably more the investment aspect that interests her. Anyway, the art angle was something Hugh uncovered on another investigation, and one reason why I was encouraged to work with him in addition to secretly aiding the task force. We hoped Hugh's knowledge of the art world would benefit our investigation."

"Talk about a tangled web," I said, moving forward to join him in the aisle. "It seems most of the people on this task force are using everyone else for their own purposes."

"It happens." Fred's eyes glinted. "It shouldn't, but everyone wants the glory associated with bringing down a high-value criminal. Even though we're all supposed to be working together . . ."

"You're actually rivals?" I looked him up and down. "Maybe you'd better talk to Hugh and let him know what's really going on. I don't think you want him to find out what you're up to before you've had a chance to explain."

"That's actually a good idea," Fred said. "Perhaps I can even nudge him to do the same thing with your aunt."

"I'd appreciate that, and so will Aunt Lydia, even if she'll never admit it." I gave Fred a knowing look. "And it wouldn't hurt your relationship with Sunny either."

Fred nodded before following me to the back door of the library. As we stepped out into the parking lot, I turned to him and laid a hand on his arm. "I wouldn't give up on Sunny, by the way. I can tell she really likes you."

Flashing me a brilliant smile, Fred strode off toward his car.

I stared after him as he drove off, thinking that I liked him too. But I was still worried that his obsession with the Esmerelda case, while understandable, might prove a stumbling block to his relationship with Sunny.

She wasn't one to dwell on the past. Forgive and forget was more her style.

I didn't think the same could be said about Fred Nash.

Chapter
Twenty-Two

Aunt Lydia had planned a dinner party for the following evening, which was Saturday, a week before the wedding—combining the meal with opening the wedding gifts Richard and I had already received. My parents had arrived early Saturday afternoon, along with Walt and Zelda, Sunny, and Karla. Aunt Lydia had invited Jim and Fiona Muir, but they'd declined, claiming that Jim had some sort of business event they couldn't miss.

"Not that I'm too upset about that turn of events," Aunt Lydia said, as she pulled a steaming casserole dish from the oven and set it on top of the stove.

"That smells great," I said, breathing in the scent of potatoes mingled with cheese. "Is it your lovely potatoes au gratin?"

"Yes. I made it especially for your dad. You know how he loves it."

"Do I ever. He could probably finish off half that dish by himself."

"It's also something Sunny can eat, although I have plenty of other vegetarian options." Aunt Lydia swept her oven mitt–encased hand through the air, indicating the salad, curried carrots, and steamed broccoli. "I just hope she won't miss not having a veggie protein dish. I'm afraid I didn't get around to that."

"She'll be fine. As long as she has all these side dishes, she won't care." I snitched a piece of raw carrot from the salad bowl.

Aunt Lydia shot me a sharp look as she stripped of the mitts. "Hands off. We'll be serving in just a minute." She glanced toward the archway that led to the hall. "Is Richard here yet? I didn't hear him come in."

"He's in the dining room, chatting with Mom and Dad and the others." I turned at the sound of the front door opening. "Would that be Hugh?"

"Not sure if he's coming or not." Aunt Lydia vigorously tossed the salad with a pair of wooden tongs. "He was invited a while back, but with the way things have been between us . . ."

"Nonsense. I can't believe he'd skip one of your dinners," I said as I stepped into the hall.

It wasn't Hugh.

"Hello, sis." Scott set down a duffle bag near the foot of the stairs before striding forward to give me a hug. "I'm cleared to be out in public again," he added as he released me.

I popped him in the shoulder with my fist. "Just in time to enjoy one of Aunt Lydia's feasts."

"Planned that," Scott said, with a smile that faded when our aunt stepped out into the hall.

"Scott Webber, it's about time you showed up. We were worried sick."

He lifted his hands in a remorseful gesture. "Sorry. I couldn't contact anyone. Orders."

Aunt Lydia tapped her foot against the hardwood floor. "Next time, I expect some sort of warning. Even if it's simply that you'll be out of touch for a while."

Scott hung his head. "I promise. Am I forgiven?" As he lifted his head, I couldn't help but notice the sparkle in his dark eyes. "At least enough to join the dinner party? The aromas are tantalizing."

"I suppose," Aunt Lydia said with a sniff. But her eyes were just as bright. "Come along and help Amy and me carry the dishes into the dining room." As Scott and I followed her to the kitchen, she called over her shoulder. "Your parents are here. You'll have to explain yourself to them—don't expect me to help you with that."

"I'll take the hit," Scott said, shooting me a conspiratorial grin.

After we carried the food into the dining room and Scott received both hugs and hectoring from my parents, I took a seat at the table between Richard and my mother.

"Glad to see I won't have to scrounge up another groomsman," Richard said, motioning with his wineglass at Scott, who was seated across the table from us, next to Aunt Lydia.

"I promise not to disappear again. Not before the wedding, anyway. Which is only a week away, you know." Scott winked at Richard. "Scared yet?"

"Not at all." Richard draped his free arm across the back of my chair. "I'm only worried that Amy will get so involved in helping with this latest murder mystery that she'll forget to show up."

I leaned back against his arm. "Not going to happen. I'd have to be locked up somewhere to miss out on marrying you."

"It's happened before. The locked-up part, I mean." Richard looked down at me, his gray eyes sparkling with good humor. "Let's try to avoid that this time."

I crossed my heart. "I promise to do my best."

"So, Scott," Karla said, "it seems you're almost as mysterious as my enigmatic sponsor, Kurt Kendrick."

Scott raised his eyebrows. "I didn't realize Kendrick was your benefactor, Karla."

Karla brushed a lock of her silky hair behind her ear. "One of them. Kurt's donated a considerable amount to support my work with physically and emotionally challenged young dancers."

"I didn't know that either," Mom said, fixing Karla with a thoughtful gaze. "He is quite a puzzle. Sometimes I think he's the most gracious man alive, but then there are other times when I catch a glimpse of his expression and get the shivers."

"He's definitely a man of mystery," Richard said. "Although perhaps we need to reserve that term for Scott now."

"But that's due to Scott's job, not a natural inclination to be secretive." Dad swirled his wine before lifting the glass. "Anyway, enough of that. I propose a toast prior to digging into this delicious food. To Amy and Richard," he said.

Everyone followed suit, repeating his toast, with Sunny adding, "Here's to my bestie and her beau."

I rubbed at my nose, using my hand to hide the blush rising in my face. "Thanks. But let's also thank Aunt Lydia for this lovely dinner."

"I'll second that," said a voice from the hall.

Turning in my chair, I spied Hugh in the doorway, with Fred Nash standing behind him.

"I hope I'm still invited?" Hugh asked, his focus on my aunt.

"Of course." Despite the coolness of her tone, Aunt Lydia's face betrayed her true feelings. Happiness mixed with caution brightened her blue eyes.

Hugh strolled over to an empty chair next to Scott. "I brought Fred along. I didn't think you'd mind."

"It's perfectly fine." Aunt Lydia looked down, arranging her linen napkin across her lap.

Sunny waved Fred over. "There's an extra chair there against the wall. Just pull it up to the table next to me. I can scoot over a little."

Aunt Lydia shifted and dug her fingernails into the tablecloth, as if bracing herself before standing. "We'll need an additional place setting . . ."

"I'll get it, dear. You've done quite enough for one day," Zelda said, before rising to her feet and bustling out of the room.

Hugh surveyed the laden table before casting Aunt Lydia a quick glance. "It all looks delicious, as always. I'm looking forward to enjoying the meal, as well as the company."

My aunt finally lifted her head and met his steady gaze. "As am I."

While the food was passed around the table, Zelda entertained us with a story from her childhood, one that also included mentions of Aunt Lydia and Walt.

"So your big sister wasn't always the picture of respectability?" Dad asked, nudging my mom with his elbow as he handed her a basket of dinner rolls.

"Hardly. Why, there was the one time I remember . . ." Mom caught a glimpse of Aunt Lydia's icy glare and tightened her lips. "But that's all in the past. Why don't we enjoy this amazing food and talk about other things? Like a certain upcoming wedding, for example."

"Or the bachelor party?" Walt said with a smile. "Do you have anything special planned to surprise Richard, Scott? Oh, and Karla too, I guess, since she is filling the best man's role."

Karla widened her eyes. "If we told you, it wouldn't be a surprise."

Richard paused with a forkful of broccoli poised halfway between his plate and his mouth. "Let me clear up one thing right now. I thought we all agreed that there isn't going to be any bachelor party."

"Or so you think." Karla batted her eyes at him over the rim of her water glass.

Richard pointed his fork at her. "I said I didn't want one, and I meant it."

"Hmmmm, I heard that. But then Scott and I had an idea that even you might approve of, Mr. Stick-in-the-Mud."

Richard placed the fork on his plate with a clang. "You'll have to drag me to any such event. Which means you'll have to find me first."

Scott grinned. "Kind of my specialty."

Richard muttered something under his breath while Sunny laughed.

I glanced at her. "I hope you aren't planning to surprise me as well. We also agreed—no silly party. I think I'm a little too old for all that nonsense."

Sunny held up her hands. "I'm innocent of any scheming, I swear. We're still going on that hike Wednesday instead of having a party. Although"—she flashed a smile at Karla—"I might be convinced to help you and Scott with your surprise."

Richard turned to me, dramatically widening his eyes. "They're all ganging up on me."

I patted his hand. "Don't worry. I'm sure my brother and your best friend wouldn't do anything that might embarrass you . . ." I lifted my fingers and pressed them briefly to my lips before adding, "What am I saying? Of course they would. You'll just have to bear it, I'm afraid."

Most of the people around the table laughed at this, although I noticed that Fred appeared preoccupied. He wasn't really looking at anyone, just using his fork to shove cooked carrots around on his plate.

Strangely, I noticed that he seemed distracted throughout the meal, barely speaking two words to Sunny, who kept shooting him concerned glances from under the golden fringe of her lowered lashes. Everyone else, including Hugh and Aunt Lydia, relaxed after the banter about the bachelor party turned into a discussion of other aspects of the wedding, but Fred remained on edge.

Sunny and Zelda helped Aunt Lydia clear the table, insisting that I stay seated.

"This is a party celebrating you and Richard, so you should just enjoy yourselves," Zelda chided when I protested.

"Perhaps Nick and Scott can carry in the gifts after I serve the coffee and cake. You can open them at the table once it's cleared," Aunt Lydia said. "I believe you brought them all over earlier, didn't you, Richard?"

"They're in the sitting room," Richard said, looking over at me. "Except for that odd one we already opened."

"That's right, the antique necklace. Hold on, let me grab that from my room. Maybe someone here will have a clue as to who sent it." I sprang up from my chair and headed out into the hall as Richard explained how we'd discovered the strange, unmarked box among our other gifts.

When I returned to the dining room clutching the white jewelry box, I was pleased to see that Hugh had left the room with Aunt Lydia.

"He offered to help her with the coffee and cake," Mom said, but I could tell by her expression that she hoped, as I did, that her sister and Hugh were finally having the conversation that would restore their relationship.

This hope seemed to be answered when, after serving the coffee, Aunt Lydia asked Scott to slide over one seat to allow her to sit next to Hugh.

My mom side-eyed me and flashed a smile as Hugh pressed his fingers over the hand my aunt had laid on the table.

"Before we all become distracted by this delicious cake and the gifts, I want to apologize. Publicly, to you"—Hugh intertwined my aunt's fingers with his and gave them a squeeze before looking around the table—"but also to others here. I should have been honest and given you fair warning about my investigation into

Kurt Kendrick. I realize he's someone who many of you know well. That was thoughtless of me."

Fred cleared his throat and settled back in his chair, leaving his cake untouched. "I need to apologize as well. I've already explained this to Hugh, but the truth is, I haven't been entirely honest either."

"Oh?" Sunny swiveled to face him. "About what, exactly?"

"Why I'm in Taylorsford," Fred said, tearing his gaze away from her to look across the table. "I explained all this to Hugh on the drive here, and I suspect he was about to confess the truth to you, Ms. Talbot, but I think I should do so instead. My lies had nothing to do with Hugh. He shouldn't take the blame."

"I'm not sure I understand, Mr. Nash," my aunt said. "Are you admitting you lied to Hugh as well as to the rest of us?"

"I did. Well"—Fred fiddled with the cake fork, absently tapping it against the tablecloth—"I didn't exactly lie. I just didn't tell him, or any of you, the whole truth. You see, I took the job with Hugh under false pretenses. I agreed to help him dig into Kurt Kendrick's business operations to hopefully discover any irregularities, but that wasn't my main focus . . ."

"It was a convenient cover," Scott said dryly.

"Very true, just like your family visit." Fred's tone held a razor edge.

Scott took a long sip of wine instead of replying.

"Anyway, just like Scott, I'm part of a team of investigators and federal agents—a task force established to track down a specific individual. It just so happens that assisting Hugh's investigation allowed me the opportunity to hide my true mission." Fred glanced at Sunny, who was eyeing him with a dubious expression. "Not that I didn't do the work that Hugh requested, I just combined it with other activities."

I cast Fred a sympathetic glance before focusing my gaze on Scott. "You told me some of this already but haven't really said whether you think Oscar Selvaggio's death is tied up in this investigation in any way."

"Because I'm not sure that it is," Scott said. "Except in a very peripheral sense. But enough shop talk. Let me grab those gifts so we can continue to enjoy the festivities." As he stood, Scott shot Fred a warning glance.

He obviously doesn't want him sharing any more information on the case, I thought. Which I could understand. If Fred wanted to explain more about his recent activities to Sunny later, that would probably be okay, but I had to agree with Scott about not sharing everything with the entire group of guests.

Walt joined my dad and Scott as they left the room, saying, "Another pair of hands can't hurt."

"Especially since there's quite a tidy little pile of gifts, from what I saw earlier," Zelda said.

"Including this one, which is the mystery." I popped open the lid and held up the jeweler's box, moving it from side to side so that everyone could see the necklace nestled inside. "Does anyone have a clue as to who gave us this?"

Despite murmurs about the uniqueness of the pendant, no one spoke up with any knowledge about where it had come from.

"I think you're going to have to ask Fiona," Aunt Lydia said. "As I've said before, it could have been one of her acquaintances. I know she likes antique jewelry, so maybe a few of her friends do as well."

"I guess that's our only option at this point," I said, snapping the lid closed and setting the box on the table. Despite my curiosity, I'd avoided mentioning the necklace to my future mother-in-law. If one of her friends had sent it and we didn't have the card, I was sure she'd blame us, not the giver. *But then again, she did pay off our catering bill.* I glanced up at Richard. "I'll ask her next time we see her."

"Which won't be until the rehearsal dinner, I'm afraid," he said. "But as long as we can eventually track down the sender to thank them, I guess the timing doesn't really matter."

"We'll figure it out," Aunt Lydia said firmly. "Now—let's get to this unwrapping, shall we?" She motioned for Scott, Dad, and Walt to deposit the gifts on the table.

"Just a minute." My mom dug through the purse she'd set on the floor next to her chair before holding up a small notebook and pen. "I thought I'd write down each gift and the name of the giver. That way there won't be any more chances of misplacing a card or anything like that."

"Good idea," I said, before handing Richard one of the wrapped boxes. "Here, you start."

After that, the conversation focused on admiring the gifts, although there were a few items, like the Dresden china figurine of a milkmaid and cow, that elicited some humorous comments.

Sunny wrinkled her nose. "What do you do with that?"

"Thank the person kindly and then donate it to the next library yard sale," I said.

"That's dangerous, don't you think?" Karla asked. "I mean, if the person who sent it sees it in a local sale . . ."

"I doubt they will. I suspect it's from someone in Fiona's social circle." I held out the card for Richard to examine.

"It is," he said. "And knowing this woman, she's probably just regifting anyway."

"Really?" Zelda batted her eyelashes. "Your mother's friends would do a thing like that? It's so tacky."

"My mother's friends definitely would. Which is why they aren't really *my* friends," Richard replied.

"But, to be fair, Fiona surprised us recently, in a nice way." I shared a smile with Richard. "Believe it or not, she actually paid off our catering bill. The entire remaining amount."

"That is . . ." My dad appeared to be searching for the appropriate word. "Very generous."

"Extremely," Aunt Lydia said. "But as I've said before, I think Fiona actually does approve of you, Amy. And your marriage."

"Which is really one of the best gifts she could give us," Richard said, his expression sobering.

I leaned over and placed my head on his shoulder. "I am prepared to like her for that reason alone."

"A mother wants what's best for her children, at least if she's any kind of mother at all," my mom said. "I feel blessed that Amy and Richard have found one another. Now"—she cast Scott a sly look—"we just have to find the right person for my other child."

"Working on it," Scott said, which made both my mom and dad sit up in the chairs and turn to stare at him. "Early days," he added, before taking a sip of coffee. "But I do have a date for the wedding."

"So do I." Sunny glanced over at Fred, her eyes very bright. "I hope."

He slid his arm around her shoulders. "Absolutely."

"So I'm the only poor soul without a plus one?" Karla fluffed her bobbed hair. "Not that I mind, especially if Amy will share Richard for a few of the dances."

"Of course. Just not the first one." I gave her a surreptitious wink.

Aunt Lydia shifted in her chair. "To be honest, I'm not sure of my status either, Karla."

"Don't worry, my dear," Hugh said, taking her hand again. "I still plan to be your date, if you'll have me."

She turned to him, a brilliant smile illuminating her lovely face. "I will."

Which was close enough to "I do" to make everyone in the room share conspiratorial, but delighted, glances.

Chapter
Twenty-Three

On Sunday, I decided to escape. The house felt so full of people, and even though they were people I loved, the closeness was getting on my nerves, already frayed by wedding preparations.

I asked Richard to come with me, but he said he had to run an errand. I was a little miffed until Dad pulled me aside and told me Richard had confided that he was actually driving into the city to pick up a special wedding gift he'd had made for me.

"I guess I'll forgive him then," I told my father with a smile.

"I think you'd better." Dad gave me a hug before I headed outside.

It was a beautiful May day. The sky was so clear that it held only a hint of blue, and the fully leafed-out trees offered counterpoints of emerald and jade. I strolled down the cracked cement sidewalk toward the center of town, noting the spray-painted lines marking the areas that were to be replaced, on Sunny's initiative, with brick pavers. She was making good on her promise to repair and replace the aged sidewalks with walkways that would blend in with the historic nature of the town.

I passed the library and continued on to the edge of the historic district, where a sprawling brick building separated the quainter part of town from the more modern section and its strip of auto repair shops, car dealerships, pizza and burger joints, and dollar stores.

The Taylorsford Inn was located in a renovated mill. The owners had seamlessly incorporated the original structure, complete with its now stationary waterwheel, into a two-story hotel. The newer section housed the guest rooms, but the owners had converted the mill into a restaurant and meeting rooms. There was also a shop that sold handicrafts, mountain music CDs, photographs and paintings of the area, and even a few dulcimers and other instruments built by local craftsman Delbert Frye. Richard and I had actually considered renting out the restaurant for our reception until the quoted cost had sent us scurrying back to the idea of using Aunt Lydia's garden.

Not interested in walking out of the historic area of town, I turned around to retrace my steps. But before I could leave the grounds of the inn, my attention was caught by the sight of someone packing a compact car with luggage.

It was Honor Bryant. I approached her with a cheery hello.

She met my gaze with a tense frown. "Hi, Ms. Webber. Sorry, but I can't talk. I want to hit the road soon." She twitched her lips into a humorless smile. "I prefer to avoid driving too late, so I need to get going if I want to reach my destination before dark."

"Where are you headed?" I asked.

Honor shifted her weight from one foot to the other. "Up north. I think I'll have more success looking for a new job in the New York or New England area."

"I see. The sheriff's department has cleared you to leave, then?"

Honor slammed down the trunk lid of her car. "Of course. Why wouldn't they?"

Looking her over, I registered her quite different look—tight and tattered black jeans, magenta T-shirt, and black leather jacket. Quite a change from the image she'd been presenting up to this point. She was still wearing the short boots, though. Now clean.

There was mud on her boots before, like someone who'd stomped through the woods, I thought. *But she wasn't wearing those boots at the party, so I have no reason to alert Brad about that.*

"I just thought, since they haven't determined who it was that poisoned Mr. Selvaggio, they might still have questions for you."

"I don't see why. I had nothing to do with Oscar's death," Honor said, her voice cracking slightly.

"It's just . . . Well, I did see you carrying a mug that could've had anything in it. One you didn't seem to be drinking from. I had to tell the authorities that, I'm afraid."

"I have no idea what you're talking about." Honor's eyelashes fluttered, drawing attention to the fact that she was no longer wearing glasses.

She looks like another person. Like she's reverted to the girl she was in those older photographs, I thought, before clearing my throat.

"At any rate, I hope you have a good trip. Looks like you'll have decent weather for the drive, at least."

Honor didn't respond to my pleasantries. "Sorry, must go," she said, casting a quick glance over her shoulder. Glimpsing something that obviously unnerved her, she tensed until her shoulders were hunched up almost to her ears and yanked a set of keys from her jacket pocket.

Following her gaze, I spied Lance Dalbec standing on the side porch of the inn. "Do you know him? He seems to be taking an inordinate interest in you."

Honor's knuckles whitened as her fingers clutched her keys. "No."

"His name is Lance Dalbec. I've met him a couple of times, and he gives me the creeps. I don't think we should ignore his obvious stalking. In fact, maybe I should call the sheriff's department." I pulled out my cell phone.

Honor's face blanched. She slapped my hand so hard that my phone flew from my grip and crashed onto the driveway pavement.

"What the hell?" I leaned down to retrieve my phone. Staring at the cracked glass and blank screen, I straightened just as Honor made a dash for the driver's side of her car.

She didn't offer an apology or even a good-bye; she simply jumped into the car and slammed the door behind her. I scurried to the edge of the driveway as she fired up the engine and backed out as if the devil himself were chasing her.

Lance Dalbec waited until Honor's car disappeared around the curve that led out of town before he strolled over to where I stood, examining my broken phone.

"Hello, Ms. Webber. I see Mr. Selvaggio's former assistant has beat a hasty retreat." He stared at me, his pale eyes opaque as frosted glass. "Do you know her well?"

"Not really. I met her at Mr. Kendrick's party and have only spoken to her once or twice since. But honestly"—I shoved the dead phone into the pocket of my jeans—"I'm surprised the sheriff's department has allowed her to leave Taylorsford. I have this odd feeling that she knows more than she's saying about Mr. Selvaggio's death."

"She did appear a bit jumpy." Dalbec's eyes narrowed as he surveyed me. "Did she say something that's aroused your suspicions?"

I met his intense gaze with a lift of my chin. "I don't think I should share anything Ms. Bryant may or may not have said with you, Mr. Dalbec. I suspect you're looking to pin Mr. Selvaggio's murder on Kurt Kendrick, and frankly, I'd rather help the authorities handle the investigation than assist someone who seems to be, in my opinion, something of a vigilante."

"Is that what you think of me?" Dalbec's smile was, in its own way, as intimidating as Kurt's.

But he's more of a hyena than a wolf, I thought, taking a step back. "You told me that you attacked Mr. Kendrick in self-defense, after he lunged at you. But I expect that's a lie. I think you actually accosted him because you believe he had something to do with Mr. Selvaggio's death. Since you aren't, by your own admission, involved with law enforcement, it seems you're not above taking the law into your own hands."

"Sometimes the law doesn't have all the facts," Dalbec said, his smile fading.

I crossed my arms over my chest. "If you have more information than they do, perhaps you should share it with them. That might be more useful than knocking down elderly men in their own homes."

A bark of laughter escaped Dalbec's thin-lipped mouth. "Are you suggesting that I was engaged in an unequal fight with a defenseless old man? Surely you know Kurt Kendrick better than that."

"He's strong, but also in his seventies. Which gives you the advantage, if only in years," I said, locking my knees to keep my legs from wobbling.

Dalbec looked me over. "As I said before, you should be careful where that man is concerned. He's much more dangerous than I suspect you realize. And utterly ruthless when it comes to protecting his own interests."

I knew this. But I also knew that Kurt's interests included protecting me, Richard, and our families and friends. Which was information I didn't feel like sharing with this man, whatever his reasons for attacking Kurt. "I do understand that, actually. But personally, I don't think he murdered Mr. Selvaggio. Not at a party at his house. It's not his style."

"People can do things out of character when pressed to their limits," Dalbec said.

"True, but again, I prefer to allow the sheriff's department to study the evidence and arrest the proper person. Neither you nor I probably have all the information we'd need to label anyone a murderer, even if we have assembled some interesting facts."

Dalbec's expression darkened. "Which I assume you've done. Perhaps with some input from people like Ms. Bryant?"

"Like I said before, I don't think that's any of your business. Now, if you'll excuse me, I intend to resume my walk." I turned away and strode off without waiting for any reply.

I reassured myself that I owed Dalbec nothing—not an excuse for my rudeness and certainly not any information I might have learned from anyone involved in this convoluted case. *He's just looking for an excuse to pin the murder on Kurt*, I thought as I walked back toward my aunt's house. *There seems to be some animosity there that his words don't really explain. Better to leave him in the dark than have him attack Kurt, or anyone else, again.*

When I reached the library, I paused on the sidewalk and considered my options. My cell phone was dead, but there was a landline in the library. I used the spare key I'd fortunately added to my personal key chain and entered the building through the staff door.

In the workroom, I grabbed the receiver of the phone extension and called Brad.

"So Dalbec is still in town," he said, after I explained my run-in with the man. "Good to know. We're trying to keep tabs on the guy, especially since his background is a little murky."

"He isn't an art broker?" I coiled the cord of the wall-mounted phone around my wrist.

"He's been involved in a few deals, but that doesn't really seem to be his profession. To be honest, we haven't been able to determine exactly what it is he does."

"You think he's a crook?" I asked.

"Let's just say his lifestyle doesn't match up with his apparent lack of employment." Brad's dry tone didn't hide his obvious distrust of Lance Dalbec. "And he appears to move around a lot. Always something to consider."

"Well, he's apparently just as suspicious of Kurt Kendrick as you are," I said. "Although I've sensed a level of antagonism from him that I don't think you feel."

"Interesting." Brad fell silent for a moment before speaking again. "You said you saw him at the Taylorsford Inn?"

"Just as Honor Bryant was leaving. I think he was watching her."

"What?" Brad's tone sharpened. "Bryant's left town?"

"Didn't you approve her departure?"

"Definitely not. We had more questions we wanted to ask her. Where did she go? Did she say?"

"Not really," I said, frowning as I realized how vague Honor had been. "She said something about New York and driving north, but that was about it."

When Brad swore, which he rarely did, I knew he was truly upset. "When did she leave?"

"About twenty minutes ago. She was in a hurry and obviously didn't want anyone from your department to show up, even when she seemed frightened by Dalbec's presence. When I said I was calling you, she knocked my cell phone from my hand."

"That's not a good sign," Brad said. "But helpful information nonetheless. Thanks for letting me know."

"Sure." I unwrapped the phone cord from around my wrist. "Obviously, Honor Bryant lied to me. She claimed your office had told her she was free to leave Taylorsford."

"Absolutely not. Like I said, we wanted to question her further." Brad hesitated before speaking again, indicating that he was carefully weighing his words. "One of the feds assisting with this case let me know that Bryant had had a few run-ins with the law in the past. Drug problems, apparently."

I held the phone away from my face and stared at it for a moment before responding. "She has a history of drug abuse?"

"Yes, although everything I've seen indicates that she straightened herself out and stayed clean for the last several years. There's no reason to think she's still involved in that lifestyle, and I don't want to smear her name without cause."

"But she could've been involved with Esmerelda's gang at some point?"

"It's possible. They operate throughout the greater DC area, and she did grow up in the District." Brad's gusty sigh resonated over the phone. "Which was one thing we wanted to question her about."

"I see." I tapped the phone receiver against my palm. Had Oscar Selvaggio hired Honor because of her association with a woman he wanted to do business with? I frowned. Maybe that was part of Lance Dalbec's interest too, if he truly was a broker for illegal art deals.

But how would some user, or former user, like Honor Bryant have developed a close connection with the mysterious woman called Esmerelda? A woman who probably never dealt with buyers directly and had obviously worked hard to remain incognito? As I told Brad good-bye, I pondered this wrinkle in my theory.

Maybe they hadn't ever met, I thought, considering that Esmerelda probably had any number of people who could've contacted Honor Bryant. Leveraging the debt one of her dealers held over Honor, Esmeralda could've remained in the shadows while still enlisting the girl into some type of criminal activity.

I placed the receiver back on the phone hook as I contemplated another possibility, realizing I could have things backward. Perhaps it wasn't Oscar Selvaggio using Honor to get close to Esmerelda—the drug dealer could've encouraged Selvaggio to hire the girl so that Honor could keep an eye on a man who was selling investments in the form of art. Maybe Esmerelda had suspicions about Selvaggio, who had a rather checkered past, and wanted him kept under surveillance. She might even have forced Honor to change her appearance to fit Selvaggio's typical assistant requirements. Someone who'd been in control of a criminal organization for so long could've certainly found out the art dealer's typical hiring practices without much trouble.

I walked over to the staff exit but paused with my hand on the doorknob as I realized that Esmerelda needn't have met Honor to set such a plot in motion either. She simply could've threatened Honor to comply with a set of instructions delivered by one of her "lieutenants."

Someone like Lance Dalbec, who perhaps didn't just work with Esmerelda but possibly worked *for* her.

Unable to unravel this knotty tangle, I headed back outside and walked home, my thoughts consumed by images of a terrified Honor Bryant, a menacing Lane Dalbec, and the unknown woman who might be the link between them.

Chapter Twenty-Four

After spending all day Tuesday working out the logistics of both Sunny and me being off work for the remainder of the week—and me for the two weeks following as well—I told Samantha that I'd realized wedding planning wasn't really that difficult.

"Not like this, anyway," I said, pointing at the document I'd created to keep track of what volunteers were covering what shifts on what day. It was color-coded by volunteer, which had turned the chart into a rainbow. "I know you've agreed to work more hours than usual, but don't let anyone take advantage of you. All the volunteers are aware that I'll be away for almost three weeks, and they agreed to step up and help keep the building open regular hours."

"Sunny's going to be pulling extra shifts starting next week too, right?" Samantha asked.

"Correct. See—she's the purple color on the graph. So starting next week until I get back, she'll be here almost full-time, as will you. But I don't want either of you stuck working by yourselves for hours at a time. If the volunteers don't show up, call and shame them."

"I'm sure Bill and Denise will be here on schedule." Samantha tapped a yellow square with her mauve-polished fingernail. "But Zelda . . ."

"Definitely call her if she doesn't show up. I know she wants to help, but sometimes she gets scattered and things slip her mind." I frowned as I studied the multicolored chart. "My aunt will be helping out too. She doesn't have a lot of experience working the desk, but she knows how to shelve, so you can set aside some carts for her."

"I'm sure it will be fine." Samantha gave me a sidelong look. "You don't need to worry."

"I will, though. I've never been away so long. Not since I started working here."

"Then it's high time you had a break." Samantha smiled as Bethany Virts approached the desk. "Find what you needed?"

"Yes, thanks," Bethany said, as she laid a book on the counter. "I know this is a kids' book, but I just love it, you know?"

Glancing at the cover, I saw that it was *The Secret Garden* by Frances Hodgson Burnett. "Nothing wrong with that. I reread children's books too, and that's one of my favorites."

"I like the idea of gardens being magical," Bethany said, dipping her head as if embarrassed.

"You do have a beautiful cottage garden." When Bethany looked up in surprise, Samantha added, "I saw it when I was chasing Shay down the alley beside the diner one day. Didn't mean to trespass or anything, but my daughter just loves to explore. We couldn't help noticing your garden, which is really hidden otherwise." She stamped a due date in the book. "It's your own secret garden, I guess. Pretty magical in its own way."

Bethany offered her a shy smile. "Thanks. I use some of the produce in the diner."

"That must be why your sandwiches always taste so fresh, especially in season," I said. "Lettuce and tomatoes harvested straight from the garden are always the best."

"I use other things too." This discussion seemed to have opened the floodgates of Bethany's typically spare use of words. "Radishes and melons and even horseradish. I make my own spicy spread with the roots."

"But not aconite, I hope," I said, with a little smile.

Bethany's face, always pale, blanched to the color of snow. "You mean what they call wolfsbane? I saw pictures of that on the news when they were covering that poor man's death up at Highview."

"That's right. It's also known as monkshood and blue rocket." I met Bethany's worried expression with a reassuring smile. "But I think it's pretty common around here."

"Yeah, I recognized it because my mom grew it in the back bed, which she reserved for flowers. She liked plants that are native to this area. Said they were hardier or something. Anyway, a lot of those plants were taller than more common flowers, and they make such a nice backdrop to my little vegetable garden, I just left that bed alone. I guess the wolfsbane is still there. I mean, I remember weeding around some tall flowers with bluish blossoms last summer."

A garden behind a shop that closes at two o'clock in the afternoon each day, I thought. *With alley access and a bed near the back that anyone could've accessed without being seen, even by visitors to Taylorsford* . . . I cleared my throat. "I wouldn't worry about it, Bethany. I'm sure no one suspects you of poisoning anyone, especially not a man you never met."

"But my garden is accessible to anyone, really," Bethany said, her eyes widening. "I've actually had some stuff stolen off the vines, so I know people do raid it sometimes. I even caught someone once—a visitor staying at the bed-and-breakfast. They said they wanted some fresh strawberries, and I had this open patch that they thought was a community garden. Come to think of it, I noticed some strange footprints in the ground around some of my beds recently . . ." Bethany shook her head. "You don't think someone stole the wolfsbane that killed that man, do you?"

Samantha shot me a concerned glance. "I doubt it, don't you, Amy? Plenty of other sources for that, including herbal stores in the city, if what I read in the paper is right."

"It is used in some traditional medicines. Although not in a concentration meant to kill." I slid the checked-out book down the counter beyond the point where the security gates would set off an alarm. "But maybe you should mention this to Brad Tucker or someone else at the sheriff's department, Bethany. Couldn't hurt to cover all the bases."

"I'll do that. Thanks." Clutching the book to her breast, Bethany bobbed her head in a silent good-bye before scurrying out of the building.

"I sure hope that stuff wasn't taken from her garden," Samantha said, her dark eyes glistening with concern. "Bethany's had enough trouble in her life. The last thing she needs is to be mixed up in this latest murder."

"I couldn't agree more. Which is why I suggested she talk to the authorities. If someone did raid her garden to concoct a poison, it'd be better that she mentioned the possibility up front."

"I guess so." Samantha straightened a display of brochures from local attractions. "As long as they don't jump to any conclusions."

"Brad Tucker won't do that." I considered the fact that Samantha, as a black woman, might have more reason to be distrustful of law enforcement than I did and added, "But maybe one of us should talk to him as well. We could let him know how horrified Bethany seemed over the idea that anyone might have used something from her garden to poison anyone."

"And that she definitely showed no glimmers of guilt," Samantha said thoughtfully. "I can do that, if you want. You should be focusing on your wedding instead of all this murder stuff."

"Thanks, that would be a help. Ask for Brad Tucker when you call. He's the one I trust the most, to be honest."

"Okay. I'll give him a call on my break." Samantha glanced over at the main doors. "Uh-oh, here comes the Nightingale. Who's turn is it to trail her?"

"Yours, but let me do it. I'll be gone for three weeks after today, so it only seems fair," I said as I circled around to the front of the circulation desk.

"Not going to argue with that." Samantha offered me a brief salute before I headed into the stacks.

*   *   *

The next day, Sunny picked me up and drove to the head of the Twin Falls trail.

"This one, really?" I squinched up my face. "I don't have great memories of this trail."

"That's why we need to hike it. Get all those bad memories out of your system," Sunny said as she threw open her car door and jumped out.

I climbed out of her bright-yellow Volkswagen Beetle more slowly. As we walked to the start of the trail, I tied my sweat shirt around my waist. It was warm in the sun, but because we were hiking in a mountain forest, I knew I might need more coverage later. "Just so we don't encounter any fae folk. I really don't want to be dragged off to their underground lair right before my wedding."

Sunny cast me a grin over her shoulder. "I thought you didn't believe in such things."

"I don't. Mostly," I replied, as I followed her into the woods.

The temperature immediately dropped a few degrees as the canopy of leaves overhead filtered out the May sun. The trail, beaten down by many feet over the years, was devoid of vegetation, but on either side of us, pines and hardwoods soared up to the sky. A tangled undergrowth of shrubs, ferns, and weeds filled the spaces between the trees, making leaving the path a dubious and—given the possibility of snakes and other wild creatures— dangerous choice.

"So what's this bachelor-party-that-really-isn't thing that Karla and Scott are planning?" Sunny asked, as I quickened my pace to walk beside her. "I heard Karla say something about it being tonight rather than the traditional night before the wedding."

"Yeah, they had to do that for two reasons. One, because they didn't want to interfere with the rehearsal dinner Friday night. Scott said they knew Richard would absolutely refuse to go out afterwards, because he told them he wanted to get plenty of sleep before the wedding."

Sunny arched her brows. "Because he doesn't plan to sleep much Saturday night?"

"Ha-ha. Very funny." I swatted her arm lightly. "Don't be rude."

"Well, I mean . . ." Sunny flashed me another grin. "But weddings are exhausting, of course. And there will obviously be a lot of dancing."

"You can count on that." I side-eyed her. "I hope Fred can dance, so you have a decent partner."

"He says he has some moves, but we'll see." Sunny glanced at me. "What was the other reason?"

"What? Oh, you mean why they're taking Richard out this evening?"

"Yeah. I mean, they could've aimed for tomorrow night."

"No, because they planned it around a special event." I cast Sunny a smile. "Something Richard will love, if I know him.

There's this hip-hop dance crew competition at some venue close to DC tonight, and Karla and Scott have gotten tickets for that."

"Very cool. Richard will enjoy it, I'm sure."

"Absolutely. And I think there's barhopping involved later, although poor Karla has to be the designated driver, so she'll miss out on that fun."

"She may be grateful for that tomorrow morning." Sunny lifted her chin and looked up into the leaves fluttering above our heads. "Beautiful day, isn't it? And from what I've seen on the weather, it should hold through Saturday."

"We did luck out with that, if the predictions prove to be true. Kurt arranged for some extra tents on standby, but it looks like it will be a clear day."

Sunny glanced at me. "Good ol' Kurt. Always ready to come through in a crisis." She frowned. "You don't really think he's capable of murder, do you?"

"Capable? Yes. Do I think he killed Oscar Selvaggio? No."

Sunny tossed her head, bouncing her long ponytail. "Someone did. Any ideas as to who?"

Slipping on my sweat shirt, I considered her question with care. "I've accumulated what feels like a lot of unrelated information, so I could make some guesses, but I don't have a solid theory yet."

"Or at least not one you want to share." Sunny stopped for a moment to tie her shoe. "Like something that involves Richard's old dance coach, maybe?"

"Why would you think that?" I said, furiously trying to remember everything I'd shared with her about Adele's relationship with Selvaggio.

"Oh, I've heard some rumors, that's all." Sunny straightened and flashed me a smile. "You know how Zelda is. She apparently saw that Selvaggio guy grab Adele Tourneau at Kurt's party and said you seemed pretty taken aback when she mentioned it to you."

I sighed. "Zelda talks too much."

"No joke, but it made me wonder . . ." Sunny strode off, forcing me to jog to keep up with her.

"She does have a history with him." I motioned for Sunny to slow down. "Even more than I originally told you, honestly." I took a deep breath before I filled her in on all the additional information I'd discovered about Adele's connections to Oscar Selvaggio.

Well, not all. I left out any mention of my late uncle.

"She tried to kill him once before? Wow, that must put her at the top of Brad's suspect list," Sunny said, when I'd shared all the facts I'd collected.

"I don't know. He still seems interested in Kurt. And then there's that weird connection to the leader of that drug operation."

"Esmerelda?" Sunny swept an errant lock of hair behind one ear. "Fred told me about her. She was responsible for him getting injured and leaving the police force and for his partner getting killed. Well, her gang was, anyway."

"I know. Which makes this whole investigation pretty personal for him. But while I can understand an interest in Selvaggio's dealings with her, I don't see why she'd want him dead. He was selling artwork, not stealing from her."

"Maybe he swindled her?" Sunny stopped for a moment, her gaze apparently caught by something off to her left. "Sold her some forgeries or something? You know that happens a lot, and he apparently wasn't the most honest person . . ."

I grabbed her arm. "Brilliant! That would explain so much. If he cheated her, someone like Esmerelda could easily have wanted him dead. She wouldn't even have had to do the deed herself. Just get one of her flunkies . . ." I closed my lips over the next words that had bubbled up to my lips. *Esmerelda or one of her henchmen could also have blackmailed someone into doing their dirty work*, I thought. *Someone who was in their debt . . .*

Sunny turned her head to look at me. "Shhhh." She placed a finger to her lips. "Someone's out there, walking through the brush."

"It's probably just an animal," I said, but lowered my voice.

"I saw something moving. Just a flash, but too tall to be an animal," Sunny whispered.

A chill peppered my arms. "A bear?"

"No, not that bulky or shaggy. I think it's a person."

"Someone lost their way? Or a hunter?"

"It's not hunting season, although that doesn't always stop people." Sunny took a few steps off the path. As she peered into the dense foliage, I heard rustling leaves and the snapping of twigs.

"Maybe we should move on," I said, tugging on her arm.

She nodded and backed away from the edge of the forest. Keeping an eye on the side of the trail, we both set off at a jog.

"There's a side path. Leads to Delbert Frye's cabin," I said, my voice breaking slightly.

Sunny gave me a thumbs-up. "Good idea," she mouthed at me, while footfalls echoed behind us.

Right before we turned onto the side trail, I glanced over my shoulder just long enough to glimpse a tall, thin, dark-haired man stepping out of the woods.

Lance Dalbec, I thought, picking up my pace. *Who has no reason to be out here, wandering through the mountain forest, unless he actually is chasing me.* "Run," I whispered to Sunny.

We rushed toward the small circle of light at the end of the trail. That was the clearing, close to a cabin owned by Delbert Frey, a hermit who, among other things, had a gun he was not afraid to use to threaten trespassers.

Who would protect us, if we could reach his house in time.

Chapter
Twenty-Five

Sunny and I raced across the short stretch of open field that separated the woods from Delbert's rustic cabin. As we clattered up the rough steps to the front porch, I stared back at the trail, but saw no one. Apparently Dalbec had not seen us turn off the main path.

Which didn't mean that he wouldn't eventually figure that out and backtrack to follow us. I pounded on Delbert's front door as Sunny leaned against one of the porch posts, her chest rising and falling under her Vista View Farms T-shirt.

The door opened a crack. "Amy Webber, what are you doing out here, girl?" said the grizzled older man who peered out at me.

"My friend Sunny and I were hiking the Twin Falls trail, but then we spied this man who seemed to be following us . . ."

The door flew open. "Get in, get in," said Delbert Frye.

I rushed inside, Sunny on my heels. Delbert, a short, wiry man in his eighties, grabbed the shotgun from a gun rack right inside the door and stepped out onto the porch.

I crossed the main room of the cabin, which was almost as dim as the forest. There were no overhead fixtures, only standing lamps that cast yellow ovals of light over isolated areas, and the small windows cut into the exposed log walls didn't provide much illumination.

"This is definitely rustic." Sunny looked around, her gaze sweeping over the handcrafted furniture that filled the room and the faded rag rugs that covered the wooden plank floors. "I like it."

I pointed up at the shelf that ran in a continuous track around all four walls. It was set far enough below the timbered ceiling to accommodate stringed instruments of all shapes and sizes. There were fiddles, banjos, and a variety of dulcimers. "There's Delbert's passion on display. Making those instruments and playing folk music."

"Beautiful," Sunny said, her eyes widening as she surveyed the shelves.

I motioned to a seating area near a stone fireplace. "We can have a seat, I think. Delbert will make sure that guy doesn't try to approach the cabin." I sat down on a pine settle draped in a woven wool blanket.

Sunny plopped down beside me. "I've heard plenty of stories about Mr. Frye. Some of them from you. I think you said he scares people off with his shotgun but has never fired at anyone?"

"Yeah, he can intimidate without actually doing any harm," I said. "He's a brilliant musician too. I think I mentioned that as well."

"I'd love to hear him play," Sunny said, examining the instruments filling the high shelves. "I bet the grands would as well."

"Unfortunately, he's very shy about performing," I said, closing my lips over my next words as Delbert entered the cabin.

Closing and locking the front door, Delbert lifted the shotgun back onto the rack. "I spied some dark-haired fellow over by the entrance to the trail, but the minute he saw me, he skedaddled."

"The minute he saw your gun, you mean," I said.

Delbert Frye's smile lit up his weathered face. "Most likely."

"I think we should call Brad," Sunny said. "Some stranger following two women on a mountain path is a bit suspicious."

"More than you even know," I said, as Delbert crossed the room and sat on a worn armchair whose springs visibly pressed against its floral-patterned upholstery. "I've encountered him a couple of times before," I added, before describing my run-ins with the supposed art broker. "To be honest, I don't think that's his real career."

"More likely some kind of criminal," Delbert said, running his fingers through the fringe of white hair that encircled his bald pate. "He had the look of a con man."

"I think you're probably right," I agreed, before turning to Sunny. "And you're right too. We should call Brad about this."

"I'll give him a shout," Sunny said, sliding her cell phone from the pocket of her yoga pants.

Delbert pointed to a larger window at the back of the house, over the sink. "Better reception over there."

Sunny nodded and walked over to the kitchen area, punching in numbers she'd obviously memorized when she and Brad were a couple.

"So, Delbert"—I pressed my spine against the wooden back of the settle—"are you going to attend my wedding or not? You haven't actually responded to my invitation. I thought maybe you were planning to escort Mary Gardener, who has sent word that she'll be there."

Delbert's face reddened, a clue, like the cinnamon streaks in his beard, to what I suspected was his original russet hair color. "Not sure. Big crowd, isn't it? And Mary has another date."

"Kurt?" I smiled. Mary Gardener, an elderly woman who kept alive the oral tradition of the area's mountain folktales, had been a housekeeper at the orphanage where Kurt lived as a child. They'd bonded there and remained friends ever since.

"Yep, that Kendrick fellow. Mary told me he asked her as soon as you and your fiancé set the date." Delbert glanced up at the display of instruments. "Truth is, I wouldn't mind coming, 'specially as my great-niece will be there with that man of hers. But I don't really feel like I'd belong at such an event."

"Nonsense," I said. "Like you said, Mary will be there, as well as Alison, and probably a few other people you'll know. And it isn't going to be a really formal occasion, so you don't have to worry about that. We're getting married in my fiancé's backyard, and the reception will simply spill over into my aunt's garden."

"All right then." Delbert met my gaze with a wary smile. "But only if I can be there as a musician rather than a guest." He pointed at the dulcimer leaning up against a stool near the hearth. "I'd feel more comfortable that way. I like to be doing something useful rather than just standing around."

"I won't argue with that," I said, as Sunny walked back across the room. "I'd love for you to play something at the wedding or the reception. Whichever you prefer."

"Really?" Sunny sat down beside me, her bright gaze fixed on Delbert's face. "You're going to play something at Amy's wedding, Mr. Frye? That would be splendid."

Delbert shrugged. "Good practice before my great-niece's ceremony, I guess."

Sunny's elbow banged into my arm. "Are Alison and Brad getting married?" She shot me a sharp look. "I hadn't heard that."

"So I'm told. Didn't think it was a secret," Delbert said, his expression sobering as he obviously remembered that Sunny and Brad had been involved in a relationship before Brad started dating Alison.

"I think that's wonderful." Sunny's beaming smile seemed to set Delbert at ease.

I shot her a sidelong look. I knew she didn't care that Brad was marrying Alison but suspected that she didn't like being the last to know about it.

"What did Brad have to say about our encounter in the woods?" I asked, hoping to divert her attention from this slight.

"He's sending deputies out to search for Dalbec. They definitely want to question him. Apparently, the sheriff's department has had some suspicions about the guy ever since he showed up in Taylorsford."

Ever since I told them a slightly altered tale about some stranger matching his description running into me and then tracking me down at the library, I thought, but decided not to voice this thought aloud.

298

"He's also sending someone to escort us to my car. They'll drive us around to the parking lot at the trailhead so we won't have to tramp back through the woods." Sunny yanked the elastic band from around her hair, freeing it from its ponytail. She flipped the loose fall of golden locks behind her shoulders. "Now, to get back to more interesting matters—what do you think you'll play at the wedding, Mr. Frye? Some real folk music, I hope."

"That's pretty much all I know," Delbert said. "That and a few classical pieces my wife liked. She used to take me to concerts when we lived in the city, long time ago." He rose to his feet to grab the dulcimer. "I can remember some of them, even though I don't know all the titles." Settling back in his chair, Delbert balanced the dulcimer in his arms. "Something like this."

Haunting strains rose from under his deft fingers. I leaned forward.

"I know that," I said. "It's Rachmaninoff's *Rhapsody on a Theme of Paganini*." I clapped my hands. "Please do play that at the wedding. That would be awesome."

As Delbert lifted his head, his smile broadened. "I loved it when I heard it at a concert with the missus, but then couldn't remember what it was called." He rose to his feet. "There's another one I also like to play, but it requires a little different instrument and technique." He crossed over to a shadowy corner of the room, returning with another dulcimer that he set on a stand. He held up two pieces of wood that resembled drumsticks, but with open filigree circles carved into the flattened ends. "Hammered dulcimer," he said, before launching into a piece I recognized almost immediately.

"Pachelbel's *Canon in D*." I sighed in delight as the beautiful music filled the cabin.

Sunny nudged me. "You haven't been happy about having the band play the traditional wedding march, but they didn't have anything else to offer. What if . . ."

I clasped her hands. "Great minds," I told her, before turning back to Delbert, who'd just concluded the piece. "That is gorgeous. Would you consider playing that while I walk down the aisle? We might have to mic you, since we'll be outside, but I think that would be so much better than the regular march that's always played at weddings. More fitting to the setting too."

Delbert's face flushed, but he offered me a warm smile. "I'd be honored," he said.

"You'll need to attend the rehearsal on Friday evening so we can practice walking down the aisle to the song," Sunny said. "But don't worry—I'll drive out here and personally escort you home."

"And there's a rehearsal dinner at Kurt Kendrick's estate after. Of course you'd be invited. We could even ask Kurt to have Mary attend, if that would make you feel more comfortable."

"Well." Delbert tapped one of the sticks against his chest. "I guess that'd be all right."

"Great," I said, thinking how delighted Richard would be with this turn of events. He'd been working on a choreographic piece featuring mountain tales and folk music for some time, so I was sure he'd be happy to have Delbert involved in the wedding.

And maybe it would even give him an opportunity to ask Delbert to participate in his new piece, I thought, knowing that Richard wanted to record tunes played by true folk musicians for his choreographic suite.

A knock sent Delbert scurrying to the door. He peered out the door before swinging it wide open.

"Your ride's here," he said, motioning toward the deputy who stood, hat in hand, on the porch.

I followed Sunny out, but not before making sure to shake Delbert's hand. "Thank you so much for sheltering us, and for agreeing to play at my wedding. I know your music will make the day extra special."

Delbert gripped my hand for a moment and looked at me, a more peaceful expression on his face than I'd ever seen there before. "I 'spect it's time I learned to rejoin the world," he said. "And I can't think of a better time than when two people in love pledge their lives to each other."

Knowing his story—how he'd lost his beloved wife and unborn child in an accident so many years ago—I impulsively leaned in and kissed him on the cheek.

He dropped my hand and stepped back, but as Sunny and I left the porch and walked out to the deputy's car, he called out a cheery "Good day" and a promise to see us Friday evening.

Chapter
Twenty-Six

The lengthening of the days as summer approached made it possible to hold our rehearsal at six in the evening on Friday, which worked with the minister's schedule as well as Kurt's plan to host a rehearsal dinner at Highview.

"To make up for the unfortunate ending of the party I held in April," he'd told us when we'd protested that he'd already done too much.

Knowing that the hosting duties would fall on my aunt if we didn't agree, Richard and I had acquiesced to this generous offer. After all, Kurt had a spacious dining room and could easily hire in a chef and waitstaff. There was no reason to burden Aunt Lydia. Even with help from me and my mom, handling the rehearsal dinner could be overwhelming, especially since she'd already agreed to provide cakes for the reception.

As I introduced my friend and bridesmaid Jessica Roman to everyone, I was delighted to see Sunny arrive with Delbert Frye and his dulcimers.

"Mr. Frye will be providing the music for our walk down the aisle," I told Jessica. "It's a little different than the usual wedding march, so I wanted us to have time to practice with him."

"Good idea," she said, fluffing her short hair, which was dyed the color of ripe persimmons.

With her bright hair, tattoo sleeve covering one arm, and multiple ear piercings, Jessica presented an even less typical image of a librarian than I did. She was shorter than me, with a curvaceous figure that she highlighted with tight tops, short skirts, tights, and boots. I knew that she didn't care that people thought she looked more like a rocker chick than someone who worked in an academic library. In fact, in library school we'd been labeled "least likely to be taken for librarians" by our peers, a nickname we both found amusing.

"Now I understand why Amy can't stop talking about you," she told Richard when he joined us at the arbor the florist had set up at the wooded edge of his backyard.

"Really?" Richard draped his arm around my shoulders. "You think maybe she's a little bit in love with me?"

Jessica snorted. "I expect you know she's crazy about you. Which is probably for the best, seeing as how you're getting married tomorrow."

"Definitely a good thing," Richard said with a grin.

I nudged him with my elbow. "As long as you feel the same."

"Pretty sure I can promise that." He pulled me close. "Among other things."

I smiled and allowed my gaze to roam the backyard. Although the event planner's crew was waiting until the next morning to set up the chairs and a runner, they had marked the center path with stakes so that we'd be able to practice walking down the aisle. At both ends of the aisle, the florist had placed standing urns that would be filled with flower arrangements before the wedding.

"I'm glad we decided to hold the ceremony here," I said. "I don't think any space could be prettier."

"And the weather seems like it will cooperate. You lucked out with that," Jessica said.

"I lucked out with a lot of things," I said, slipping my arm around Richard's waist.

Jessica looked Richard up and down. "Obviously."

"He's not just a pretty face either." I wrinkled my nose as Richard looked down at me in mock dismay.

"Glad to know I'm not simply arm candy," he said, tapping my nose with one finger.

"Although you fulfill that requirement quite well." Jessica gave him a wink. "But don't mind me. I appreciate good-looking people on an artistic level, but I'm really no threat."

"Not into guys?" Richard asked with a lift of his eyebrows.

"Not into anyone. Not that way." Jessica held out her right hand, displaying a black ring on her middle finger. "I may dress a little provocatively, but it's all in fun. I'm actually asexual." She fixed Richard with a speculative stare. "Hope that's not TMI, but

I thought I'd better share before you try to fix me up with one of your groomsmen or something."

"No worries. I only have one groomsman, and he's gay, and my best man is actually a straight woman, so you can rest easy."

Richard's genuine smile seemed to relax Jessica, who gave a thumbs-up gesture before dropping her hand. "Good to know. And thanks for not expressing shock or confusion."

"Easy enough. I don't really have any," Richard said. "You have to remember, I work with a wide variety of artists, including dancers, designers, and musicians. If I was going to be shocked by anything, it would've happened many years ago. Besides, I have no interest in telling other people how to live their own lives."

"That's right, you're a choreographer." Jessica widened her brown eyes. "I bet you've planned some sort of fabulous grooms-men dance for the reception."

Richard shook his head. "Again, I don't have a whole crew. But I might have a little something planned with my best man—excuse me, best woman."

"His dancing partner," I told Jessica. "I think I've mentioned her before."

"The gorgeous goddess over there?" Jessica pointed toward an area that bordered a rose-draped fence.

Following her gaze, I noticed that Karla was providing instructions to a small crew setting up a portable dance floor next to the risers where the band would be seated.

Karla looked up and waved. "Almost done here," she called out, as Aunt Lydia led the minister through the rose vine–covered arch that separated her garden from Richard's yard.

"Good, 'cause I think we're ready to start," I said, raising my voice so Karla and the other people milling about could hear me.

Giving me a little nod, Jessica jogged over to where Sunny was assisting Delbert with setting up the stand for his hammered dulcimer.

I slid out from under Richard's arm and tapped him on the chest. "I need to join Sunny and Jessica and head over to Aunt Lydia's."

"And I need to wait here. I know." Richard's expression grew solemn as he studied my face for a moment. "Tomorrow it will be the real deal," he said softly, before leaning in press a kiss against my lips.

"I know. And I'm a little scared too," I replied, before returning his kiss. "But I want this," I added in a whisper. "More than anything."

"Me too." Richard brushed a lock of my hair behind my ear. "So let's get this rehearsal over with and move one step closer to the real thing."

I gave him another kiss before breaking away and crossing the yard to join Sunny and Jessica.

My mom and dad were waiting on Aunt Lydia's back porch. "We're starting here, right?" Dad asked, as Sunny opened the door.

"You and I are. I'm getting ready here, along with Sunny and Jessica, and we'll be walking into Richard's yard through the archway in the fence between the two houses. Richard and Karla and Scott will dress at his house so they can walk up to the arbor from his back porch." I glanced over at my mom. "You and Aunt Lydia will need to leave here a little earlier, so you can be seated before the music starts."

"What about Fiona and Jim?" Mom asked, as Aunt Lydia entered from the hall.

"They just drove up," my aunt said. "Looked to me like they were confused about where they were supposed to be, so I sent Hugh out to lead them around to Richard's backyard."

"I'm glad Hugh and Walt offered to act as ushers, since that was something I forgot," I said with an apologetic smile. "I guess I thought everyone would wander in and sit down wherever, but the planner informed me that we really should have close family members escorted to their seats."

Mom bustled over and gave me a quick hug. "It'll all work out," she said, with a quick glance at my father. "Now, Lydia and I had better head next door and make sure the Muirs are properly situated, among other things."

Things progressed smoothly after that. As arranged with Sunny earlier, Delbert played a loud flourish at the end of his version of Rachmaninoff's *Rhapsody on a Theme of Paganini*, alerting Sunny and Jessica that he was about to launch into Pachelbel's *Canon in D*.

We rehearsed the procession a few times, coached by the minister, who suggested that we slow our steps to better match the music. As Richard and I held hands under the arbor, listening to the minister's instructions as to what would happen during each portion of the ceremony, I sneaked a glance out at the small group of people standing in the neatly trimmed yard.

My dad's eyes were glistening with unshed tears, while my mom shared happy glances with my aunt. *They're all going to cry*

307

tomorrow, I thought. *Well, maybe not Aunt Lydia, although Hugh looks like he's trying hard to maintain his composure. And, of course, not Richard's parents. Jim Muir just looks pained, like he'd rather be anywhere else. But Fiona . . .*

I lowered my lashes to shadow my eyes and shot another quick glance at Richard's mother, confirming my earlier suspicion that she actually looked pleased.

Maybe she really is happy about our marriage. The thought made me promise to engage her in a real conversation over dinner.

When we concluded the rehearsal, Richard rounded up everyone to arrange for carpooling and hand out directions to Highview.

"You go on, since you're going to drive your parents. I'll be along a little later," I told him, as most of the rest of the group headed for their vehicles. "I want to freshen up and maybe change into something a little nicer." I swept my hand through the air, indicating my plain cotton slacks and top. "This was fine for the rehearsal, but your mother and Aunt Lydia are so decked out . . ."

Richard lips twitched into a smile. "Feeling underdressed? I can understand that, since my mom is in her pearls, although I think you look fine."

"Regardless, I should probably make more of an effort. I am the bride," I said, with a smile I hoped hid my real agenda. I actually wanted one more chance to practice the rumba with Karla, who'd agreed to run through the dance one last time before we drove to Kurt's house.

"All right. But how are you getting to the dinner? With Lydia and Hugh? Or Sunny?"

"No, Lydia and Hugh are riding with Mom and Dad, and Sunny is driving Delbert so she can transport him and his instruments safely home after the dinner," I said, tossing this off with a glance over at Sunny, who was in on the deception. "Karla's riding with me."

"Okay. I'll see you there, then. Don't be too late." Richard traced the line of my jaw with one finger. "We can't start without you."

"I promise not to take too much time. But do go ahead with cocktails and hors d'oeuvres as soon as you arrive. I'm sure Kurt will insist on that, and I don't mind." I tipped my head to look up at him. "I should probably skip the drinks before dinner anyway. A hangover tomorrow would not be good, for my appearance as well as my head."

Richard gave me a kiss before striding off to join his parents, who were hovering near his car.

As soon as everyone left, Karla and I headed into Aunt Lydia's house, where I quickly changed into my poppy-print sundress and touched up my lipstick and mascara.

We planned to rehearse, without music, just running through the steps, but before I could join Karla on the back porch, the landline phone in the hall rang.

"Hi, sorry to bother you," Brad Tucker said as soon as I answered. "I know you're probably busy with wedding stuff, and I did try to reach you earlier on your cell phone . . ."

"It's still broken, and I haven't gotten a replacement yet." I waved at Karla, who'd poked her head around the door that led onto the back porch. Seeing me on the phone, she placed a finger to her lips and backed off.

"Oh, right. Well, that brings me to the reason I wanted to call. Since you gave me a good tip about Honor Bryant fleeing

Taylorsford, I felt you should know that we have a lead on her whereabouts. Some of my colleagues in Maryland tracked her to a hotel in Baltimore. They should have her in custody soon, which means we'll be able to question her more thoroughly."

"And she's a more likely suspect now, I take it?"

"Unfortunately, yes. You know she apparently had addiction problems in the past."

"You were the one who told me that."

"Right. Well, now someone on Scott's team has uncovered the fact that she actually did owe quite a bit of money to one of Esmerelda's dealers. Apparently, some informant spilled that info just today."

"So she really could've been forced to do something?" My mind raced as I remembered Honor carrying that mug at the party, as well as the mud on her boots. Perhaps she'd even been the one to harvest the aconite used to poison her boss and then deliver it to him in a mug of cognac.

"Could be. Which is why we definitely need to talk to her."

"Interrogate her, you mean." I twisted the phone cord around my wrist.

"Yes." Brad's voice had taken on the cool, professional tone he always used when seriously discussing a case.

"What about that Lance Dalbec guy?" I unwound the phone cord and glanced at my watch. Although I was anxious to hear more news on the Selvaggio case, I didn't want to be late to my own rehearsal dinner. "I'm not sure he wasn't also part of the murder in some way."

"I agree he may have been involved, but unfortunately he seems to have skipped town as well. At least, we haven't been able to track him down yet."

"That's too bad." My fingers clenched the receiver. "I don't trust the guy, especially where Kurt Kendrick is concerned. Maybe you should keep an eye on Highview for a few days."

"Already thought of that. Which was another reason for my call. I know Kendrick is hosting your rehearsal dinner tonight and wanted to give you a heads-up. Don't be alarmed if you observe some departmental presence in the area. We're trying to keep our surveillance on the down low, so I hope none of the guests actually notice anything, but if they do . . ."

"Just tell them that it's part of the ongoing investigation into Oscar Selvaggio's death? Understood, Chief Deputy, sir."

"Brad will do," he replied, in a lighter tone. "Now I should let you go. I expect you need to get to that dinner."

"I do, but thanks for the heads-up," I said, before telling him good-bye.

"See you tomorrow, almost Mrs. Muir," he added, before hanging up.

I hurried back to the porch, where I told Karla that we really didn't have time to rehearse and would need to just hope for the best.

"You'll do fine," she told me, while I locked up behind us before leading her to the car I shared with my aunt. "And just remember, tomorrow you'll have a partner you can rely on."

As I slid into the driver's seat, I thought about her words, realizing how accurate they were.

And not just for one dance, I thought as a wave of happiness swept over me.

Chapter
Twenty-Seven

When we reached Highview, the circular parking lot was already filled with vehicles, so I took the narrow driveway that led to a smaller lot and detached garage behind the house.

"I don't think Kurt will mind if we park here," I said. "Especially since I doubt he'll need to go anywhere until after we leave."

Telling Karla to circle around to the front door while I locked the car, I took the opportunity to survey Kurt's backyard and woods. I didn't see any sheriff's department deputies lurking about, but that didn't surprise me. I assumed they'd probably keep their distance.

They might not even come onto his property, I thought, as I dropped my keys into the pocket of my white linen jacket. *Probably not, come to think of it. I bet they're parked farther up the road. Just keeping tabs on who's coming and going from there.*

A flash of movement in the trees caught my eye. Maybe it was one of Brad's deputies after all. Strolling to the edge of the woods, I peered into the shadowed undergrowth.

I didn't see an officer but did notice something odd—what looked like a hand poking through a small window in a stone outbuilding. As it was almost obscured by the thick growth of shrubs and trees, I hadn't realized there was another building in the woods behind the house until now.

That can't be a person, I thought, fumbling in my other jacket pocket until I realized that I still didn't have a cell phone. With this week's busy schedule, I hadn't bothered to get mine replaced yet. It didn't seem critical—I could simply use Richard's phone when were in Italy for our honeymoon.

Convinced that my eyes were just playing tricks on me, I decided I'd simply call Brad once I got inside the house. Turning around to head for the front door, I slammed straight into someone's chest.

Lifting my head, I met the heavy-lidded gaze of Lance Dalbec.

"Pity," he said, gripping one of my upper arms with fingers as strong as steel clamps. "You weren't meant to be part of all this, but now . . ." He swung the switchblade he was holding in his free hand through the air.

I opened my mouth, but Dalbec cut me off before I could scream.

"None of that," he said, giving me a rough shake. "Not if you want your friend to live."

"No phone," I managed to squeak out as he poked at my jacket pocket with the handle of the knife. "And what friend?"

"Old-lady dancer."

"Adele Tourneau?"

"That's the one." Dalbec spun me around, still holding me tight. "I'm afraid you'll have to join her. Don't want you raising any alarms at this point." He shoved me forward, forcing me to walk into the woods.

"My other friend just went inside. She'll expect me to have followed right behind her," I said, fighting the tremor in my voice. "Someone's bound to come looking for me soon."

"Unfortunately for you, your tall friend will have been stopped at the front door." Dalbec tightened his grip on my arm while he unlocked the shiny padlock fastened through an older metal clasp on the weathered wooden door. "We have someone posted there who will've told your friend that everyone in the house had better stay inside and avoid contacting the authorities if they hope to see Ms. Tourneau alive again." Dalbec flashed me a humorless smile as he yanked the stiff door open. "They're to sit tight and wait for our next message."

"But there's a back door, you know," I said, my thoughts jumbled as I attempted to process this turn of events. It was obvious that Dalbec was working with at least one other person, and that they planned to use Adele, and now me, as hostages in order to lure someone from the house out into the woods. Recalling Dalbec's previous run-in with Kurt, I suspected that the art dealer was their target.

"Someone's keeping an eye out from the woods, so we've got that covered," Dalbec said.

I considered kicking him in the shins but remembered the knife. "Who's this *we*, and why are you holding Adele?"

"None of your business," Dalbec said as he shoved me inside. "Just be quiet and maybe you and Ms. Tourneau will live through this," he added, before slamming the door.

I jiggled the latch, but he'd already fastened the padlock. The door rattled but wouldn't open beyond the merest crack. Wiping my damp hands on my jacket, I turned around.

"Amy! Oh my dear, how did you end up in here?" Adele's voice rose up from one of the shadowy corners of the small room.

"The real question is, how did you?" It took a moment for my eyes to adjust to the dim light. As I picked my way across the broken flagstones paving the floor, I almost tripped over a lip of stone that surrounded a circular pit.

Not this again, I thought, averting my eyes from the black depths of the stone circle. It appeared that this was an old well house, complete with a narrow runoff trough that led to a metal grate in the far wall.

Adele was huddled next to the grate, her fingers scraping over the perforated metal. "I thought if I could pull this free or push it out . . ."

I knelt down in front of her. "Neither of us can fit through that opening."

"But maybe someone could hear us shout, when they search the woods. As I'm sure they will, eventually." Adele looked up at me, her eyes glistening with fear. "All the other windows are too high up, except that one at the front."

She was right. The narrow windows that pierced three of the stone walls were placed right below the wooden rafters. Only the window in the front wall was lower. Unfortunately, it was still situated above my head. It could be reached only if I stood on

315

tiptoe, and even then, I could probably only stick my hand through the small opening and wave, as Adele had done. It was too high for me to look out, even if I stretched as tall as possible.

"I didn't mean to involve you or anyone else in this," Adele said. "I just thought if anyone saw my hand waving through the window, they'd immediately call the police."

"Sadly, I don't have a phone on me right now." I examined Adele with a critical eye, noting the bruise discoloring one of her delicate cheekbones. Her hair had tumbled out of her bun to hang about her face like skeins of pale silk thread. "I don't think that grate is moving. Looks like the screws are rusted shut. The front window is probably a better bet." I helped her to her feet. "After all, I could see your hand poking through, all the way from the back driveway. We could try that again."

Adele rested her slight weight against me before straightening. "I doubt that will work a second time. That awful man will see it now. I think he's keeping a watch out front."

"You don't know him?" I asked as I moved to the center of the room.

"No. I mean, he looks a little familiar, but I'm sure we've never met. Do you?"

"Only slightly. His name is Lance Dalbec. He says he's some sort of art broker, but I'm not sure that's true, even though he does appear to know Kurt. But I've heard . . ." I hesitated, remembering I probably shouldn't share this privileged information, entrusted to me by Brad, with someone who was still a suspect. "Anyway, I'm not sure that's his real profession or name."

"You mean he may be a criminal? I had assumed that already." Adele brushed off some damp bits of mortar clinging to her black dinner dress. "I must look a fright."

"No worse than me," I said, glancing down at my jacket, now stained with mildew where I'd wiped my hands. "But that really isn't important. What I want to know is—how and why were you brought here?"

"That man—Lance Dalbec or whoever he is—grabbed me when I stopped at one of the minimarts outside of Taylorsford. I was only inside for a minute, buying a bottle of water. He was waiting for me as soon as I stepped back outside, so I suspect he must've followed me all the way from the city." Adele shoved her tangled hair behind her slender shoulders. "He came up beside me, grabbed my arm, and told me he had a knife. He claimed he'd use it if I screamed or otherwise attempted to escape."

"Then he drove you here?"

"Not directly. He didn't use Kurt's driveway. He turned down a dirt road—a path, really—somewhere farther up and then forced me to hike through the woods to this spot." Adele slid a lace-edged cotton handkerchief from the pocket of her dress and dabbed at the perspiration beading her upper lip. "There was a trail, even though it was terribly overgrown."

"He must've scouted that out ahead of time." I glanced down at her feet. Her black leather pumps were gouged and scratched, and one shoe was missing a heel. "But why did he kidnap you, of all people? Did he say?"

Adele shook her head. "He didn't talk much. Just made some obscure comment about finally getting revenge for some wrong committed in the past."

"Not by you, surely," I said, before I remembered Fred's revelation about Adele's attempted murder of Oscar Selvaggio. But why

Dalbec would want to punish Adele for such a thing was a mystery. *Unless . . .*

"You said Dalbec looked familiar. Do you remember where you might have seen him?"

"Not him, exactly." Adele crumpled the handkerchief between her fingers. "There was someone once, but that was so long ago."

"Like forty-five years or so ago?"

"Yes," she said, her eyes glazed as if she was staring at memories instead of me. "But that man already had a few years on me, and this one looks like he's only in his fifties. So it couldn't be the same man."

"It could be his son, perhaps? Or some other close relative?"

"I suppose." Adele lowered her head until I couldn't see her eyes. "I saw that other man once or twice, when I was involved in a court case. He was in the gallery, sitting with some rather nondescript woman, during part of the proceedings. I only remembered him because he did have such a striking appearance. Pale and skeletal, with dark hair and light eyes, just like our captor."

"That must've been during the suit you brought against Oscar Selvaggio because you felt his actions contributed to your father's death." I softened my tone when Adele shot me a startled expression. "I read about your case when I was doing research for the sheriff's office."

Adele wiped the dampness from her eyes with her handkerchief. "His reckless actions did cause Dad's death. I know they did. Oscar Selvaggio sold my father illegal property, and when Dad tried to get an insurance appraisal on the item, he was caught up in a criminal case. As an honorable man, it simply crushed him."

"From what I've read, he had a heart attack. That was a natural death . . ."

"But brought on by the unbearable stress he was under. He'd always been healthy before that. Before his reputation was destroyed." Adele squared her shoulders in a dramatic movement that betrayed her dance training. "I encouraged my siblings to join me in a civil suit against Selvaggio, but it was later dismissed for lack of evidence."

"I know, and I'm sorry." I examined her for a moment. "I'm still curious, though. Why were you so jumpy when I saw you fixing that drink at the party, and why were you out tramping through the woods right around the time Oscar Selvaggio was killed?"

Adele's face crumpled like old paper. "The drink was for Kurt. Sort of a bribe, I suppose. I wanted to ask him for another donation to one of my dance charities, and I thought I should butter him up beforehand." She sniffed. "I hate doing that It's the worst part of charity work, but inevitable, I'm afraid. And honestly, right before you saw me with the drink, I'd just had an unpleasant encounter with Selvaggio."

"He grabbed you, like I heard?"

She cast me an apologetic look. "I'm afraid I lied to you about that before. But I had provoked him, I'm afraid. I was terribly rude. It was even worse because we'd already argued before the party . . ."

"When you ran into each other at the bed-and-breakfast?" I held up my hands. "Someone saw you and told me about it."

"Yes. I totally lost it during that first encounter, so having another fight at the party just felt"—Adele pressed one hand to her heart—"so cheap and tawdry. I wasn't being the person I wanted to be, the person I'd fought so hard to become. So I decided I had to apologize."

"Which is why you went out looking for Mr. Selvaggio at the party?"

Adele nodded. "I saw him rush outside. I didn't follow immediately, but he looked so unwell that I thought I should see what was wrong. And apologize, of course. It seemed like the right time to do that, when maybe I could help him or something."

"But you never saw him?"

"No. I suppose he'd headed directly for that shed, for some type of rendezvous or something. Anyway, I checked the area behind the house, but"—she shrugged—"saw nothing."

That explained her appearance in the woods, and the drink, but not her apparent recognition of Lance Dalbec. "Getting back to our captor, let's assume it was his father in the courtroom . . ."

Adele's eyes narrowed as she stuffed her handkerchief back into her pocket. "But why?"

"I don't know. Maybe Dalbec's father was somehow involved with Selvaggio and was in the courtroom to keep tabs on the proceedings or protect his interests or something." Seeing Adele's haunted eyes, I decided to go ahead and share more. "Our chief deputy, Brad Tucker, told me that Dalbec has a questionable past. Maybe his dad did too."

"Perhaps. But it still doesn't make any sense. I never did anything to Mr. Dalbec, or the man who was possibly his father. If he was a thief who was involved with Selvaggio in selling stolen goods to my dad, how could I have ever done him any wrong? It's more likely that he was involved in harming me." Adele pressed her hands to her temples. "I'm sorry, but I don't see the connection."

"Neither do I, but there must be one." I looked her over. "You honestly don't have any idea why you were abducted?"

"I just thought it might be as bait." Adele dropped her hands and rubbed her bare forearms, as if warding off a chill. "Dalbec did mention something about Kurt protecting me. I think he plans to lure Kurt out here by threatening me with harm."

"Which would work." I took a deep breath before continuing. "Kurt's done it before, you know. Stepped in to save you. Back around the same time as your court case."

Adele's forehead creased as she stared at me. "What do you mean? Kurt has been a generous benefactor in terms of supporting my dance charities, but I wouldn't call that protecting me, exactly. And we didn't actually meet until a few years after the court case."

It was too late to back away from the revelations now. I met Adele's puzzled expression without faltering. "I've been told that Kurt was the anonymous donor who provided you with the best possible legal help, among other things, when you tried to kill Oscar Selvaggio for what he'd done to your father."

Adele took two stumbling steps backward. "What? How could you know such a thing?"

"Research. And some information from the authorities. As I said, I've been assisting them with gathering information related to the recent murder of Selvaggio. And"—I clenched my hands until my fingernails dug into my palms—"Kurt himself told me some of this."

"Why would he do such a thing? He didn't even know me."

I took a deep breath before speaking again. "Don't misunderstand—it wasn't all about you. I believe Kurt did want to help you, but he had an ulterior motive. One that involved my late uncle Andrew Talbot."

Adele pressed her palm to her forehead. "I'm so confused. What does your uncle have to do with anything?"

Stepping forward, I laid my hand on her arm, tightening my grip as she wobbled when I explained the connection between Kurt, Andrew, and the Kelmscott Chaucer. "You see, it wasn't really Oscar Selvaggio who sold your father that copy of the Kelmscott Chaucer. He was involved, and he did cover up the truth when Kurt pressured him to do so, but he wasn't the real instigator of the sale."

"Kurt helped me in order to cover up his own deeds, then," Adele said, her tone icy. "As an expiation of some of his sins, I suppose."

"Partially." I forced myself to hold her intent gaze without faltering. "But it was really because of my uncle's involvement. I think Kurt would've taken the rap if it had only involved him, but you see . . ."

"He loved Andrew? I knew there was someone, sometime in his life. There had to be." Adele's expression softened. "He betrayed himself once, when he didn't think I was looking. He was watching a particularly beautiful performance by Richard and Karla.

The piece was about loss—specifically losing a loved one. I glanced over at Kurt's face and couldn't help but notice this look, like he'd lost something, or someone, he'd treasured more than life." Adele straightened her shoulders, casting off my steadying hand. "I know that look. I should. I've seen it in my mirror often enough."

"You're right, he loved my uncle. I think he still does, in a way. But I also know he feels sorry for having contributed to the circumstances that thrust your family into such a horrible mess."

"He helped me avoid jail. I suppose that's something," Adele said, thoughtfully. "And I imagine it's one of the reasons he'd do almost anything to protect me now. Maybe Dalbec knows about Kurt's involvement in selling my dad that awful book and chose me as a hostage for that very reason."

"Kurt undoubtedly feels he owes you." I frowned. "Not long ago, Dalbec came to Highview and attacked Kurt. I suspect he may have wanted to kill him but couldn't manage it then."

Adele's eyes widened. "You think he plans to do so now, by luring Kurt out here?"

"With us as bait. I bet Dalbec plans to stab him and then disappear before anyone realizes what's happened. Dalbec could send a message for him to come alone or else, and Kurt would agree."

"To keep us safe."

"Right." I gnawed on the inside of my cheek. "Dalbec has a getaway car he can reach by escaping through the woods. But only we know that, and by the time we're freed, it might be too late to catch him."

"And we're stuck in here, unable to see anything," Adele said in a defeated tone. "All we'll have is our suppositions if Dalbec does kill Kurt. We can't be true eyewitnesses, which means he could get away with it."

I crossed to the front wall. "Not if we can find a way to see out that window. That's crucial. And not just to see what happens, but also to warn Kurt before he gets too close."

Glancing over at the well, I considered my options. If I climbed onto the rim of stones, I might be able to gain enough height to peer through the front window. Unfortunately, that meant balancing on a narrow ledge of mossy stone, and I knew the slippery surface could prove treacherous. One wrong step could send me plummeting into the darkness yawning below. Not a prospect I relished, especially with my past history.

But I had to try. I didn't want Kurt Kendrick to be harmed while protecting me.

I smiled grimly as I kicked off my shoes. I'd never been sure how I felt about the enigmatic art dealer. Sometimes he seemed like family, sometimes an adversary. Sometimes I thought he was my guardian angel, and sometimes I didn't trust him at all.

But whatever my feelings, I had to admit that the last thing I wanted was for him to die.

Chapter
Twenty-Eight

With Adele providing a steadying hand to help me balance on the rim of the well, I was able to lean forward and grip the iron bars that formed a grille over the open window. Looking out, I caught the glint of sunlight flashing off a knife blade as Dalbec lifted his hand at the thud of approaching footsteps.

It was Kurt, strolling up to the other man with a nonchalance belied by the stoniness of his expression.

"Kurt, be careful!" I shouted, before Dalbec told me to shut up if I wanted to live.

"That seems unnecessarily rude," Kurt said, as he faced off with Dalbec. "Although I don't suppose good manners are really your strong suit."

"You can shut your trap too," Dalbec said, slicing his knife through the air. "I'm not alone in this, you know. I can signal for backup any time. So don't think you have an advantage."

Kurt's predator smile held no humor. "I'm not surprised you aren't alone in this. You couldn't manage to kill me by yourself last time, so . . ." He shrugged his broad shoulders.

"Don't flatter yourself, old man. I would've finished you off that day if I hadn't heard someone at the door. I only left you alive because I'm not stupid enough to risk getting caught in the act."

"Stupid enough to try again, though, after I've already informed the authorities about your first attack." Kurt casually adjusted the cuffs of the lavender shirt he was wearing under his ivory cotton sweater. "I hope you have a solid getaway plan, since you are now definitely on their radar."

"Don't worry, they won't catch me." Dalbec pointed the tip of the knife at Kurt. "Anyway, you'll never know one way or the other, as I'm afraid you're going to be quite dead soon."

Kurt's bushy white eyebrows arched. "You intend to stab me? I doubt you can actually overpower me with that little penknife."

"Like I said, I have backup. And they have a gun. But I want to give this method a try first. Seems only fitting, since you murdered my father with a knife."

"Murdered? Not quite. It was self-defense, after he came at me during what should've been a civil conversation."

"Don't give me that. You sought him out to strong-arm him into following your demands."

"If you mean to stop him from selling drugs to my friend, Andrew Talbot, then you're correct." Kurt's sardonic expression morphed into a fierce glare. "I warned your father, several times, before I attempted to convince him by more . . . physical means."

"Convince him to do what? Not pursue his own business interests? Which was really hypocritical, since you sold drugs yourself."

"I did, although unlike you and those I suspect you're now in league with, I no longer do so. But even back then I never tried to push a recovering addict to resume his or her habit." Kurt's hands, hanging at his sides, clenched into fists. "Andrew was finally clean. He desperately wanted to stay that way, but unfortunately, he was still too fragile to resist your father's blatant temptation. Offering him a free taste to get him hooked again or whatever else it took—despicable."

Kurt spat out this last word with such vehemence that Dalbec took a step back. "So because your friend was so weak willed, you decided to kill my dad in cold blood. Leaving me fatherless at age eight, and plunging my mom and me into poverty."

"As I said, I didn't plan to kill your father. But when he lunged at me with a knife"—Kurt shrugged again—"what could I do except turn it back on him? Anyway, I know for a fact that he'd already abandoned you and your mother, so don't give me the grieving-son act. He'd been living with another woman for a couple of years before his death. The very woman I suspect you're partnering with in this little escapade."

"Yeah, well, don't think you're going to throw me off my game with that news. I know all about Esmerelda and my dad. She's already explained the whole situation to me."

"Quite convincingly, I imagine. She always had a gift for twisting words to her advantage." Kurt looked Dalbec up and down. "What did she tell you? That they were just business partners and he only got in the drug game to make the money for his family?"

"It's the truth," Dalbec said, but I noticed the hand gripping the knife wavering slightly.

"If you say so. At any rate, I suppose I can imagine why you'd want to kill me, for revenge if nothing else. But why'd you dispatch Oscar Selvaggio? He wasn't mixed up in your father's death."

Lance Dalbec sneered. "Shows what you know. I didn't kill that thief. Which he was, so don't try to paint him as some legitimate businessman. He sold stolen artwork to plenty of people without a qualm."

"Including your partner? That does explain a few things." Kurt unclenched his fingers and shook out his hands. "Foolish old Oscar. I knew he dealt in items with questionable provenances, but to sell them to someone like Esmerelda was a dangerous proposition. I assume that's why she wanted him dead?"

"Of course, but like I said, I didn't kill him. She had someone else lined up for that little job."

Glancing down at Adele, I said, "Well, that clinches it. Given all the facts, I think it had to be Honor Bryant."

She tightened her steadying grip on my leg. "Why do you say that?"

"Brad Tucker told me that Honor had a drug problem in the past and owed Esmerelda, or at least one of her dealers, a lot of money. I expect they used that fact to blackmail her into poisoning Mr. Selvaggio."

Adele shivered. "That poor girl, driven to such extremes. And yes, I hated the man, but I wouldn't have wished that fate on him.

Even if I did try to shoot him that one time." She looked up at me with an abashed expression. "I wouldn't have gone through with it, I swear. I wasn't in my right mind at the time, but even so, I really just wanted to frighten him."

"I know," I said, ashamed I'd ever thought of her as a possible murderer. "Wait—I think Kurt's asking Dalbec to prove that we're okay."

"If you bring them out, unharmed, I will turn myself over to you," Kurt said.

Dalbec snorted. "Like I trust anything you say."

"I think you'll have to, if you want your revenge. Let Amy and Adele go, and you can have me without a fight." Kurt's tone was as unyielding as granite. "Or we can wait until the sheriff's deputies arrive, which I suspect they will, sooner rather than later. I know they're watching the estate for any strange occurrences, if only from afar. I imagine if I were to shout loud enough . . ."

"All right, I'll bring them out. But if you move one inch, or make any sound, at least one of them will die." Dalbec pantomimed the slice of his knife across a throat.

Kurt crossed his arms over his chest. "Understood."

"Help me down," I said to Adele, slipping on my shoes as the padlock rattled.

Dalbec threw open the door and marched in. Grabbing Adele by the arm, he shot me a warning look. "Try to run or scream or anything like that and I cut her. Get it?" He pressed the knife against Adele's throat.

I swallowed back an epithet and nodded.

"You stay close," he told me as he hustled Adele outside.

The glare of the sunlight made me blink as we walked out of the woods to face Kurt. "Sorry," I mouthed at him.

He gave me a warning shake of his head. "Now let them go," he told Dalbec.

"Not until you walk into the well house."

Kurt dropped his arms to his sides. "That isn't the deal. How will I know that you won't harm them once you lock me in?"

"You won't. But it's really their only chance, I'm afraid." Dalbec slid the knife across Adele's bare neck—not cutting deep, but still raising a thread of blood.

"Lower your blade first." The naked anger in Kurt's face was something I'd seen only once or twice before. It was just as terrifying this time.

"Walk in that building and close the door behind you. I'll let these two go before I deal with you."

"No you won't," said another voice.

I cast a quick glance at the edge of the woods, where a woman stood, surveying the scene.

It was Cynthia Rogers. Puzzled over why she'd been lurking in the woods, I debated whether I should shout a plea for her to run and call for help, but the knife at Adele's throat silenced me.

And, I thought, as realization widened my eyes, *Dalbec said his partner was watching from the woods . . .*

And Cynthia Rogers is the right age to have been a contemporary of Kurt back in the '60s. I swallowed back a hysterical bark of laughter as I realized the truth.

Cynthia Rogers—the talkative, inquisitive, but pleasant tourist—*was* Esmerelda.

"Ah, there you are," Kurt said, his expression once again filled with sardonic humor. "I wondered when you'd show up."

I looked from him to the gray-haired woman and back again. "She's Esmerelda, isn't she?" I said, before I could stop myself.

"Yes, although I didn't immediately recognize her when she showed up in Taylorsford. Too many years have passed, and the alteration in her appearance . . ."

"I cut my hair," Cynthia Rogers, aka Esmerelda, said, strolling forward until she was standing in front of Lance Dalbec, Adele, and me, directly facing Kurt.

"I think there are a few other changes," Kurt said, his bantering tone at odds with the cold fury in his eyes. "But I suppose we've all grown older, if not wiser."

"Indeed we have, although you seem remarkably well preserved, Karl." Esmerelda casually lifted her right hand, as if in greeting.

A very dangerous greeting, I thought, as I realized that she was holding a gun. I sucked in a breath as Kurt gave the weapon a cursory glance before focusing back on the older woman's face.

"Have you informed your little lieutenant here of your real intentions, or were you saving that as a surprise?" Kurt asked.

"What do you mean?" Dalbec lowered the knife but kept a tight grip on Adele. "What's he talking about, Ez?"

"Oh, I think Karl, excuse me, Kurt, is just trying to stir the pot," the woman who went by the street name Esmerelda said.

"Not really," Kurt said. "I just think that Mr. Dalbec might want to know that you intend to kill all of us and frame him for the murders. Which won't really matter, I suppose, since he'll be dead."

"What an incredibly difficult person you are." Esmerelda stepped forward, her gun aimed directly at Kurt's chest. "Always have been, haven't you? First, interfering in my dealing back in the day . . ."

"That was just a business rivalry," Kurt said.

"I could allow that. But killing my partner was a step too far."

"He tried to stab me. I was just defending myself." Kurt shot a glance over Esmerelda's shoulder, catching Lance Dalbec's eye. "And let's be honest—you were really upset because he was your lover. You could always find another partner. But I suppose even you might have cared about someone enough to be hurt by their death."

"He was the only man I ever loved!" The words exploded from Esmerelda's lips.

"You should've thought of that before you sent him to kill me. I know it was your call. He admitted that much before he died."

Esmerelda's string of words, damning Kurt with a variety of colorful epithets, was interrupted by a short, stocky man who'd jogged around from the front of the house. "You okay here?" he asked.

"Everything's under control," Esmerelda said. "I hope the same can be said for all those people in the house."

"They've been warned not to come out if they want their friends to live," the man said, with a quick glance at Adele and me. "What now?"

Esmerelda waved him aside. "You go. Cut through the woods and find our cars and make sure they're fired up, ready for a quick getaway. Lance and I can handle this."

The stocky man gave her what almost looked like a salute before dashing off into the woods.

"You really think no one inside called the authorities?" Kurt said, his tone mild as milk.

"I expect they may have by this point. Which is why I'm going to have to dispatch all of you more quickly than I planned." Esmerelda raised the gun. "Starting with you. Time for the Viking to fall. No more interfering in my affairs. And no more assisting the feds with their feeble attempts to capture me."

Kurt flashed a wolfish grin. "If only I could've seen that through, I would die a happy man."

"Now you'll just die, happy or not," Esmerelda said grimly.

I glanced at Lance Dalbec and Adele. Obviously confused by this turn of events, he'd lowered the knife. I caught Adele's eye. "Try," I mouthed at her.

She lowered her eyelids in silent acknowledgment. Lifting one leg in movement that exuded strength as well as grace, she kicked to the side before swinging her leg back in a circular motion that slammed her foot into Dalbec's legs.

A dance movement I'd seen Richard execute many times before, although not with quite the same results.

Dalbec tumbled forward, falling so fast that he didn't have time to adjust his grip on the knife. Mixed in with the thud as he hit the ground was the sickening sound of a blade sinking into flesh and bone.

I didn't wait to see if Dalbec was dead or alive, just flung myself at Esmerelda's back.

She wasn't a large woman, and she was no longer young. Only the gun gave her power over us, and that was torn from her fingers when I tackled her. It skidded across the pavement, landing at Kurt's feet.

He snatched it up in one smooth scoop and took aim at Esmerelda, who had rolled away from me but was still sprawled across the ground.

"Get up, Amy, and move behind me," Kurt commanded. "You too, Adele."

Adele, walking past the prone figure of Lance Dalbec, who was clutching his stomach and groaning, gave him another little kick.

"Good work," Kurt said, as we circled around to stand behind him. He shot me a look of approval before turning all of his attention on Esmerelda, who'd climbed unsteadily to her feet. "Now you both go inside and let everyone know you're okay. And notify the sheriff's department, of course. I'll keep these two here until the authorities arrive."

"What about the feds?" I asked, slipping my arm around Adele's trembling shoulders.

"Just tell Scott. He'll know what to do. Now go." Kurt fired the gun up in the air before training it back on Esmerelda. "That should alert the deputies who are staked out up the road."

Keeping my arm around Adele, I guided her to the front of the house, where we were met by the slam of the front door.

"Amy!" Richard flew down the porch steps to greet us. "We heard a shot and thought . . ."

Adele slid out from under my arm and stepped to the side as Richard flung his arms around me and pulled me close.

"I'm fine," I managed to say, between kisses. "Perfectly fine."

Scott and my parents rushed out onto the porch, the rest of the guests pressing up behind them.

Richard finally let go of me to check on Adele. Seeing the thin ribbon of blood at her neck, he yelled for someone to call 911, while Adele protested.

"It's just a scratch," she said, pushing Richard's hands away. "But there is a man around back who might need some medical attention. He was holding me captive, but then he unfortunately fell on his own knife."

Richard eyed her with wonderment. "How'd you manage that?"

Adele lifted her chin and struck a pose that could've come straight off a poster for the Ballets Russes. "Simple. I rond de jambe'd him."

Karla cast a glance over her shoulder at Richard's parents. "And some people claim dance isn't worthwhile," she said, before flinging out her arms to acknowledge her former dance coach. "Brava!"

Adele, smiling, responded with an elegant curtsy.

Chapter
Twenty-Nine

After Brad and his team, joined by some of Scott's colleagues, carted off Esmerelda and Lance Dalbec, I had to endure another round of questions. Staggering out of Kurt's study, which had been requisitioned as one of the interview rooms, I was greeted by Richard.

"So much for the rehearsal dinner," he said, taking my arm as we descended the stairs to the main floor.

"Oh dear, all that food gone to waste." I glanced into the dining room, noticing that the table had already been cleared.

"Not exactly. Kurt asked the chef and her crew to pack it up and carry it over to Lydia's house. She invited anyone who didn't want to just make a beeline for home to stop by and enjoy a buffet-style meal."

I shook my head. "Sounds like Aunt Lydia. Always the gracious hostess, even during a crisis."

"That's where everyone is, I think. Of course, I waited around to take you home. And Adele too, although Brad told me that he's going to drive her so they can stop by that minimart to retrieve her car."

"Sounds good." As I looked over at the entrance to Kurt's living room, I was surprised to see him standing in front of a tall occasional table, examining something. "You coming?" I called out.

"I don't think so," he replied. "I believe it would be best for me to just stay here tonight. Not all of Esmerelda's crew have been rounded up yet."

"You think they might try to attack you again?" I headed into the living room, Richard at my heels.

"If they do, they'll get a surprise." Kurt met my concerned gaze with a smile. "The chief deputy has left a solid contingent of deputies stationed around the estate."

"So more of a trap than protection?" Richard asked, with a lift of his dark eyebrows. "Don't you ever get tired of being in danger?"

Kurt shrugged. "I'm used to it by now. Anyway, I just got this earlier today"—he motioned to the object on the table—"and want to spend some time admiring it before I lock it in my vault."

I stared at the beautiful leather-bound book. "Is that what I think it is?"

"Indeed. A Kelmscott Press edition of the works of Geoffrey Chaucer. The very one Oscar and I were vying to buy. Come, take a closer look." Kurt held up one of his hands, clad in a white cotton glove. "I'll flip the pages."

Richard and I stood close together as Kurt stepped to one side to open the book and slowly turn the pages.

"It really is gorgeous," I said, staring at the hand-set type and elegant borders surrounding the text. "The Burne-Jones lithographs are just stunning."

"Yes, a true treasure." Kurt closed the book and shot me a look from under his pale lashes. "But not worth anyone's life."

Richard nodded. "For sure, which makes me glad it wasn't actually the cause of Oscar Selvaggio's death. That would've tainted it, don't you think?"

"Wouldn't have been the book's fault, in any case," Kurt said. "But yes, I'm glad it wasn't the Chaucer that cost Oscar his life."

Richard took my hand. "Sounds like it was his own bad decisions. Selling forgeries to a notorious drug dealer is a risky proposition."

"No question about that." Kurt pressed his gloved palm against the back of the book. "Sadly, I think Oscar had gotten away with so many questionable deals in his life, he thought he could pull off anything. Hubris"—Kurt narrowed his eyes—"always the downfall of those who've simply been lucky before."

"What are you going to do with this, now that you have it?" I asked.

"Have a case made and display it in here, I think," Kurt said, looking around the large room. "Although I plan to make special provisions for it in my will." He flashed Richard and me a smile. "I thought perhaps the Clarion University library might like to have it for their rare-book collection."

"I'm sure they would," I said, as Richard tightened his grip on my fingers. "I'm glad you let us see it, but now we should be getting along. We need to visit with our other guests before the party breaks up at Aunt Lydia's house. Thanks for providing the food, by the way."

"No problem." Kurt stepped back and looked us over. "Tomorrow's the big day. I'm looking forward to being there."

"It's great that you can make it," Richard said.

"Yes, so fortunate that you're not dead," I added with a sly smile.

Kurt grinned. "I couldn't allow that. I wouldn't want to spoil your wedding day. Oh, by the way, I convinced Mary Gardener to accompany me."

"I'd already heard about that from Delbert Frye, and wholeheartedly approve," I said, before dropping Richard's hand and impulsively throwing my arms around Kurt.

"Maybe I should try to get almost killed more often," Kurt said as I stepped back from my unplanned and, I had to admit, rather exuberant hug.

"Maybe not." Richard pointed a finger at the older man. "I don't care what you do in your business dealings, but don't you dare try to steal my bride."

"As I've assured the authorities, my thieving days are over," Kurt replied.

"I'm not sure I believe that," Richard said. "But I'll trust you this once."

I placed my balled fists on my hips. "Anyway, I'm not property, so no one can steal me." I shot Richard a sharp look before turning back to face Kurt. "I'm not your Kelmscott Chaucer. You can't put me in a vault or under glass."

Kurt gave me a wink along with a little bow. "Understood, my dear."

"But you are priceless," Richard said, before leaning in to give me a kiss.

* * *

When we arrived back at Aunt Lydia's, some of the guests had already left, including Sunny, Karla, and Jessica. According to my mom, they'd headed out to hit some night spots closer to DC.

"They were going to wait for you," Mom said, "but I told them I didn't think you'd be up for a girl's night out, despite the excellent company. I hope I said the right thing."

"Definitely." I gave her a hug. "Besides, I don't want to look like death warmed over tomorrow."

"No, I imagine you need some rest after that ordeal."

I turned around to meet Fiona Muir's steady gaze.

She almost looks . . . concerned, I thought. "I certainly do. By the way, I know Richard has already thanked you for so generously paying off the remainder of our catering bill, but I want to offer my thanks as well."

A tinge of pink colored Fiona's cheeks. "Oh, it wasn't so much. Anyway, Jim and I wanted to contribute something toward the wedding expenses."

You did, you mean. I doubt your husband was involved. "It was still a lovely surprise," I said, studying her face. There was a softness in her eyes I'd never noticed before. It made Richard's resemblance to her much more evident. "Wait a minute, there's something I need to ask you. I keep forgetting."

"Not surprising," my mom said. "What with all the kidnapping and rogue drug dealers and such."

"Something I can help you with?" The quirk of Fiona's eyebrows was so exactly like her son's that I had to swallow back a foolish comment. *Maybe they're more alike in other ways too,* I mused as I turned and headed for the staircase. "Yes, it's a gift we received in the oddest fashion. It just showed up in our pile of wedding presents." I paused to lean over the balustrade. "There was no card attached, so we have no idea who sent it. I wanted to check with you because I thought maybe it was from one of your friends. Hold on, I'll be right back."

As I clattered up the stairs, I heard my mom explain to Fiona that the gift was a piece of antique jewelry and that no one had any idea where it had come from.

Grabbing the white box, I headed back down to the hallway, where Mom and Fiona were discussing, of all things, Mom's collection of rare seashells.

"Here it is," I said, handing the box to Fiona.

She flicked the hinged lid open with one of her perfectly manicured fingernails, then shocked me by voicing a swear word.

"Where did you find this again?" she asked, her hand trembling as she snapped the lid closed and pressed the box to her breast.

"It was lying in a pile of gifts that one of the cats knocked off the desk in the back room. Richard and I were both confused, because neither of us remembered receiving it. Not to mention it wasn't wrapped and had no card." I shared a puzzled look with my mom before looking back at Fiona. "Have you seen this necklace before?"

Fiona took an audible breath. "Many years ago." She squared her shoulders and looked me directly in the eyes. "The truth is, the last time I saw this pendant was when Uncle Paul showed it to me on his deathbed."

I was my turn to swear. "It belonged to Paul Dassin?"

"Yes, although he told me he'd had it made for someone else."

My mom's dark eyes widened. "For Eleanora Cooper?"

Fiona nodded. "That's right. He said he commissioned it during her trial, and planned to give it to her when she was acquitted. Which she was, of course, but then she disappeared. He never saw her again."

"But he kept the necklace, always hoping he would," I said, speaking slowly while my thoughts raced. "Forget-me-not. That was his message to her."

Fiona dipped her head and stared at her now steady hands. "But it was really his fate to always remember her, wasn't it?" When she looked back up at us, I was surprised to see tears welling in her gray eyes. "Uncle Paul was a good man. I enjoyed visiting him when I was younger, because he allowed me to . . . be myself. Not something I experienced at home. My parents were wonderful people, but they had a lot of expectations they thought I should fulfill."

Aha, I thought. *There it is.* Like her son, Fiona had been an only child and, it seemed, had also been forced to meet a set of rigid standards.

Fiona rolled her shoulders, as if casting off some unseen burden. "But Uncle Paul always seemed so sad. Even when he smiled, there was this wistfulness in his face . . . Anyway, I didn't know anything about his feelings for Eleanora Cooper until the moment he showed me that necklace."

I brushed an errant lock of hair behind my ear. "And you never saw it again, until today?"

"No." Fiona pulled a tissue from her pocket and dabbed at her damp eyes. "Uncle Paul asked me to put it back in the drawer of his nightstand, which I did. But when I cleared his home after he died, I couldn't find it. I thought it was lost, because we definitely cleaned everything out of the house before we rented it. At any rate, none of our renters ever mentioned discovering that necklace, and apparently Richard never found it when he was doing renovations to the house. So how it has appeared again . . ."

"Another mystery," my mom said, offering Fiona a sympathetic smile. "Not one we're likely to solve right now either, so how about you and I head to the kitchen and grab a cup of coffee instead. Or wine, if you prefer."

"Coffee would be good," Fiona said, before holding out the box to me. "I think, all things considered, this belongs to you now."

"Thank you." I popped open the lid to gaze down at the necklace. "I will wear it tomorrow," I said, looking up and locking eyes with Fiona. "To honor your side of the family."

"I'd like that," Fiona said, before offering me the first genuine smile I'd ever received from her.

Chapter Thirty

Dad squeezed my hand as the dulcet strains of the Rachmaninoff *Rhapsody* hung in the air for a moment before they were wafted away by the breeze. It was our cue to line up on the path that led from Aunt Lydia's garden into Richard's backyard.

Soon to be my backyard too, I thought, as I looked up to meet my dad's watery gaze. His eyes had welled with tears the moment I'd walked down the steps in my wedding gown and veil, prompting my mom to stuff a few extra tissues into the inside pocket of his suit jacket.

"Ready?" he whispered.

I nodded before fixing my gaze on the back of Sunny's head. I couldn't help but admire her upswept hairdo—a loose chignon threaded with tiny braids plaited with peacock-blue ribbons. As if sensing my focus, she lifted her bouquet in a little salute.

Our nosegays were similar, although Jessica's and Sunny's arrangements were composed of greenery, Queen Anne's lace, and white roses, trimmed with white ribbons. My bouquet included more color—lilac sprigs and purple wisteria were interspersed among the greenery and white flowers, and my ribbons included all the colors worn by my bridesmaids and Karla.

As Delbert Frye launched into his hammered dulcimer interpretation of Pachelbel's *Canon in D*, I took a deep breath. I knew that as soon as Dad and I walked into the adjoining backyard, following Jessica and Sunny, I would see Richard waiting at the arbor.

He would see me too, and I was anxiously anticipating his reaction. I knew that I looked splendid, with the natural makeup applied by the cosmetologist Zelda had recommended. It was a lovely look, enhancing my features without appearing overdone. My dark hair had also been professionally arranged—softly curled and swept away from my face with the help of delicate gold barrettes. The barrettes, once owned by my grandmother Alice Litton, who'd tragically died when my mom and aunt were young, had been given to me by Aunt Lydia, who'd also provided a pair of her pearl-drop earrings as my "something borrowed." Of course, my "something new" was the rest of my wedding ensemble, including the veil that trailed from my fresh flower–decorated headpiece.

My "something old" and "something blue" were reflected in the necklace that had once belonged to Paul Dassin. *More than fitting*, I thought, *since I am marrying his great-nephew at Paul's former home.*

Sunny cast a smile over her shoulder before she stepped through the rose-draped archway to follow Jessica.

My dad offered his arm, which I clung to tightly. As much as I wanted to marry Richard, I was suddenly overcome with a sense of panic that made my mouth go dry and my heart flutter like a bird beating its wings against a cage.

Dad and I stepped through the archway and walked behind the last row of white folding chairs to reach the white carpet runner covering the center aisle. All the chairs were filled, and I vaguely registered the faces of people I knew as well as a few—the Muirs' family and friends—that I didn't. But all that faded when I focused my gaze on the white lattice arbor placed at the far end of the aisle.

Scott, quite handsome in a light-gray suit with a mauve waistcoat, dark-gray tie, and crisp white dress shirt, caught my eye and gave me a wink along with a smile. Karla, wearing a one-shouldered draped silk dress the color of a purple twilight sky, truly looked every inch the Greek goddess I'd always imagined her.

But it was the man standing beside them who attracted all my attention. Richard was wearing a gray morning suit with a white shirt and a tie the color of the wisteria in the airy fountains of flower arrangements decorating the area around the arbor.

I gripped my dad's arm, almost stumbling when I made eye contact with Richard and saw the look that suddenly suffused his handsome face.

Sunny and Karla had been right—although his expression was joyful, he also looked like he might pass out. As if sensing this reaction, Karla reached out her hand, which he clutched blindly, his gaze fixed on me.

Jessica and Sunny lined up on the other side of the arbor, and the minister stepped forward when my dad and I reached the front row of chairs. As Dad leaned in to kiss my cheek, I felt the dampness on his face and patted his jacket. "Tissues," I whispered, offering him a warm smile as he turned away to take a seat between my mom and Aunt Lydia.

I handed off my bouquet to Sunny before facing Richard. Taking hold of his outstretched hands, I kept my eyes lowered, not daring to catch a glimpse of his face until the minister began speaking.

When I finally looked up, the pure, powerful, love shining in Richard's beautiful gray eyes almost undid me. It was just as well that he was gripping my hands so tightly, or I might've been the one to sink to the ground. As the ceremony progressed, our clasped hands shook like leaves in the wind. Not sure if it was my fingers trembling or his, I kept my eyes locked on his and held on for dear life.

We made it through the vows without breaking down, but after I slipped the ring on Richard's finger, I glanced up and caught him dashing away tears with his other hand. Which made my own eyes well up.

When Richard reached out and wiped away the tear skidding down my cheek with one finger, I heard a sob erupt from somewhere. Glancing out over our assembled guests, I caught my dad clutching a damp wad of tissues and openly weeping as my mom passed clean tissues to both my aunt and Hugh.

Richard leaned in to whisper, "I'm told I can kiss you now." He gave a little nod of his head toward the minister. "Shall I?"

"Please," I said, rising on tiptoe to meet his lips.

* * *

After the ceremony, we posed for a round of photographs while Hani Abdi directed the guests over to Aunt Lydia's backyard. It

347

had been transformed into a reception space by the addition of a large, open tent placed at one side of the garden and a variety of small tables and chairs scattered along the gravel paths. Under the tent, long tables held the buffet supplied by Hani as well as a selection of drinks. Aunt Lydia's slices of cake were artfully arranged on a tiered silver tray, creating a luscious centerpiece.

I tossed the bouquet, guided by hand signals from Mom to angle my throw so it landed where I wanted it—in the hands of Alison Frye. Then, with Richard at my side, I mingled with our guests before we engaged in the traditional cutting of the cake and champagne toasts. Delbert Frye, seated on a small platform at one corner of the tent, provided background music on his dulcimers.

Standing behind the cake table, Richard tapped his champagne flute with a fork to get everyone's attention. "I almost forgot, but before we head back over to my yard for the dancing, I understand there's a newly engaged couple here," he said, as the crowd fell silent. "I think we should toast them as well." He lifted his glass. "To Brad Tucker and Alison Frye—congratulations!"

Brad, standing nearby, turned the color of the red roses in the garden, while Alison slipped her arm through his and leaned into him, beaming.

"Congrats, you two!" Sunny shouted, clinking glasses with Fred before they both took a long swallow of champagne.

"Yes, congratulations, my dears," Zelda said, her eyes sparkling. "Now we just have to work on a few others." She cast a significant look at Hugh, who shared a smile with Aunt Lydia, before she spun around to face Scott and Ethan. "Doesn't this give you any ideas?"

"Yes," Scott said, throwing his arm around Ethan's shoulders. "It gives me the idea that we should dance."

Zelda made a disgruntled noise and waved him off, while my parents and some of the other guests laughed.

"Scott has the right idea," Richard said, circling around the table to grab Karla's hand. "It is time to dance. And maybe"—he cast me a warm smile—"offer a little surprise for my bride."

"I'll go get everything set up," Karla said, dropping his hand and hurrying off.

Richard crossed back to me and offered his arm. "Shall we?"

"What's this all about?" I asked, as we walked out of the tent and made our way into his yard.

He glanced down at me, his eyes sparkling. "Oh, just one of my surprises for you."

"One?" I asked, arching my brows.

"You didn't think I'd limit myself to one, did you?" He kissed me before leading me to one of the folding chairs, several of which had been rearranged to face the temporary dance floor. "Hold this for me, will you?" He stripped off his jacket and laid it over my lap before kicking off his dress shoes.

Karla held up a pair of jazz dance shoes, which Richard slipped on as soon as he joined her on the dance floor, while I detached the trailing veil from my headpiece and laid it and Richard's jacket on the chair to my left.

"This should be good," said a familiar voice.

I glanced at the speaker as he settled in the seat to my right. "Where's Mary?"

"Resting in a chair over in the tent," Kurt said. "She tires easily these days, and anyway, she and Delbert Frye wanted a little time to catch up."

I studied him, imposing in a pearl-gray suit cut to fit his large frame perfectly. "You look quite dashing today."

"And you look gorgeous," he replied, taking hold of one of my hands. Lifting it to his lips, he kissed my fingers. "I confess to being a bit envious of Richard today."

"Ha," I said, wrinkling my nose at him. "Like you'd ever tie yourself down. Although"—I curled my fingers around his hand— "I do think you might give love a try again, after all these years."

Kurt's eyebrows disappeared under the fall of his thick white hair. "But I have done so, my dear, many times. Just because it didn't last doesn't mean it didn't happen." The twinkle in his eyes faded. Fixing me with an intense stare, he lowered our clasped hands to rest on the adjacent arms of our chairs. "And one thing I've learned, after all these years, is that there are many kinds of love. Not all of them end in marriage, or are even romantic, but all can mean quite a lot. Or at least"—he released my hand and sat back, his focus shifting to the stage—"enough."

Noticing that Richard and Karla were getting in position for their dance, I didn't reply.

The song was one Richard had shared with me before—Josh Groban singing "Won't Look Back." Richard had told me it was how he felt about our upcoming marriage, which had made me tear up at the time.

This time, as he and Karla danced together in a performance that showcased all the brilliance of their partnership to lyrics that promised a lifetime of real, and realistic, love, I cried without shame.

Kurt handed me a cotton handkerchief halfway through the performance, demurring when I tried to give it back to him at the end.

"Keep it," he said. "You might need it again today."

"And you won't?" I said, after swallowing back a hiccup.

"I have another," he replied, standing. "I came prepared."

"Don't you always?" I said as I rose to my feet to join the applause for Richard and Karla.

Kurt just grinned and asked me to save him a dance before striding off.

Richard leapt off the low platform to run to me. Sweeping me up in his arms, he gave me a long, passionate kiss. "Did you like it?" he asked, as he set me back on my feet.

"I loved it. But now it's time for our first dance, don't you think?" I motioned to the assembled crowd of guests. "Then everyone can join in the fun."

"Absolutely." Richard took my hand and guided me over to the dance floor. "Did you already tell the band what we wanted?"

I caught Karla's eye as she stepped down onto the grass beside the platform. "Yes, they know what to do," I said, giving her a wink. "Just tell them it's the first dance and we'll be all set."

Richard led me onto the dance floor before giving the band their cue. As the opening bars of "Sway" rang out, he turned to me in surprise.

"What's the matter?" I asked, widening my eyes in fake innocence. "Not up for a rumba?"

He laughed before taking me in his arms. "You little sneak," he whispered in my ear as we began to dance. "You rehearsed this. With Karla, I bet."

"You are correct, sir," I said, tightening my grip on his shoulder and hand. "Now dance."

It was glorious, I had to admit. I'd learned the basics with Karla, but in Richard's arms, with him guiding me, I felt a freedom I'd not experienced before. It gave me a little peek into his world and helped me understand, for a brief moment, what he must have felt so many times—the power of movement to express what words could not.

When the dance ended, we were met with applause from all the guests and shouts of "Bravo! Brava!" from most of Richard's dancer friends, including Adele, who rushed forward to offer us her special congratulations.

"You know that now you've proven yourself, you're going to have to dance with me much more often in the future," Richard whispered into my ear as we took another bow.

"Gladly," I said, pressing closer to his side.

"Okay, now that we've demonstrated our skills, it's time for everyone to get up here and show what you can do," Richard called out, waving a hand to draw the guests onto the dance floor.

The platform was soon full of couples, some trained dancers who put on quite a show, some—like Scott and Ethan, and my parents, and Aunt Lydia and Hugh—amateurs whose enthusiasm made up for their lack of professional experience. Even Fiona and Jim Muir, I noticed, managed a respectable foxtrot and waltz.

Sunny and Fred, waltzing beside us, made Richard and I switch partners for half a dance.

"You weren't lying, you are pretty good," I told Fred, before spinning into the arms of Brad, who'd handed off Alison to Fred.

"I hate to talk shop today," Brad said as he expertly patterned me across the crowded floor. He stopped at the edge of the platform near the rose-laden fence. "But since you did help us with research and other information, I wanted to let you know that we apprehended Honor Bryant, and she confessed to digging up the aconite from Bethany's garden, as well as handing Oscar Selvaggio the tainted cognac. But she didn't distill the poison—that was one of Esmerelda's flunkies, who gave Honor the finished potion to douse Selvaggio's drink."

"I guess Esmerelda wanted him dead because he cheated her by selling her forgeries."

Brad nodded. "She wasn't the type to put up with that. But she was clever. According to Ms. Bryant, Esmerelda pretended to be interested in acquiring that Kelmscott Chaucer. She even told Selvaggio that things would be square between them if he got the book for her."

"I assume she asked him to attend Kurt's party, saying she or one of her flunkies would meet with him there to finalize details?"

"Yes, and she commissioned Lance Dalbec with the task." Brad looked down at me, his expression grave. "He sent the text to Selvaggio, telling him to meet out in that garden shed."

"Was he the one who actually killed Selvaggio, then?" I asked, hoping, for Honor Bryant's sake, that this was true.

"No, the guy was already poisoned when he stumbled out to the shed. Ms. Bryant says that Dalbec was just supposed to keep him there so he couldn't get any medical help." Brad's blue eyes narrowed. "We assume Dalbec watched Selvaggio die, then confiscated his cell phone, threw that tarp over the body, and ran off into the woods."

I smiled at my parents as they danced by us, but my thoughts were elsewhere. "Dalbec must've parked on that back road and taken the path through the woods, like he did when he kidnapped Adele yesterday."

'That's the theory." Brad shrugged. "Dalbec isn't saying much, although he swears he never intended to kill anyone but Kurt Kendrick. He says he meant to let you and Ms. Tourneau go after he dispatched Mr. Kendrick and then just disappear somewhere. Apparently, he'd set up some sort of escape plan."

"Leaving Honor Bryant to take the rap." I fiddled with the glass pendant of my necklace. "I suspect she was forced into poisoning Selvaggio because of her debts to Esmerelda's gang."

"Unfortunately. She told us they threatened her life, as well as the lives of her family, if she refused." Brad stared into the swirling crowd of dancers. "That and her testimony against Esmerelda may help her avoid the worst sentence for her crime, but of course she won't escape completely unscathed."

"Sad." I looked up into his pensive face. "You are a good man, Brad Tucker. I hope you know that."

A flush colored his cheeks. "Thanks." He stepped to the side. "But here's Richard, ready to reclaim you."

Richard held up his hands. "I have no claims on Amy," he said with a grin. "Except those of love, of course."

"The best kind," said Kurt, as he stepped between Richard and me. "I do believe I was promised one dance."

Richard moved aside. "I'll allow that."

"You'd better," Kurt said, flashing one of his wolfish smiles before he spun me off in a fast foxtrot.

"Good heavens, I can't keep up," I told him as we danced past Hugh and Aunt Lydia.

"Nonsense. Just follow my lead." Kurt quick-stepped me to the edge of the dance floor. "Although I could understand if you want a breather." He lifted me up and set me down in the grass next to the platform. "You wait here. I'll grab you another glass of champagne."

I looked back at the dance floor, which had cleared as the band launched into a vigorous jive. Only Richard, Karla, and some of the other professional dancers remained, indulging in swings, jumps, and dips that the less accomplished couldn't hope to match.

It was fun to watch, though. I applauded their efforts with enthusiasm but was happy to stand quietly by, sipping the champagne Kurt had brought me before he wandered off to talk to Adele.

Sunny strolled over. "The most awesome wedding ever," she said, throwing her arm around me.

I gave her a sidelong smile. "I do think it's going rather well."

"Absolutely the best." She laid her head on my shoulder. "I'm so happy for you, I could bust."

I slid my arm around her waist. "And I'm happy all the people I love are here. Especially you," I added, hugging her close.

"Bestest day for my bestest friend," she said, shooting me a bright-eyed glance from under her golden lashes. "I ordered it up specially, you know."

"Did you? Thanks." I leaned my head against hers. We stood like that for several minutes, watching the dancers.

As the band took a break, Richard jogged over to the edge of the platform. "Can I steal her away for a minute?" he asked Sunny.

"I think that sounds like a fine idea," she said, stepping away from me. "I probably should check on Fred anyway. Last I saw of him, he was talking shop with Scott and Hugh. I bet Lydia and Ethan will appreciate it if I break up that convo."

"Definitely sounds like an important mission." Richard jumped down onto the grass and hugged Sunny before giving her a little push. "Off you go. And tell those guys this is a wedding, not one of their task force assignments, okay?"

"Will do." Sunny gave him a mock salute before hurrying off.

Richard pulled me close. "How about you and I sneak away for a minute?"

"Another surprise?"

"Could be." Richard stepped back and took my arm. "Come on, we can take the secret way."

He escorted me past the arbor, into the woods that bordered his lawn. Lifting my long skirt, I followed him down a narrow path that required us to walk single file.

It led to an old arbor, groaning under the weight of ancient wisteria vines.

"Our special place," he said, as he pulled me into the center of the tunnel-like arbor that connected his land to the woods behind Aunt Lydia's house.

I looked up at the tapestry of dark-green vines and clusters of deep-purple blossoms. "It's blooming again."

"Yes, perfect timing on our part." Richard kissed me before stepping back and pulling a small box from his pocket. "This is the other surprise," he said, handing it to me.

I opened the box to reveal a brooch—a delicate filigree of gold studded with emerald chips that looked like leaves and amethysts that mimicked the chandelier of blossoms overhead. "Oh," was all I could say, before snapping the lid shut and throwing myself into his arms.

After several more minutes lost in kisses, Richard lifted his head to study my face. "So I guess you like it?"

"It's perfect," I said. "I love the way it tells our story."

"But only the beginning." Richard cupped my face with his hands. "There's so much more to come."

"And I can't wait to write that epic," I said. "With you as my coauthor, of course."

"One thing's for sure, it will be guaranteed to have a fascinating plot and many lovable side characters," Richard replied as a breeze whistled through the arbor, showering silken flower petals over us like a fragrant drift of snow.

"We don't know the ending yet, though," I murmured as I laid my head against his chest.

"But I know it will be happy," he replied, and then kissed me until I was convinced that his words were the indisputable truth.

Acknowledgments

T ossing bouquets of thanks to:

My amazing agent, Frances Black of Literary Counsel.

Everyone at Crooked Lane Books, especially my editor, Faith Black Ross. Also, thanks to Matt Martz, Jenny Chen, Melissa Rechter, Madeline Rathle, and Rachel Keith.

Richard Taylor Pearson, a great author and critique partner. Also thanks to author Lindsey Duga for her advice and support.

Booktubers Angela Hart of *Books are My Hart* and Courtney of *Courtagonist*.

Podcasters Kristine Raymond of *Word Play* and LeAnna Shields of *The Cozy Sleuth*.

Bloggers Dru Ann Love from *Dru's Book Musings* and Marie McNary from *A Cozy Experience*.

All of the other bloggers and reviewers who have mentioned, reviewed, and recommended my books.

My husband Kevin, my son, Thomas, and the rest of my family, who support me as well as my writing career.

My friends, including the online writers' community.

My readers. Without you, these books could not exist!